WINGS OF FLESH

"Gotholic Warfare"

Written by
Edward Francis Nyahay Jr.

WINGS OF FLESH: *Gotholic Warfare*

Dedicated In Loving Memory of

ZYLA FAUSTINA PELAGIA NYAHAY
(12/21/2000 – 6/28/2023)

ROSEMARY JEAN BARATTINONYAHAY
(12/5/1947 – 5/6/2024)

"My life is not a song, it is a story."
~Zyla Faustina Pelagia Nyahay

"You can't even imagine how beautiful the afterlife is, you can't even imagine."
~Rosemary Jean Barattino Nyahay

Modern Day Saints: In the Society of Victim Souls

Zyla Faustina Pelagia Nyahay

Rosemary Jean Barattino Nyahay

On July 24th, 1999, Edward and Jacqueline Nyahay married at St. Charles Borromeo Catholic Church, North Hollywood, CA, where Edward was a Sacristan. Jacqueline converted to Catholicism, and both did prison Ministry through the LA County Jail. Nine months into their marriage, Jacqueline conceived, and their winter solstice, the year of the dragon baby, Zyla Faustina Nyahay, was born in Ft. Lauderdale, FL, on December 21st, 2000. Zyla's original name would be Zyra, the lead character of this book, but then Edward and Jacqueline found the Hebrew name, *Zila*, meaning *"Shadow of God"*. Zyla was baptized on the first Divine Mercy Sunday, the canonization of St. Faustina, Zyla's middle name, which in Spanish means "Lucky." So Zyla Faustina Nyahay "Lucky Shadow" was born. Pelagia was Zyla's confirmation Saint.

Eternal joy, overabundance of love, and happiness filled the air. However, one of Zyla's earliest memories was 911, and later found out, Zyla, Jacqueline and Edward literally lived down the street from one of the terrorists, and shopped in the same grocery store, in Coral Springs, FL. Then two years later, Zyla got to pay her respects, and experience New York (2003-2005) before settling in Burbank, CA. At one and a half years old, Zyla starred in her first film, "Krush The Serpent" Little Lost Productions. Zyla attended St. Charles Borromeo School where she excelled at Mock Trial, winning MVP Defense Lawyer, issued by Judge A. Cole, LA County Court. Zyla also completed over two hundred service hours during her adolescent and teen-age years. She was an honor-roll student and started acting at 10, but from 7 years old, Zyla started her own reality show, ZYLA'S WORLD on YouTube, which documents her life, up through her high school years.

Zyla gave 110% to everyone she ever encountered, on every occasion. She became SAG-AFTRA in 2012 and acted in over 100 TV shows/films (Netflix); including acting with her favorite celebrity, Selena Gomez, on "Wizards of Waverly Place" and more recently, "Shameless". Zyla lived three lifetimes in one. Zyla was on top of the world, heading for a bright future, before she received test results, stating she had stage 4 terminal cancer, one out of five million, Fibrolamellar Carcinoma. Zyla was a true Artist and Saint, in all aspects of these words. She created from love and passion, and was able to explore the darkest sides of humanity, spreading love and light, at the same time as expressing her kindred spirit to the most elite. Zyla encompassed all. She is a true Saint, who suffered greatly, who expressed her love for life through many mediums: fashion, painting, drawing, jewelry, acting, dancing, gymnastics, and writing…here is one of her last poems.

ZYLA'S POEM

Birds are chirping
I listen while slurping
The water brought by me
As the birds watch and see
Rebirth is an interesting theory
The idea of rising from the dead
Is dreary
How do we prepare for it?
Meditate in front of a candle-lit
Butterflies fill my soul
This feeling is new to me
Love carried me out of this dark hole
As you are down on one knee

Now being guided from within, I see and feel differently. Zyla is an eternal source of inspiration. A bond between a father and a daughter is very sacred. My baby girl was the perfect blend of Jacqueline and I. God designed Zyla perfectly. I know that is why He called her home early, to lead the way for my precious mother, Rosemary Jean Barattino Nyahay, who also suffered for many years. Their journey together in the afterlife is also accompanied by my grandparents, Anita Bernadette Giordanella Barattino and Army Officer, Lt. Col. Emanuel Joseph Barattino, whom I was blessed with the gift of helping guide each of these precious souls home to heaven during their last week of life, catching their last breath, and tears, making sure it is a peaceful exit from here and smooth transition handoff to Jesus Christ. Four of the most Saintly souls to have ever walked this planet, the souls that create infrastructure within my heart, granted me the title of *Death Doula.* I know each soul is in Heaven, my job was to make their journey as peaceful and loving as possible, as I removed their taunting spirits, sending them to the foot of the cross, yet caring for my own flesh and blood. Death is equivalent to giving birth, it will be your most difficult labor in this existence. For the last 7 days of my Mother's precious soul allowed to breath here, I was present. The first three days were spent on a 24/7 Facetime connection, until I landed there on May 2nd, 2024. I never left her bedside, only to keep up with the necessities.

Rosemary Jean Barattino Nyahay was truly the greatest Mother, not to just me, but to all she encountered. I compare her heart to the Immaculate Heart of Our Virgin Mother Mary, but with a New York twist, and modern day vocabulary, and well, with a habit of being late. She ruled with a wooden spoon, making sure I was disciplined at all costs. Growing up with having to get my priorities straight from her Dad, I was always kept in line, as I continued to walk it on a daily basis. Tough love, well needed. She did it with a loving heart that grew beyond what her physical heart could handle. My Mom taught us all so much how to live life. How to find the humor in situations that demand attention, or never casting judgement upon the core heart and soul of an individual. There may have been situations or actions that she did not agree with, and with Heaven behind her, she released her point of view upon you. That's my Mom. A pillar of light in this darkened world. A woman who touched so many lives. The hole in my heart, the entrance into Heaven, keeps expanding. First pierced with the sword from my grandmother's passing, then next with my grandfather, followed by 16 years later, my daughter, and again ten months later, my Mom. Both my Mother and Daughter, as well as my Wife, are all Sagittarius. Yes Sagittarius's are storming Heaven. My wife connecting this earthly sacred triune. I am grateful for the time, love and memories created with these two most precious souls. Until we meet in Heaven, St. Zyla Faustina and St. Rosemary Jean pray for us!

Although, Zyla never read my book that my Mother edited, WINGS OF FLESH: EXPEL YOUR DEMONS ENJOY THE FLIGHT, she 100% guided me through this rewrite.

There is something very magical about this photo on the left. It was taken on February 12th, 2022 at the Colony Theater, Burbank, CA. Zyla's very close friends, Lauren and Connor, put on a fundraiser magic show for her, and this was the amount of money raised, so Zyla could live her best life. If you read the amount Zyla raised from right to left, that is her death day…6/28/23…

God Bless Zyla & Rosemary! May your wings of flesh transition into spirit. I Love You Both & Miss You!

Modern Day Saints: Society of Victim Souls, Pray for Us!

Saint Zyla Faustina Pelegia Nyahay, Pray for Us!

Saint Rosemary Jean Barattino Nyahay, Pray for Us!

Saint Anita Bernadette Giordanella Barattino, Pray for Us!

Saint Emanuel Joseph Barattino, Pray for Us!

First Printing, 2024 Gotholic Ink

WINGS OF FLESH: GOTHOLIC WARFARE

Dedicated to the Loving Memory of

ZYLA FAUSTINA PELEGIA NYAHAY

(12/21/00 - 6/28/23)

My Daughter is a Saint!

Jesus Christ needs Zyla for His return!

ROSEMARY JEAN BARATTINO NYAHAY

(12/5/1947 – 5-6-2024)

My Mother is a Saint!

Jesus Christ needs Rosemary for His Return!

A

Novel

Wings of Flesh

"GOTHOLIC WARFARE"

By

Edward Francis Nyahay Jr.

Based on his Novel

Wings of Flesh

"EXPEL YOUR DEMONS ENJOY THE FLIGHT" ~Xlibris

ISBN: 1-4010-9802-9

THE BOOK OF REVELATIONS

"Inside every soul, Gotholic Warfare!"

~Edward Francis Nyahay Jr.

"And war broke out in Heaven: Michael and his angels fought with the dragon, and the dragon and his angels fought, but they did not prevail, nor was a place found for them in Heaven any longer...."

"Now when the thousand years have expired, Satan will be released from his prison..."

~The Book of Revelation

AUTHOR'S NOTE

Welcome my soulprint friend, to a world of inspiration, mysticism, power, choices, and living in faith, truth, and love, Gotholic Entertainment LLC. I will guide you through situations where decisions push the boundaries of the imagination to new creations. I, Edward Francis Nyahay Jr., author of "Wings of Flesh," have a beautifully haunted story to reveal. I started writing this story twenty-five years ago. My words have traveled through space and time, and yet the words that fill these pages now will be remembered. After facing and conquering many demons in my life, a story so real, so tangible, and so determined to be told, has risen to the surface once again.

ZYRA JORDONELLO, my main character, rockstar vampire witch, or something like that, shares common characteristics with yours truly. All of the above, none of the above, all in your head? Many writers say if you want to be a writer, write every day, and if want to be a great writer, write what you know. Creating a character somewhat true to life, yet still encompassing his interpretation, forced me to bring to your attention, a world within worlds. Yes, a deeper understanding of the concept of the Kingdom of Heaven within. Within each of us is the door to eternal life. If we choose to live our existence never opening this door, a world of fulfilling spiritual pleasure and enlightenment will never be known to us. The soul must feed on spiritual food for it to grow. Holy Communion and the word of God is my spiritual food. Channeled illumination from the other side, through the heart of truth and love, is where I receive my inspiration to create. And real-life dreams, of course. I started writing Wings of Flesh after I had a dream of a horrific beast washed up on shore. You will meet this beast. Another dream that is real is the only premonition that manifests in Zyra's life, that's my clue.

The absence of fear turns on Zyra as he tries to live as a God-fearing man, only after he is dragged through the incantations of hell. Handing over my body, mind, and soul to this creation, my story represents self-fulfillment through Righteous Guidance. If I have done my job correctly, I shall bring you on a journey, not too far from your own heart and within your mind. These words I wrote over twenty years ago. They still ring true. But now written with even greater love, more than I could have ever felt then. You will see why in a moment.

Hell, that fiery brimstone place beneath the surface of our skin, lives within each of us. Always be aware of what drives the choice, love or hate. You have the freedom of choice, which energy flow to tap into and manifest from. Monsters, demons, and entities of the worst kind exist! They *GNAW* at the mind. Be BRAVE, as I take your hand, gently squeeze, and hold tight as I introduce to you my devilishly handsome Antagonist, a friendly deceitful man/demon-beast (Satan) known as BABEL. He has the power to transform into the deadliest creature of all time, DRAGON-WHALE, manifesting as the largest most frightening beast, past present, or future, to survive on this planet for any length of time.

I want to thank God the Father, God the Son, God the Holy Spirit, and all of Heaven, Angels, and Ancestors, who supported and loved me, through this crazy journey called life. My wife, Jacqueline Lovell, who inspires me, loves me unconditionally and truly manifests her deep intense love for our beautiful daughter, ZYLA FAUSTINA PELAGIA NYAHAY. This book is dedicated to this most precious Saintly Soul, who entered Heaven way too soon on June 28th, 2023 at 10:48 am. Zyla was born on December 21st, 2000, and was my inspiration to turn this story, my first feature film, WINGS OF FLESH, under Zalman King's mentorship, into my first novel, WINGS OF FLESH: EXPEL YOUR DEMONS ENJOY THE FLIGHT (Xlibris Publishing). My second loving memory dedication, ROSEMARY JEAN BARATTINO NYAHAY, my Mom who I was blessed to help guide her soul to Heaven at the end of her precious life. Born December 5th, 1947, two days after Ozzy Osbourne's birthday. Her soul entered Heaven May 6th, 2024 at 10:12am. Her body came to rest at 5:37pm that same day.

Now, Zyla is my inspiration to rewrite this story, but her directing me from the other side. Zyla never read my book; she knew it was loosely based on our lives, and did not want to read about any intimacies that may take place between the two lead characters, Zyra Jordonello and DEZERAE NELSON, Zyra's love interest. But now she has a different perspective, and will truly guide my words written, as I feel her with me, every moment of the day. Special gratitude towards my family and friends, my Mom and Daughter who taught me how to love unconditionally, for everyone's love and support, especially during the most difficult times of our lives. May God Bless you all, and if you are reading my words, thank you, enjoy the ride! See you on the other side!

Mystical Playground, Gotholic Warfare, consume my thoughts, enhance my vision, may I never be alone again! Jesus, protect me! Jesus, I trust in you! Jesus, I love you! "As I walk through the valley of the shadow of death, I will fear no evil, for thou art with me." Psalm 23:4

FOREWORD

CARRIE MAGALSKI

Thank you for taking this soul journey with us. I introduce you to the story of "Wings of Flesh". A story of inspiration, mysticism, power, choices, and living in faith, truth, and love. A story that is inspired by the life of my brother and author, Edward Francis Nyahay Jr. A story that is also dedicated to the memory of his daughter, my Godchild, and niece, Zyla Faustina Pelagia Nyahay, who left this world too soon, but continues to guide us from the other side.

My name is Carrie Magalski, President of Inspirit Press, the publisher of this e-book, but without the visual works of art presented here, and for only pennies from your pocket, you can access WINGS OF FLESH: *Gotholic Warfare* anytime, anywhere!

Our mission is to publish and produce books and creative multimedia works of art that inspire, instill, enlighten, and encourage.

I decided to publish this book after my brother rewrote the second edition following the death of his daughter, our beloved Zyla. The pain and suffering that he and my sister-in-law, Jacque endured as the cancer torturingly stole their only child's life was something no parents should ever experience. Pouring his grief into his writing, singing, and producing has given his works of art a harrowing depth that will vibrate your soul. Creating art and conveying their story through various mediums is a way to honor her memory, as well as share his message of hope and redemption with the world.

This book is not a typical fantasy novel. It is a spiritual adventure that explores the inner and outer realms of existence, the power of choice, and the consequences of our actions. It is a story that challenges us to face our fears, our demons, and our true selves. It is a story that beckons us to explore the Kingdom of Heaven residing within ourselves. It intricately weaves together with the anticipated return of Jesus Christ, bridging Heaven and Earth. Through this union, order and peace are restored to creation, and we are encouraged to embrace the divine potential inherent in each of us—a purpose for which we were uniquely crafted.

The main character of this story is Zyra Jordonello, a complicated soul with great talent. He is a complex and conflicted hero, who struggles with his identity, his destiny, and his love for Dezerae Nelson, a human woman who holds the key to his salvation. Zyra is also pursued by Babel, a cunning and charismatic villain, who can transform into a dragon-whale, the most terrifying creature ever created. Babel has a sinister plan to unleash hell on Earth, and he will stop at nothing to achieve it.

Will Zyra be able to overcome his inner and outer enemies, and fulfill his divine purpose? Will he be able to protect Dezerae and the world from Babel's evil scheme? Will he be able to find peace and happiness in his life? These are some of the questions that this story will answer, as it unfolds in a series of thrilling and surprising events.

To my brother, God could have never chosen a better brother for me. Thank you for being the most high role model for unconditional love, strength, courage, and faith. Amongst so many other ways I could describe you, these are the virtues that form the foundation of truth from which you live your life and that guide you in all your ways. You are a brilliant artist who has no fear of going deep into the depths of darkness to save a soul and bring them to the light. I love you with all my heart and soul and honor you as a brother, father, son beautiful husband, and man of God that you are. There are no words for how much of an impact you have made on so many lives that you have touched. God truly had a plan for your life when He created you and every day you live up to His highest expectations for you being a shining example for us all. Every day you choose God, you choose love, you choose life and you live it to its fullest purpose no matter the odds that are against us or the challenges life brings us. The pain and suffering you have endured will give you the wisdom you need for the next chapter of this life on earth. We thank you eternally for taking up your cross with dignity and grace.

To our readers, I hope you enjoy reading this book as much as I enjoyed publishing it. I hope it inspires you, entertains you, and touches your heart. I hope it makes you think, feel, and grow. This book is the author's life's work and a masterpiece with an unending finale. I hope it helps you to expel your demons as you enjoy the freedom of the flight.

Thank you for choosing this book. Thank you for joining me on this journey. Thank you for being a part of this story. God Bless you All!

Table of Contents

WINGS OF FLESH: *Gotholic Warfare*

PROLOGUE

My name is Zyra Jordonello. If you are one of those blessed souls who obtain wisdom by reading between the lines, my story will entertain you. Some have told me it is amusingly *scary*. You can make up your mind. Have you ever heard the expression, I have been to hell and back? Well, now it is my turn to make you dance on the fiery flames, and open your mind's eye to a place only known to the supernatural. There is light at the end of the tunnel, predestined to live forever, but now that I have proclaimed my faith in God, my darkest, blackest desires, waged war against me, and all those I love, forcing me into a transcendental state of being, within the spirit, to participate in the spiritual battle, Gotholic Warfare. Gotholic, my genre, my world around me, combines my Catholic beliefs and Gothic influence, creating the Ancestral Congregation, fans living and deceased who partake in this movement.

Yes, money can be the root of all evil, and yes money brings positive change to others. I learned this very valuable lesson from my dear old friend, well, guardian angel, Nazareth. He is the Angel destined to guide and protect me from my self-created hell. He came down upon me with the wrath of God, and instantly my life was changed. To be more precise, what changed first, was my awareness of His Presence. I still gave into temptations in the beginning, and I am sure I will fall again, but as once told to me by a priest, "Even Jesus fell three times."

I want to start my story when I was eighteen, a true beast/"Animal," a Knick name I earned back in high school from Sterling Palmer, who eventually became the middle linebacker for the Washington Redskins. I went against him in high school football practice, and, well, he also taught me how to throw shot-put and discus. Anyways, now eighteen, the world is my oyster, living in the mid-western corn fields. If you are familiar with "Children of the Corn" your mind is enraptured correctly. This cold desolate Indiana climate familiarizes itself to our imagination, as wind bounces off the tips of its vegetation. These wintery months grow old, spring finally arrives, then leaves us with weather from the hottest parts of Hades, summer. As the sweat pours down my face, my determination to seek the truth will unfold before your very eyes. And remember my guardian angel, Nazareth, well you will hear his voice. You will know it is him speaking when he describes my inner thoughts and framework.

Chapter 1

ZYRA

"It's not just another hot, sunny day on June twenty-eighth, in the dry climate of Bloomington Indiana…the sun is a bit brighter today, ravens scatter as birds chirp, just at the right moment, painting, no manifesting the perfect scenario into existence…,"

Says a deep male voice, DJ IOU, over the radio airwaves, with a hint of country music behind him. The rolling hills spread across the horizon in this highly educated, little town called Hanover, the southeast corner of the state. Hanover College protrudes high above the tree tops, overlooking three bends in the Ohio River. This practically Ivy League College is named after this small provincial town, which possesses a National Winning Division Three Football Team, PANTHERS. The underdeveloped intellect of the locals is made up for by the high intellect of the students and faculty.

This all comes together at the local pub, a mile off campus. Garth Brook's music lingers from the broken windows of this aged, dusty cement square. The neon sign above reads "or pub." Five tired, yet youthful young men, stroll in, as one of them looks up, and reads the sign.

"What the hell is or pub?"

His buddy squints at the lettering, then tells him to look closer.

"Oh, Corn Pub. How long has the 'c' and 'r' been out?"

He blows a snot rocket onto the ground. His buddy slaps off his cap.

"That's gross, man!"

He starts cracking up and wipes his hand off his ripped jeans.

"It's better than swallowing it." They walk inside.

Sports channels play on the two televisions above the pool tables. College students and toothless locals downing beers, fill the atmosphere—the music roars through, the musty scent of alcohol, farmers, and sweaty football players. Many drunken tones fluctuate through the air, as one obnoxious singing voice takes control.

"...I got friends in low places where the Whiskey's right and the beer chases my blues away...,"

This one haunted, angry, deep-toned voice, in the likes of King Diamond, Ozzy Osbourne, Sopor Aeternus, and Marilyn Manson, all intertwined into one, is Zyra Jordonello. Next to this goth rocker, dressed in a pair of cotton shorts and a weight lifting competition t-shirt is Andy, one of Zyra's fraternity brothers, singing his ass off, toasting a 20-ounce. Their arms are wrapped around each other, forming a line of twelve drunken football players. A few locals oversee, and converse, about their high school football days, in the good *Ole' Town of Madison* they cheer! Madison is the larger town adjacent to Hanover.

Andy slams his glass into Zyra's, spilling the beer everywhere. They both die laughing. Andy barely gets out.

"This is for two-a-days, the two weeks of football HELL."

The players grunt out loud like they're in a huddle. Even though Zyra seems to stick out, some of his closest friends are here sharing this moment. Zyra has always been the type of character that took in moments well. He made himself and others live life to its fullest. A perfect example is what he is going to do right now. He stands up from the chair and walks away. Andy puts down his drink and screams out.

"Where are you going?"

Zyra turns around, smiles, and presses numbers on the jukebox as if he already knew what he wanted to hear. The guitar kicks in as Zyra starts to sing.

"*I, I, I, I,...Crazy, but that's how it goes, millions of people living exposed, maybe yeah, yeah, it's not too late, to learn how to love and forget how to hate.....*"

Andy screams at the top of his lungs.

"OZZY RULES!"

The players break up, jam out, singing the rest of "Crazy Train." Some locals get disgusted and leave, as Randy Rhoads's guitar solo rips through the air. A voice cries out.

"Zyra you always raise hell!"

Another player gets in Zyra's face, then stumbles back to the group in a drunken stupor, and raises his can of cheap beer.

"Zyra, I want to go where you go when I die."

Zyra looks at him in disbelief, smiles, throws his arms around him, and kisses him on the lips.

"Thanks, man. God Bless you."

The football player freaks out.

"Dude, I don't swing that way!"

Andy interjects.

"You said you wanted to spend eternity with him."

Everybody cracks up.

"You're so stupid"

Somebody throws out. Two-a-days, for anyone who does not know, are truly gut-wrenching days for football players all around the country, the last two weeks of summer. Back in the mid-90s, these memories were lived, as a dream come true, for Zyra. His foster parents needed to get him out of the house, and his coach promised to get him a scholarship, if he raised his grades, which he did. The dark and twisted memories of his youth, which we will get into later kept Zyra trapped for many years.

Now, for the first time, he can explore life on his own, and there is no turning back. If it wasn't for football, he would have taken his anger out in other ways, probably putting him behind bars. Getting others to reach his insanity, is what he lived for, daily. *Not conforming*; was his motto, it's never an option. Being the life of the party, driving his closest friends to the brink of sanity, yet, composed and focused, was and still is Zyra's hidden talent. Zyra's desire to play professional football was intense enough for the big leagues, however, his 210-pound soaking-wet body, flattened any kind of future in this field. There was one Saturday afternoon, in particular, against their rival, which made this realization apparent.

But before we get into that, let's look through the window of time, and get a glimpse of Zyra's life, before this occasion, which changed the direction of his life forever. He spent his first year at Hanover College drunk, stoned, and passed out in front of Sororities, after acting out wild fantasies with mid-western women, as adult cartoons played on the TV; Life was beautiful. The fraternity he became brotherhood to was "Phi-Delta Theta." Zyra always talked about what his frat brothers used to say.

"You don't call your country a cunt, so don't call your fraternity a frat."

You could imagine the high intelligence that charges forth from fifty beer-guzzling brothers. In between the partying, he somehow found the time to lift weights and become a raging beast, breaking all the school's records. Playing sports was his catalyst to release the hidden anger and demons that built up throughout the years. It caused a lot of sorrow and pain at first, because winning is all he cared about, and would do anything to achieve it, nothing would change his philosophy. The three-foot, National Weight Lifting Competition Trophy, still stands tall in the wooden glass case, in the foyer of the Phi-Delt Theta house.

Getting back to this one particular game that changed Zyra's life forever, it all started on special teams, kick-off return. It is the position when one team kicks the ball to the other, at the beginning of a game and after each touchdown. Well, Zyra, was the guy on the front line who got a running start to knock the crap out of anyone he set his eyes upon. It was fun. When he was not playing kick-off return, he was starting offensive guard. If there is any position in football that allows you to be powerful and intelligent with no recognition, it is an offensive guard. The sounds of bones and helmets crushing are a recurring experience for him. But being forced to succumb to all the wrath he dished out, has once again, returned to strike against him, and change his destiny.

The smashing of helmets, the cracking of bones, and the ripping of muscles, immediately follow the whistle, if you ever paid attention to the sounds produced, once the ball is hiked. Zyra lived by the motto, *Protect the quarterback, kill the opponent.* The coach normally put the kind of guy in the front line, who was willing to face death, with a superior attitude. Needless to say, Zyra became very good friends with the other lineman and still is to this day. Forced to think a certain way, and believe the philosophy preached, is a lifestyle Zyra and Andy breathed.

The morning of this rival game, Andy told Zyra his name stood for Angels Never Die Young. Zyra's response was "Man, if you're an Angel of God, then I'm the Angel of Death." And sometimes, Zyra tried to live these words on the field. *What makes a man, can break a man, if his philosophy is wrong,* his father's words rang through his head.

DJ IOU, is back on the airwaves, broadcasting the game.

> *"The roar of the crowd fills the stadium, folks, as kick-off and kick-off return take the field. Something flies differently in the cool breeze; something not right. How else to explain it, but it's a gut feeling. Hopefully, I'm wrong..."*

The stadium is full like always for the first game of the season. Everyone charged and drunk as Zyra stood in the middle of the field, waiting for the Referee to blow his whistle. The energy is high. Zyra's blood boils, raging can be seen in his gator yellow eyes. Zyra focuses in on his opponent, who he imagines dead in his coffin. Zyra shakes the vision, drool drips from his mouthpiece. Anticipation, the calm before the storm, the eye of the tornado ready to strike. Zyra turns to poison waiting to release his wrath on the poor soul in front of him. He wants blood, he can taste it in his mouth, and will not stop until he gets it. Just as the Referee blows the whistle, Zyra faintly remembers hearing his coach scream, "Zyra, watch the middle guy."

Only one word echoed in his mind, *Kill...kill...kill*, as he locks eyes with his prey, charges at him with a vengeance summoned from legion below, POW! Zyra is blind-sided. He was knocked to the floor. As his last memory of being lifted, then smashed head first, plays in his mind, he blacked out.

The helmet splits in two, feeling like his skull. Instantly, cracking down his spine, rolls his eyes to the back of his head, darkness, Zyra's soul lost in the world familiar to him. Flash images of his father enter his brain like lightning. His body convulses. An image of his dead, bloody brother shatters the father's image. He was throwing Zyra into another convulsion.

The roaring of the crowd fades. Silence, as Zyra's body lays motionless. The trainer runs onto the field with the assistants trailing behind with a cot. The coach stops them from entering, "The whistle didn't blow!". The running back runs toward the sidelines with the ball. Instantly, Zyra pops up to his feet and is leveled one last time by the defense. The face mask slams against his face, and blood splatters from his nose as the helmet flies off in two different directions. Zyra hits the ground as dead weight, with a force strong enough to indent the field, are the thoughts before the whistle blows.

Zyra was rushed to the ER. His next awareness occurs when he wakes up in a hospital bed, to the sounds of his sobbing fling, unfortunately, he does not remember her name.

Lies and more lies fill his head as he lays in the hospital bed trying to convince himself he will one day play again. *"What is going on with me?! I will play again…*I will play again" mumbles from his mouth as he passes out. His girlfriend looks perplexed.

Blaming his father for the aggression stored in his soul, left him in a deceitful web of lethargic dreams. He tries to force them down and keep them locked away, but his memories arise from deep within. Yes, the medications, the doctors have him on, could have very easily opened these doors. Zyra's dark past, where the shadows dance with his father's wretched spirit, full of maggots, flashes before his eyes. Within the half-dead words that linger off his lips, Zyra wakes from a deep slumber, "God knows he tried infesting my brother and me with his dark, layered, diseased soul. Witch, he was a witch." She squeezes his hand, he falls back to sleep.

Time passes and Zyra heals with a year of rehabilitation, but he is never allowed to play football again. During this time, nightmares haunted him to the point of bone-shattering fright, as he awoke many nights in a pool of sweat. To try and fill this huge void in his life; Zyra submerged himself in his artwork. He drew and painted the most surreal, darkest images his mind could summon. Many were convinced his works of art were a cross between Salvador Dali, the king of surrealism, and H.R. Giger, the creator of the creatures from the movie "Aliens". Searching for answers through this new world, acted as a catalyst to expel demons in his life. Once he was able to express himself through melting faces, disfigured bodies, and portraits of demons, Zyra found himself continuing to indulge in mind-altering drugs, the only world he felt safe in.

Up until this point in Zyra's life, he had not experimented with drugs, just alcohol. Once he got a taste of the forbidden fruit, LSD, his mind was open to receiving information only known to these other dimensions. His friend Russell Vinda, was the first to introduce him to this wonderful cartoon world. Tripping became his pastime and all because of a little piece of paper no larger than the size of a pebble. Zyra's first experience with acid was his most intense. Growing up listening to the Godfather of Heavy Metal, Ozzy Osbourne, Metallica, Van Halen, Motley Crue, and all of the other heavy metal bands of the eighties, enhanced his escape from reality. But these bands mentioned were not the ones he experienced his first hit on. GWAR, medieval demon-screaming freaks were playing in Indianapolis at the time when Russell and Zyra drove two and a half hours to see what was one of the most interesting, yet terrifying, concerts he ever attended. This is the show that changed his fate.

Darkness settles over the roaring crowd as a cavity of human snakes made up of skinheads and metal heads is ready to mosh. The testosterone in the air is very strong. The stench of sweat, body pressed against the body, somehow leaves an erotic feeling in the belly of the beast. Zyra, on the other hand, was starting to peak, and if you cannot relate, just allow your mind to open and drift. The sound of an angry guitar accompanied by medieval demons, walks out on stage. The drums kick in and the crowd starts to sway. As one group, one mind watching and listening to GWAR reminded him of no picnic at the beach, except for the chick who came prancing out on stage in her spiked bikini going down on the lead singer.

Needless to say, the mosh pit went from crazy to insane. One punch to the head, followed by a bone-crushing thug to the ribs as everyone started to look like oversized lizards. Russell's words, *it will be an experience you will never forget*, rang over in his head. After seeing an eight-foot version of the pope walk out on stage, and be beheaded with one swing of a battle axe, Zyra knew his calling as blood splattered from the darkness upon his body.

Watching it in slow motion and through strobe lighting, made him feel a surge of evil, he had not felt since his brother died. Getting caught up in the moment and forgetting it was a stage show, Zyra goes crazy in his head, swinging and punching anyone and everyone around him. At this moment of peaking, hundreds of screaming psychotic GWAR fans backed away giving him his space. He falls to his knees crying out to Heaven, clenching his hair, and screaming from the deepest part of his soul, which arose his new destiny. He will become the most surreal, terrifying, controversial rock star this world has ever seen and heard.

After the show, he told Russell what happened. Russell wanted to be part of the band. He knew Zyra was serious.

"Zyra, I want to go where you go when I die."

Zyra shakes his head.

"Why does everybody keep saying that to me?"

He immediately responds by telling him to pick up his guitar again and they'll jam. The cheap little acoustic Russell once owned was soon replaced by a mean-ripping KV1 Jackson. He talked as much about Dave Mustaine from Megadeth who created that guitar as Zyra did about Ozzy and Randy. Russell always said if there's one guitar in the world he wants to play, "Give me the KV1...". "One" rang in Zyra's head for about a minute. Talking about Dave Mustaine, Russell says.

"Anyone who can hold a note like that and still play as fast as he does is one hell of a man, Dave's KV1 Rocks."

These words spontaneously combusted from Russell's mouth after just confessing that he grew up on a farm and was ready to experience the world. As much as Zyra may have respected Russell's reason for picking up a guitar, he had many arguments about how Randy Rhoads put the Concorde on the map, with the more aggressive headstock design, which became the staple for the Jackson brand.

"None's better than Randy though."

Zyra believes Russell was in his life to motivate him and redirect his anger to achieve a bright future. The next day, Zyra and Russell went to the woods to trip and jam out. After playing for about an hour, and from what he can remember, it was one of the most spiritually shocking experiences of his life. During what he did not realize was going to be his last trip with Russell, Zyra conversed with the spirits of fire. As he stared deeper into the flame, the flickering stops as the presence of the flame expands. Within the flame, spirits come to him. Among them, is his brother, Gabriel. Zyra is deep in a trance.

"Gabriel, is that you?"

Zyra receives confirmation within his mind.

"I miss you, brother."

"Zyra listen to me,"

Gabriel telecommunicates.

"Stay focused, I the sideshows you see in your peripheral are demons trying to steal your soul…also, remember this…"

A flash image of Zyra as a child, being held down against the bed, his neighbor, three or four years older, has his way with him. Zyra in his mind's eye sees his eyes as a child bulge with fear, and confusion, then his hand is laid on a Torah, and a voice echoes in his head, "Say it…say it…say it…" Zyra as a child hears himself whisper among his fear and tears, "I will never tell." Zyra snaps out of the vision, scared to death. His heart is pounding, he looks around and doesn't see Russell.

Russell had gone out to meditate on a tree branch hanging over a 120-foot drop. Russell hears faintly his name being called. Russell awakes from the meditation and finds Zyra huddled over by the fire. They stare at each other, realizing they both finished their experience with the other realm, and their discussion seemed a bit, how shall I put it, different. Russell stares down into the flame about to die out.

"Nature is so beautiful."

Zyra looks up from his hypnotic stare.

"I couldn't disagree with you more. I don't know what you see. I see skulls and moaning souls buried deep within the flames. Not to mention…oh forget it."

Russell looks at him disturbed.

"Sorry to hear that man, not to mention what?"

Awkward silence, changing the subject.

"Through my eyes, the colors of nature are so vibrant, I feel truly alive for the first time. And I love it. Come on Z, let's get out of here."

They both stand up and hug each other, Zyra whispers in his ear.

"Thanks for trippin' with me brother."

Russell pushes him away laughing.

"Get away from me."

Russell picks up his guitar and Zyra picks up his book of lyrics as they walk back to campus.

Months passed as their celebrity status grew in the local bars. Quickly becoming a popular local band, Zyra sent out demos all over the United States trying to get a record deal. His frustration built as the rejection letters returned. Not knowing where else to turn, he buys an OUIJA board and gets many of his peers to join in. At first, this medium was just a game, but the more Zyra believed, the more everyone else believed, and not before too long, his interest in the occult grew. Zyra started his seances in his dorm room, where he would black out the room, and have one candle lit.

He had Skinny Puppy on ration in his CD player, creating an eerie ambiance. He had fifteen or so souls in the room and had them all sit in a circle holding hands. Only two in the middle with their hands on the Ouija board. A circle around a circle. Zyra would make up a prayer, getting everyone into the spirit realm. He had them do breathing exorcizes and concentrate and focus all of their attention on the manifestations of spirits. Zyra was able to channel ancestors of people present, offering them solace and peace where there was hurt and confusion. Zyra warned people not to do this alone or without him involved because if not done right, entitles would take over. That is exactly what happened.

Zyra, one night received a phone call from a person who was present at the seances, letting him know that one of the sorority girls was just rushed off-campus in an ambulance because she went crazy doing the séance alone in her room. That same night, Zyra receives another phone call. This time it is from CEO, Alex Rimmington of Dilemma Records, Boston Massachusetts.

Zyra runs over and answers the phone as people party in the background.

"Hello, What I can't hear you. Who do you want to speak to? It's him. Who's this?" Zyra quickly turns the music off and kicks everybody out of his dorm.

"OUT, everyone out now!"

People exit the room.

"Hi, I'm sorry, my friend was blasting the music and I couldn't hear."

The male voice over the phone says.

"I think there is a market for your music."

A smile brightens Zyra's drunken face.

"So you liked it ha, Mr. Rimmington? Cool. Do you want to fly me out? When?"

"As soon as possible, like tomorrow."

Zyra finishes off his bottle of beer and throws it away.

"Okay um...tomorrow I have class until 2 pm, but I can probably catch the five twenty flight. Great, wow, thank you. Hey, witchcraft is big in Boston, right?"

The voice over the phone hesitates and then answers.

"Um, well Salem is where all the witch trials were held years ago."

"Salem is where I want to be. I've been doing some reading on Wicca as if you couldn't tell by my lyrics. It's interesting stuff. Well thanks for the info., see you tomorrow."

He hangs up the phone, ecstatic. He runs out to the hallway and tells everyone the news. Russell looks at him with disappointment and runs off. A friend of theirs questions Zyra.

"What's his problem?"

Zyra drops his head forgetting about Russell when he was talking to the record label.

"He never asked about Russell. He just wanted me to fly out."

He puts his arm around Zyra.

"Don't worry about it man, he'll get over it."

Zyra loses his excitement.

"Yeah, I guess."

This did bother Zyra, that the person who helped him get to this place, was now not going to be part of a life he might have.

Chapter 2

DEZERAE

Meanwhile, across the United States over on the West Coast, we find ourselves in the middle of an old run-down warehouse, deep in the San Fernando Valley, rented out to an independent production company. They are currently in the middle of filming a movie, "Attack of the Killer Lady Bugz," starring Dezerae Nelson, the starlet B-Movie Horror/Erotic Actress in Hollywood. Lining up film after film, Dezerae has a personality unlike any other. Her unique, natural acting style makes Cameron Diaz look like a Barbie doll. Dezerae has no fears, watch her as she stops the director from shooting this scene.

"This whole headless, whale-human thing being eaten by my character is just a bit too weird for me. So how about I just take off my shirt for the roach scene, and get that over with? Since I can't think about anything else, so please, can we just move on."

Her gut-roaring scream as she finished her sentence could have moved mountains. The director walks rapidly over to Dezerae lifts and shakes his finger at her. She bites down on the tip of his finger, as shock strikes his face. She sucks it like a lollipop and kisses it when she is done caressing.

"Charlie, be a good little boy and move your crew to the nude location."

She hisses at him and then continues.

"... because I cannot take it anymore. Do you understand me?"

Charlie nods his head falling prey to her whims.

"Good."

She walks off set and grabs a handful of M&M's as the director says under his breath.

"No, you're gonna get fat."

Dezerae turns around, stares him dead in the eyes, pops the handful of candy into her mouth, and chomps down exposing brown mush, as she opens her mouth, and wriggles her tongue.

"Am I?"

Dezerae has reached a point in her career where she has reached the top of her Industry. She wants to pursue higher-quality films. So, she knows after completing this project, she will be moving on to bigger and better things. It was a Tuesday afternoon when she scheduled her appointment with her agent to discuss her new future in A-List films. She walks into Newhart Talent Agency in Beverly Hills, and takes a seat, as the secretary files her nails and chomps away on her gum.

"And you're here to see...?"

Dezerae looks up at her, in complete disgust.

"Excuse me, do you always file your nails and chew gum like a cow, or are you just that absent-minded?"

The secretary throws her hands down on the desk.

"You are the rudest person I have ever met."

Dezerae mimics her, then laughs it off. Just then, Dezerae's agent, William Newhart, walks in.

"Dezerae darling, how are you, my dear?"

He gives her a French welcome, kissing her on both sides of the cheeks. Dezerae smiles and looks over at the secretary.

"You my dear, are one cute girl, but you need to stop chewing bubble gum, 'cause it's allowing too much air into your head."

William is taken back at first but then chuckles as they both walk into her office. William takes a seat behind his desk, as Dezerae lays down on the leather couch. Movie posters with Dezerae and other working clients cover the walls. William clears his throat.

"Please take your feet off the freshly polished leather."

Dezerae sits up.

"Sorry."

William continues.

"So I just got off the phone with the director of your last project, Attack of the Killer Lady Bugz..."

She cuts him off.

"He's an idiot."

William takes a sip of his coffee.

"He may be an idiot, Dezerae, but he is one of the top directors for your genre, and he is paying the bills."

Dezerae leans in, takes out a piece of gum, puts it into her mouth, and offers one to William.

"No thank you."

Dezerae tries to figure out the best way of saying what she needs to say.

"I'm sick of shooting B-films. I had to do a shirtless scene the other day, as this half-human, half-roach licks my tits. I'm done with this shit."

William laughs at her directness.

"Well, I can see nothing has changed, you still speak your mind, in a very direct manner." Dezerae gets up and throws away her gum wrapper. She looks up at her movie poster.

"Eating Your Heart Alive, now that was an interesting film."

William looks at her quizzically.

"It grossed over two million dollars, Dezerae, that's serious cash."

Dezerae takes a seat on the couch.

"What do you want, Dezerae? Why did you call me in a panic?"

Dezerae moves her fingers over her lips, as to tell him she… hesitates for a moment, then answers his question.

"Eating Your Heart Alive, Attack of the Killer Lady Bugz, Spread Your Legs and Die, do you see a pattern forming here, William Newhart? Every movie I star in is about death, metamorphosis, cannibalism. You know after doing this for five years, it kinda takes a toll on your soul. I mean, listen to the way I speak to people these days. I don't care. I was never like this. I came from a Christian background."

William lets her ramble on.

"Who the hell knows what ever happened to that? I want to do wholesome films, now. Put me against Cameron Diaz, people say I look like her. I could play her sister."

William shakes his head.

"Dezerae, you have fans all around the world. You can't let them down."

She jumps in.

"Screw the fans. The people who like my work sit in their trailer parks, plotting out murders, and masturbating. Do you see my point? I want to move people with my work. I want to star with Brad Pitt or Tom Cruise. They can't take me seriously as an actress, if the only films you send me out on, are these damn low-budget cult films. I need to grow spiritually, as a human being, and in my craft, and these kinds of movies stunt that growth."

William leans back in his chair and then stands up.

"Well if this is how you, *truly feel*, then our work is done. In these movies, you are queen, and they pay your bills. People would die to be in the movies you're in, Dezerae. You have a niche, milk it, because one day, the milk will run dry."

Dezerae stands up very upset, and slams her hand down on William's desk.

"You know what, Mr. William Newhart, founder of Newhart Agency? You're all the same! All you care about is money. You said it yourself. There is more to life than just money, and if you don't see that, then you're going to burn in hell, with all the rest of them!"

William approaches Dezerae.

"Excuse me, are you threatening me?"

Dezerae grabs her purse and throws it over her shoulder.

"No, just stating the truth."

She walks out and slams the door behind her, the secretary jumps from fright. She composes herself, then sarcastically says to Dezerae.

"Ahh, did someone get fired?"

Dezerae turns her head, and locks eyes with the secretary, controlling the wrath within her soul.

"You know what, honey, keep on fucking your boss, he might just actually give you a part in his next porno."

She walks by a potential teenage client sitting next to her mother in the lobby.

"You may want to reconsider."

Dezerae leaves. The secretary's mouth drops to the floor, as elevator music continues to play in the lobby. The mother turns to her daughter.

"Come on honey, we'll find another agency."

They get up and walk out.

For the next year, Dezerae must have met with every major agency in Hollywood. All of them say the same thing.

"You are very talented, but we cannot represent a person with your kind of background."

The frustrations build as Dezerae does not know where to turn. She spends her days at coffee shops, spends her money on smoking pot, and partying. Her environment, was chaotic whereas before it was organized. Her big bank account, soon becomes next to nothing, leaving her in a state of depression. With nowhere else to turn, she calls home for the first time in five years.

"Hello, Mom? It's me, Dezerae."

Her face turns from natural nervousness to fighting back tears, as she tries to think of the next thing to say.

"Yeah, I know it's been five years, I'm sorry."

Her mother's voice echoes in her mind questioning if she made the right choice to call.

"No Mom, I'm not in trouble, and I'm not just calling because I want money."

About to hang up, Dezerae realizes this is not a place where she is welcome.

"You know what, Mom? You're no different than all these assholes out here. I'm sorry for hurting you, but I have no one to turn to."

Her mother hands the phone to her father.

"Honey, listen to me…"

"Hi, Dad….Yeah, I know, but if I can't even call home, and be spoken to as a human being, then where can I turn?"

A long pause proceeds as her father says.

"Listen Dezerae, why don't you come home for a while and take a break from California."

Dezerae holds the phone to her ear not saying a word. She can hear her mother screaming in the background.

"She's not welcome here."

She finally speaks.

"You know what Dad, thanks for taking the time to talk to me, but I made a mistake thinking I was going to hear a friendly voice. I don't have a person in this world that I can trust. But that's okay. I've been on my own for a while now, and I'll deal with it."

Her father tells her mother to be quiet and then turns back to the phone.

"Dezerae, you are always welcome here. I would love to see you again if you want to come home."

Dezerae wipes the tears from her eyes.

"My rent is due and I can't afford to pay it. I have been trying to find a job this whole year, and everywhere I turn, it seems like I'm being blackballed from the Industry. I'm sorry Dad for hurting you and Mom all this time."

Dezerae's mom screams out in the background, "Go to church!" Dezerae chuckles to herself.

"Funny you should say that, I've been going to church lately, and I believe it was God who gave me the strength to call."

Her Dad takes in her sincerity.

"I will buy your ticket home, but if you leave, you will have to pay for it on your own." Dezerae smiles.

"Thanks, Dad, I'll sell my stuff, to make a few extra bucks, so I'll have some money when I get back to Indiana."

Her father motions to the mother to keep her mouth quiet.

"I love you, sweety, I always have and I always will."

"I love you too, Dad, thank you. I'll see you soon."

She hangs up the phone with a glimmer of hope in her eyes.

The next couple of weeks kept Dezerae very busy, having garage sales outside her apartment building. Finally, the moving day arrives. One of her friends who lived in the apartment downstairs, approaches.

"I'm gonna miss you Dezerae. So many people move here every day to fulfill their dreams, and you did that. I'm so proud of you! I will never forget you."

Dezerae gives her friend a long hug goodbye, then gets into her ride for the airport. They pull away. The driver looks at Dezerae through the rearview mirror on their way to LAX.

"You know, you look familiar. Are you an actress?"

Dezerae looks up at him.

"Yeah."

He continues.

"What have I seen you in? No wait don't tell me, I just saw Attack of the Killer Lady Bugz, Dezerae Nelson, that's you, right?"

Dezerae laughs for the first time all year.

"Yeah, that was me."

The driver gets so excited.

"This is so crazy, when I saw your name to pick you up, I didn't put two and two together until now. I think you were awesome. You're so funny."

He then quotes a line of hers from the film.

"Killer ladybugs, huh, I'm your queen ladybug!"

Dezerae's face contorts for a moment, as she finds herself smiling for the first time, in a while.

"Wow, you even know my lines."

"Of course, where are you headed?"

She sits up in her seat to talk to him.

"I'm going back to Bloomington Indiana where I'm from."

The driver exits off the 405 highway and heads towards the airport. He looks back at her when they stop at the red light.

"How long are you going for?"

Dezerae looks surprised as if she never thought about that.

"I don't know, for good probably."

He presses on the gas.

"For good? What kind of movies are made in Bloomington Indiana?"

She reaches for her purse to grab the money.

"How much do I owe you?"

He pulls up to the curb outside the airline.

"Don't worry about it. It's not every day I get to meet one of my favorite movie stars. So you never answered me."

Dezerae shakes his hand.

"Thank you for the ride, and to answer your question, I'm done with acting."

He keeps holding onto her hand as if he doesn't want this moment to end.

"That's a shame. I wish you well in whatever you decide to do."

Dezerae overwhelmed by his kindness, fights back her tears.

"Thank you, what's your name?"

He lets go of her hand and smiles.

"I'm John, John Williams."

She opens the door and grabs her luggage.

"I'm Dezerae. It was very nice to meet you, John Williams Newhart."

His smile gets bigger making it obvious that he is very grateful to have met her.

"The pleasure has been all mine Dezerae Nelson. See I told you I knew you."

She closes the door shaking off her disbelief as she says to herself.

"Where have you been hiding John Williams?"

Then the thought hit her.

"Hey, are you related to William Newhart?"

He gets in the car, doesn't answer her question, and takes off. Dezerae, completely perplexed, *How is that even possible?* She thinks to herself, then enters the airport with her luggage.

Chapter 3

DILEMMA RECORDS

Zyra gets out of the overstretched black limo, looks up at the very high building in front of him, and tips the limo driver who refuses. The busy street corner of downtown Boston seems typical, as people rush by in their suites and sneakers on their lunch breaks. Looking back up at the very high black glass building, Zyra takes a deep breath and walks in. In front of him is a security desk which he approaches.

"Hi, I'm looking for Dilemma Records."

The security guard points him in the right direction, Zyra thanks him and enters the elevator. As the elevator door closes, a messenger sticks his hand in as the doors close and reopens.

"Sorry, I'm in a rush."

He looks over at Zyra dressed in all black leather and in his Boston accent asks.

"So are you going to Dilemma Records?"

Zyra surprised that he was talking to him, finally answers.

"Yeah, I just got signed and I'm meeting with them for the first time."

The messenger finally puts down the heavy package.

"Congratulations, is your lawyer already up there?"

Zyra gives him a puzzled look.

"My lawyer?"

The messenger presses the top floor button as the elevator starts to move.

"Yeah man, I hope you don't sign a contract without your lawyer looking over it first." The tension builds as they climb higher and higher.

"Yeah, my lawyer's up there. How do you know so much?"

The messenger laughs.

"Where you from the mid-west or something?"

The doors open upon a huge lobby that reads Dilemma Records. They both step out, the messenger walks up to the counter, drops off the package, and says to the secretary.

"Take care of this guy will ya, Anne?"

Anne laughs and replies.

"Whatever you say, Tommy."

He turns back to Zyra on his way out.

"You're in good hands. Don't worry about the lawyer thing, I was just kidding. Congratulations, man."

He enters back in the elevator as Zyra stands there confused. Anne breaks his confusion.

"Can I help you?"

Zyra walks up to the counter.

"Um..yeah, I'm here to see Alex Rimmington."

"And you are...?"

Zyra touching his long dark hair, answers.

"Zyra Jordonello."

She smiles holding out her hand as he shakes it.

"So you're the guy everyone's been talking about?"

Zyra not knowing what to say, answers hesitantly.

"I guess."

She laughs at his indecisiveness.

"I thought you would have been different, pompous, you know like all the rest of the rock stars."

She picks up the phone and dials Alex's office.

"Hey Cindy, Zyra is here to see Mr. Rimmington. No problem."

She hangs up the phone.

"Just have a seat and he'll be with you in a moment."

Zyra responds.

"Thank you, Anne…"

He takes a seat and picks up a rock magazine, that has their company on the front page. As he skims through it, he hears Anne's voice.

"I like your voice, but the music isn't dark enough."

Zyra looks up and looks around to make sure she's talking to him.

"Excuse me?"

Just then Alex walks out and greets Zyra. They head back towards his office as Anne smiles staring at Zyra's backside. Alex introduces him to everyone they pass. Zyra is a bit overwhelmed by this experience but takes everything in like a professional. They enter Alex's office.

"Please have a seat. Welcome to Boston. How was your flight?"

Zyra crosses his legs, and sits back in the black leather chair, as he takes in the sight of all the gold records hanging on the walls.

"Good. Thanks for asking. Um…before we get started, do I need a lawyer?"

Alex laughs not expecting this question.

"What'd you do wrong?"

Zyra sighs in relief.

"Nothing I just didn't know."

Alex picks up his phone.

"Well, before we start talking business, would you like some coffee?"

Zyra quickly responds.

"No thank you."

Alex talks into the phone.

"Cindy, can you bring us two lattes, please? Thanks, Sweety."

He looks at Zyra after hanging up the phone.

"If you don't want yours, I'll drink it. I gotta have my caffeine buzz to get me through the day."

Zyra smiles.

"Thanks, I'll take it."

Alex grabs the remote sitting on his desk, leans back in his chair and presses play. Zyra's cd plays over his sound system sounding better than ever. Zyra comments.

"Oh my God that sounds awesome on this system."

Alex nods.

"State of the art. So here's the story Zyra. I love your voice and your lyrics, but you got to lose that band."

Zyra remains quiet. Alex continues.

"I don't have time to waste and I only want to work with people who see things my way. Do you understand what I am saying?"

Zyra runs his fingers through his hair about to speak. Alex cuts him off.

"Shh...before you say anything, I want to tell you what I think. Your voice can be uglier than Marilyn Manson's, your pitch hits notes higher than King Diamond and your whole feel is darker than Ozzy, Alice Cooper, and Metallica. And your lyrics, well, I believe they'll create more controversy than Howard Stern. You are unbelievable. You will sell millions. I do not doubt that, but not with this band. I have a band for you. They have been playing together for five years and you were made to front these guys. Listen to this and tell me what you think."

Alex presses the remote again as a slow eerie guitar and keyboard kick in. Instantly a sound comes from the speakers heavier than any band out there. Zyra starts rocking out loving every second of it. He starts singing whatever lyrics come to him. Alex freaks out.

"See that's what I want. You get what I'm talking about. I knew you would."

He flips to another song. Each song gets better and better. In Zyra's mind, he drifts off seeing the audience as he sings on stage putting on a show he always knew was inside of him. A tear comes to his eye. Alex, puzzled, asks what's wrong and Zyra responds.

"I grew to love Russell. It was because of him that I even wanted to get into music. How do I just drop him?"

Alex, dealing with this kind of thing all the time, stands up and gestures for him to rise. He puts his arm around Zyra and walks him over to the window, which overlooks the whole city.

"Tell me what you see."

Not knowing where he is going with this, Zyra answers.

"Buildings, people, cars, the city of Boston."

Alex smiles.

"You know what I see?"

Zyra shakes his head no as Alex continues.

"I see thousands of screaming fans crying out 'ZYRA, ZYRA'. I also hear hovering above all this chaos, your music being played on the radio stations, not only here but across the world. That's what I see. There is nobody else those people are going to want but you."

Cindy walks in holding two cups.

"Here are your two lattes."

She lays them down on his desk smiles at Alex and locks eyes with Zyra. She walks over to him and seductively kisses him on the cheek. Alex steps back.

"See what I mean. So what do you say?"

Zyra takes in a deep breath and releases it.

"What do I have to do?"

Alex laughs.

"I knew you'd come around."

Cindy caresses Zyra's face with her hand.

"It will be my pleasure working for you, Zyra. Anything you want from me is yours."

Zyra nods his head.

"Thank you, Cindy."

She walks out of the room looking back at him. Zyra walks back to the leather chair and takes a seat. Alex pulls out a contract and goes over it with him. Zyra agrees to work six days a week in the recording studio, twelve hours a day until the album is complete. As far as touring, they will start in Boston, sweep across the nation, and come back around the southern route. A European tour is also being plotted out.

With one week to pack his stuff from Hanover, and move everything to Boston, Zyra had his work cut out for him. They are giving him a penthouse down the street from the studio. Even though this was the most exciting time for him, sadness was present in his heart as he said his goodbyes to all his friends and professors at Hanover. Russell eventually said goodbye to him on his last night there.

"Hey brother, I understand. If roles were reversed, honestly, I'm not sure what I would have done, but you deserve all the success in the world."

Russell hugs Zyra goodbye. Zyra wondered on many occasions *what if the roles were reversed.*

* * *

Upon returning to Boston, Zyra enters his new world, all laid out for him. Leopard print couches, state-of-the-art modern, yet gothic, furniture with an industrial twist. To his left, stands four gargoyles holding up a black leather table. Red velvet lines the intricately carved chairs. On the other side of the room, in the corner, overlooking the whole open area is a seven-foot medieval knight, holding a shield and sword. The only words that rise from Zyra's diaphragm.

"Holy Shit. This is cool."

Right behind him, Alex walks in with Cindy.

"So what do you think?"

Zyra turns around and goes over and hugs Alex.

"Thanks, man. I never expected anything like this."

Alex pushes him off, laughing.

"Alright, alright, save that for the girls."

Cindy interjects.

"I picked out your medieval guardian."

He smiles.

"I love it. Thanks."

Alex walks in and takes a look at the refrigerator. It is full from top to bottom with beer and food.

"Zyra, come here."

Zyra walks over and looks in the refrigerator.

"Oh my God."

Alex smiles.

"Tonight is your night, signing party. You had to be prepared."

Zyra offers a beer to Alex and Cindy, then pops one open.

"So when do I get to meet my band?"

"In about an hour…"

Cindy says as she drops her hand down his back. Zyra looks at her with interest.

"Really?"

Alex interjects.

"Now hold off kids until tonight."

They both laugh as Zyra's hazel eyes lock with Cindy's crystal-clear blue soul. The heat begins to rise. Alex pops open his beer, turns on the top-of-the-line stereo equipment, and plays Zyra's music.

"I am very excited about your album. You will have the freedom to write your lyrics."

"I know. Thank you. So what are these guys' names?"

Zyra asks. Cindy makes herself a rum and coke by the stained glass bar, which overlooks the city. The window extends from one end of the room to the other, as black and red curtains divide the window panels. Alex finally answers.

"Well, the guitarist is Snitch."

Zyra laughs.

"Snitch? Who else?"

"Your bassist is Kunt."

Before Alex can finish Zyra jumps in again.

"Are you for real?"

"Oh yeah, your keyboardist is Wicked Bad and the drummer, well when you see him you can ask him yourself."

Cindy takes a sip of her drink.

"So we have Wicked Bad, Kunt, Snitch, a no-name, and Zyra. I'd pay to see you guys." Alex raises his bottle.

"Exactly."

So far it seems Zyra is in for a night he will never forget. As they down a few more drinks, a buzzer goes off. Zyra gets up and answers the intercom.

"Yeah."

"It's Snitch open up."

Zyra presses the button and lets them in. A few minutes later a knock on the door can be heard as Zyra gets up to answer it.

"So here goes nothing."

He opens the door and before his eyes, stands Snitch, dressed in jungle leather pants and a black silk shirt. Behind him enters Wicked Bad dressed in a black leather skirt, thigh-high boots, long blond hair, and fangs. Zyra cannot control himself.

"Are you a dude?"

Wicked Bad plants a long wet kiss on Zyra's lips.

"I go both ways, cutie."

"Holy Shit!"

Zyra replies as he enters. Kunt walks in wearing skin-tone leathers with an extremely large female organ painted on his crotch. Zyra, not needing a doctorate to figure out this was the bassist.

"You must be Kunt."

"What gave it away?"

Each guy walks in with a beautiful girl draped over their arms, one more beautiful than the next. Finally, a seven-foot

African American Male with dreads passed his waist, walks in with two chicks on each arm. Zyra looking up at him says.

"Well, you must be the drummer."

"Damn straight."

"What's your name?"

Zyra asks as the drummer looks over at Alex.

"Yo Alex, you didn't tell my main man my name? Shame on you."

He walks past him and asks where the booze is located. Zyra points towards the kitchen. He grabs a beer, chugs it, grabs another, pops it open, and walks over to the rest of the party. Zyra's music continues to play in the background, as Snitch walks over to the sound system, and picks up Zyra's CD.

"You look bad-ass. I can see why Alex thought you'd be perfect for us."

He turns to Zyra seeing Cindy all over him like a wet suit.

"Slow down killer. So have you heard us yet?"

Zyra walks over to Snitch leaving Cindy behind.

"Yeah, you guys are fuckin' awesome."

The drummer walks over to the window and looks out towards the city.

"Great place you got here, man. I'm glad you like our shit. We've been together, five years, give or take, and must have gone through what about ten different singers. No one can seem to keep up. We'll see if you last."

Alex interjects.

"Oh, not only will he last, but he'll bring you guys to the next level."

Kunt, laying down on the couch, humping it like no tomorrow.

"Good, cause I'm sick of trying to sleep my way to the top."

The chick that came with Kunt laughs as Alex throws them a look of disapproval.

"What's wrong with you, man? Respect the man's shit. We paid a lot of money for it."

The drummer walks over to Alex.

"You gotta be shitin' me, you bought this place for him and I'm still livin' in some shit hole."

The intercom buzzes again, as Zyra looks over at Alex.

"Who's that?"

Wicked Bad runs over to answer it.

"I invited a few friends to liven up this place."

He lets them in. Zyra makes a comment to Cindy about this starting to get out of control. She grabs his face and kisses him passionately.

"You have no idea."

Kunt starts grinding with the girl he brought over and says to Zyra as he's doing it.

"So you just came from college right, man?"

Zyra answers the door as a group of people holding liquor walks past. One of them says.

"So this is the Dilemma Records party, right?"

Zyra nods as they walk past. He turns back around, as Cindy grabs his crotch and kisses his neck. Zyra, puzzled, tries to answer.

"Um, yeah Hanover."

Kunt responds.

"Where the hell's Hanover?"

Alex steps in.

"Indiana. He's a football player."

The drummer overhearing the conversation interjects.

"I played pro ball until I fucked up my knee and couldn't play any longer. My music back then was just secondary."

Cindy grabs another drink from the bar as Zyra approaches the drummer.

"What team did you play for?"

The drummer looks down into his eyes.

"I was second string linebacker for New England, fucked up my knee real bad, in summer training. I was so depressed, I started drumming my ass off and joined a bunch of bands. That's how I met this loser."

He points to Snitch.

"Who played a Jackson like I never heard before? We've been together ever since."

Zyra grabs another beer as he screams out to the drummer.

"So what the fuck's your name, man?"

Finally, he answers.

"Anaconda."

One of the girls walks over to him and grabs his manhood.

"I can vouge."

Zyra laughs it off thinking *what did I get myself into, only if the guys back at Hanover could see me now.*

"I'm in a band named after the human organs."

Cindy massages Zyra's shoulders.

"Loosen up, it's not so bad."

He turns around and locks eyes with her.

"So I take it we're supposed to hook up tonight. Normally, it's me trying so damn hard, but you make it easy."

Cindy slaps his face, then runs her fingers down his torso, then kisses him as she grabs him.

"You're mine asshole."

On that note, Alex downs his last drink and heads out.

"See you guys bright and early tomorrow morning. Don't get too fucked up tonight."

He leaves as Anaconda whips out the largest blunt any of them have ever seen.

"You sure you don't want to stay?"

He lights it, Alex nods his head, and exits. Anaconda takes a big hit and passes the blunt.

Chapter 4

PRODIGAL SON

Upon arriving home after a long five years, Dezerae gets out of her father's car, grabs her luggage, and looks at the outside of the house, taking in the memories as they flash before her eyes. Sitting on the porch, waiting for their arrival, is her mother and Dezerae's old boyfriend, Zack. Throwing her off guard, Dezerae walks up the creaking wooden steps, leading to the porch. She puts the luggage down, her mother walks inside the house. Zack hugs Dezerae, that awkward moment, trying to comfort her, but the unwelcoming feeling from her mother was too prevalent. Her father, feeling the tension, approaches her, and picks up her luggage.

"Honey, it's ok, she'll warm up."

A tear drops from Dezerae's eye. He walks inside with her luggage. The oak trees in their front yard are encased by the white picket fence; an old wooden chair hangs from the branch. Dezerae, lost staring off into the front yard.

"I remember swinging on that swing as a little girl. I thought to myself, one day, I'll get outta here, and become the biggest movie star ever."

Zack finally breaks the tension.

"Well, you did do that."

She looks at him.

"Sort of, in your way, right?"

Dezerae drops her head.

"Oh, what do you know about that?"

Zack steps in closer.

"I watched every one of your movies, Dezerae, I have every magazine article ever written about you."

"Wait, what? Really?"

Dezerae gives him a twinkle in her eye.

"Dez, I missed you."

Dezerae hugs him.

"Hey Zack, I didn't realize you still kept in touch with my parents."

Zack walks down the steps towards the oak tree. He sits down on the white wooden swing. Dezerae stands at the top of the steps. Zack swings, then finally gains the courage to speak.

"How did you expect me to stay away, when you just left me five years ago? We were engaged, Dez, to get married."

Dezerae drops her head.

"Yeah, I know. I guess an apology is long overdue."

Zack stares out into the yard, lost in a memory of them squirting each other down with a hose, as they washed the car. He laughs.

"You know, you never even said goodbye to me. Your mother found your engagement ring on your dresser, the next morning."

She thinks back to that night when she made her decision, to just pack her bags, and head out to the closest Greyhound station, in the middle of the night. Zack felt the awkward silence.

"Your mother has the right to be upset with you. She thought you were *dead* or something. She read me the note you left. She gave it to me, saying I would probably want it."

Tears in his eyes, he reaches into his pocket and grabs the letter from his torn jeans. She looks into his blue eyes, touches his dirty blonde hair, and gently caresses his cheek.

"I'm sorry for hurting you, Zack, but I knew if I didn't get out when I did, I would have grown up in this little town barefoot and pregnant."

A tear drops from his eye.

"What's wrong with that? I would have supported you. I have a good job now. I'm finally the manager of the hardware store."

She smiles at him, trying to control her laughter. His facial expression says it all, and she immediately responds.

"Good for you, Zack. I knew you could do it."

He looks down trying to understand.

"You know I still love you."

An awkward silence again, Zack continues.

"When your mom told me you were coming home, I thought maybe..."

She cuts him off.

"Zack, when I moved out to California, the land of opportunity, things happened for me. I became a pretty big star, like you said."

He perks up.

"I know. I never told your parents about them, cause I didn't think they would approve, being Christian and all."

She grabs his hand and squeezes it.

"Thank you, Zack, that means a lot to me."

Her father comes out with a tray of food and drinks in his hand.

"I thought you kids might be hungry."

Dezerae looks up at him and grabs her plate.

"Thanks, Dad."

Zack also thanks him as he grabs the plate and glasses of lemonade from the tray. He walks back inside as her mother can be heard screaming.

"Let her get it herself."

Dezerae shakes her head and thinks back to the passage in the Bible about the Prodigal Son.

"I wonder if I was her son if she would accept me back?"

Zack looks confused trying to understand what she is talking about.

"You remember, Zack, from Bible class, the story of the Prodigal Son."

He smiles.

"Yeah, I remember, so what are you going to do now with your time?"

She thinks about his question, never really putting any thought behind it before this moment.

"You know Zack, I don't know."

"I'll hire you at the store, so you can get by for now."

He stands up from the swinging chair and approaches the bottom of the steps. She smiles at him.

"Thank you, Zack, I have to think about it, but thank you, that was sweet."

He leaves, and she enters the house.

This moment in Dezerae's life was the lowest she ever felt. Contemplating the rest of her life and what she was going to do after all the success she had, made her wish that she never left. The cliche of having success, and it being taken away, is worse than never having it at all, her existence. Her thoughts. *Where does a person go from here? Suicide,* crossed her mind many times, but the hope of one day returning to Hollywood kept her alive. She knew that allowing this to get her down, would put her deeper into an abyss, which if she was not careful, would swallow her whole.

As the days passed, Dezerae spent many of them in bed, reliving the memories of being on set in Los Angeles. She knew if she did not get out of bed, there could not be a brighter future. The only thing that kept her going was the fact that she rose to the top on her own, and no one stopped her before. But why couldn't she break into the mainstream? Was a question she pondered many times over. She knew she had the talent to succeed, but why would none of the agents represent her? For days, Dezerae wrote in her journal, documenting exactly what had happened to her in the City of Angels. For the first time in five years, she started to question her own religious beliefs. Even though, she had gone to church towards the end of her career in LA, something was missing, that true faith that she once knew. The faith that drove her to pack her bags, and head out west to begin her new life. But where did it go, and at what point did her own goals become greater than the eternal plan?

Zack would stop by her house now and then, to check up on her, but Dezerae just wished he would move on. Her father was more caring towards her than ever before. Her mother softened a little bit, but she kept telling her husband.

"Dezerae will do it again, that's why, I'm so harsh, how will I be able to forgive her, if she rips my heart out again?"

Her mother, heartbroken, fights the feelings of wishing she were dead, so she didn't have to feel the pain, instead of just appreciating what she has at the moment. As time continued to pass, days turned into nights and Dezerae's will to live slowly grew stronger. She finally decided with her father's pleading, to attend church with the family once again. Being an only child, made Dezerae realize, that not having the support of her parents, could only end in misery. She struggled with her own choices but finally came to submission when the local Parish Priest had a long talk with her after a service. His point of view on life, also an only child, helped Dezerae relate to her mother. The most impactful information he offered, was when he admitted to her, that his parents were very upset to find out their only son was never going to have children, and they will never know the joys of being grandparents.

Indirectly, this comforted Dezerae by opening her eyes to seeing God's plan for each person's life, was not always the plan the parents had in mind for their children. This was an internal conflict she dealt with daily. She believed in her heart at one point in her life, the destiny which was plotted out for her was that of superstardom. However, God's plan to get her to this place was different, than what she expected. By allowing God to once again, work in her life, blessings will overflow her cup. The Priest repeated many times, that for this process to start, she must believe it, because only in faith and love is God present.

After soul searching for close to a year and not working, her parents finally gave her the ultimatum. If she does not find a job, and pay rent, then she will be out on her own. Dezerae at this point in her life, still had no money, so she called Zack for that job he offered her the day she came home.

"Bloomington Lumber how can I help you?"

After hearing his voice and hesitating to talk, she finally conjured up enough courage to ask.

> "Zack? Hey, it's Dez. Good. The reason I'm calling is, remember last year when I came home, you offered me a position at your store?"

His soft-spoken voice reflected a hint of sarcasm.

> "You want to work for me Dezerae? After what you've done to me now, you ask me to help you?"

There is silence on the other end of the line, Dezerae thinks to herself *this was a mistake.* His voice speaks again.

> "I don't know why I'm doing this, but I do have a night shift open if you want it. You will have to close the store."

"That's fine, I'll take it, Zack. Thank you. Hey, I'm sorry for everything."

He immediately responds.

> "I don't have time to talk about this right now. Come in tomorrow, and you can start your training."

> "Thank you, Zack. Again, I'm sorry for hurting you."

She hangs up the phone as an excitement she has not felt in years rises. She runs into the living room, where her parents are watching television. She grabs her mother's hand, looks into her eyes, and apologizes for all the pain she has caused.

> "I don't expect you to forgive me Mom, but I hope maybe one day you will be able to."

Her father turns his head in disbelief but with a pleasant smile across his face. Her mother sits there not saying a word. She lets go of her hand and sits down on her father's lap.

"I'm sorry Dad. Do you forgive me for being the worst daughter in the whole world?"

The smile in his eyes says it all, but the words that accompany this smile are even more powerful.

"I love you Dezerae. I always have and I always will. I forgive you, and you have made me very happy to hear you ask forgiveness from your mother."

Tears swell in his eyes. She blurts out.

"I got a job."

Her mother turns to look at her acknowledging what she said.

"Really?"

"Yeah, Zack hired me. I start tomorrow. I'll be working nights closing the store."

Her mother smiles.

"I always liked that boy."

"I know, Mom. I know you did, and still do."

Her father puts his arm around Dezerae.

"See Honey, I knew she would come around. These things take time."

Her mother stands up, walks into the kitchen, and pours herself a glass of red wine. She enters the living room sipping her addiction.

"A glass of red wine a day keeps the heart attacks away. In Italy, the elderly outlive many other cultures because it makes their heart pump easier."

Dezerae giving her father a look of where that just came from, proceeds to ask.

"Mom, will I ever be able to make you happy?"

Her mother takes another sip of her wine.

"We'll see."

She turns on the twenty-year-old television. Dezerae gets up and walks out of the room.

That night, Dezerae flips through her journal, reliving the memories from what she documented over the past year. She noticed a pattern in her mother's behavior. She always used the television as an escape from her reality. Dezerae decides to try and make amends one last time. She goes to the local mall and window shops for the best large-screen television money can buy. After an hour of looking, Dezerae sets her eyes on the video, audio device she believes will win back her mother's love. Not being able to purchase the television just yet, she decides to put away, however, many paychecks it will take, to bring this state-of-the-art entertainment system home.

For months, Dezerae worked this crappy nighttime job, putting her hard-earned money into a bank account. Zack finally found another girlfriend, which eased the tension she felt between them. Having to deal with the locals of this somewhat backward town, drove her to work even longer hours, so she could eventually get back to California.

The day finally rose on her mother's birthday, when she had saved enough money to buy the television. To her advantage, the store was running a huge sale on all their digital equipment, purchasing and getting it delivered for half of what she thought it would be. Excellent morning so far. As the afternoon crept on, they were cutting the mother's birthday cake, and the doorbell rang. Dezerae asks her mother to get the door.

"Who would be coming over for my birthday?"

Dezerae looks over at the clock hanging on the wall.

"Mom, It's your birthday present from me."

Her mother gives her a disturbed look, mumbles under her breath *you should not have spent any money on me* and refuses to answer the door. Her father, not being able to deal with the knocking, gets up, and approaches the door. As he opens it, they can hear him from the dining room.

"Oh my God, Honey come here. You're never going to believe this."

The delivery person confirms the Nelson Residence, then wheels this monstrosity into their home. Her mother freaks out telling the guy to put it back on the delivery truck.

"Sorry ma'am, but it has already been paid for. Where would you like it?"

Dezerae points him in the right direction.

"Over there please."

He dollies it over to the living room and places it where Dezerae is pointing. She tips and thanks him for bringing it in.

"Dezerae we can't keep this."

Her mother replies as she can't take her eyes off of the gift.

"What is it?"

Dezerae and her father rip open the box, as this huge large screen TV stands erect in the center of the living room. The father immediately responds.

"This is amazing."

Her Mom shakes her head in disbelief.

"How in the world were you able to afford this Dezerae?"

"It was nothing Mom, I just want you and Dad to enjoy it."

Her mother fights back the tears and eventually gives in.

"Thank you Dezerae. I've been hard on you this year. I'm sorry."

She hugs her daughter for the first time in years. Having not felt this kind of compassion from her mother, tears swell in Dezerae's soul. Healing has now started to begin.

A few more months passed by, and Dezerae had finally saved enough money for her return to Los Angeles. The people she once knew were no longer there, so the feeling of going out to Los Angeles for the second time was similar to that of the first. She had to start all over meeting new faces, something she was not looking forward to. This obstacle is tough for any human to overcome, especially when there is already a past, and no one to share it with.

So for her to set things right this time, Dezerae made her proper goodbyes. She started by thanking Zack for the opportunity to raise enough money to get back on her feet and set things right with her Mother. The day she informed Zack she was leaving, he told her he was getting engaged to his girlfriend, and a little more.

"I will always love you, Dezerae, but I'm no longer in love with you. Thank you for allowing me to heal."

Tears swell in Dezerae's eyes. She admits that this trip back home taught her many valuable lessons.

"I'm ready to live God's Will for my life, Zack, and to read the Bible cover to cover." They laugh.

"By being centered in my faith again, I've realized, patience is a virtue for those who truly live the existence."

He remained silent in thought, as she kissed him goodbye on his cheek.

"I promised to keep in touch with you this time."

When it came time for her to say goodbye to her parents, their peace of mind was comforted by their support for her decision. Dezerae was finally able to move back to California, confident in her ability to succeed. The fear she once knew, was now transformed into a courageous spirit. She hugs her parents goodbye, and hops in her ride to the airport, anxiously awaiting her new bright future, she waves to them through the back window, as the car pulls away.

Chapter 5

TRANSCENDENTAL STATE OF MIND

Back in Boston, the following morning, after the signing party, the sun rises, piercing through Zyra's apartment. Zyra leans over Cindy, who is curled up in a fetal position, with her back against him, to answer the ringing phone. His gigantic headache pounds, as Alex's voice radiates throughout his brain.

"Wake up sleepy head, and get your ass over to the studio now."

Zyra brings his hand to his head.

"What? We're recording now."

Alex screams on the other line.

"Get your hung-over ass out of bed, get into the shower, and get over here NOW."

Zyra looks over at the clock.

"Dude, it's like seven in the morning, and the rest of the band is passed out in the living room."

Alex hangs up the phone after his final words.

"Good, I'll be right over."

Zyra jumps out of bed.

"Shit, Shit!"

He runs into the living room with a towel wrapped around his waist. All the members are sprawled out on the floor and couches. Bodies are everywhere. Zyra walks over to the stereo and blares the music, waking everybody up.

"Get up, Alex is on his way over."

Snitch sits up, rubbing his pounding head.

"What time is it?"

Zyra kicks out the bodies he does not know.

"Let's go, guys, we have to be at the studio."

Anaconda grabs his shirt lying next to him.

"Alright, alright just turn that shit off."

Zyra lowers the music as everybody gets up, and proceeds towards the door, stumbling trying to find their possessions. Empty beer bottles are scattered throughout the place. Cindy walks in dressed in pearl white silk lingerie.

"Oh my God, look at this place."

She turns to Zyra.

"I'll clean up as you get ready."

Zyra thanks her as he enters the shower. The door buzzer rings as Alex's voice asks to be let in. Cindy lets him in and unlocks the door. The band members, discombobulated, are still getting their stuff together as Alex opens the door, and lets himself in, whipping them into shape.

"Look you have breakfast waiting for you at the studio, you guys need to head over there now."

Wicked Bad rubs his eyes.

"I thought we weren't recording until nine?"

Alex quickly responds.

"Did you hear what I said? Don't argue with me."

They head out the door, as Zyra comes out in a towel and wet head.

"Hey, Alex. I'll be ready in a few minutes."

"Zyra, we have breakfast waiting for you guys at the studio. Drink a bunch of water to get the oxygen back into your brain, and we'll have honey, lemon, and tea waiting for you before you warm up."

Zyra dries his hair with another towel.

"No problem."

He walks back into the room.

"Good morning Cindy looks like you had fun last night."

Cindy smiles and rubs the sleep from her eyes.

"Yeah, I'm gonna stay behind and clean up this mess."

He takes in her image as light pierces through the curtains accenting her perfectly firm body.

"I never knew you looked this good without clothes."

She laughs from embarrassment and quickly comes back.

"Well, I'm glad I look better than what you imagined."

He throws her a surprised look as she continues.

"I see you undress me every morning with your eyes."

Alex grins.

"And I thought I was being inconspicuous."

Cindy smiles as she starts to clean up the mess. He walks over to her, as she bends down, tickling up her spine.

"Don't get too attached. He won't be with us forever."

He then calls out.

"Zyra, I'll see you at the studio."

"Alright, man."

Zyra responds as Alex leaves. Their first day in the studio was a success. They wrote their first song together as a band and awaited the following day with excitement. The name of the band, "Sacred Witch", rose to the surface as they all agreed that Zyra sounds like a witch when he sings.

After a month of recording in the studio, the marketing department had successfully got the town of Boston hyped up about this band. Having only one day off and his nights free, led Zyra to Salem every waking moment he could. He dove into studying the occult, and the different witch trials that took place in Salem. This beautiful small spiritual town, which sits on the Harbor, welcomed Zyra to many of the healing masses, and ceremonies that took place in local homes, and churches. Sacred Witch revolved around crystals and spells, and performed ceremonies and rituals on stage as part of their show. They quickly caught the media's attention as "Sacred Witch" was being played on Boston radio airwaves.

Almost instantly, Zyra felt the rush of fame. His ideas grew immensely, both musically and on stage. The voice coach who showed up to the studio every day worked wonders for Zyra's sound. Opening him up to notes he never knew were possible. He found his master voice and soon the world would either love or hate him. Either way, Dilemma Records was sure they found a gold mine. Sacred Witch climbed the music charts, all across America with their number-one hit single, "Fantasy Spell."

Shooting their first music video was an experience, Zyra and the band would never forget. It took place in a warehouse in New York City. Turning it into a nighttime forest with sacrificial ceremonies and snake-eating humans. This horrific sight struck America with a fear summoned from the heart of the beast. Zyra's demented crippled walk and diabolic smile became famous on every talk show and magazine cover. Growing faster than Marilyn

Manson, these guys rose to the top within the first year of being together.

Zyra spent his weekends working with Shamans, and witches learning how to use the earth's energy. His honesty and abruptness grew stronger each day. Using the anger buried deep within from childhood, Zyra was able to enhance his craft to new levels in every single performance. His image and what he represented took on a power of its own. No other band in the history of the world possessed the power that Sacred Witch was tapping into. Soon Dilemma Records had a monster on their hands too big for them to handle.

After doing a nationwide tour, the president of Haunted Shadow Records, Amir, located in Los Angeles, a much larger label, called Alex wanted to buy Sacred Witch.

"Listen to me Alex, this band is too big for you. I am making you an offer of five million dollars. This is more money your company has ever grossed in a single year. Take the money and find another star."

Alex's eyes get larger.

"Look, you did it once, you can do it again. Zyra needs to be on the West Coast. You know I have the largest metal label in the world. Zyra will be signed to us."

Alex leans back in his chair, contemplating the offer, as the phone is pressed to his ear.

"Amir, I must admit your offer is very tempting, but I need more time to think about it." Amir's voice ends the conversation.

"I'll be on a flight first thing tomorrow morning."

Dial tone, Alex hangs up the phone.

"Damn it. I should've asked for more."

Alex picks up the phone.

"Cindy, call Zyra, and tell him to get here immediately."

Zyra arrives shortly after, dressed in top-of-the-line, stylized black gothic clothing. Alex gestures for him to take a seat. Cindy brings in two lattes as normal. She flashes Zyra a look of sorrow, as if she knew what Amir wanted, thinking back on Alex's words *don't get too attached, he won't be here long*, then leaves the office. Zyra turns to Alex.

"What the hell was that about?"

Alex gets out of his chair, walks over to his bookshelf, and grabs the latest "Rolling Stone" Magazine. Flipping through the pages, he lands on the article about "Haunted Shadow Records." Alex throws it down in front of Zyra. He picks it up and sees an image of Amir.

"What's this?"

Alex shakes his head in disbelief.

"Don't you ever read?"

Zyra skims through the article and reads out loud.

"You can quote me on this. When I say I will have Zyra on Haunted Shadow Records, you better believe I will have him."

Zyra throws the magazine back at him.

"Who cares? He's talkin' shit again."

Alex takes a seat on the edge of the desk in front of him.

"You don't understand. I just hung up with Amir, he will be here tomorrow."

Zyra keeps his eyes locked on Alex.

"So you're selling me out as a whore?" silence proceeds, "This is fucked up man. Is that all I am to you a quick million?"

Alex drops his head breaking the stare.

"You're not a quick million. You have to remember, I am a businessman..."

Zyra cuts him off.

"You have to remember, I'm a bloody fuckin' rock star."

Alex continues.

"You're a bloody fuckin' rock star who is too big for my company."

"What the fuck does that mean?"

Zyra shoots back at him.

"I thought you would want somebody in here to bring your company to the next level. I owe you everything man, and now you're just going to pawn me off because some rich guy with a bank account makes you an offer?"

Alex tries to calm him down.

> "Listen to me Zyra. Just take a deep breath and listen to me. Amir can do things for your career that I can't. He can book you on international tours, and get you into movies if you want. You're just too big and controversial for Dilemma Records."

Zyra stands up and looks out the window.

> "I don't get you. You're the one who supported me in whatever I wanted to do, and now you're saying, I'm too controversial for you. I thought we were in this together."

Alex walks over and puts his hand on his back.

> "We are in this together. I thought you would have been happy."

Zyra pushes him off.

> "You think I'm stupid, Alex. I'm not going to have any creative freedom now. It's not about the money to me, it's about creating worlds that only exist in the imagination and manifesting it into reality. If I'm singing someone else's songs, he might as well call me Zyra Vanillie."

Alex laughs at his joke.

> "Zyra you are very talented. You have moved up faster than any other musician in the world. If you want to keep on climbing, you have to go where the ladder is. And right now you are at the top of my ladder."

Zyra locks eyes with him.

"How much is he offering you?"

"That's not the issue"

Alex replies.

"How much did he fuckin' offer you?!"

Alex looks him dead in the soul, with a cold blank stare, and a deep voice.

"If you don't drop it, you will be escorted out ."

Zyra shakes his head in disbelief.

"Holy Shit, I'm outta here."

Zyra storms out. Alex chases after him, and catches him in the lobby, waiting for the elevator.

"I own you Zyra. It's in your contract. That means I can do what I please with you, and nobody can do a damn thing about it."

The elevator doors open, and Tommy the messenger walks out carrying a big box. He sees Zyra and acknowledges knowing him.

"Hey remember me from about a year ago? You got huge man, I loved your show." Zyra thinks back to that first day in Boston and remembers what he said to him about a lawyer. "You were right, man, I should have gotten a lawyer."

He walks passed him, enters the elevator, and descends.

The following day, Amir shows up at Dilemma Records asking for Alex. Cindy is in awe of this man.

"I read the article in Rolling Stone about your company."

Amir smiles as he rests his arm on the counter, and his silver gothic finger ring points at her breast. She reaches out to touch the point, he grabs her wrist.

"Be careful, it's sharp."

She pulls back breaking the hypnotic spell he seemed to cast on her.

"Sorry...I, I didn't know."

"It's ok Sweetheart. Are you free tonight?"

She gasps, not expecting him to be so forward. Just then, Alex walks in and greets Amir.

"Welcome to Boston. It's nice seeing you again."

They walk into his office and take a seat on the couch. Amir pulls from his briefcase, a contract, and hands it to Alex. He looks it over seeming to fulfill his satisfaction, and asks for the check. Amir tilts his head, raises his finger to Alex's cheek, and serpentines down.

"Do you think, I am going to hand over five million dollars without a signature?"

Alex gives a nervous laugh.

"Of course."

Amir hands him a silver gothic-looking pen, with see-through red liquid inside. Alex examines the pen.

"This is very unusual."

Amir says with a straight face.

"It's my blood."

Concern strikes Alex's face as another nervous laugh rises. Amir does not seem entertained. Alex signs, as Amir hands over the check. A transfer of energy takes place in the room. A gust of wind sweeps through.

"So where's my boy?"

Alex clears his throat.

"Cindy called him, and told him to be here."

Just then, Cindy announces over the intercom that Zyra is here. Alex responds.

"Let him in, please."

Moments later, Zyra enters his office wearing all-black leather, trench coat and platform knee-high boots. Amir stands up, puts both hands on his cheeks, and kisses Zyra on the lips.

"It is time to make you a superstar my beautiful young man."

Zyra backs away.

"I recognize you from the picture in Rolling Stone. You must be my pimp 'cause what, I'm your whore."

Alex laughs at the abruptness.

> "Well, Zyra, you're going to have to have everything packed up, and out of the penthouse by tomorrow morning."

Zyra clenches his teeth staring Alex in the eyes.

> "You've done this before."

> "Yes."

Alex admits as Zyra walks over to the gold record of *Sacred Witch* hanging on the wall.

> "So I take it all these gold records you have hung on your wall are now Amir's property as well."

Amir picked up on Zyra's irritation.

> "Zyra, Alex, and I have been in business together for many years. It's better this way, not telling the artists their destiny."

Zyra looks over at Amir.

> "Why?"

Amir walks over to Zyra, puts his arm around him, and casts his eyes upon the city.

> "What do you see?"

Zyra laughs and looks over at Alex.

"You know what, you can't even come up with your lines."

Alex drops his head as Amir answers for him.

"He learns from the best, Zyra."

"So you're the best, Amir?"

Zyra asks as he takes out a joint, and lights up. Amir widens his eyes at his response. Zyra continues.

"Ok, I get it. Alex, I still think you have no backbone, but I understand, and I do want to thank you for everything you've done."

Amir sits in Alex's seat and puts his boots on the desk. The sweet smoke aroma fills the air as Amir confronts Zyra.

"You plan on passing that?"

Zyra hands the joint to Amir.

"So are you a witch, Zyra, or is it just a gimmick?"

Amir takes a hit as Zyra thinks for a second, and Amir passes the joint to Alex. Zyra finally responds.

"How do you think I rose to the top so quickly? I was, how would you say this, born into it."

"Wisdom beyond your years."

Amir says as he blows out the smoke. Alex takes a hit and passes it back to Zyra.

"So now that I'm your dirty little whore, what happens from here?"

Zyra takes another hit and passes it to Amir.

"You have to stop saying that. You will be a millionaire. I have you booked for a movie called 'The Lizard' starting in a couple of months. It's a lead role about a human lizard who gives birth to a new species, as he is being crucified to a cross. You will wear the crown of the new lizard king."

Zyra looks over at Alex, then back at Amir.

"What are you talking about?"

"Today, artists need to be able to jump into any medium. Getting you into films while the iron is hot, is most lucrative for everyone. In the meantime, you will work on an album called, *Kanniballations*, and the soundtrack for *The Lizard*. Alex has been documenting everything you've been through this past year. I have a ghostwriter who already started writing your biography. You will read it, fill in what has been left out."

Zyra takes the joint and inhales as he comments.

"This is unbelievable. So a...what, this is how Hollywood works?"

He blows out a huge hit in Alex's face. Amir and Alex remain silent.

Cindy walks in and smells the air.

"Excuse me, Alex, would you like me to lock the doors for lunch break?"

Alex agrees.

"Thanks for looking out Cindy."

She walks back out, Amir watches her every move. He looks over at Zyra.

"Have you hit that yet?"

Delivering an evil grin.

"Of course you have. Tonight we both taste the bittersweet."

Upon the midnight dream, elevate the scream, blood fiend, witch vamp desire.

Chapter 6

HOLLYWOOD

Dezerae's driver pulls up to the main strip in Hollywood, California. The door opens, and Dezerae steps out onto the Hollywood pavement. People of all cultures, shapes, and sizes walk the streets paved with Hollywood stars. Dezerae, holding her bag over her shoulder, quickly enters the shuffle. Down the street, she sees a local cheap motel and wanders over. As she enters, an Arabian woman behind the desk greets her, asking how long she will be staying. Dezerae responds.

"Just a couple of days, until I can get on my feet."

She gives her the money and receives the key. Walking through the parking lot, Dezerae sees two suspicious characters, who look to her like they are making an illegal deal. She mumbles to herself.

"Dear Lord, get me through this safely."

She receives a burst of confidence and enters the room. The first phone call she makes is back home, to let her parents know she just got in, and for them not to worry.

Further down the street, on Hollywood Boulevard, Zyra and Amir pull up to Haunted Shadow Records. Zyra looks around, not believing he's on the soil where legends are made.

"You know Amir, Hollywood looks better in the movies. This place reminds me of Crack Ville or something."

Amir opens the door for him, looks him square in the eye, and says.

"They are building this place up again. You should appreciate it."

They walk up this long dark stairwell, walls filled with framed posters of rock bands, as Zyra stops, touches one of the posters.

"Wow, hmmm, I didn't realize they were on your label as well."

Amir looks back.

"There's lots to learn. Let's go."

They approach the office at the top of the stairs. Above the door, a neon sign reads, "Haunted Shadow Records." Amir responds.

"I saw you play at *The Whiskey* last year, you make it sound like you've never been here."

"For one night, and I didn't leave the hotel room after the show. I was in and out of here so quickly, it was like just another bar I played."

They walk past the secretary, who seems a bit more liberal looking, with piercings on her face, and multicolored hair, compared to Cindy.

"This is Duppy." "Duppy? Now that's interesting."

Duppy looks up at Zyra.

"Nice to meet you Zyra, my name means ghost or spirit, am I real, or am I not? Welcome to Haunted Shadow Records."

Zyra looks at Amir.

"Oh, I like this girl."

"She's off limits, let's go."

They enter Amir's office.

His domain seems like something out of a horror film. Alien, demon, and monster creatures line the black shiny walls, in between the gold records, which encompass twice as many hits than Dilemma. The window behind Amir's desk overlooks the Hollywood sign. Zyra immediately responds.

"That's so cool, just in case you forget where you are."

Amir laughs. Zyra takes a seat in Amir's high-back red velvet chair, something off the throne of hell.

"I can get used to this."

Amir turns on the stereo which is tuned to the local rock station.

"Zyra, tomorrow you will be meeting with your acting coach. I got you the best in the industry. After you read the script tonight, start memorizing your lines. Trust me, you need to know them, backward and forwards before you step on set. The coach is getting paid big bucks to make sure you do."

Zyra nods his head.

"Who am I acting with?"

Amir picks up his phone, dials voice mail, and jots down the necessary information. He looks up at Zyra.

"The casting director just called and said Cameron Diaz is out of town on emergency, and will not be back for a month."

Zyra leans forward in his chair.

"I was acting with Cameron Diaz?"

Amir dials the casting director.

"Not anymore."

Focusing his attention on the phone.

"Hey, we just got back into town...It was good. So what are we going to do?... I will not put Zyra against a no name....No, we need someone with more depth. Someone who will make this role believable, not cartoony. I don't know, that's your job."

Zyra is hanging on to every word.

"Zyra's meeting with Bobbie Shaw Chance tomorrow, maybe he knows somebody. Call me tomorrow."

He hangs up the phone.

"You believe this crap, they want to put you against some no name."

Amir turns up the radio as 'Crazy Train' from Ozzy and Randy blares. They both start singing. Amir smiles at Zyra.

"Ozzy and Randy, Baby, my boys."

"Ozzy and I go back many years."

Zyra looks up at him.

"You know Ozzy, personally?"

Amir laughs.

"Personally enough to be invited to his home on several occasions."

Zyra freaks out. Amir looks at him.

"Hey Zyra, listen to me, you need to cut all of the star-struck, mumbo jumbo, out. Do you understand me? People are going to go from, thinking they've heard of you, to fuckin' worshiping the ground you walk on. Do I make myself clear?"

Zyra lights up a joint.

"Understood."

"Cool, so let's think. What starlet can we get to co-star?"

* * *

Meanwhile, as the sun begins its descent, darkness, restless winds, something uneasy in the air. Dawn creeps upon, Dezerae grabs her coat, from the bed podium, and heads down the street to Starbucks. The local musicians dressed in ripped clothing, hung over and barefoot, fill the atmosphere, with their harmonic sounds, singing about soul redemption. Dezerae glares at them with a kindred spirit, flips them some money, and keeps walking. She looks at the clock reading 5:15 pm.

"That makes it 7:15 in Bloomington."

She laughs to herself. The waitress behind the counter recognizes her.

"Hey I know you...you look so familiar... aren't you that chick from 'Attack of the Killer Luv Bugz'?

Dezerae smiles, not expecting someone to recognize her.

"Um...yeah, you saw that?"

The girl freaks out screaming to the guy, at the other end of the counter.

"Hey Rob, this is the chick from that killer luv bug movie."

Rob hands the two customers their drinks and runs over to Dezerae.

"You don't understand, we love you. When we heard you left the industry a couple of years back, a few of my buddies formed a huge website, a fan club for you."

Dezerae looks at the girl.

"Is he for real?"

She has a smile across her face brighter than any star in the sky.

"Yes, Ms. Dezerae Nelson. We love and respect you. You are always welcome here."

Dezerae is taken aback by their kindness, yet, still hesitant about believing them.

"Well, thank you. If this is how you *truly* feel, I appreciate your support. What is the website called?"

The waitress looks over at the guy behind the counter, giving him a look like should she tell her.

"Well, Johnny made it up."

She points at the guy. Dezerae, anticipation rising.

"What is it?"

Johnny answers.

"www.dngmwd.com"

"What the heck does that stand for?"

Johnny tries to hold in his laughter.

"I never thought I would ever meet you, especially not at work."

Dezerae orders her favorite drink.

"Raspberry Mocha Frappuccino, please…"

Dezerae continues to demand an answer. Johnny finally gives in while making her drink.

"Dezerae Nelson gives me wet dreams."

She looks at him allowing the moment to pass.

"I'll take that as a compliment, even though it's borderline rude."

He jumps in immediately.

"Take it as the highest compliment."

She laughs gaining his respect back. He hands her the drink, she offers money.

"Nah, you know what, it's on me. It's not every day, I get to meet my favorite actress." Dezerae looks back, nods her head, smiles.

"Thank you…"

She takes a seat outside overlooking Sunset Strip.

At the cross light, in plain view of Dezerae, Zyra runs out in front of a car, which *squeals* its brakes, almost breaking his legs, as the car swerves around him. The guy sticks his head out the window screaming.

"ASSHOLE!"

Zyra laughs, then pretends a fake limp, holding his knee. Dezerae laughs to herself, *That guy's nuts.* The script falls from Zyra's hand, and Dezerae *screams out.*

"Your script!"

Zyra looks back, tires peel over it. He picks up the tire-tracked script, cursing under his breath, and walks across the street. After entering the coffee shop, Zyra orders an extra-large, triple shot, caramel macchiato, and a muffin. He sees Dezerae, staring at him through the glass, thinking to himself, *she looks familiar.* He receives his drink and heads out towards her. The guy behind the counter comments.

"He thinks he's gonna get Dezerae. Watch this looser."

Their eyes widen, and Zyra takes a seat next to Dezerae. She holds out her hand, waiting to shake his, he grabs a joint and places it in his mouth.

"I'm Zyra."

They shake hands. He lights his joint.

"Are you crazy, you just can't light up a joint in public."

"Why not?"

Dezerae takes in his response, and smiles deep down within her soul, almost as if butterflies start to tingle.

"I'm Dezerae, nice to meet you Zyra."

"So how long have you been in town?"

Zyra asks as Dezerae sips her Frappuccino. She looks up at him.

"Is it that noticeable?"

"Yeah, most people around here aren't that friendly, from what I've been told."

He replies.

"Well, I just got back into town today. I was gone for two years."

He gives her a strange look.

"What kind of look is that?"

She gestures to him for a hit. He hands it to her.

"I don't mean to freak you out. It's just, that I moved here today *too*, from Boston. I guess more than one person moves to this city every day."

They laugh. Dezerae's curiosity gets the best of her.

"What's that script, that you almost got yourself killed over?"

He searches through it.

"It's called '*The Lizard*.' It's a pretty cool character."

She picks up on his non-human movements.

"You, or the Lizard?"

She makes him belly laugh, something not too many people do. His mind wanders, trying to figure out why she looks so familiar.

Dezerae waves her hand in front of his face.

"Hello Zyra, stop staring through me, you're giving me the creeps."

Zyra snaps out of it.

"Sorry, that was weird."

Her concerned expression directs him to share dialog about his fantasy.

"Have you ever acted before?"

She takes another sip of her drink.

"Why have you got a role for me?"

"I'm serious, you look so familiar, and I *can't* figure it out. I don't want to be rude, but you almost look like this erotic B-movie star, I love."

She remains silent.

"Wait, you said your name is Dezerae, the actress I'm talking about is Dezerae Nelson. Is that you?"

She lets the joy and laughter slowly build up inside.

"Anyway, we need a female, who looks like Cameron Diaz, and you sort of do. *Can you act?*"

She finally answers.

"Yes, I'm Dezerae Nelson, you moron…"

She bursts out laughing.

Still not sure, "Okay, Dezerae Nelson, what movies have you been in?"

He touches her arm. She takes back control and seduces him to his core.

"Um, Zyra Jordonello, I've done many movies, that obviously, you've seen."

"Wait a second, I never told you my last name."

"You don't think everyone here knows who you are?"

Zyra looks around and sees people whispering to themselves pointing at them.

"I've done a lot of independent films, and men's magazines, actually that's why I'm here, to make my come back, but this time, mainstream."

Zyra leans into her, very interested. The people behind the counter, are in disbelief, as they watch their love story develop, in the distance, through the glass.

"My last movie went straight to video, DVD, and online streaming, so I haven't quite made it to the big screen yet, except as an extra in Forrest Gump."

Zyra begins to like her.

"Really? You were in Forrest Gump?"

"It wasn't a big deal or anything, I just walked by, holding a baby, as Forrest Gump sat on the park bench."

"I think that's so cool. I liked that movie."

She wipes the foam off his lips and licks caramel off her finger.

"Sorry, but, that looked too good."

Zyra jumps up with excitement, and passion gleams in his eyes.

"Attack of the Killer Luv Bugz, I'm the queen lady bug…"

He laughs and continues.

"I couldn't remember that damn movie!"

"Damn movie?"

"Well, you know what I mean."

Dezerae gives a nervous laugh.

"Yeah, that's me, queen ladybug."

Zyra continues to freak out.

"I just saw your movie like three weeks ago. I'm telling you, I loved it. You know, you might be perfect for this role."

She leans into him.

"Really what's the role?"

As they sit and read the script out loud together, a chemistry neither of them expected grows like the tree of life. An hour and a half later, Zyra shuts the manuscript.

"So what do you think?"

Her mouth is open, speechless as she tries to summon the words to fit this most incredible journey.

"This is the strangest, yet, most thought-provoking script, I ever read."

Zyra smiles.

"So you like it?"

"Like it, I'd die for this role. This role is me, and against your character, watch out world, life's about to change."

She looks up at the sky, lips the words *thank you*. Zyra grabs her hand, pulls her from her seat, and they walk away.

"You have to meet Amir."

The next couple of weeks, for both Zyra and Dezerae, were life-changing. Dezerae's struggle between leading the ideal Christian life, and giving in to the sweet temptation of lust and love, was inevitable, as they made love anywhere and everywhere. Dezerae was offered the role in "The Lizard," her largest budget film to date. Things were going their way. Zyra was happy for the first time in his life. She gave him hope, fulfilling a part in him that was empty, for so many years. The City of Angels somehow makes irrational thoughts, rational, as they take a trip to Vegas to elope.

Wedding bells transform the Vegas nightlife, as this about-to-be newlywed couple, Zyra and Dezerae, make their vows before Gene Simmons at the KISS Chapel. Just as Gene is about to pronounce them man and wife, Zyra gets locked into a vision.

A flash image of this horrifying white slimy beast swims passed his eyes. Zyra screams. Gene looks over at him.

"Is that an I do?"

Zyra locks eyes with a perplexed Dezerae.

"I'm sorry, I'm sorry, yes, of course, I do."

Gene hands them both a chalice of blood.

"Drink!"

Zyra takes a sip and hands it back to Gene.

"Drink."

Gene hands chalice to Dezerae. She takes a sip and hands it back.

"By the power invested in me, I now pronounce you man and wife. You may KISS your bloody bride."

He sticks out his long tongue as Zyra and Dezerae lock lips. Gene finishes off the blood in the chalice, letting it flow down his chin, and chest.

The next morning, Dezerae looks over at Zyra, sprawled out naked across the bed. She smiles, kisses his toes, and tickles his legs, arousing him once again. Her long blonde hair travels up his rock-hard body, as she grabs him, and inserts him into her. Their passion increases as Dezerae rides him, arching her back, the desert sun pierces through the window, overlooking the main boulevard. Their moans of ecstasy rise through the air, intermixing with the never-ending clanking of the gambling machines. Zyra rolls Dezerae over, with a smile larger than life.

"I love you my beautiful wife, Mrs. Jordonello."

She whispers in his ear.

"I love you, my beautiful husband."

"So, where would you like to spend, the first day, of the rest of our lives together?"

He cradles her face with his hands.

"You're looking at it Mr. Jordonello."

They continue to make love, never leaving the bed, except to shower, which passion continues there, as water runs down their bodies, minds, and souls, intertwining as one.

A few days pass, as we see Zyra and Dezerae, moving into their new home in Malibu. This extraordinary mansion stands tall on a cliff, the ocean breeze off the Pacific rushes against the window walls, viewing the Pacific Coast Highway and the beach below. For miles stretching out as far as the eye can see, the sky meets the ocean creating the horizon line. Tears of joy stream down Dezerae's face, as she thinks back over the past month, and how her life just sort of happened so quickly. Zyra walks up behind putting his arm around her.

"Are you okay?"

She turns around and looks into his soul.

"I never thought I could be this happy."

He smiles.

"I love you, Sweety."

Dezerae pushes away for a moment.

"Hey Zyra, what happened on the altar?"

"On the altar?"

"Yeah, when we were getting married, something happened to you, like you were locked in a vision or something."

Zyra walks over to the window.

"Yeah, there's something out there."

She walks up behind him.

"We have a busy schedule, with filming this week, and you having to record your album."

Zyra raises his arms above his head, stretches, and yawns.

"I know."

Alternating days between shooting "The Lizard" and recording, "Kanniballations," Zyra has been sleep-deprived, slowly wearing himself down. Their lives, moving quickly, getting caught up in the hustle, not thinking about the message being produced, from both the movie and album. Another morning arrives, on the TV, as Zyra and Dezerae, are getting ready for set, Holly Gossip, the news anchor assigned to follow this newlywed celebrity couple reports.

"Controversy grows like a fungus, ripping through people like rapid fire, changing the course of history forever, as we tune in behind the scenes of "The Lizard, and "Kanniballations.""

Dezerae stops to watch.

"Oh wow, we made the news again, honey."

Zyra walks in, and on the TV, Bobbie Shaw Chance enters.

"She's old Hollywood."

"She knows what she's doing."

She turns off the TV.

"I wanted to see that."

"We're gonna be late, let's go."

They rush out of the house.

Chapter 7

ANGELIC DREAMS

Hours after the sun settles, Dezerae and Zyra stroll in from set. Zyra strips down, pours himself a glass of wine, takes a sip, and hits the bed. Dezerae takes off her clothes, grabs the Bible from her nightstand, and hops into bed, reading where she left off. Zyra looks over at her.

"Why do you keep reading that before bed?"

She looks at him, conjuring her words.

"Well, it's like a sheep led astray. I'm the sheep, and this book is my guide back."

He looks at her, not sure how to respond, but he lets it pass. They kiss good night, he rolls away with his back facing her. Dezerae continues to read.

We enter into Zyra's mind where he dreams of the thick brown cloud, hovering over the City of Angels. The sounds of church bells, in unison, playing "Amazing Grace." Multi-colored paints streak across the sky, greys complement the pinks and purples, and rays pierce through the darkness and dance on the ocean canvas. Seagulls spread their wings, and glide with the breeze, as people manifest along the beach fronts; some are building sand castles, others blissfully sin in the cold brisk water. Lifeguards, believed to be beach gods, patrol the area, as their eyes remain on the surfers, indulging in their fantasy. Bikini babes jog on the beach, their footprints left bloody, as lookers, bugged-out eyes, drool over God's beautiful creations. But something's not right.

Instantly, thunder ROARS, shaking the sky, with heavenly desire. Lightning electrifies, reaches down as fingertips, and scatters the living creatures. A voice echoes in Zyra's mind, *"Can you feel the rain?"* The rain, heavy as tears of God on Good Friday, pours down upon the earth. Life-filled pearl-white wings, sprout from the core of the sun, gripping the air with conviction, crawling forth, pulling a spirit bridge, from the other side. Harmony accompanies the voices of angels passing through, elevating Zyra's awareness, as the sound of the bridge continues to grow.

Hovering the spirit bridge in the center of the sun, a being of light, waits anxiously for his wings, as the breeze from the bridge growing, rips across his long blond hair, striking his chiseled cheeks, and golden hazel eyes. A familiar voice charges forth from behind the sun, giving life to the wings at the end of the bridge; doves blazing with fire escort this Angel to the edge.

"Go Nazareth. Complete your mission!"

Anticipation and excitement, to its greatest extent, is Zyra's spirit as he waits for the Angel to jump. Nazareth settles back into his wings and spreads them far and wide. Immediately, he separates from the bridge, his back slightly arched, his feet dangling above the earth, thousands of miles below. The sun closes behind him, the bridge disappears, and he *free-falls* clumsily, tossing, turning, flipping out of control. The 120 mph wind presses against his face, as he enters the earth's atmosphere.

The earth enlarges, and his stomach rises to his throat. He looks up, and the sky retrieves further away, the sounds of angels are nothing but wrathful screams, guiding his flight. Finally, both wings catch the air at the same time, slowing him down, as he swims playfully through the air. Within the reflection of the aqua-blue waters, the bottom of his wings curls, as he somersaults backward through the sky.

The sky and ocean, transpose into mirrors, and he tucks his arms and legs in, increasing speed, traveling through this new infinite reality. His thoughts bounce around, like numbers of a lottery, his wings engulf him, curling him into a ball; his dizziness, a logical state of mind, almost does not allow his voice to echo, from this world to earth, where Zyra dreams his dream.

"Here I come, Zyra."

Under the black and white satin leopard print sheets, Zyra *jolts* awake, and watches Nazareth dive from the ceiling mirror, into his own eyes. He jumps out of bed and looks at the alarm clock, 4:20 a.m. His eyes, bloodshot, slightly open, as he wipes the sleep away with his middle finger. The moonlight pours through the window, spotlighting his face. Nazareth, wings outspread, stands tall in the corner of his room. Catching his balance, Zyra grabs the half-drunk glass of wine.

"What the hell was that?"

Zyra downs it, and Angel disappears. The only words that rise from his half-dead soul, linger out into the room.

"Cool dream."

Dezerae still lies motionless next to him, with the Bible open on her chest.

* * *

Meanwhile, the streets of Los Angeles are full of dope pushers, prostitutes, and nightlife authorities busting those they can. A quiet little street in Hollywood, Sycamore, slithers down a slight incline, underneath tall trees and houses to keep it dark. An obnoxious drunkard, Garth Blackwood, the type who would sell his soul for fame, mumbles to the cat crossing his path.

"You know, I've killed for less than that."

He laughs to himself, grabs his keys from his pocket, and opens the door to an old white Sunbird. He enters his car, sprawls out across the back seat, and locks the door with his foot. Before passing out, he looks at the clock on the dash.

"4:20, shiiiiit...I got a couple of hours..."

He lets his head fall against the seat.

* * *

Zyra slams his head back down onto the black feather pillow.

"I got a couple hours."

As his head sinks back down into his pillow, he renters the dream; back through the infinite mirrors bouncing off the infinite reality. He finds himself straddling a black Harley Davidson which vibrates between his black leather thighs. He rides fast without fear, through the winding streets of Los Angeles. His right hand firmly pulls back on the throttle, and his knees tighten against the engine, forcing life into every part of his being. Through his dark visor, he sees a car approach, skipping the hands of time, it lays on its horn, echoing throughout his dream. As he flies around a turn, his right knee barely touches the ground, he continues to feed this wild boar gas, until the bike straightens out, and the front tire lifts; thoughts of death excite him.

The ascent of his tire while riding this black hog, continues to elevate higher, trusting the air beneath the rubber skin, as the earth sends excitement throughout his soul. His back wheel rides the incline against a winding, snake-like road as his left arm rises in victory. His scream echoes throughout the night, as the moonlight dances gracefully around him. The ocean spans out across the horizons, hundreds of feet below his moving bike, riding the wings of Nazareth.

Nazareth's spirit leaves Zyra, rises above the trees, then watches the bike drop back down onto the pavement, and drive away. His calm soothing voice.

"I'll see you later."

Fear grips Zyra's soul, then releases as he feels this presence vanish. Nazareth, now free, flies west over the homes following Mulholland Drive, the winding path along the peak of the hills. To his left is the valley and to his right, subdivisions of Los Angeles. In front of him, the infamous sign reads, "HOLLYWOOD."

In the distance, Nazareth spots one of the doves that escorted him just beyond the bridge. He communicates through osmosis…the dove is paralyzed by discernment then turns its head and looks his way. The dove flies towards Nazareth, landing on his pointer finger in front of the sign. He cradles its head petting down its neck.

"Your feathers are smooth as silk."

The sun shines bright illuminating their presence, as they lock eyes and interlock spirits. The dove slightly turns its head again, takes in the information, and flies off.

Nazareth gravitates towards the ocean, where his spirit regains energy. Angels and demons fill the atmosphere above the ocean. Two opposing forces within the same realm, a dichotomy that creates a brisk breeze, making the hair on the back of Nazareth's neck rise. He takes in a deep breath, and presses his fingers against his temples, concentrating and internalizing vision through his mind's eye. As he vacillates, within the ocean breeze above the sea, he spots Zyra riding in the distance, through the gliding eyes of the dove, hovering above him.

* * *

Below the ocean surface, still within Zyra's dream, the vast brine bottom fluctuates for miles. Coral reefs and bright-colored plants fade into view. A school of exotic fish are spotted in the distance, targeted as prey. Submerged life quickly scatters, as a large presence rapidly butterflies through, and in one gulp, its hunger is satisfied; hundreds of fish slam into the back of its throat, forcing down its long anaconda-like neck. Its green fork tongue traps them in its mouth as large canine fangs rip apart those unfortunate rarities, caught in between its upper and lower jaw.

A "GROWL" from the bowels of this inner beast, vibrates throughout the ocean. The water ripples on the surface. All ocean life knows this beast, as the ruler of the underworld. Warm blood caresses its body from the half-eaten fish. Its long white dragon wings, protrude out, guiding the beast up through the frigid water, to the surface. The sun beats down upon its back, warming its body. This beast is DRAGON-WHALE.

Nazareth absorbs the image and descends in flight for a better view. The disfiguration in his face gives away his confusion and curiosity. The wing span alone of this obscure mammal exceeds seventy yards. Its white slimmed coat has a jagged neck, the size of a full mature anaconda, the body of a blue whale, and the tail of a dragon, close to the size of its wing span. Making this beast, larger than a football field. Nazareth cannot restrain from commenting on this creation.

"Lord have Mercy."

I've never seen anything like it. I can't make out its head, Nazareth thinks to himself fully absorbed by this creature.

Water shoots up from Dragon-Whale's back, and slams into Nazareth's feet, with a force flipping him mid-air. Through the eyes of the dove, Nazareth sees Zyra, drop into a ditch, in the middle of the road, his bike flips into an on-coming car, CRASH, head-on.

Nazareth's head snaps back with great force, swallowing too much water from Dragon-Whale's back. Guilt overwhelms him, as he thinks of his regret of leaving Zyra, *why did I leave him?* He coughs up water, tears stream down his face, and rage boils in his blood. He clenches his teeth, and veins pop from his neck and forehead, as he tries to regain composure.

"Augh...You distract me..."

He CHARGES the beast without fear. For the first time, it raises its head from the water and expels fire from its breath. Nazareth, face to face, SHOCK, paralyzed as a ball of fire jets straight for him. Nazareth snaps out of it, his wings catch the force, pushing him through the air. The fire *burns* his eyes, and he enters his mind, through the eyes of the dove, now watching Zyra SMASH into the car windshield.

The bike FLIPS over the car, CRASHES onto the ground, and rolls to a stop. The car SLAMS on its brakes swerves through the streets, and Zyra is thrown from the hood. Zyra lands on the ground, motionless. The *skidding* tires stop inches from crushing Zyra's skull.

Nazareth shakes off the vision, the wind and mist press against his face. Trying to fly away, Nazareth is not going anywhere, locked in by razor-sharp teeth, clamped down onto his wings, where they attach to his back. As Nazareth lingers from the jaws of death, his feet skim across the ocean surface, traveling at high speed. Dragon-Whale turns its head, lifting Nazareth up and over its body. Now pressing forth backward, water shoots up from Dragon-Whale's back, and SLAMS Nazareth in between the legs. His wings *are* slightly from his back, he PUKES into the water. Dragon-Whale releases him, and Nazareth *tumbles* through the air, in the opposite direction. Closing his wings around him, Nazareth uses healing energy to restore his wounds. After composing himself, Nazareth CHARGES the beast.

Dragon-Whale's white slimy tiger head, with black oval alien eyes, rises from the ocean, and faces Nazareth, nose to nose; water fans from Dragon-Whale's jaws *...ROARS...* with fury. Nazareth's eyes widen, his jaw drops, and fear permeates his being, taking in the sight of Dragon-Whale's head. Its green serpentine tongue, slithers out, SLAMS, Nazareth upside the skull, BLACK OUT. Dragon-Whale ROARS from the *depths of hell*. Inside Nazareth, blurriness fades in from the darkness, vision is granted, followed by a deep echoed voice, Arabic drives from the tiger's mouth, and penetrates Nazareth's soul.

"Have a safe flight."

With precision and innate quickness, Dragon-Whale's tail, rises from the water, POUNDS Nazareth, sending him back across the ocean, toward shore. Nazareth's wings protect him, as he is forced onto the beach *skidding* to a stop, he blacks out again. A flicker of fire light in the darkness, opens Nazareth's mind, to see through the eyes of the dove, encircling Zyra's accident. The back tire of the smashed Harley spins awkwardly. The California license plate, barely hanging on reads, "ZYRA."

An Asian woman, in her mid-50s, quickly jumps from her car, and runs over to Zyra who is lying flat on his back, motionless; his helmet, pressed against the tire. The stench of burning rubber, and metal aromas the air, as layers of dirt cover his body. The woman panics and drops to her knees.

"Oh my god, you ok? Hello, hello…"

A classic black fancy vehicle pulls up to the accident. A mid 40's, or so, African American male, BABEL, dressed to kill, in an antique white Victorian three-piece tuxedo, gets out of his car, and calmly walks over. The woman, shaking from the accident, looks up at the man with distressed tears in her eyes, and a quivering bottom lip.

"I didn't see him."

His cold stare, yet warm smile, confuses her fragility. He speaks sedately with confidence.

"Don't touch him."

A red Wrangler reduces its speed and approaches the accident. A young actor type in sunglasses fronts his concern.

"Is everything alright?"

The man in the suit turns around and locks eyes with this individual. The driver, being an idiot, says the first thing that comes to his mind.

"Where'd he learn to drive, crash course 101?"

He cracks up at his indecisiveness to care, pushes his sunglasses up his nose, and guns it. Babel says to himself.

"Pride is your demise."

The jeep flies around the turn, spins out of control, and rolls off the cliff, crashing to his death.

The woman wipes her tears away, finally calms her nerves under his spell, as she listens to the birds cry with sorrow accompanying the crash. Babel kicks Zyra in the helmet. Shocked, the woman's eyes display panic, snapping from the spell for a brief moment, "What are you doing?" as she moves closer to Zyra. His frigid stare accelerates her fear, as he reaches around her, fists the back of her dark oily hair digging his rings into the back of her head, *"Move On."*

A sinister smile slithers across his face, exposing his gold teeth, as he forces her to her feet. The dove, Nazareth was using, *dives down* and presses against the man's face. He throws the woman back down to her knees, grabs the dove by the wings, pushes against the spine, snaps its back, lifts it to his mouth, bites off its head, and spits it out, bouncing it off Zyra's helmet. Zyra opens his eyes, staring back at him, the soulless eyes of the dove. Nazareth *screams* out to the heavens, as the eyes of the dove slowly fade to black.

The man throws the headless bird at the woman, splattering blood all over her. She backs away in fright. The surrounding birds cry as they vacillate above their dead companion. The woman, terrified, looks down at her hands, with submission in her eyes, and looks up at him, "Who are you?" He licks the blood from his stained teeth, and pulls a feather from his mouth, "You better worry about your kid." He flicks the feather in the direction of her car, turning her around to see her child's face, smashed against the inside of the cracked windshield. As reality hits, submission falls into tragic sorrow, she runs back to the car in defeat and leans her bosom against her dead son's bloody body.

Zyra, still in the dream, wakes up within the surrealism, after another blow to the head, from Babel's snakeskin boot; his vision becomes clear as Babel kneels and flips open his visor. Zyra, trying to make sense of the situation.

"What do you want?"

Babel reaches down noticing his reflection in the visor, clenches Zyra's vest, lifting him off the ground, seducing his way into his soul.

"You're my bitch Z. I'm gonna teach you to bark."

The Asian woman pulls her child's face from the shattered glass and rests her lifeless son against the seat. Chunks of hair, blood, and brains, remain dangling from the splintered windshield.

"God help me..."

She lays him down and gives him CPR. As she breathes life into his collapsed lungs, she finally pounds her fists onto his chest, lost in perpetual sadness, still no air circulates.

Zyra finds the strength to lift off his helmet, and SLAMS it down on Babel's forehead, ripping open the skin. Babel shakes off the shock, as blood pours down his face. He wipes it with his middle finger and puts it into his mouth. During this distraction of tasting his blood, the wound miraculously heals, Zyra gets up, and limps off, disappearing into the nearby woods. The sound of the Asian woman's sighs echo in Zyra's mind.

"Eloi, Lema Sabachthani? "Eloi, Lema Sabachthani?"

The overcast releases rain, as another woman's voice enters, familiar to Zyra.

"And what do we do?..."

A BEEP from Zyra's alarm clock faintly enters; the rain thickens; the female's voice crescendos.

"...We kill His only begotten Son."

As if time stops, Zyra looks around and then continues to run through the muddy forest. Another BEEP can be heard. His foot catches in between the roots of a tree, and falls to the ground, twisting his ankle. He can feel the presence of Babel getting closer. BEEP from the alarm summons his presence. *Am I dreaming?* he thinks to himself. Releasing his ankle, the pain subsides, and he becomes fully aware of his state of mind. He takes off running again, and a tree branch from out of nowhere, SLAMS him in the face, shattering his head like broken glass. At this same moment, the female's aggravated voice, Dezerae, screams.

"Damn it, Zyra, get up!"

The alarm clock "Beeps" again. *I'm trying,* he thinks to himself. Instantly on the thought, the surrounding trees become liquefied mirrors reflecting the inside of his bedroom. Dezerae is cleaning up the broken glass from their wedding frame, that was knocked over by Zyra during the dream. His spirit dives through, and drops from his ceiling mirror, into his body, which is sleeping in fetal position.

The Bible was moved to the nightstand where the wedding frame used to be. The passage illuminates "Blessed is he that reads, and they that hear the words of this prophecy...for the time is at hand."

Zyra sits up breathing heavily, and looks over at the clock which reads, "7:07 a.m." The morning sun shines brightly through the silver blinds, which reflect their image. His hands rise blocking the light from his perturbed look.

"I can still snooze for ten more minutes."

"Oh no you don't. Get up. We're going to be late."

Zyra looks at Dezerae.

"I think we're gonna upset a lot of people today."

He slams his head back down on the pillow, and closes his eyes; he's out like a light, and sees Nazareth, disheveled, lying in the sand. Nazareth sits up, brings his hand to his throbbing head, and looks out at the ocean. His eyes widen, in disbelief, from the image produced before him. Protruding up from the water is Dragon-Whale. Its long neck and tiger head are drawn back in strike position. It spreads its wings and speaks.

"I AM YOUR GOD. You will have no other gods before me."

After turning itself around, it shoots water from its back and dives into the sea. Nazareth's wings flutter, breaking him from this darkened paralysis; he rises to his feet, and with great fury roars back.

"BLASPHEMER!"

Meanwhile, Dezerae is in the shower singing her morning prayers, shampoo glides down her body, into the drain. Zyra turns in his sleep, stops singing, and raises her voice above the shooting water.

"I think you're right, maybe we are going a bit too far with this movie. I just looked at it as an opportunity."

He grabs the pillow and puts it over his head. Back in Zyra's dream, he is still in hot pursuit, running for his life, through a spider web, spun between two trees. He stops, and looks down, trying to pull webs from his face, a thorned branch GASHES a piece of flesh, from his upper arm, and a black widow crawls up his cheek; he throws it off in frustration. He palms a handful of mud and places it in the wound. The bleeding clots, as the ground swallows his feet, keeping him dead in his tracks. A young elf-like boy with long dreadlocks, peaks out from behind a tree. Before Zyra can react, the boy tugs on his vest.

"Hey mister, you that Nephilim everyone's talking about?"

Zyra breaks the incantation by acknowledging the face of evil.

"No, I'm not a fallen angel."

As he tries to turn and run, his feet stay planted, and the momentum brings him to his knees. Rage within fury, becomes vengeance, for the little boy; his skin catches fire, burning off the flesh, and exposing his natural form.

"It's your desire I deserve, now KILL'EM!"

He screams out to the others, as his fingers and teeth grow and sharpen. His dreadlocks harden into horns, and his eyes roll back into his skull, exposing a tunnel of fire. It releases a horrific sound and grows black wings of flesh. Zyra is lost in the seduction of this transformation, the demon grabs Zyra's thigh and BITES a chunk of meat from his leg.

"Augh!"

He reaches down, grabs the demon's lizard-like legs, and yanks it away. A chunk of meat tears from Zyra's thigh, dangling in between the demon's teeth. Zyra lifts the demon over his head, just as he's about to slam him down, hundreds of demon children step out from behind the surrounding trees. Lightning strikes the gloomy mood.

Fear manifests into power, as Zyra ferociously, repeatedly SLAMS the demon down, onto a tree root, splitting open its skull, and splattering blue blood everywhere. The demon claws at Zyra, however, its unsuccessful attempt keeps the others away. He slams the demon a final time.

"DIE DEMON!"

As the blood touches the children's flesh, it spreads like a rapid disease turning the children, back into their demonic form. Their breath blackens the air, dark wings expand from their backs, and they circle Zyra chanting.

"My heart broke. My heart broke."

Zyra throws the demon at the others, it instantly decomposes mid-air. Its spirit descends, its peers pay homage, then charge Zyra, spreading their wings over him; blackout. Strange sounds and the smell of death encompass his surroundings. Zyra jumps out of bed.

"Holy shit...I'm up, I'm up!"

Dezerae stands in the bathroom doorway, wrapped in a towel, brushing her teeth, shaking her head in disbelief. He gets out of bed and limps past her.

"What's wrong with you?"

"I don't know. My leg hurts."

"You didn't hear anything I said, did you?"

"Yes, I did. You said um...something about uh..."

"Whatever, get ready."

Dezerae finishes brushing her teeth, and Zyra grabs the towel from her. He kisses the back of her neck, pressing himself against her. She turns to him and kisses his lips.

"Take a shower. We have an eight o'clock call time."

They quickly get ready and rush out the door.

Chapter 8

THE LIZARD

The morning sun dances across the red brick, movie studio, on the busy street of Ventura Boulevard in San Fernando Valley. Outside the building, a Production Assistant (PA), the lowest man on the totem pole in the hierarchy of the film industry, dresses hip-hop style, puffing away at his joint, leaning against the wall. A little person actor, dressed in black coattails, a red lacy shirt, and shiny red shoes, sips his coffee, standing next to him. PA calls out.

"Yo Midget, what's up with the craft service chick? Does she put out or what?"

The smoke blows from his inquisitive facial expression and dissipates around the little person's red velvet top hat. Little person's deep ruffled voice, butts against PA's sudden cough attack, as he laughs at his joke. The daggers from the little person's eyes said it all.

"Give me a hit". PA passes the joint to him, "She'd crush your sorry ass."

PA stops coughing and takes another hit. The little person reaches above his head and grabs the lit joint from PA's mouth. His silver dragon, diamond eye, and full-finger ring catch the sun's rays, sparkling in PA's face.

"I ain't done."

PA blocks the light and presses down on his top hat.

"'Under the Rainbow."

The little person shakes his head, lifts the top hat over his eyes, and spits out, "Always a smart ass in Hollywood."

"I thought actors were supposed to be rich. Look at you, bumming a hit."

The little person clears his throat, makes a funny face, brings it into his mouth, and spits out a huge loogie, onto the ground.

"I only get half the pay."

PA cracks up. He wiggles his stubby fingers in his face. Over the walkie, the assistant director (A.D.) speaks.

"Back to one."

PA shakes his head.

"They don't give you time to take a shit around here."

He gets on the walkie.

"Copy."

He looks at the little person.

"They want you back on set."

Little Person takes one more hit and stamps it out.

"Can't even finish a joint around here."

He opens the back door to the studio and enters. Sunlight shines in, giving a glow to the darkened atmosphere, Zyra stands off to the left, turning his cell phone, like he just hung up talking to someone. The computer printout sign, above the doorway, reads, "The Lizard." PA follows, closing the door behind him. People hustle to set.

Hair and make-up are in a small room, touching up the Skeleton actors, sitting in director's chairs, in front of the mirrors. The craft service, located to the left of the exit door, is full of snacks, everything from M&M's to bananas, dried fruit, and doughnuts. Little Person walks by, grabs a handful of M&M's, and throws them down his throat. The craft service girl, Natasha, a six-foot Afro-American, stares him down. Her right hand rests on her hip, as the other lengthy middle finger, picks at her teeth, while she thinks, *I wonder what that little man's like in bed.* Little Person mumbles under his breath, just loud enough for Natasha to hear,

"Nothing like smoking good chocolate after a hard day's lay."

He grins proudly, laughing to himself, and continues to walk. Natasha catches up to him and slaps the top hat off his head. He looks up, perturbed.

"Whatchu say, little man!?"

He grabs the front of her thighs, sticks out his tongue, and wiggles it. She bends down, picks up his hat, and pushes it down past his head, onto his shoulders.

"You're lucky I don't scratch those beady little eyes out."

She pushes him to his knees, his butt protrudes in the air.

"Now that's funny shit."

She laughs and walks back to her table.

The other Production Assistant, a nerdish type with certain behavior issues, nicknamed *"Eurkal,"* his first day working in the industry, walks over to the little person. With slight hesitation, and uncertainty in his tone, he spastically grabs his crotch, out of nervousness, blinks extra hard, squeezes.

"...Um...little person, excuse me, little person, it's time to go to set...Um…Mr. Sting, the director, is waiting...Um, seriously dude, stop messin' we got to go!"

Little Person wobbles his way back to his feet, punches Eurkal, in the groin, and keeps on walking. Eurkal leans over in pain. His confused mind questions reality, *why does he keep doing that*?

Little Person laughs taking in a deep breath, and walks along the yellow air conditioning duct, leading to the set. He mumbles under his breath, "A midget gets no respect. A midget gives no respect."

The three skeletons walk past him onto the set. The make-up lady grabs Little Person before he enters. Over Eurkal's walkie, the 2nd Assistant Director A.K.A. "A.D." in charge of talent screams, "Eurkal, turn off that damn air conditioning now. How many times do I have to tell you? and get Little Person in here now." Eurkal, close to losing it, gets on his walkie,

"Copy."

The make-up lady grabs the base sponge, from her bag, and presses it against Little Person's face.

"Let me touch you up before Sting stings my ass."

Noticing his discomfort, "What's wrong with you?" He lifts off his hat, she puts the base over his sweaty bald head. She grabs a black makeup pencil and touches his go-tee. He finally answers.

"Nothing you need to worry about, sweet nips."

He walks onto the set, into a red-illuminating chapel, with religious stained glass crosses. The first A.D. screams at him.

"Little Person, where the *hell* have you been? Sting's been waiting ten minutes for you."

Refusing to put up with the sarcasm, Little Person raises his right hand, waving him off, like he doesn't want to hear it.

"Whatever, I was only gone for two..."

The first AD stands like a tyrant over him.

"Put your hat on, let's go. PLACES. PEOPLE! Time is money, let's go!"

The actors go to their first marks. The script supervisor sits next to Christopher Sting, the director, an aging man with a black baseball cap, behind the monitor. The camera assistant, Garth, whom we met the night before, passed out in his car and slated the camera. The Director of Photography (D.P.), the person in charge of the camera and lighting, gets comfortable on the dolly. Sting speaks.

"Actors ready...Roll sound..." he waits to hear, *Rolling* from the sound man, and proceeds, "And...Action..."

He points to the miniature black and white monitor. Little Person walks backward on the long white rolled-out carpet, tossing black and red rose petals, from a basket. He throws some into the air as he sings.

"Here comes the bride…All dressed in white…Da dant da da dant…Da da dant da da..."

Through the monitor, the rose pedals, hit the carpet, in slow motion, turn into lizards, and skitter away. Blue Doc Martin's, which look black, enter the frame. As the D.P. tilts the camera up, exposing the bride, wearing a shredded white wedding dress, Dezerae walks down the aisle. Wedding music from deep within Zyra's darkened soul creates the atmosphere.

A grayish-black veil covers the bride's face, holding in her hands, an empty thirty-gallon glass terrarium, illuminated in neon blue. In the front of the chapel, beyond the carpet, stands a black wooden altar, with a carved distorted image of "The Last Supper" on its face. The characters are human lizards, eating the head of Christ.

Little Person reaches the end of the carpet and places the basket down. Three skeletons with painted faces, one red, the other blue, and the last one green, each wearing black velvet cloaks, kneel, then hammer nails, into the cross, using metal skulls. The skulls slam down, in unison, against the head of the nails. Sparks fly, blue blood squirts onto their faces, and nails drive deeper through Zyra's hands, and feet into a black wooden cross, now turned blue. The muscles contract as blood pumps life through his veins.

Zyra's face contorts and screams. His veins pulsate from his neck, pushing his head back, against the black wood. His eyes bulge and roll back into his skull. One skull slips off the nail and crushes his fingers.

Zyra takes in the surge of pain, and releases it through his eyes, making it look, as if he is being electrified. His silver green-blueish scaled lizard skin, covers every part of his body, except his hands, feet, and half his face. His hips thrust forward, his tail whips around, and he releases another horrifying scream, accompanied by many hellacious sounds. The Little Person picks up the black leather Bible, sitting on the podium, next to the altar. The red skeleton brings his final blow, to the metal nail, blue blood STRIKES, Little Person's face, and top hat from Zyra's wounds.

"Damn you."

He throws a look at the skeleton.

Demonic laughter from the skeletons, mix in with the music. They finish nailing Zyra to the cross. Little Person wipes the blood from his face, and finds his place, at the end of the carpet. The bride stands erect, holding the terrarium, before the foot of the cross. Little Person is between the bride and Zyra. The skeletons lift the cross, sliding it into position.

It SLAMS down into the hole. Zyra's lizard-like body jerks forward tearing his flesh. Again, he holds in the pain, as it shoots up his legs, through his torso, into his hands, and out through his skull. His head jerks to the right, pressing it against his shoulder. He lets out another forbidden yell.

"AAAAUUUUGGHHGHGHG…"

The veins and muscles in his neck enlarge life courses through his veins. He squirms, trying to find a comfortable position. His face contorts, his eyes bulge, his eyebrows raised, and his lizard tongue rapidly slithers in and out, as green saliva drips from his mouth. The pressure from his body weighs heavily against his hands and feet. They slowly tare the piercings, surrounding the nails. His hands and feet clench onto the nails, as he lifts himself to keep from suffocating. He gasps for air.

Blood drips down from Zyra's left hand, onto the handle of the flower basket. The blood creeps over the edge, onto the bed of rose pedals. Little Person hands the black leather book to the red skeleton. The other skeletons stand behind the bride. Little Person speaks diabolically reading from the book.

"We are gathered here today, to unite this new species, The Lizard King, to a human"

Followed by a sinister smile.

"…Bride…"

Rolls from his tongue, shooting a look at the green skeleton, who then walks over to Zyra, and presses a bob-wire crown, onto his head. Zyra, feels the penetration into his skull, as Little Person looks up, into the eyes of Red Skeleton, and commands him to wipe away the blood on the book. The skeleton uses his cloak, which smears it over the page. Little Person, enraged gestures for the skeleton to fall to his knees. He grabs him by the neck and shoves his bony cheek against the page.

"I'll rip your head off and eat your spinal cord for dinner, if you mess up one more time, now lick."

The Red Skeleton submits.

"Yes Father", and cleans the page.

The Blue Skeleton lifts the veil off the bride, exposing Dezerae's bleached-out face, blue hair, and blue eyes. Her serene smile has a touch of menacing thoughts. She squats down, placing the terrarium, under Zyra's bleeding feet, and kisses tenderly his pregnant stomach. The Little Person picks up a handful of rose petals and throws them into the terrarium. The three skeletons semi-circle behind Zyra. In unison, they begin to sing…

"On this day

We are gathered

For the birth of the lizard

On this day

We pay homage

To the birth of our lord"

Christopher Sting, behind the monitor, can't contain himself.

"CUT, PRINT! I LOVE IT! MONING ON!"

* * *

At the same moment, inside a nearby crowded shopping mall, two old ladies wearing sun visors and tennis shoes, walk rapidly along the shops, following the mall's every turn. The heavier one, Bertha, has blue veins popping from her swaying thighs. The thinner one, with loose skin, carries a book in her right hand.

Two young punk kids, Spike and Mohawk, Spike has blue spiked hair, and wears a "Sacred Witch" T-shirt, while orange Mohawk wears a "The Lizard" T-shirt, walk out of the record store, *ripping* open their news cd's. Mohawk opens the sleeve to "The Lizard" soundtrack. On the cover, an image of Zyra as the Lizard King hangs on the cross.

"This is gonna be awesome. Look at him, man."

He shows Spike. Spike opens up the sleeve to the "Kanniballations" CD. On the cover, bleeding hands pierce through the sun, bleed down upon Zyra, and the band standing, in a desert bloodbath. In the distance, a rattlesnake strikes at the inner thigh of a beautiful, naked female wrapped around a sharp thorned cactus. The name of the cd reads, "Kanniballations."

"Holy shit! Look at this. I can't wait to pop this in."

Mohawk grabs the "Sacred Witch" CD from Spike and gives him "The Lizard."

"Let me see."

Spike responds with a look of disgust, but then gets into the imagery of "The Lizard."

"What the hell man, this dude's nuts! Look at this" he flips through "The Lizard" sleeve.

Both of them ooze with excitement. Spike screams out.

"I can't wait to see this movie."

"Let's go right now, but first we should light up a big fatty."

Spike slaps Mohawk upside the head, as they continue to walk, not paying attention.

"It doesn't come out 'till March 2nd, dumb-ass."

Boom, Spike hits the ground, and Mohawk's cd goes flying. The thinner old lady hits the ground, at the same moment, her book goes flying.

"Oh my God!"

The heavier woman screams, she leans over and tries to pick up her friend.

Spike gets up, walks over, picks up the CD, turns back to the old lady, and stares her down.

"Watch it Bitch!"

Mohawk cracks up, and they both take off running through the mall. The record store manager walks out of his store, bends down, and helps the old lady.

"Are you okay, ma'am?"

The heavier lady comments.

"These damn kids have no respect for the elderly."

The thinner lady's bones crack, as he lifts her to her feet. The heavier woman steps back, as her friend lets off steam.

"I'm getting too old to be in the same place as these wild youngsters."

A middle-aged Italian woman, Elizabeth, dressed in tight shorts and heels, who saw the accident, runs over to her. She bends down and picks up the lady's book. On the cover reads, "Zyra, Across the Painted Sky" with an image of him, riding his Harley Davidson, under the sunset. Her fingers painted red, with gold rings, brush off both sides of the book, she takes a deep breath, and hands it back to her.

"Excuse me, I believe this is yours."

The thinner lady finishes wiping off the dirt from her white shorts and then takes the book.

"Thank you."

Elizabeth cannot help but be social, after hearing her sweet tender voice.

"May I ask you, how far along in the book are you?"

She finally stands upright, gains her composure, and is ready to deal with people again.

"This is my second time reading it. I normally enjoy reading on my walk breaks, but I will never return to this mall again, to get my exercise."

The heavier woman interjects.

"We'll be back tomorrow. She's just upset. You know how women get. Kids these days have no respect for the elderly and when I was a child..."

"Alright already, Bertha, they don't need to hear about the time when your mother slapped your face for being fresh to your grandfather."

The Italian woman and manager laugh, and then she continues with her thoughts.

"Is the book *that good* that you need to read it twice?"

The Italian lady pulls out a new copy of the book. "I would have bought it sooner, but I've been really busy."

The thinner lady responds.

"It's the best book I ever read. He lives such an exciting life. He makes you feel as if you are on this journey, reliving the moments with him. What's your name young lady?"

Bertha interjects.

"I'm Elizabeth, nice to meet you."

"Well, Elizabeth, his butt's not too shabby either."

She giggles to herself.

"Isn't this the same guy who plays "The Lizard?""

The manager asks as he pushes his glasses back onto his nose.

Elizabeth answers.

"Yes, he is the same person, however, the movie is not out yet". The manager politely responds. "I know, March 2nd. Everybody is Lizard crazy these days. Kids walk into my store all day doing the Lizard. I even saw a father doing it to his little girl. It's so strange. I can't even distort my body and face the way he does. All of this is based on a trailer."

Bertha pops into lizard mode as if she has been practicing it for weeks.

> "It's on the trailers, commercials, t-shirts, everywhere. I even saw an interview with Zyra on Jay Leno. He was talking about his drug problem."

The thinner old lady slaps her arm out of embarrassment.

> "She does this kind of thing all the time. I don't understand the whole human lizard thing. He tries to explain it in the book but it's just beyond me."

> "Well on that note, I think I'll get back to work" the manager laughs to himself, and walks back into the record store, past a life-size cardboard image, of Zyra as the Lizard.

> "Well, I too have to go. It was nice chatting with you both."

Elizabeth waves and walks away passing the bookstore. At the entrance, a life-size image of Zyra on his motorcycle reads *ZYRA – Across the Painted Sky - The Autobiography Now Available!* The old ladies continue their walk chatting to each other.

* * *

Back on the movie set, Zyra's thoughts and words, become one, as he hangs on the cross. His breath, is barely audible, as his last words finalize his death.

> "Forgive them Father for they know not edwhat they do."

Dezerae is on her knees in front of his bleeding feet, absorbing the sound of the blood, dripping into the terrarium. She looks up at his distorted torso, then into his lost defeated soul, with hatred and love. Her vengeance breaks the silence.

"Praying for our forgiveness, as you give birth to human lizards?"

She laughs sinisterly.

"You're not evil, you're naturally pathetic."

A whip *strikes* Zyra's pregnant stomach, releasing a horrific sound. Nausea rises from his gut, as the little metal balls connected to the whip, rip open his skin. Green puke flies in his mouth. Movement from within his womb is accompanied by baby lizard cries. A small tail pokes through and dances back and forth. The moment plays out, then the director screams.

"And Cut!"

On the monitor, the lizard king hangs on the cross, and Dezerae stands up, while Little Person and the skeletons walk off frame. Sting sits on his director's chair mesmerized by what he saw.

"INSANE! If this doesn't metaphorically represent what is going on in society right now, then nothing will."

The crew laughs. The first AD stands next to Sting and confronts Garth, the camera assistant who slept in his car the night before.

"Alright, check the gates."

Garth checks the lens.

"It's good."

The first A.D. shakes off the mood and talks into his walkie.

"It's a wrap, everybody. Listen, same time tomorrow. Don't forget to grab your call sheets from P.A."

He turns back to Garth, "You know, you look like shit. You need to get more sleep."

Garth laughs, knowing that's impossible during production, then continues to dissemble the camera, as the first A.D. helps Zyra, down from the cross. Garth confronts Zyra, trying to make small talk.

"I saw the preview for *this* film the other night. When's the release?"

Zyra thinks to himself, *small talk?* But he does what everybody seems to do in this situation.

"March 2nd, my birthday."

"Doesn't give you much time."

Garth responds as he places the camera in the case. Zyra shakes his head and thinks *I need a joint,* then he continues.

"They just have to throw in the pick-up shots, dude. We'll be done shooting tomorrow."

The first A.D. finally gets Zyra down from the cross.

"Thanks."

Zyra takes off his pregnant pouch and lizard tail and hands it to the first A.D..

"What's your name again?"

The first AD throws him a look of disbelief.

"Rick Spark."

Blowing it off, Zyra responds.

"Oh yeah, it's been a long day Rick, sorry. You gotta joint?"

Garth pulls a joint from his bag and hands it to Zyra as Rick responds.

"I don't smoke."

Zyra confronts Garth.

"Thanks, man. Got a light?"

Garth flicks back his Zippo, lights Zyra's joint, slams it shut, and puts it back in his pocket.

"You're welcome."

Rick takes off his headset and walkie hands it to PA who is walking around collecting them in a box.

"I need your headsets. Don't leave without giving them to me, or I'll kick your ass."

Three electricians walk past PA, and place their walkies in the box.

"Thanks."

Rick speaks to Zyra.

"So you're all set for tomorrow. You have your call sheet?"

Zyra sees Dezerae walking off set, but deals with Rick first, "Same time tomorrow, right?" Rick screams out to Eurkal, "Eurkal, get over here now." Eurkal quickly hands a call sheet to Natasha, and marches over to him, with the call sheets in hand. Rick grabs Eurkal's arm.

> "You make sure Zyra, Dezerae, and Sting are always the first people to receive the call sheet. Do you understand me?"

Eurkal nervously responds, blinking heavily, he spastically grabs himself again.

> "I did…I mean I was."

Rick lets go. He gives Zyra the call sheet. Rick continues to reprimand him.

> "If this is something you can't handle, I'll find someone capable of handing out paper. You should've learned this shit in kindergarten. Now get the hell out of here."

Eurkal puts his head down and walks off. Zyra laughs to himself and takes a hit from his joint.

> "Rick, lighten up on the kid." Rick stares Eurkal down as he walks away.

> "Kids make me sick these days. They think by working one day in the industry, they know everything and deserve to be discovered."

Garth throws him a dirty look. Zyra walks towards Dezerae, as he responds to Rick's rudeness.

"Whatever! One day you'll be working for Eurkal."

Dezerae waits for Zyra by the craft service table. She grabs some dried fruit and pops it into her mouth.

"What are you rambling about?"

Zyra grabs his chin.

"I'm sick of people's bullshit."

Dezerae laughs. Garth runs up to both of them, on their way to the trailer.

"Media's hyping 'The Lizard' to be your most controversial film yet."

Zyra turns to Dezerae, throws her a subtle look, of *what the hell*, and ignores him, as he opens the door for Dezerae. They walk outside as Garth follows. Zyra stands on the first step of his trailer; Dezerae opens the door and walks inside the star wagon. Zyra confronts him.

"That's what sells tickets. Gives them something to complain about."

Garth takes a hit from Zyra's joint, blows it out, and nods his head in agreement.

"Yeah, I guess you're right."

Zyra ends it.

"Look, man, I don't want to be rude, but I want to get out of this make-up, and grab a bite to eat. Thanks for the joint."

Zyra takes his last hit and flicks the joint away from the trailer.

"No problem, it was nice talking to you." Glancing over at Zyra's Harley, "No way is that the hog from your commercial?"

Zyra thinks to himself, *alright already*.

"Jesus Christ, what the hell? Yeah, nice talking to you."

Zyra opens the door and enters his trailer.

Dezerae is in the bathroom, talking to Zyra, through the reflection of the mirror, as she throws water onto her face.

"I didn't want to disturb you while you were talking to Garth."

Zyra unzips his lizard costume.

"Who?"

Dezerae grabs a towel and wipes her face.

"The Camera Assistant guy, Garth."

Frustration builds as he peels off the rubbery costume.

"Can you help me, please?"

She starts laughing.

"You look like you're shedding skin."

She throws the towel down.

"Oh my God!"

He lashes out. She walks over and helps him out of the suite. The inside is soaked from sweat.

"Calm down."

"I am calm…"

He hangs the lizard costume up, huffing and puffing, jumps in the shower, and speaks over the running water. The blue blood drips down his thighs, into the drain.

"I didn't know his name."

Dezerae gets out of her wedding dress and hangs it up next to the lizard costume. She takes off her black see-through G-strings, and jumps in the shower with him.

"Baby, we have no room."

He finishes washing off and gets out. She shakes her head.

"You're so romantic."

Zyra grabs the towel and dries off. Dezerae finishes her shower, turns off the water, and gets out. She grabs Zyra's butt, whispers playfully in his ear.

"He's nice. He introduced himself to me and said he admires my work."

"Who the hell are you talking about?"

"Garth, the camera guy."

"Yeah, I'll bet he does."

Zyra throws the towel down, grabs his black leather pants, from the closet, and puts them on. She puts on her black bra, grabs his hand, he squeezes her hindside.

"Ooh...don't touch, not until you pick up your mess."

She leans her head back and kisses him on the lips. He bends down, picks up the towel, and folds it perfectly, as he sarcastically responds.

"Hey, you're a real natural playing Smurfette gone goth."

She puts on a white button-down halter top, and brushes her hair.

"*What*? I can't believe you. At least my character's original, unlike *The Lizard King*."

Zyra puts on a baggy white, button-down shirt, and fixes his long black hair. She puts on her black leather pants. Zyra quick-wittedly comes up with.

"Jim Morrison may have come up with it, but it's all in the eye of the beholder, and frankly my dear, my interpretation has never been done before."

She grabs her purse and walks out of the trailer. Zyra follows.

"Fine, I'll give you that. I'm starving. Where are we gonna eat?"

They walk over to Zyra's Black Harley Davidson, which was payment for the commercial, parked next to the trailer. Zyra hops on the bike, Dezerae puts her purse in the compartment, jumps on the back, and wraps her arms and legs around him. Zyra turns to face her.

"McDonald's or Sushi Bleu?"

She smiles.

"You know me so well…McDonald's."

He hands her the black helmet with blue flames, she grabs it and puts it on. He puts on his black and silver demon vs. angel air-brushed helmet, throws down the visor, and kickstarts the engine.

"Had I known you were going to say that?"

He starts up the bike, revs that massive engine, shaking the environment around him, and pulls out of the parking lot.

Chapter 9

SUSHI BLEU

The city lights of Los Angeles accentuate the cool breeze coming in off the shore and around the pier protruding out into the water. People, dressed in their party satire, walk along Pacific Coast Highway (PCH) to the local clubs. Street musicians and performers, entertain the diverse group, hanging out at Third Street Promenade.

One block over, Zyra and Dezerae, pull up to the drive-thru of McDonald's. She orders a cheeseburger, to hold her over, then scarfs it down. Zyra pulls out onto the busy street, drives a few blocks to PCH, hangs a left, and pulls up to L.A.'s finest hot spot for sushi. A blue neon sign reads, *Sushi Bleu*, over a pink neon tuna.

This rustic Japanese fisherman's wharf creates its reality. A white wooden bridge, over a stream of water, in a Japanese Garden, paints the landscape of this beautiful foyer. Twinkling blue and white lights, line the exterior, as live jazz plays over the speakers. Zyra pulls up to Valet, turning heads with his loud revving engine. They get off the bike, the Valet takes their helmets and keys. He hands Zyra a ticket, and Zyra slips him a ten.

"Take care of her."

He puts his right hand around Dezerae's waist and slides it into her back pocket. The Hostess opens the door, and they enter, and walk past a dozen people or so, sipping cocktails and enjoying conversation, in the garden waiting to be seated.

The restrooms are to the right when you first enter. To the left, against the left wall, is a huge blue-lit liquor bar. The center of the restaurant is a circular silver mirrored sushi bar, with neon blue lights. Outside on the deck, overlooking the water, the live jazz band plays. Round and triangular tables, covered in black and blue Japanese Dragon print, are scattered throughout the restaurant.

Above the blue booths, that line the walls, opposite the bar, are mirrors enhancing the illusion of the size. The waiters and waitresses wear black and blue, Japanese Dragon print uniforms. The hostess, an early 20's, delicate Japanese woman, greets them.

"How many will it be, two?"

Zyra answers.

"We have reservations for three under Zyra."

Dezerae surprisingly looks over at him.

"Three?"

Zyra does not acknowledge her comment. The hostess crosses them off the list.

"Oh yes, your third party is here. Follow me."

She walks from behind the podium with two menus. Zyra and Dezerae follow as he thanks her. Dezerae stops Zyra from walking and makes him answer. A waiter walks by with a tray of sushi. Dezerae keeps her eyes locked on Zyra.

"Who's the third party?" she demands with slight irritation in her tone.

Zyra nonchalantly answers.

"I invited Von Hildonberg."

Annoyed, Dezerae continues.

"What for?"

Zyra pulls her along trying not to make a big deal about it.

"Because of those dreams, I keep having. He said he wasn't busy, and he'd meet us here for dinner."

She sighs, throws him discontent, and decides to deal with him later. Zyra feels the discomfort.

"What? You're the one who hooked me up with him."

Dezerae lashes out under her breath.

"Not after *working* all day. I'm *tired* Zyra. I don't feel like socializing."

Zyra tries to dissipate the tension. Dezerae thinks to herself *God forgive me.*

"What do you want me to do? Do you want to leave?"

She shakes her head in disbelief.

"I just wish you would have told me."

Zyra lets the tension pass as she moves on.

"Sorry. I called him last minute. I wasn't thinking."

They reach the corner booth, next to the fish tank, containing exotic fish. A fluorescent black lamp, lights the water, stretching across the whole back wall. Dr. Von Hildonberg, the older gentleman, dressed in a yellow suit, and thick black glasses, puts his glass of wine on the table and stands to greet them. She squeezes in under her breath loud enough only for Zyra to hear.

"That's the problem, you never think."

The doctor's German accent weighs heavy. Dezerae gives a half smile.

"The beautiful couple. Modern-day Tommy and Pamela. Anyway, you both look great. Please have a seat. I got the best Merlot in the house."

"I hate Merlot."

Dezerae sputters as she slides into the booth. Zyra shakes his hand, shoots Dezerae a look of daggers, and retreats with a smile. She keeps her back straight, head down. Zyra slides in next to her, as she looks at the exotic fish tank.

"It looks like they have more fish than last time. Oh my God, look at that one."

She points to a fluorescent purple and pink spiked fish. The hostess places the menus on the table. Dezerae stays focused on the fish for a bit longer, then deals with her situation.

"It's a weird fish. I wonder what it is?"

Dr. Von Hildonberg embarks upon her one-way conversation.

"That fish had one too many sex on the beach."

They laugh, and finally the tension breaks. Dezerae turns back around and picks up the menu. Zyra picks up his menu and locks eyes with the Doctor.

"That's pretty good, Doc."

Dr. Von Hildonberg turns to the hostess, pointing to the bottle of Merlot.

"Get rid of this. Bring me your best..."

"Beaujolais," Dezerae says, her head still buried in the menu.

"...Auh, Beaujolais..." as he responds with his pointer in the air.

The hostess responds.

"I'm not your waitress. I only get paid to look cute."

Dr. Von Hildonberg smiles to be polite. Dezerae does not tolerate her rudeness.

"Well, then why don't you take your cute..."

Dezerae bites her tongue, not wanting to later regret what she might say. Zyra tries holding it in but cannot. He busts out laughing. The hostess, stunned by their manners, fixes her disposition, walks away.

"I'll send your waiter, *right over.*"

She shrugs her shoulders and shakes her hips.

"Think she's sleeping with the owner?"

Dezerae blurts out, Zyra continues laughing, and the Doctor finally comments.

"People in America can be very rude."

Dezerae seems to be on fire tonight.

"Only non-working actresses, who sleep with their boss, to get them an extra role."

Dr. Von Hildonberg analyzes every word.

"How is she…awe extra roll, I see what you did (chuckles). You are very witty, my dear."

Zyra looks around the restaurant and sees many celebrities. The owner, Chi Jung, is greeting all of his guests.

"Hey Doc, look around you. You have Jenna Ortega dining with Oliver Stone. A couple of tables down, the guy in red leather pants, Marilyn Manson dining with Johnny Depp. Look over at the bar. Be discreet, Angeline Jolie and Kelly Osbourne, sipping their Long Island Ice Teas. So, as you can see, the owner, Chi Jung, must be doing something right, building a rapport with these people."

Von Hildonberg takes in his surroundings, "I've never seen so many celebrities before at one restaurant."

Dezerae jumps in.

> "I'm sure you heard stories about how 'so and so' made it big because producer Paul decides to give a waitress a break. That's sugar-coated Holly Gossip crap. Nobody in this town gives some peon a break, not unless favors are being exchanged."

Zyra adds.

> "I've done it all Doc., you better believe, before I give a person a break, I need to know he/she did their time. It's the way of the world. Why should I help you, if you can't help me? What it boils down to is a…the almighty buck."

"No, what it boils down to is having faith in God, and allowing Him to run your life."

Dezerae takes a sip of her wine smiling at her advice. Dr. Von Hildonberg listens deeply as he takes a sip of wine, and looks at the menu. A few moments pass, and Zyra confronts the real issue of why they are here.

> "I'm having these crazy dreams again, Doc. I don't know what they mean."

Dezerae chimes in.

> "Dr. Von Hildonberg, I woke up this morning, took a shower, and brushed my teeth, all before Zyra got out of bed, *screaming* at the top of his lungs, *Alright, I'm up...I'm up.* Screaming Doc."

Zyra cracks up as Dezerae gives him the evil eye, and turns back to Dr. Von Hildonberg, "You have no idea what we've been going through."

The doctor takes off his glasses, cleans them with his napkin, rubs the inside of his eyes, and puts them back on, "Zyra mentioned that incident to me over the phone earlier."

Zyra notices Von Hildonberg's attentiveness and decides to open up a little more.

"I feel lost, Doc. I feel *evil* around me…It's like *standing* in the middle of a *massacre*. I don't participate, it's just happening all around me."

This strikes a chord in Dezerae.

"It's revelations unfolding. The sign of the times. The writings on the wall. You know all the cliches."

Zyra shakes his head. The waiter brings over two glasses of water. Zyra nods, and takes a sip, the waiter waits for an opening, as Zyra says his last thought.

"I don't know where you come up with this crap, Dezerae."

The waiter interrupts.

"Are we ready to order?"

Dezerae speaks.

"I haven't had time to look at the menu."

"I'll be back, take your time."

He walks away. Dr. Von Hildonberg confronts his curiosity.

"Are you religious, Zyra?"

Zyra looks at Dezerae, and she shrugs. He turns back and locks eyes with the Doctor.

"Not you too, Doc. Look, I believe people need to *believe in something* greater than themselves. My wife takes it to the extreme, reading the bible every night."

Dezerae defends herself.

"That's not fair. You told me, Zyra, on many occasions, you believe only in yourself."

"That's true, Dez. I live in truth, not fantasy."

Dezerae quickly responds.

"You live in controversy."

"Controversy is truth, the purest form," Zyra shouts.

Dr. Von Hildonberg interjects, "How do you figure?"

Before Zyra gets a chance to answer, Dezerae's hot tongue flares.

"You're blinded by your ego-centric stupidity. That's the truth."

Zyra controls his temper and confronts her. Tension increases.

"Controversy are elements of truth, out of order. Chaos heightens emotion and causes immediate reactions. At this moment, truth is in its purest form. *What will you do?*"

Dr. Von Hildonberg leans forward.

> "Listen to what you just said, Zyra. Controversy, elements of truth, out of order, chaos. Very profound, however, in this state of mind, pieces of truth make up the larger picture and are still in their box. That's controversy, scattered pieces of truth. When you lay the pieces out, in the proper order, each piece complements the next. At this moment, truth is prevailed, by presenting the story. Why do you think, Christ Himself, who is truth, spoke in parables? He placed pieces together. People saw the truth and were scared. They killed the truth."

Silence follows. A thick energy presence is felt. Zyra finally speaks.

> "In my dreams, a horrific beast tells an angel, *I am your god, you will have no other gods before me.* Now that's a commandment, right? I remember DeMille's *10 Commandments.* Anyway, the angel screams, **'BLASPHEMER'.**"

Zyra's fists SLAM down on the table. Dezerae jumps. Dr. Von Hildonberg's body jolts, and the waiter approaching THROWS the tray of drinks in the air. In slow motion, or so it seemed, it crashes down on the couple next to him.

> "What the...?"

Screams the bodybuilder, dressed in a nice pair of tight slacks, skin skin-tight pink tank top, white blazer.

> "Let's get outta here, baby."

They get up and walk out without paying. Silence. The waiter apologizes.

"I sorry, I sorry, I got scared, I jump, I got scared."

Everyone's attention is focused in their direction. Enraged, Dezerae lifts the menu, above her head, clenches her teeth, and mumbles under her breath.

"So much for being discreet, Zyra."

Zyra stands up, looks around, and takes a bow.

"Sorry everyone, sorry."

He sits. The waiter cautiously approaches, and Dr. Von Hildonberg is speechless.

"I'm Chung Ho. I will be your waiter. Are you ready to order?"

Dezerae speaks as fast as possible, "We're going to split the California roll, rainbow roll, freshwater eel, spicy tuna roll, and fried vegetables, please, oh, and edamame."

The waiter checks off each item and turns to Dr. Von Hildonberg.

"And for you, sir?"

He responds.

"Um...California roll and rainbow roll, please. Zyra, do you want to split a large Saki?"

"Sure. A large one please, oh Chung, my wife will have another glass of Beaujolais."

The waiter stands straight up, and locks eyes with Zyra, keeping him on the edge of his seat.

"No Beaujolais, sir."

Zyra looks over at Dezerae who quickly orders, "Chardonnay please."

"I'll be right back with your drinks."

He walks away as Zyra's hands come together, rubs back and forth, then finally interlocks fingers.

"Doc, you know what I forgot to tell you? A child was killed in my dream, last night. His mother's words..."

Searching for the right tone to describe the experience, he blurts out.

"'Eloi, Eloi, Lema Sabachthani."

There is silence in the restaurant, from the surrounding tables, whose mouths are dropped to the floor, as they see Zyra, standing on top of the table, in a lizard pose. He gets off, sits down, and continues to speak.

"I don't know what I just said, but they were the words from my dream."

Dr. Von Hildonberg takes a sip of his wine and repeats his words.

"Eloi, Eloi, Lema Sabachthani."

Dezerae and the Doctor, at the same time, say, "My God, My God, why have you forsaken me?"

As they say these words, Zyra receives a flashback of his dream. FLASH: He speeds on his Harley Davidson through the winding streets of Los Angeles. He pops a wheely, screams for joy, lands in a ditch, and slams into a windshield. His right pressed against glass, as the boy's face, smashes on the inside, shattering it. Their eyes interlock for a second, and the boy's soul leaves his body, FLASH…Zyra snaps out of the hallucination, with a frightened yell, then says.

"The mother cried like a milk less baby."

Dr. Von Hildonberg absorbs the situation.

"Zyra, these are the exact words spoken just before Christ died on the cross."

Dezerae sips her water as her confused thoughts verbalize.

"But why would they appear in Zyra's dream?"

Dr. Von Hildonberg nods his head, and moves his shoulders around, to try and relax the tension.

"I don't know Dezerae. In the Book of Revelations, as you mentioned earlier, Lucifer is described as a beast…"

Zyra cuts him off, not willing to tolerate the religious talk.

"Are you my psychiatrist or bible teacher? Look man, my brain's all messed up right now, and the last thing I need, is you and my wife talking crazy Jesus talk. I won't tolerate it. No wonder you suggested him Dez."

Dr. Von Hildonberg tries to calm him down, but the more he speaks the angrier Zyra gets.

"Zyra, nobody is preaching to you. We are just trying to analyze your dream. A mother loses her child. Christ loses his life. You Zyra, may be losing your soul."

Zyra loses it.

"You're gonna sit here and judge my soul!"

Dezerae grabs his right arm and *digs* her nails into his flesh.

"Stop it now. You're embarrassing me."

Zyra pulls away and sees Dezerae in a crazed stare. He stands up, puts both hands on the table, and gets in the Doctor's face.

"I get enough religious talk from Dezerae. I take enough criticism from the public. I'll be *damned* if I'm going to sit here and take it from some Nazi Christian, telling me, *I'm losing* my soul. Let's go Dez, we're out of here."

The waiter brings out the food and wine and places it on the table. Dezerae grabs the glass of wine, downs it, grabs her purse, and scoots out of the booth. Embarrassed, she apologizes for her husband's behavior.

"I'm sorry Doctor, now you see what I have to live with."

She storms out as Zyra reaches into his front pocket, pulls a fifty from his money clip, and throws it down on the table, the waiter walks away. Dr. Von Hildonberg is left dumbfounded not knowing where things went wrong.

"Have a nice meal."

Zyra mumbles as he walks out, and passes by Marilyn Manson and Johnny Depp's table. They stop him.

"Zyra."

Zyra turns around.

"You alright?"

Manson asks as Zyra responds.

"It's cool. Hey, if you're not doing anything tomorrow, stop by the studio. It's our last day shooting."

He acknowledges.

"I'll be recording all day tomorrow."

Zyra asks.

"You guys will be at the premiere, right?"

"Yeah, we'll be there."

Zyra nods, exits the restaurant, and hands the ticket to the valet. Dezerae walks over to Zyra, her arms crossed, shaking her head.

"You just make me so mad. Sometimes I can't take it."

Zyra reaches into his pocket, grabs a joint, and lights up. He blows out the smoke, she remains silent. The valet pulls the bike around and hands them their helmets. They put them on, and get on the bike, Dezerae puts her arms around Zyra's waist, and he takes his last hit, and flicks the joint. He checks for traffic and pulls out onto PCH. The quarter moon glimmers off the black ocean, dimly lighting the highway as they ride.

Chapter 10

TARTARUS

This same quarter moon shines over the peaks and valleys of Bel Aire, the city of the elite. Multi-million dollar mansions, cuddle into the landscapes, estates engaged by their security. This surveillance community with grand entrances, can only be entered by those who live there or those invited. The transportation that sits in the driveways consists of all high-end vehicles: Mercedes, BMWs, Porches, Jaguars, Lamborghinis, Ferrari, and most definitely but not least, Limos. If the wardrobe is not Armani or Donna Karen, you must be the maid.

High on the hills, a mansion is nestled in its forestry off of Fontenelle Way. A black BMW rests on the grey cobblestone driveway, leading up to two huge cement gargoyles, guarding the home. The exterior is strong in presence, and dark in color, as purple and red stained glass windows block light from entering. The backyard displays an indoor/outdoor pool with a waterfall, gargling multi-colored water, into a black shiny tiled pool.

The grey cobblestone paves the yard, to the black wooden cabana, infested with red roses, sitting on this spikey metal deck, just beyond the waterfall. Chains, interlaced with red glass, dangle down over the pool water, separating the inside from the exterior. A fancy black bar, with a mirror background, stands independently overlooking the pool, as the bartender in a black tux, black shirt, and top hat, sets up the bar. A statue of the Virgin Mary, crying black tears, is honored in the beautiful Japanese garden, set back in the corner of the yard, while statues of angels, ward off statues of demons, rising from the ground. Lights twinkle, throughout the yard, and heavy incense aromas, this dark twisted wonderland.

Sitting in the Jacuzzi, in the center of the garden, naked with long black hair, a metallic blue face, blacked-out eyes, and fangs, is Tartarus. On either side of him, sit two beautiful flesh-exposed playmates. One strokes his masculinity, while the other kisses his neck, and scrapes down his shaven chest, with her fingernails. Sacred Witch's eerie sounds of *Kanniballations* play over the speakers. In the distance, a falling star shoots down the sky. Opposite the trio, in the tub, Garth's fleshed-out tattooed body sips his Jack and coke.

"Tartarus, I think it's going to be a little more difficult than what I expected."

Tartarus' eyes cut through the steam, penetrating his soul.

"No it's not."

One of the playmates gets on top of Tartarus, and rides. The steam increases the sensation, just as Tartarus is about to climax, he still controls his words.

"Garth, you will do as I say...the full moon is in a couple of days...uh.."

His eyes glaze over, in his moment of ecstasy. The playmate squeezes her breasts into him, as she also enters bliss.

Garth never breaks eye contact with Tartarus, as he sits with his enlargement, and sweat pours down his face. Tartarus continues.

"If you don't show up, with Zyra on this very sacred night, you will never have to worry about showing up again. Do you understand?"

The blood on Garth's face drops, transposing him into a ghostlike complexion, he fights back the urge to get sick. He dashes out of the jacuzzi, runs behind the bar, and releases his insides. The playmate gets off Tartarus, and the other hops on. Tartarus throws the second one off and gets out of the jacuzzi. Garth looks back seeing Tartarus fully aroused hovering over him.

"There is no time to waste. This world will be a better place once we're through with Zyra."

Garth grabs his clothes and runs out. Tartarus receives a flashback image of himself, receiving the blood of an innocent child, given to him by the original Tartarus, Zyra's father.

Chapter 11

WINGS OF FLESH

During the same hour, Zyra and Dezerae ride up a winding road, which borders a cliff, to their house. Zyra relives the evening in his mind, as Dezerae's voice fades in like a dream.

"...now you know what I have to live with..."

Dr. Von Hildonberg's voice fades in.

"...You, Zyra are losing your soul..."

Dragon-Whale's voice fades in.

"...you will have no other gods before me..."

Images rampage through Zyra's mind, meshing into one moment, one reality. His blood boils with anger and confusion. No matter how hard he fights the negativity, he is being drawn further into an abyss of insanity, where he can hear roaring darkness, and feel an intense hatred for life. This confusion attacks his mind, like a bullet from a barrel, exploding. His spirit welcomes death, as he accelerates the gas, at the same moment of snapping back into reality. They approach the driveway, Zyra turns to Dezerae, seated behind him, and releases from under his breath.

"The things I'm gonna do to you tonight...."

They pull into the driveway and idle the bike as he gives off a sexy sinister smile. Dezerae opens the compartment, pulls out the automatic door opener, and opens it. Zyra drives in and turns off the engine. They take off their helmets, and place them on the shelf, against the wall. Zyra hits the button and shuts the garage door. They enter the house, and as she walks by the living room, Zyra grabs her, pulls her into him, and hugs her as tears stream down her face.

"I'm sorry."

She doesn't answer. Zyra releases the snakes from his mind.

"Do you want to make love tonight?"

Through the living room glass wall and skylights, the quarter moon and starry night, illuminate their alien-colored skin. She replies sadly.

"No. I'm tired."

She kisses him on the lips, and walks past the black leather couch, into their bedroom. The gothic/angelic decor compliments the mood. Zyra gets a glass of water from the kitchen, gulps it down, and walks into the bedroom, passing by a hanging plant with dying leaves. He mumbles.

"The plant needs water."

He spits in the pot, laughs, and unbuttons his shirt, exposing his ripped stomach and tattoos. He lets the shirt slide off his shoulders, catches it before it hits the ground, walks into the bedroom, over to the closet, and hangs it up. Dezerae's voice lingers.

"I'll water the plants tomorrow."

He unbuttons his pants and takes off his platform boots. After hanging his leathers, he throws his socks, into the hamper, and walks out naked. Dezerae lays nude on the bed, reading the Bible. She looks up at him as he gets into bed.

"Why are you like this?"

"Like what?"

"Hot and cold. It's like you expect me to move on and forget, that we just walked out of a restaurant."

"I'm sorry."

"See what I mean."

"What else do you want me to say?"

"Nothing. Forget it."

She turns her back, and curls up in fetal position, pressing the Bible to her chest.

"Does this mean you don't want to make love?"

Silence as Zyra throws the covers over his head, turns his back against hers, and curls up in the fetal position. Dezerae, still dealing with this, decides not to go to bed angry, and tries to resolve it.

"Zyra, please don't turn away from me. I want to talk to you."

He stays in this position.

"All you want to do is read your *damn* Bible. I thought Christians are supposed to put their spouse first."

She responds genuinely concerned.

"You don't think I do."

Zyra sits up.

"I didn't say that. You know, I've been having these night terrors lately, that scare you know what out of me, and nothing scares me Dez, I'm the person who instills fear."

Dezerae grabs his hand.

"Everything in my life is pandemonium. I have no control, Dez. The reason I freaked out tonight is because Dr. Von...berg, or whatever the hell his name is, listened to me for five minutes, and within that time, he spoke a truth to me, that I couldn't put into words before. When he said 'You, Zyra, may be losing your soul', I felt chills rise my spine. I felt like he tapped into my nerve endings, and played them like a harp. How do you explain that?"

Dezerae leans over, kisses Zyra.

"I love you. I think you should give Dr. Von Hildonberg another chance. I believe he is the one person who can help you, only if you want to be helped."

Zyra throws his legs around, sits at the end of the bed, opens up the drawer, pulling out a bag of weed. He rolls himself a joint and lights up. He places the lighter back in the drawer, next to the bag, and closes it. He hands it to her.

"Want a hit?"

She doesn't take it.

"You know I'm trying to quit."

Zyra takes another hit and blows out a lot of smoke. He coughs, trying to catch his breath.

"I didn't know he was religious, Dez,..."

The aroma of marijuana clouds her mind, she gets lost in her thoughts, and his voice fades. *Mmm, one hit won't hurt, but I've been doing so well. If I take a hit, we'll be on the same wavelength, but the perfect example is sobriety. God, what do I do?*

Zyra fades in.

"Dezerae...Dezerae."

She snaps out of it.

"Yeah."

He hands her the joint.

"Do you want a hit or not?"

She takes the joint and sucks in a large hit. "That's my girl." She grins, ear to ear, frustration filters, through her eyes. She inhales, holds it, and coughs it up.

"That's some good shit."

Zyra laughs, takes the joint, flicks the ash in the tray, and takes another hit.

"My baby's back."

Dezerae takes the joint, and starts laughing, thinking about the doctor, in his yellow suit, and black glasses.

"Dr. Von Hildonberg is intelligent, he can carry on a conversation, even about spiritual healing..."

Zyra cuts her off and imitates the doctor's German accent.

"Is that what you would call it? 'You Zyra may be losing your soul'. What the hell is that?"

She laughs louder, harder.

"I can't believe we just left him sitting there. Oh shit, did we even pay for our food? I'm starving. I forgot we didn't eat dinner."

He answers her concern.

"I threw down a fifty."

He hands her the joint, and she grabs it, with her pointer and thumb, brings it to her mouth, slowly, wraps her lips around it, inhales, and releases the smoke, slowly from her lips, it rises making her eyes bloodshot. She finally responds.

>"Good. I'm going to read myself to sleep. We have to get up early. No better yet, I'm going to get myself a glass of wine."

She gets out of bed, stumbles into the wall, turns around, and speaks slowly.

>"Um...What was I going to do? Oh yeah, do you want some...wine?"

He looks up into the ceiling mirror, at her naked reflection, and lets his words roll off his tongue, seducing, attacking her every fiber.

>"Yeah, I want some."

They both laugh, and she walks out of the room. Zyra leans over, grabs the Bible, from her nightstand, opens it, landing on 2 Esdras 9:38, he reads to himself.

>"While I was saying these things to myself, I looked around and saw a woman on my right. She was weeping and wailing, terribly upset; her clothes were torn, and there were ashes on her head. I immediately put my troubles out of my mind, turned to the woman, and asked, "Why are you crying?" Why are you so upset?"

>Tears fill Zyra's eyes, as he feels these words sink in. The song "Return to Innocence" from Enigma, plays over and over, in his mind, as he enters a vision walking slowly as a young boy, through a dark hallway; spiders crawl up the walls, and green and white snakes slither in between his footsteps. A doorway flooded with light shines up ahead.

Dezerae walks back into the room, with a bottle of wine and two glasses. She sees Zyra, sitting Indian-style on the bed, staring up at his reflection, lost in his eyes, tears creeping down his cheeks, and the Bible is left open on his lap. She takes in the moment, and one of the glasses falls from her hand and *shatters* on the floor. The music in his mind stops. They both snap from their seduced spellbind. Zyra, fluttered, closed the Bible, and quickly placed it back, on her stand.

Dezerae, wide-eyed, speaks.

"I'll be right back. I'm going to get a broom."

Zyra does not say a word, she places the bottle and glass on the floor and walks out.

He looks back up at his reflection, feeling his heart pound, and mouth slightly open, as he speaks to himself.

"What do you find so interesting about love, sex, drugs, snakes? Deity? Witchcraft? Why so sad? Why so many tears?"

She walks back into the room, with another wine glass and a mop. She cleans it up, never mentioning what happened, then pours another glass of wine, hands it to him, and sits next to him on the bed.

"I love you", she whispers into his ear.

Zyra takes another hit.

"Oh my god."

Choking back the hit.

" I'm messed up, this shit's good. Do you want the last hit?"

She grabs it from him, takes the last hit, and puts it out in the ashtray. They hold up the glasses and tap them together, and love surrounds both of them. Dezerae rises to the occasion and makes a toast.

"To love."

Zyra responds.

"To love."

She continues, "To laughter." Zyra laughs, "To laughter."

They interlock arms and sip from their wine. As their arms separate, they meet in the middle and lock lips. After a very long passionate kiss, Zyra downs his glass of wine, places it on his nightstand, and lays on his back, finding a comfortable position. He falls into deep thought, entering a deep abyss, surpassing souls as he slowly fades away.

"Good night, my love."

He closes his eyes, and she grabs her Bible and continues to read.

"Good night, my love."

Zyra hallucinates a flickering light, swimming towards him, which manifests into a fish, face to face with him. Its tail swings back and forth, and Dr. Von Hildonberg's face manipulates its way onto the fish. The Doctor's thick German accent, seeps through the words, underwater.

"Eli, lema sabachthani."

He hears his voice, and he thinks out loud within this realm.

"What the hell was I thinking, inviting him for sushi? Back to my dream, why would a parent, who loses a child, say these words?"

In his mind's eye, an alien dog, attacks the fish, eating it whole. The water circles this alien dog, forcing Zyra into a deeper state of hypnosis, A flash of lightning *strikes* his vision, *This weed's insane…I'm losing my soul…*He tries to remain still, concentrating on the vision.

Laughter from children, in their mother's womb, holds their breath in between giggles, forming waves of revelation in his mind. *If my soul is exposed, and I'm aware of my surroundings, I will grow and learn as babies do.* The imagery and atmosphere change, as he takes another deep breath. *Now that smells amazing.* For as far as the eye can see, forests of marijuana trees, fill the horizon. He runs through the plants, elevating his spirit, up an invisible ladder.

He runs faster and faster, and the trees liquefy below his feet, as he glides down, a mist presses against his face. Below his flying spirit, the ocean passes beneath his feet. A protective air bubble surrounds his body, allowing him to breathe, as he *dives* into the water. He absorbs the clarity of the ocean and then descends into the deep darkness. Within this high-pressure blacked-out vision, a school of brightly colored exotic fish swims through him.

"I feel them swimming through me."

Echoes throughout his mind. A purple and yellow striped blowfish, puffs up, in Zyra's face, fighting the currents, as their eyes remain locked. Mentally, communicating to the fish.

"I'm just like you..."

Zyra jerks in his sleep, and the fish explodes in his face. In the distance, Dragon-Whale spots Zyra's state of delirium and decides to take advantage. In one gulp, Zyra is swallowed by this beast. He slams into the back of the tiger's head's mouth, forced down its long neck. Zyra screams, as his hands press against its slimy insides, forced to total darkness and suffocation, as the beast brings him into its belly.

His horrific scream, tackled by rushing water, pushes his body further down into the center of the beast; he enters a moist large cavity and pounds against its ribs. Now inside the body of Dragon-Whale, debris, fish, coral anything and everything rush past Zyra. He is thrown around, trying to survive, and *slams* up against the roof of its body. The gut-filled water continues to rise, and his eyes widen. Zyra is firmly pressed against the soft tissue, above his head, water bubbles release Zyra's last breath.

Light pierces through the opening hole, in the whale's back, forcing the excess water out. As the food consumed starts being digested, Zyra fights his surroundings, punching, kicking grabbing the organs at work, bites down. Dragon-Whale opens its back wider and shoots him out his blow hole, spinning on top of the excreted water.

Zyra free falls break through the ocean's surface, and sinks. He fights his way to the top, gasping for air. In the distance, Nazareth is on his knees praying on shore. Fatigue takes over Zyra's body, and an undertow brings him down. Nazareth rises to his feet, and screams, "ZYRA!" watching the water settle above Zyra's head.

Under the water, a wave, SLAMS Zyra's head against a rock, blacking out. Within the darkness, strange demonic sounds, permeate his mind. Zyra slowly opens his eyes, and sees before him, beady red rays of light. No longer in this place, he realizes, he is back in the forest, being attacked by those winged demons, from his previous dream. His heart palpates, and tears fill his eyes, trying to wake him from this nightmare. He finally decides to cry out for help from God, knowing he cannot break this realm.

"GOD HELP ME..."

Back in his bedroom, Dezerae is trying to wake him up, as he fights for his life. Zyra finally settles down, we reenter his dream.

Nazareth pleads forgiveness in Arabic, to the heavens, raising his fists, *roaring*, his face, red from the vigorous veins in his neck, strained from exhaustion. He flares his wings open and rises to his feet, looking towards the sun. Church bells ring in the distance, energy surges through his body.

The core of the sun, once again sprouts wings and pulls forward the spirit bridge, further along its path. The sound of a bridge being pulled from the sun can be heard. The rapid breeze crosses the water, creating choppy waves, slamming onto the shore. Chills rise Nazareth's spine, he looks around cautiously and thinks to himself, *I feel the presence of evil.* He looks out towards the ocean.

At that moment, Dragon-Whale shoots straight up. Its black oval alien-eyed, white tiger head, pumps its long serpentine neck, larger than a blue whale, Dragon-Whale RISES from the water, flapping its huge dragon wings, its tail is in rhythm, elevating into the air. Its gills flair and its tail rotates, spinning the beast mid-air. No words from Nazareth, silence, awe, open jaw.

Dragon-Whale's wings fully expand, then its tail curls underneath its body, as six bear-clawed feet, spread its toes. The tiger's head GROWLS, with force summoned from the center of the earth, black breath, and fire shoot from its mouth, ending inches from the wings at the end of the spirit bridge. After this horrific beast reaches its peak, it ducks its head, and flips its body, diving down towards sea. The wings gear its descent, and Nazareth snaps out of it.

"He'll expose Atlantis."

The head and neck slice into the water, as the body enters, SPLASH, creating a tidal wave, blocking Nazareth's vision. The moving wall of water, forms a face of Babel, "HE'S MINE!" then crashes down on Nazareth, forcing him to his knees. The soaking wet angel, rises, shaking off his body and wings. He hears the sound of thousands, maybe millions of bees, in the distance. He looks where Dragon-Whale entered the water, from the swirling center, a tower of bees circulates, building its base, claiming its throne, and climbing towards heaven. The spirit bridge continues to grow even further across the sky.

The sun closes, the bridge disappears, and day to dusk instantly. The sun becomes black, the moon bleeds red. The tower of bees, continues to soar, illuminating a false light. From the base of the bees, an opening appears Babel in a white three-piece tux, top hat, and cane of souls, walks out. He glides on top of the water, towards shore, palming a swarm of bees, under each hand. His devil glide music can be heard. Babel approaches Nazareth, a suave look across his face, as Babel communicates telepathically through his infinite burning eyes. Nazareth is hypnotized by Babel's grand entrance.

"Quite an introduction, Babel."

Babel circles him, and nods his head, as his deep dark seductive voice lingers.

"The show has just begun."

"And who do you, proclaim to be?"

Babel grins, showing off his gold teeth, and water skims across his feet, back into the ocean. The bees beneath Babel's palms, enter his flesh. His eyes roll back, exposing bees rising from the light, within his eyes. They fly out from his eyes and circulate Nazareth.

"The 'Tower of Babel' has been reconstructed. This is my new creation, the 'Tower of Bees."

Nazareth's understands Babel's strategy.

"First off, you'll never have enough power to intercede the bridge. That's exactly what you're doing, and second, Zyra is protected."

Babel springs forth, with the look of death, locks eyes with Nazareth.

"Zyra's faith is dead. Do *you* think, you are going to restore it?"

Nazareth quickly responds.

"Dezerae's faith is alive. They are one under God. I cannot restore anyone's faith, they have to do it on their own."

Babel's eyes turn from infinite black to fiery red.

"God? God is dead. Zyra is mine."

His words penetrate Nazareth's soul, leaving him weak in the knees. He maintains his composure, not showing fear. Babel turns around, and instantly glides over the water, entering the base of the tower of bees. He disappears within the walls of the tower of bees, it dissipates. Nazareth arches his back, raises his arms to the sky, spreads his wings, and releases frustration toward heaven.

Thunder rolls in, as lighting strikes from the sun, shattering the darkness, colliding into

Nazareth's chest. Energy *radiates*, from his fingertips, and his body convulses, becoming one with this power. The voice of God can be heard throughout his mind, trembling the earth, as rain starts to downpour.

"GO!"

Nazareth is lifted into the sky as a lightning bolt, then *strikes* down through the forest, electrocuting the winged demons encircling Zyra. They fly back, isolating Zyra as Nazareth, now enters Zyra's body as the lightning, making the two become one. Zyra's eyes roll into the back of his skull, he bleeds tears. His fingers distort, quivering as his body is being possessed by this angelic lightning. The energy radiates from his body, forcing him off the ground, into the air, and keeping space between the demons and himself. Nazareth then speaks through Zyra.

"RUN!"

His legs and arms pump a mile a minute mid-air, as he lands face down in the mud, which swallows his fore-arms and feet. The rain pours down even harder, as he pulls his hands from the mud suction, and rips off his black leather vest crying out in agony.

"What's happening to me?"

His feet are heavy, practically cemented in, but he summons the strength, breaks from its grip, and then continues to run. Fatigue drops him to his knees, he arches his back, and his fingers claw down his face, leaving trails of mud and blood. He tries dealing with the excruciating pain concentrated in his upper back. His watered eyes reflect the weight of the world.

"I CAN'T TAKE IT!"

Tears pour from his bloodshot eyes, and a cold sweat breaks from his body. Blood rushes to his upper back, whitening the rest of his carcass. Nubs form in his upper back, as the muscles cramp, pushing out the skin, deforming, reshaping, and eventually *ripping* through his flesh. The piercing scream from Zyra's lungs, causes the surrounding animals to cry with sympathy. The raw pink, white, and red moist texture of muscles and bones, grows from his back. A skeleton frame, creating wings of flesh, from Zyra's back is being born. T

he cracking of the bones, within a mucus, accompanies Zyra's perpetual tears, and deafening cries. Nazareth's wings continue to grow, through Zyra's back, as every ounce of energy, is released through Zyra's wings. Zyra's jawbone is driven down, his eyebrows are forced to the middle of his forehead, and his tongue shakes vengefully, releasing horrific sounds.

* * *

Dezerae, scared to death, jumps out of her skin, and flips on the light.

"What the hell is going on!?"

Zyra is in the same sleeping position, but the bed is soaked with sweat, underneath his body. The muscles throughout his body, are cramped, as if they had ached for months. Pain shoots up his back and out his chest. Dezerae grabs his trembling arm, trying to wake him.

"Zyra get up! Zyra, you're scaring me, get up!"

He doesn't budge, only his spastic muscle cramps, with strange sounds coming from his sleep. Her heart races, tears swell, and she releases his arm, out of the room panicked.

* * *

Back into his dream, Zyra's wings are almost fully mature, as they start to heal, from his upper back, working out towards the tips. The itch and sting of the raw muscles, force Zyra to roll over and dig his wings into the mud, releasing an insignificant amount of misery. The muscles in his legs contract, bringing his knees into his chest and pushing the blood into the wings. Veins, and nerve endings, wrap around each other and layer the muscle within his wings. He bites down and releases a grunt, summoned from the depths of his being.

The wings move back and forth, digging deeper into the mud, calming the itch and pain. The muscle spasms, throughout his body, ungodly as the last layer of the wings, complete their growth. His body fidgets and contorts into many positions, but finally, his wings of flesh, are fully mature. The rain offers a small amount of relief, and eventually, the pain subsides, Nazareth, within Zyra's mind, tells him what to do, as they face their enemy.

"Stand up, glide."

His voice gives him strength. Instantly, Zyra rises like a vampire out of a coffin, and together, Zyra and Nazareth, as one body, mind, and spirit, hover over the ground and glide through the swampy forest.

The demons try to regain their composure, after just witnessing this freak of nature. Babel, stands in the distance, watching, fire intensifies in his eyes.

"GET'EM!"

The demons savagely attack Zyra. Zyra turns around and summons energy from within. His fingers protruded, forcing distortion in his face, and his stomach muscles raged with fury. Passion and desire to combat the enemy take over his body, Zyra flaps his wings, releasing electrical surges from his fingertips. His eyes reflect the moving clouds, as he screams out.

"ELOI..."

The energy expelled through his fingertips charges forth, *zapping* the demons, and forcing them back. Their grunts and growls are magnificent. The storm continues to rage, as Zyra shakes and screams, a venom to the demons, which is love, with the intent to save souls, shoots from Zyra's mouth, blood, soaks the demons, forcing their souls into a state of judgment, their creator.

* * *

In the bedroom, at this exact moment, Dezerae runs back with a glass of water to throw at him. The room is cold. As she is about to throw the water, Zyra sits up, and throws up blood all over the bed, sending the glass of water, and Dezerae flying back in pure terror as she screams.

"JESUS!"

Practically going into convulsions, Zyra tries to shake the evil presence. He slams back down on the pillow, his arms and legs jolting, convulsing, in the air. His strained muscles force blood to surge through his veins, like lava before its eruption. His disjointed fingers shake, and his face is beat red, but in a cold sweat. His chin drops, as a deep psychotic grunt escapes from his ruffled throat. Dezerae *jumps* on top of him, and grabs his arms and legs, trying to control the spasms.

"WAKE UP!"

Zyra becomes more possessed, stronger, and more violent. He takes her on as if he is wrestling a demon.

* * *

Back in the dream, electrical surges expel, pulsating from Zyra's hands. He lifts the demons by their blackened hearts, and aims them toward the sky, reflected in his eyes, they burst into flames. His wings flare wide, drool and blood, escape his mouth, drops to the ground. His feet are planted, and his body frozen, as his long, wet-stringy black hair, strikes his chiseled cheeks. His vest lays next to him, in the mud, accumulating the rain. A glimmer of joy strikes his heart, as the demons turn to black ash, and are blown back towards the trees. Zyra's animalistic, surrealistic, and raw energy is ready for battle.

Babel does not interfere, allowing Zyra's quest for power and destruction to explode from his soul. *One step closer to your eternal fate with me,* Babel thinks to himself.

Zyra searches the grounds for more demons. Thunder roars in the distance, Zyra turns around and glides through the trees, of the moody green forest. Babel, sees a branch up ahead, with a swipe of his finger, the branch sweeps down, and slams Zyra to the ground, stopping him dead in his tracks, *Why does this keep happening?* Zyra shakes it off, gets back up, continues on course, and sees a familiar wooden cabin up ahead, highlighted in the sun, breaking through the clouds and trees. He is drawn to it as if he belongs there, and approaches. Zyra blesses the door, as a cross of blood, materializes, protecting whoever lives there. Zyra pounds on the door.

"Open the door, let me in."

The door unlocks and Gabriel, his younger brother, a typical stoner pre-teen, opens the door. Zyra's wings close, and disappear into his back.

"Zyra?! Dude, let me see your back."

Zyra storms past Gabriel, his mother screams from the other room and stands in the foyer.

"Who's there Gabriel?"

Before he can answer, she is in Zyra's soaking wet face, pressing her right hand against his cold cheek. His mother looks like Elizabeth from the mall, we met the other day.

"Zyra, you alright? You look like crap, son. Come in."

His lost, confused crazed stare, sends chills up her spine, as the rain pours down in the doorway.

"Shut the door!"

She commands Gabriel.

"Get your brother a towel before he gets sick."

Gabriel shuts the door and leaves. The same old coat rack, from his childhood, stands in the corner, holding the father's grey hat, collecting dust.

"A detective Babel, is here looking for you. What'd you do wrong this time, son, huh?"

She slaps him upside the head.

"I don't know, ma. I don't know a Babel."

Zyra responds.

Gabriel comes back with a towel, and a lit joint, and hands the towel to Zyra as the phone rings. He grabs the towel, wraps it around his shoulders, and looks up at his mother, as she runs to get the phone.

"That's your father. He's coming to get you."

She runs into the kitchen and answers the phone. A mustiness rises from the mildewed rugs, as Zyra locks eyes with his brother. Cobwebs line the walls and ceiling.

"Dad's dead. What's she talking about?"

"I'm telling you, man, she's been messed up in the head ever since you left." Gabriel takes a hit from his joint.

"You're too young to smoke. Give me that."

Zyra grabs the joint from his brother's hand, and takes a hit, as Babel's deep voice radiates the room.

"Zyra Jordonello."

Any warmth that was in the room quickly chilled to the sound of his voice. Zyra stands at attention, feeling the presence of evil, as the hair rises on the back of his neck.

"Something is...not right."

"He's cool," Gabe answers.

Zyra cautiously enters the dining area, Babel, dressed in his white three-piece tuxedo, flooded with gold, offers his right hand. Babel's thick black fingernails, out-stretch his flesh.

"I'm Detective Babel."

Zyra is not capable of responding, thinking back, face after face, why this man looks familiar. He only stares, but then finds the words to speak.

"You look familiar."

Gabriel hits Zyra in the arm.

"Dude, he's a cop, shake his hand."

The coo-coo clock in the kitchen strikes eight times, Babel never blinks staring into Zyra's soul.

"Some want you dead, my friend. I'm here to protect you."

The second Babel speaks, Zyra remembers him as the man that *kicked me in the head,* then hears Nazareth inside his spirit say, *He is not who he says he is.* Zyra keeps his composure, knowing he is in a dangerous situation, but needs to let it play out. Elizabeth hangs up the phone and reenters the dining room.

"That was the strangest call."

Babel pulls a gun from hell, from his coat, and with his arm outstretched, he aims it at Zyra. His mother screams, "What's going on?!" not understanding. Still locking eyes with Babel, Zyra answers, "Back away, Mom." Babel's low, yet calm tone, addresses the situation.

"Watch scripture come alive, Ma'am. The dog is turned to his vomit...wallowing in the mire."

He turns swiftly, and SHOOTS Gabriel in the head. Gabriel drops to the ground, and blood *splatters*, striking Elizabeth across the face and chest. In slow motion, her soul cries out, she drops to her knees in terror.

"Noooooo..."

She cradles her faceless son, as Zyra leaps for Babel, clenching his fists around his neck.

"I'll kill you!"

Just as Zyra's thumbs pierce through Babel's esophagus, Babel disembodies, and crumbles to the ground as dust, leaving a haunted shadowed laugh behind. Zyra hits the ground, scattering away the dust.

A fainted alarm clock, BEEP, penetrates his dream. The front door of the cabin kicks open. Another BEEP can be heard, slowly bringing Zyra out of this dream state. A young punk demon boy, with blue spiked hair, stands in the doorway, leveling a red laser gun, on Zyra's forehead. Zyra's helpless eyes, look up, as he drops before the demon, standing over him.

"You're no different than us!"

The demon shouts, as another BEEP pierces through.

Exhausted, Zyra drops his face to his knees and cries like a baby in his demise. A final BEEP wakes Zyra from this nightmare.

He jolts up, waking him into reality, his heart still pounding, he leans over, and turns off the alarm. His swollen eyes, see Babel's ghost, manifested at the foot of his bed. Zyra's heart pounds even harder. He looks over at Dezerae's Bible, sitting on her nightstand, and starts praying for the first time in years.

"Our Father...in Heaven, Hallowed be Thy kingdom in Heaven...forgive us, deliver us from evil..."

Babel's ghost dissipates, and Zyra wipes the sleep from his eyes.

"I...I haven't prayed since...I was a little boy."

Dezerae, with swollen crying eyes, is sitting in the corner of the bedroom, holding her knees, rocking back and forth, scared for her life. Zyra keeps his eyes locked, on the place where he saw Babel, manifest.

"You ever have a dream so real, even after you wake up, you're in it?"

Dezerae, still paralyzed in fear.

"I'm going crazy. Babel just stood at the foot of our bed, manifested from my dream."

She blinks for the first time and tries to summon the strength to speak.

"Who's Babel?"

Zyra answers.

"I don't know, but he killed my little brother."

Dezerae stands up, falls against the wall, and catches herself.

"I hate you."

She walks into the bathroom. Zyra, oblivious to the night he put her through, confusingly asks.

"You don't believe me?"

Just before she shuts the bathroom door, "I don't know what to believe."

Zyra looks down, noticing for the first time, all the blood he threw up, during the night. He puts his hand to his head and lays back down.

"I am not looking forward to today. In a few hours, I'll be giving birth as the Lizard King. My life is so strange."

They eventually get ready, and head out the door for set.

Chapter 12

BABEL

The sun rises over the Hollywood Hills. On the airwaves, we hear on the airwaves.

"Early morning traffic is backed up on Sepulveda and Ventura Boulevard, once again folks. Keep that air conditioning on, it's a hot one."

This deep male voice seeps its way into every car, sitting in bumper-to-bumper traffic. We see Zyra and Dezerae, weaving through traffic, on his motorcycle. The typical chaos that exists on early morning sets, is unbearable today, especially under the hot scorching sun. By the catering truck, the Second Assistant Director, in charge of the talent, is frantic, as the PA returns late with cold cappuccinos, for the talent and crew. The 2nd A.D. grabs the cappuccino from PA's hands and takes a sip.

"Jesus, what the hell? Was the air conditioning blowing in your car?"

PA takes a sip of his cappuccino, as steam rises through the sip hole.

"Mmm...look asshole, I don't get paid enough to put up with your crap. There's no reason why you all couldn't drink the coffee here. Sending me out in this heat, with all that traffic, then being ungrateful."

Zyra and Dezerae pull up. PA confronts them.

"Guys, get into make-up, I'll bring you food."

They rush off to make up. He then turns to the 2nd A.D.

"I just did your job for you. What do they pay you for, man?"

Sting overhears their conversation, and chuckles at PA's directness. The 2nd A.D. walks away humiliated. PA approaches the catering truck.

"I need two breakfast burritos for Zyra and Dezerae, please."

The caterer responds.

"Coming right up."

Zyra, dressed in his lizard costume, with wildly spiked orange and blue hair, sits next to Dezerae at the make-up booth, getting the final touches done. Silverish, blue-green Lizard skin, covers half of Zyra's face, to match his costume. PA walks in with two plates of food.

"I'm a man of my word."

Handing the plates to Dezerae and Zyra. PA walks away, as Zyra calls him back.

"Hey dude, what's your name?"

PA smiles, turns around, and proudly answers.

"I get it, I'm new and all, but you are the first person to ask me that, everyone just calls me, PA, but my name is Edward."

"Well Mr. Edward, may I call you Eddie?"

"My family calls me Eddie."

"Eddie it is, anyway, I liked the way you handled yourself back there. You don't deserve to be treated like that, no one does. You made me laugh too, thanks man."

Zyra pats him on the arm.

"Man, I'm sick of being treated like shit, you know. I just couldn't take it anymore. Honestly, I don't care if I don't get rehired."

Zyra smiles at his spirit of courage.

"What do you want to do? I know you don't want to be a production assistant your whole life."

Edward, in awe that he is conversing with one of his favorite stars, makes himself extra aware of the words he chooses before he speaks.

"Direct, I'm the storyteller."

Zyra comes back with another question.

"Have you ever directed before?"

"Just student films, and some independents…"

An embarrassed smile strikes his face, as he checks his walkie. Garth walks by, and slaps Edward on the back, making his head jerk forward. Edward shakes it off. Garth laughs and makes himself, part of the conversation.

Zyra turns back to Edward.

"You any good?"

Edward laughs.

"My Mother always told me, I'll be the next Spielberg, or die trying."

Zyra smiles.

"I like her faith."

Zyra just received a strange feeling, realizing his vocabulary, is now starting to change, and his compassion and empathetic spirit have expanded. Garth, quickly interjects.

"Every mother thinks that about their kid, except mine, anyways..."

Edward ignores Garth. Over the walkie, the 2nd A.D. is screaming for PA to get on set.

"They're calling me on the walkie. It was nice talking to you, Zyra."

Zyra nods, "Keep that fire alive, Brother."

Edward walks away fired up. Zyra finishes his breakfast burrito and gets out of the director's chair. Zyra turns to Dezerae.

"See you out there, babe."

He blows Dezerae a kiss and walks out. Garth follows.

"Hey Z...what are you doing tomorrow night?"

Zyra keeps walking to set, "I'm busy."

Garth persists.

"We're having a party, in Bell Aire, you should come."

"Sorry, I don't do parties anymore."

"Well, it's not a party, it's more like, you know...underground."

Zyra looks bewildered, yet slightly intrigued, and shakes his head no.

"Not."

Garth hands him a card with the address.

"If you change your mind."

Zyra looks at this shiny black card, with dull black letters, reading, *Nephilim.*

"Nephilim? Like the fallen angels?"

Garth answers.

"Exactly, like the fallen angels."

"I...forget it."

"You what dreamt about it?"

Garth quickly responds. Zyra shoots him a look of discontent, instantly upon him.

"What the *fuck* did you just say?"

Zyra throws him up against the wall. Garth pushes him away.

"Hey Brother, hey…just come, ok."

Zyra calms down.

"I'll think about it."

Zyra walks away, leaving Garth to recompose himself. The First Assistant Director approaches Zyra.

"So are you ready to give birth?"

Zyra, still thinking about the Nephilim party, gives him a funny look.

"No."

Garth laughs at his unbelievably sincere tone and approaches them.

"Did you see the 2nd A.D. get *reamed* a new asshole by PA?"

Zyra corrects him.

"His name's Edward. He's a director. Watch out, you may be working for him one day."

Garth drops his head.

"Nah, I don't think so."

They walk onto the set, which looks identical to yesterday, as the lighting technicians are setting up lights. The Director of Photography and the Gaffer, the chief electrician, is directing the lighting technicians. Sting walks onto the set sipping, his hot water.

"Where're my actors?"

The 2nd A.D. responds.

"Zyra's behind you, Dezerae's getting final touches in make-up, and the skeletons are flying in."

"Great. Where's Little Person? Let's go folks, we have a movie to make. Get Edward on set."

The second gets on his walkie.

"Ed, fly in with Little Person, now." Edward's voice answers over the walkie-talkie.

"Copy."

A few moments later, he walks on set; Little Person, dressed the same as yesterday follows. The 2nd A.D. gives Edward a look of death, with a tone to match.

"Sting wants you."

Edward, nonchalantly, walks over to Sting.

"Sting, you wanted to see me."

He turns around and puts his hand on his shoulder.

"Yeah, I want you on set at all times. Watch everything I do. If you have any questions, ask."

Edward grins ear to ear, as the second A.D. interjects.

"He can't. I need him to watch the back door."

Sting points to the back door.

"You watch the back door, I want Eddie with me."

Sting puts his arm around Edward.

"This is such garbage."

He *storms* off the set. Edward, in complete, disbelief.

"Thank you, Sting, (*chuckles*) My family calls me, Eddie."

"It's your day, Eddie. Alright everybody, let's go. Places."

Edward screams out.

"Places people, we got a movie to make. Let's go. First position."

Time passes. Lunch comes and goes. The day creeps into the night.

First A.D. looks over at the Prop Master, Rand, an average-looking guy, wears ripped jeans and a Sacred Witch t-shirt.

"Rand, bring in the remote control babies."

Rand, carefully walks the lizard human robots, onto the set. Zyra walks over to the cross and out-stretches his arms. The special effects make-up girl puts the blood on his wounds.

"Are you ready for this?"

Zyra looks down at her, while she touches up his feet.

"No."

Rand laughs, as he places these horrific, realistic, slimmed, bluish-green lizard humans, into Zyra's stomach pouch. Zyra distorts his face, entering into his lizard face.

"These feel weird, man."

The special effects make-up girl stands up.

"You're all set. I'll do the final touches when Rand is done. I want you all to myself on the cross."

Zyra looks down at her breasts, hanging out of her shirt.

"Sounds kinky."

Dezerae walks onto set, with the hair and the make-up girl, led by the nerdish PA, Eurkal. The First A.D. asks Edward for Dezerae, and he responds.

"Right behind you, Sir."

First A.D. spins around and takes a double look.

"Wow, you look amazing."

Dezerae's face bleached out, blue lips, and blue eyes, strike her infamous sexy cat pose, and then *purrs*.

The First A.D. screams out to Sting.

"We have ourselves, a femme fatal here."

Sting grabs Dezerae's hand, kisses it, and locks eyes with her.

"My star, so beautiful. Too bad you're taken."

Smiles a wicked grin, Zyra screams out from the cross.

"Yeah, that's right, by the lizard king up here."

Dezerae blows Zyra a kiss and gets into the first position. Everyone clears the set, except the actors. The skeletons find their first positions, in between the lit torches. Little Person finds his first position, as the First A.D. checks in with the talent.

"Everyone knows what to do, right?"

Little Person responds.

"We rehearsed a million times already. Let's go."

The First AD runs off-set, and stands behind Sting, staring at Zyra on the cross on the monitor.

"This looks great. We're ready when you are."

Sting nods his head at the First A.D., who shouts out.

"Sound."

The sound mixer screams from off-set.

"Rolling."

Edward screams out.

"Quiet on set."

Eerie music from Sacred Witch creeps in, as *Rolling...*can be heard. Edward repeats.

"Rolling…"

Into the walkie while on the monitor, Garth slates the camera.

"The Lizard. Pick up shoot. Scene 82, take three."

The slate falls, and then Garth sprints off-set. Zyra hangs nailed, to the cross, as the pregnant Lizard King. The skeletons gather around the cross, smoke rises, and green-blue and red lights, illuminate the atmosphere. Sting says, "Action."

A bloody appendage pierces through Zyra's womb. The Skeletons' moans mix in with the music. Every muscle in Zyra's body is distorted. His tongue, skitters in and out, of his mouth. His head moves slowly up, to the right, taking the pain, as his newborns, enter the world.

Dezerae kneels at his bleeding feet, which drip into the terrarium. Colored guts and blue blood, ooze from the baby lizard's hand. The gook falls, from Zyra's stomach, landing in Dezerae's hands. She squeezes his insides, gushing out from in between her fingers, then takes in the scent, and licks her hand clean.

The human baby lizard, lets out a demonic hissing, as it claws its way out of the womb, and up Zyra's chest, leaving trails of his insides, dangling from Zyra's torso. Dezerae gasps with excitement, while on her knees, she follows the newborn, with her hands and eyes. Sting off stage whispers.

"Now."

Zyra looks down at Dezerae, who is wide-eyed and evil, yet still possesses motherly compassion. She cradles the baby in her hands as if she was holding a little puppy. Tears of joy, crawl down her face, leaving trails of black from the mascara.

The chanting from the skeletons, intensifies, as the baby lizard *skitters* away, and crawls up Zyra's neck, onto his face. Another human lizard baby tries to make its escape, from the womb but is unsuccessful. The red skeleton, grabs a black leather whip, with tiny fish hooks at the end. He raises the whip, and strikes down, tearing open Zyra's flesh. Zyra internalizes the pain, which causes regurgitation down his chin.

Dezerae grabs the baby from Zyra's face and releases a death-hurling scream.

"STOP! You idiot! These are my babies, don't hurt them."

She places the baby in the terrarium, as the skeleton jerks the whip out of Zyra's flesh. The second human lizard gets caught on the fish hook, and flies out of the womb, dangling on the end of the whip. Dezerae, furious, freaks out, grabs her stillborn baby, from the hooks, and kisses its soft, scaly-slimy body.

She places it in the terrarium. The other lizard baby nibbles on its dead sibling's carcass. Dezerae grabs the skeleton by the throat, and throws him down on the altar, as the remaining two skeletons, drop to their knees, in worship.

"Little Person, bring me the hammer and nails, NOW."

Little Person brings them to her, and with a commanding presence, she speaks.

"Hold him down."

Little Person jumps on top of the skeleton's chest, holding down his hands. Dezerae nails the skeleton to the altar. She spreads her legs around him, drops down upon him, and gets in his face.

"I'm not through with you."

Dezerae walks back around the cross, reaches into Zyra's stomach, and grabs one of the remaining two babies. She cradles it in her hands, it *squirms* as she gently lays it in the terrarium. Immediately, it joins the others in their feast. She reaches back in, and pulls out the last baby, lifting it to Zyra's face. Tears swell in her eyes.

"Look at our beautiful child. He looks just like you."

Tears fall from Zyra's eyes, as she presses the baby's face, a smaller exact version of Zyra's face, against his cheek.

"Kiss Daddy. He's going bye-bye."

She pulls it away and looks into its cute little miniature Zyra eyes. It speaks.

"Da-da."

After kissing it on the head, its tail wraps around her wrist.

"I know you're going to miss your Daddy, but he wants me to take care of you."

The Lizard King focuses on his dizziness.

"Let them go."

The Little Person grabs the baby from her hands.

"Let me see."

In one motion, Dezerae snatches the baby back, *slams* Little Person in the head, knocking him over, and then gently places it inside the terrarium. She squats over Little Person on the floor of the chapel, gets down into his face.

"How dare you!"

The skeleton nailed to the altar, moans in the background. She looks up.

"Shut up!"

Dezerae screams, as she clenches onto Little Person's shirt, and lifts him to his feet.

On the monitor, through the glass of the terrarium, Sting watches the two babies, cuddle next to each other.

"And cut."

Sting shakes off the mood.

"Dezerae, you're nuts."

Commotion builds as Edward quiets everyone down.

"QUIET! We're going right away."

The First AD shouts out to Rand.

"Rand, make sure everything is set up for the fire scene."

Rand is already on set, having the red skeleton, replaced with a prop dummy, "I'm on it." The fire marshal stands off to the side, as everyone sets up for the next shot. Sting leans over to the First A.D.

"If everything goes according to plan, this is the martini shot."

The First A.D. walks on set and screams out.

"Alright folks, martini shot."

Rand and the red skeleton walk off-set. Someone shouts.

"Yeah right, that's what you said last time."

"Places."

The First A.D. screams as he walks off-set, and stands next to Sting. Sting looks at Zyra and Dezerae through the monitor.

"Zyra, Dezerae, you guys ready?"

Zyra responds.

"Can you get Eddie to light me a joint? I need a hit before we start."

Edward waits for Sting's okay, lights up a joint, and runs it onto the set. He places it in Zyra's mouth. Zyra takes a few hits.

"Thanks, dude."

Edward nods his head, takes a hit, stamps it out, and runs off. Zyra screams out.

"Thanks Sting. I'm ready now."

Sting responds.

"Good. Roll sound."

Edward gets on his walkie-talkie.

"Rolling."

Sting says.

"Action."

Dezerae, controlling her rage, saunters over to the burning torch, and grabs it. With demon-flared nostrils, she marches over to the red skeleton. Robotically, she turns her head, towards Little Person, standing at attention, holding open the sacred book.

The Grip pushes the dolly around the track, as the Director of Photography films a close-up of Dezerae. Sacred Witch's hell-bound music fades in.

Dezerae turns back, facing the skeleton, as Little Person walks over with the book in hand. Dezerae speaks to the red skeleton.

"From the power of your darkness, you will lose your life forever. I will not be judged as these flames release your soul."

She drops the fiery torch under his feet. His cloak catches fire, spreads up his torso, his jaw drops, his chest pops up, mind torturous screams, envision severe pain, as the air fills with burnt flesh. Black smoke rises, and Red Skeleton's soul is released, through his blackened eyes.

The flames devour his whole body, as his nerves force the empty cavity, into convulsion. Little Person watches the body burn, craze rises inside of him. Unexpectedly, he reads a different passage, one that illuminates from the page.

"The Lord will carefully examine everything you have done, and bring you into judgment. On that day, you will be thrown into utter confusion; all your sins will be publicly exposed, and the wicked things you have done, will witness against you. What will you do then?"

Zyra's eyes burn, tearing up from the smoke, as it seduces its way through his eyes, and into his mind. His vision blurs, flames flicker, and the spectral snake of smoke, releases a sinister smile, and evil cackle. It materializes into a black cobra, as its head transforms into Babel's face. No longer a ghost without a grave, Zyra travels through Babel's mind.

Babel laughs at the poor soul, as his grip of death, tightens. Zyra tries to fight off the vision manifested, jerking his head, back and forth, as he hangs on the cross, fighting for his life for real. Everyone thinks Zyra is performing for a lifetime. Zyra's lips tremble his tongue skitters.

Deeper into the fiery abyss, Zyra's mind is lost, tormented by souls, reaching out as his spirit *passes* through. Sweat expels from Zyra's pores, he looks around the set and sees Babel's face, appear on every person. Notions of life pass through Zyra, intertwining with Babel's internal laughter. His body convulses, as The Lizard King. He blinks, trying to shake off the vision. His one ounce of energy left is spent summoning the darkest, lowest tone, man has ever heard.

"Leave me!"

Babel, fully human with wings of a cobra, laughs at Zyra's effort, as he hovers in front of him, amid eternal flames. Sting, completely immersed in the scene, allows the moment to play out, then shouts his excitement.

"MORE! Gimme more!"

Zyra's head jerks back, Sting's words press against his body, as he continues to fight for his soul. The piercings through his hands and feet *are* even further, and more blue blood creeps down. Babel's snake-like slither, sedates Zyra, rhythmically in perfect unison, to the eerie music.

"I'm not leaving. And only you know I'm here. I am the darkness within you, Zyra."

Zyra barely summons enough strength to confront the beast.

"In the name of Jesus, leave me."

Babel waits, nothing happens, and he chuckles. Sting turns to the script supervisor.

"Is that scripted?"

She shakes her head no. Sting looks puzzled, and grins with approval. Zyra hears the faint sound of bees coming from afar, as his lizard-like movements, and distortion, jerk his head, back and forth. His neck stretches to its furthest extent, as his words roll out from his soul.

"What do you want from me?"

Babel's split tongue, slithers from his mouth, as his eyes move in a circular motion. His drool, mellifluous as honey, drips down his chin, confronting Zyra.

"Just your soul. Innocent yet guilty. Blaspheme, for ticket sales? You are my boy."

Bees fly from Babel's mouth and ears, instantly upon Zyra. Zyra screams but is drowned out by the *buzzing* of the bees. Zyra's bloodshot, lizard-like crying eyes, are the only things not covered by the bees. Babel laughs wholeheartedly.

"Look at you, crying like a baby, as you once did."

Zyra receives a FLASH, of his younger self, crying away his Gene Simons' KISS make-up, one Halloween night, that changed his fate forever. He snaps out of the vision, congers up strength, shakes off the bees and lets out a god-awful hurl.

"Shut up! I'll kill you!"

Zyra tries to break from his bondage, like an angry ape, shaking its cage. Sting turns to the script supervisor, and whispers with excitement.

"Is he fighting for his soul, for real?"

Babel opens his mouth, and the bees slam down his throat, disappearing into his body. His cobra wings flare, then encompass his being, as his words echo through a hiss, from within his snake-like body.

"Time is at hand, my friend. No one can save you."

The flames disappear, Babel transcends into smoke, and slithers back through the air, mixing in with the black cloud, lingering above the ashes, from the red skeleton corpse on the altar. Zyra, exhausted, looks towards heaven.

"Father, into Thy hands I commend my spirit."

He drops his head and passes his ghost. His body weight falls, pulling on his hands and feet. Gravity, summons his intestines, from his torn gut and *plops* into the terrarium. The baby human lizards prey on their father's organs, growing rapidly as they eat. The skeletons shuffle over to the burning torches. The illuminated blue light simmers against the red chapel walls. They drop the front end of the torches, to the bottom of the black cross, and flames slowly consume, raising the holy black wood, devouring Zyra, the lizard king.

Little Person throws the book into the flames, raises his arms above his head, and chants the tribal beat, of Zyra's dark Sacred Witch soundtrack music. He dances around the burning cross, praising his god.

Dezerae picks up the terrarium, and watches the scene, through the slimy glass. The burning Lizard King reflects in her unhinged eyes. The two skeletons drop to their knees, and stretch out onto the floor, towards the cross, singing praise.

"We desire the end

Praise the undead

Deceased cannibal half-human lizards

Free our mind

For the chosen spirit"

They rise to their feet, as Little Person is completely lost in his dance. Possession takes over his body and throws him into the flames. He screams, bear hugs Zyra's legs, not letting go. The cross dissipates, and both bodies burn to ash around the bones. Greyish-black dust, falls to the ground, in a pile of ashes.

The clanking of the bones descends scattering the ashes. Dezerae looks down at her babies and grins with her sinister smile. The Skeletons march her out of the chapel.

On the monitor, the bones scattered ashes, and hot embers, pop, and fly into the air. The camera closes in, on the lizard humans, eating the head of Christ, carved on the front altar.

There's a beat, and then the Director screams.

"Cut!"

The First A.D. turns to Edward.

"Turn on the air, it's hot in here."

Edward runs, and flips on the switch, as the cool air charges through the yellow duct, and out onto the set. Sting shakes his head in disbelief.

"I can't believe we pulled this off. I never, in the history of filmmaking, have seen a scene like this."

The First A.D. screams to Garth to check the gates. Garth screams back.

"They're good."

Sting looks over at First A.D., and nods his head. The First A.D. screams out.

"It's a wrap! Congratulations Zyra, Dezerae, and all of my talent and crew. There's drinks in the coolers, but first, make sure everything is cleaned up."

Zyra shakes the cross, as he still hangs on it, and yells out.

"Somebody get me down from here."

Rand walks over to him and releases the nails from the back of the cross. Zyra pulls his hands away and steps down. He stretches out his cramps, as rage oozes from Zyra's head. Garth pats him on the shoulder.

"Great job. You're on fire, man."

Zyra throws him a look of death.

"Whatever, dude, just giving you a compliment."

Garth walks away mumbling to himself.

"He's nothing like his father."

Dezerae overhears Garth's reaction to Zyra, concerned, she puts the terrarium down and follows him storming off. He rips off the stomach pouch and throws it against the wall. Rand, the Prop Master screams out.

"Hey, Zyra, please, that's expensive, let's have some respect."

Zyra nods and keeps walking. Rand walks over, picks up the pouch, and places it on top of the prop table. Dezerae catches up to him. He slams the back door open, and they exit. Dezerae follows him, up the stairs, and into the star wagon.

"What's wrong with you? You were amazing. That was the best work I've ever seen you do."

Zyra fidgets with the door handle, and more anger builds up, finally, it opens, annoyed, and he walks through, trying to get out of his lizard costume. Throwing his arms around, not being able to remove the costume, he has a mental breakdown. He falls to the ground crying, hands over his face.

"Can you help me, please!?"

"Stand up, I don't understand you at all."

She unzips him from the back, he steps out of the costume and kicks it off with his right foot. The costume remains on his foot, pushing Zyra off the edge. He bends down, ripping it off his foot, and throws it as hard as he can, against the trailer wall.

"GOD! What is wrong with me?

Me vibrates from his throat, as he *convulses* with anger. Dezerae sits back, at the make-up table, watching him throw a fit, allowing his torment to haunt her. He grabs a towel, wraps it around his naked body, and sits down on the bed, clenching his hair, and teeth. He catches his breath, and calms his nerves enough, to confront Dezerae. Tears swell in both their eyes, and he finally speaks.

"I saw him again."

Dezerae quietly asks, "Who?" His eyes squint with anger, his lips protrude out.

"Babel, Satan, Death, The Collector of Souls, any of the above, all of the above."

Dezerae tries to connect.

"From your dreams?"

He answers spitefully.

"Yes Dez, from my dreams."

She shakes her head, giving him a look of, *does not even go there*, he breaks eye contact and puts his head down in shame.

"I'm sorry," getting choked up, "I was covered in bees."

He shakes off the feeling, and asks again, "What's wrong with me?"

"Sounds like a bad acid trip."

He lifts his head.

"I'm not high."

He stands up, pulls his leather pants, off the hanger, reaches into his pocket, pulls out a joint, and lights up.

"Want sum?"

"You know I quit."

She walks out of the trailer, letting him finish. He gets into the shower.

Chapter 13

UNEASY RIDER

The city lights paint the contour, along the beachfront at night; a few hours have passed as Dezerae, holds onto Zyra's waist, on the back of his Harley Davidson. He travels up the winding road, weaving in and out of traffic. Cars lay on their horn, he cuts them off. Dezerae lifts the visor on her helmet, as her left arm is still pressed against his stomach. Wind howls, vibrating her face, calling out to him with her dry lips.

"Slow down! You're scaring me."

Zyra pulls back on the acceleration; they whiz around another car, riding along the edge of the cliff. In his peripheral vision, he looks back at Dezerae and speaks with excited fear.

"It's just like my dream."

Turning back around, he screams.

"Where are you now BABEL?"

He passes another car and pulls back into his lane, a truck lays on its horn, traveling past them downhill. Zyra's delirium manifests.

"YEAH!"

Dezerae presses against his stomach, to try and get his attention.

"Stop the Bike!"

He continues to ignore her and does just the opposite. His rage and psychotic impulses, drive him to POP a wheely, Dezerae holding on for dear life. Tears fly from the corner of her eyes, and she screams again.

"STOP THE BIKE!"

Zyra drops down, and his back tire *skids* out, he catches it, and peels around the turn. She raises her right hand and punches down hard against his shoulder.

"STOP!!!"

He finally decelerates downhill and stops at the bottom in front of a restaurant. Dezerae *jumps* off the bike, *rips* off her helmet, and *throws* it at him. Zyra blocks the helmet, from hitting him in the head. The sting in his hands, surges up his arms, turning his grin, into discomfort. He takes off his helmet and confronts her.

"I thought you liked living on the edge."

Rage pumps through her veins, turning her face red, she strides over to him and slaps him across the face.

"ASSHOLE! I'm not dying like this. I don't know what your problem is, but I can't take it anymore," getting choked up, she falls to her knees in tears, "I don't deserve to be treated like this!"

She drops her head to her knees and puts her hands over her face. Zyra stands alone, dumbfounded. An older couple walks out of the restaurant and stares at them. Zyra puts the kickstand down, gets off the bike, and walks over to her. He kneels, and puts his arm around her, as his thoughts oppose his words.

"Sorry, did I do something wrong?"

She jerks his hand away.

"I'm sorry, Dezerae."

He backs away. She sniffles and wipes her running nose, still buried in her knees.

"Don't touch me! You need a priest to exorcize you. You're *possessed*!"

He instantly becomes psychotic, lashes out, his fingers disjoint, and shakes neurotically. His face beat red, and his eyes, bugged out, exposing his teeth.

"MAYBE I AM!"

He enjoys his outburst, but then retreats, trying to reason.

"Look Dez, you're just upset. I didn't mean to scare you."

The older gentleman finally interjects.

"Excuse me, Ma'am, is everything, okay?"

Zyra throws a dirty look, and answers, with a stern tone.

"Yeah, she's fine."

The gentleman takes a step closer and persists.

"I was asking the young lady. Are you alright, Ma'am?"

The older wife, tugs on the gentleman's arm, giving him a look, *forget it*. Zyra fires back with vengeance.

"I said she's fine, now get the *hell* out of here!"

"I didn't ask you, hey, aren't you..."

Recognizing him from the news, Zyra gets in his face. By this time, people are gathered outside the restaurant, watching the scene.

"You want to start with me old man, 'cuz I'll rip your head off, shit down your neck."

Zyra's breath, evil eye, crawls into the man's soul, *instilling* fear. Dezerae looks up, mascara bleeding down her face finally answers.

"I'm fine, Sir. Thank you for asking. That was very kind."

The gentleman gives Dezerae his utmost respect.

"You're welcome, Ma'am. You don't have to take it, you know."

His wife pulls him away.

"Let's go..."

The older couple retreats and walks back to their car. The wife confronts him.

"People have guns these days, Manny. You can't be the hero, all the time."

The ones gathered outside the restaurant, enter back in. Zyra looks up at the half-moon, and grabs his hair, trying to make sense of this night. Garth's words repeat echoed through his mind *The Nephilim. Fallen Angels.* He drops his head and confronts Dezerae.

"You make no sense to me. You think you have all the answers."

She sits Indian-style, wiping off her mascara, with her forearm.

"No Zyra, I don't have all the answers. I took wedding vows to be with you, in good times and in bad, but I cannot walk through, the valley of death, with you, especially when you choose to go there yourself. I'm fighting my demons."

Silence builds, invading Zyra's world. He breaks down, repentance fills his eyes.

"I'm sorry. I gave in to the fear of losing control. So I attacked it because that's what I do, and that scared you."

Dezerae stands up, and locks eyes with him, questioning his existence.

"What are you going to do?"

Cars continue to drive by in the background. His hands rise, halfway to his face, he drops his head, closes his eyes, takes a deep breath, and conforms.

"Fine, I'll see Von Hildonberg tomorrow. Maybe he can help me."

Dezerae allows his apology to affect her.

"You prayed for the first time in years this morning…that's faith. That's what's going to save you, not some doctor. Come to church with me tomorrow."

"Church? I didn't say anything about that. I'm not ready."

She stands up, puts out her hand, and asks for his keys, he responds in jest.

"You've never driven a hog before."

She takes off walking through the parking lot, entering the darkness, on the side of Pacific Coast Highway, mumbling to herself.

"Fine. I'll walk then."

A trucker drives by honking his horn, Zyra walks over, bends down, and picks up Dezerae's helmet. He screams out to her.

"I'm not letting you walk."

She continues to walk.

"Shit!"

He approaches his bike, straps on the helmet, revs the engine, and catches up to her. Speaking above the engine's roar.

"Why are you doing this?"

She doesn't answer, her eyes focused straight ahead. Cars pass by, he pulls up in front of her, gets off his bike, and waits for her. He walks it uphill, alongside her.

"God, you're impossible."

She throws him a *sarcastic* look.

"How generous. It's only pitch black out."

Zyra is getting tired, stops for a moment, then carries on.

"Damn it! Can you please wait?!"

She stops, and the moon silhouettes her. He looks down, marching the bike uphill.

"Thank you. I'm scared, Dezerae."

His voice cracks.

"You know me. I've never been afraid of anything. Or if I was, I confronted it, immediately, like when I was a kid, I went bungee jumping, skydiving, just to conquer my fear of heights."

"Where did that fear come from?"

"When I was at Hanover, one of my friends, fell to his death. He skipped football practice, went hiking, and slipped on moss, 120 feet. Saw it on the news."

Dezerae finds compassion.

"I'm sorry Zyra. That's horrible."

"Well, it seems as if death likes to follow me. These visions I keep getting, I have no control, I don't know how to confront this."

She strikes a dismal grin.

"Quit doing drugs, Zyra. That would be a start."

Knowing she is right, and no time like the present, Zyra puts the motorcycle on its stand, pulls out a bag of weed from his pocket, and empties it over the cliff. The wind catches the buds and scatters them. He shoves the empty bag, back into his pants, looks up at her, with puppy dog eyes, and pleads.

"Forgive me Dez, I wasn't high when I saw Babel, today on set."

She presses her lips together and thinks for a moment.

"Um, wait a second, that's not true, we all had to wait, while Edward brought you a joint."

Zyra shrugs his shoulders.

"You know what I mean."

She walks over and hugs him.

"I forgive you, I love you.

"

She whispers into his ear, giving him the chills. Her tears moisten his face, and he gasps.

"I feel my heart pour into yours. I love you Dezerae."

They both smile, embrace in a kiss, she squeezes him tighter. The moonlight illuminates their presence. They get on the motorcycle, he unhooks her helmet, hands it to her, and pulls away.

Chapter 14

THE NEPHILIM

Meanwhile, under the same almost full moon, the eerie presence surrounding Tartarus' mansion, is even thicker inside tonight. The black and red cross-shaped tiled floor leads down into the living room pit, where there is a fireplace, next to the pool, which leads under the stained glass, and into the backyard. The stained glass reflects a scene, which looks like a human sacrifice. Zyra's music blazes through the sound system. A closer look, reveals Zyra being the human, that is being sacrificed.

Black and red lights, enhance the mood, as naked bodies in the pool, drink their poison, and others stand. Some sit in the built-in, black leather couches, around the fireplace. Garth, dressed in black leather, and a blue silk shirt, puffs on a crypt joint, laced with LSD. He passes it to the beautiful blonde, Sarah, dressed in skimpy, black and red lace, standing next to him. She takes a hit, which sends her eyes to the moon. Zyra's vocals through his transcending half-dead voice, parallel the scene.

"Take a hit, hold it in, pass through the darkness to a world of sin."

Garth sings along.

"I'll rape your mind, destroy your thoughts, eat your soul, as you lose control...Welcome to the lair of my world."

Reflected in Garth's eyes, Tartarus, dark presence glides into the room, dressed to the nines, Victorian-style, sporting a black velvet cloak. His dark mysterious eyes, and metallic blue face, stand firmly above a silver medallion, of a fallen angel, which hangs from his neck. The dry ice, around the pool, alludes to a dream-like state. Tartarus enters, confronting his guests.

"I am glad everyone is enjoying themselves. It's only the beginning of tonight's festivities. More fun to come."

He smiles and walks out of the circle of guests. A tall lengthy waitress, dressed in a black G-string, French maid's attire, presses her red stilettos, in between the fingers, of one of the guests, sitting in the pool. He looks up at her long legs, past her mini skirt, and sees a valley between her breasts, as she passes the drink.

"Dry martini?"

"Thank you."

Smiling ear to ear.

As the night progresses, everyone's buzz starts to reach its peak. Tartarus calls for his guests to strip down to their evening garments. His servants, now no longer guests, do as he requests, then line up, and one by one, enter a black and gray cobblestone rainbow, leading to the dungeon. The narrow stone spiral stairwell is dimly lit, with torches lining the walls. One of the women grabs onto the man's shoulders in front of her. The train of people is guided, by one of the servant's burning torches. Sarah, was excited, sandwiched between two bodies, yet mystified.

"Spooky Sexy."

The guy behind her rubs his firm manhood against her leg reaches around, massages her breasts, and whispers into the back of her neck.

"You haven't seen anything, yet."

All sixty-nine guests enter the dungeon. The caboose servant, slams the stone door shut, leaving no escape. The only light, burning torches, that cut through the thick fog, shine off the sharpened medieval axes, hanging on the walls. The smell of burning incense, the chill in the air, hardens nipples. Dangling down the walls, in between the flames, chains connected to handcuffs cuffs. At the far end, a cement stage, dressed with dark red velvet curtains. Murmurs fill the air, bodies gravitate to the center of the dungeon. Sensual goth music, teases the atmosphere, as the chosen servants, silence the room. As curiosity and ambition, rise to their peak, filling the silence, the curtain slowly opens.

On the stage, two cages, each embodying a tiger stripe, full-body painted female. They are positioned in a way, which reveals their ravenous lust. A man crawls out from between the cages, on his hands and knees, in a black leather mask, covering his whole head. A chain connects his neck, to the dominatrix, who has her stiletto pressed into his back. She *whips* him, creating a heap of excitement, as he crawls closer, to the edge of the stage. Arousal is heightened as she pulls his head back, and shaves down his neck and chest, slicing the skin, just enough to create blood, with a skeleton handle, and metal blade. As the music crescendos into a tribal beat, two drugged male tigers, slowly walk out, chained to two females in black and red latex. They guide these beats to their cages. One of them roars, surging a wave of fear, the tiger stripe female, caresses its face, as they enter the cage, shut the doors behind them, *clank*!

The dominatrix, throws the girls in latex, to their knees. They attack the man, in the mask. One of them throws the man on his back, grabs the blade, and shaves around his throbbing blood-filled organ. The Dominatrix grabs the back of the other girl's head, and forces it upon her, giving her pleasure. The dominatrix lifts her thigh-high boot and presses the heel into the man's chest. The people watching, rub against each other, finding a partner or two to play with.

The tiger girls within the cages caress the cat's reproductive organs, with their breasts. Their long lengthy fingers, gently stroke, exciting the tigers even further. The crowd, in disbelief, gasps at the sight, as the slaves drugged state of mind, is heightened once again, by this debauchery. The dominatrix grabs the back of the girl's head, lifts her to her feet, hands her a burning candle, and commands her to pour the hot wax over the man's body.

Chanting can be heard, as he fidgets from the burning sensation. She commands the other sex slave, to get on top of him, and ride. The ladies in the cage, release the tigers ' organs from their mouths, and squeeze the caged bars, as they press their faces against the cold metal, and raise their curved backs into the air. The tigers climb on top, resting their paws on their backs, as the females guide them inside.

The people watching, touching, feeling, moaning, and pressing against each other, enter the beginning stages of demonic ecstasy. Some cuff themselves to the walls, as their partners divulge in pleasure. On the other side of the dungeon, opposite the stage, black wooden doors open, exposing an altar, with two burning flames on each side. Gothic framed images of Tartarus,

Zyra, and Zyra's father, line the wall, behind the altar, set up as some kind of shrine. Behind the altar, arms out-spread, watching his creation, Tartarus opens a black leather-bound book and holds up an image of Zyra. Standing on either side of him, six muscle-bound males, dressed in black leather masks, straps around their bodies. Each one of these twelve men, holds an axe in their hands, covering their mid-section. Tartarus begins to speak to the sixty-nine souls.

> "I Tartarus, found in the Bible, 2 Peter 2:4, known as the dark abode of woe: the pit of darkness in the unseen world and '...as far below hades as the earth is below heaven' am here in honor of the founder, Zyra's father the first original Tartarus, of our cult, 'The Nephilim.' We will summon his presence, to possess his son's body, on the full moon tomorrow night."

Tartarus increases his volume, matching the mood.

> "Who are the Nephilim?"

The servants answer in unison.

> "The offspring of the fallen ones."

> "Why are we here?"

> "To bring them back from hell."

> "How shall we do this?"

> "Through the sacrifice of the son of the original Tartarus."

Tartarus smiles, about to bring his people, into the spiritual world, but commands another answer.

"Who built the Ancient Monuments?"

The servants reply.

"The Nephilim."

Tartarus continues to read from the book.

"The Great Pyramid at Gaza?"

The people answer.

"The Nephilim."

"The Stonehenge?"

"The Nephilim."

"The 'face' on the Planet Mars?"

"The Nephilim."

Tartarus proud of their responses continues his speech.

"To the legends of every ancient cultural tradition on the planet Earth: Samaria, Assyria, Egypt, Incas, Mayan, Gilgamesh, and many more who all believe this. We now offer up the sacrifice of sixty-nine souls, for the return of our original leader, Tartarus. Tomorrow night on the full moon, his soul will be resurrected and will enter into the body of his son. It is then, that we will be reunited, with our ancestors, the demi-gods. "

Just as he finishes his ceremonial statement, and closes it with an unholy blessing, with an upside-down cross, everyone engages in this sacrificial orgy. Tartarus orchestrates the moans. At the peak of ecstasy, as a whole, Tartarus screams out.

"NOW..."

The music heightens into its finale, his twelve muscle-bound men, raise their axes and *charge* at the people with horrific roars.

Their swings come down, chopping up the bodies of these sinful sixty-nine souls. Sarah looks up in her state of orgasmic pleasure, an axe swings down, and slices her head in half, splitting her face and neck in two. Tartarus' possessed eyes, with fire in his soul, take in the sight. Blood splatters across his body, as massacre fills the air.

Blood crawls to the center of the room, pouring down the drain, as the music calms itself and fades into silence. The sounds of bodies and blood-hurling screams diminish. As soon as the twelve men, finish their job, they stand over this crippled scene, covered in blood and guts.

Tartarus raises his hands, above his head, blood drips down his body, and speaks to his servants left standing.

"Our job here is done until tomorrow night."

The man with the mask, who was seduced by the dominatrix, and two sex slaves, unzippers it, removes his mask, exposing Garth. Staring at this terror-struck, blood-bath, Garth vomits off the side stage. Tartarus confronts him.

"Garth, you *will* have Zyra here, tomorrow night."

Garth knowing he is in over his head, stares at him in shock, and nods his head in agreement.

Lost in the serpent's kiss, sacrifice, hit or miss, now your soul will never be the same. New reality. Who's to blame, is it love or shame? 69 souls.

Chapter 15

MORNING VOODOO

The sun creeps upon the horizon, the following morning, reflecting the deep blue sky, and white clouds of the ocean's surface. A wind sweeps across the water, cooling the air front, and waves break on the shore. Flapping wings, glide out from the center of the sun, pulling forth the spirit bridge. Its continued passion, drives across the sky, and maintains its bright reflected glow, which shadows upon the sea. Tiny stars twinkle within its illumination, as the bridge lifts and ascends, excelling rapidly, across the sky.

An airplane flies through this glitter light, it floods the interior of the plane, blinding the passengers for a moment. An angelic choir unravels, in each of their minds, paralyzing them in beauty, not a word is spoken, as the passengers witness this supernatural phenomenon. The plane flies through.

At this same moment, Church bells summon the congregation, walking quickly towards the beautiful gothic-style entrance of St. Charles Borromeo Catholic Church, North Hollywood. This once Arch-Diocese basilica stands firm with dark oak wood, a life-size crucifix hanging twenty feet above the altar, human size statues of the Pieta, the Virgin Mary holding Jesus' corpse after the crucifixion, the infant of Prague, area as well, and a statue of Jesus, holding out His hand, with a kneeler before it, just to paint the picture. The center aisle stretches over a hundred feet. Outside the open gates, Father O'Donnell, an older Irish priest, dressed in a green vestment, greets the parishioners. A young boy wearing shorts, a shirt, and a tie, tugs on the back of Father O'Donnell's vestment. Father turns around, and welcomes the little boy, with a smile and pat on the head.

"Good morning Gerald."

Gerald responds.

"Good morning Father."

His mother grabs his arm and pulls him into the crowded church. Gerald's concerned voice holds Fr. O'Donnell's attention.

"Father, when is the next funeral?"

He retrieves it with a look of surprise.

"I...I'm not sure, why?"

Gerald's mother pulls him again, as other parishioners scurry past.

"I want to serve, so I can get bread from the dead."

Father holds in his laughter. The mother slaps the boy upside the head.

"I can't believe you. Apologize to Father."

The boy's chubby face, squishes together, as she digs her nails into his forearm.

"Owe, fine. Sorry, Father."

She looks Father in the eyes, embarrassed but addresses the issue.

"I...never taught him to speak this way. Come on, Gerald."

Father shakes his head, with a forgiving smile, as she practically *rips* his arm from the socket, pulling him along. Among the late-comers, Dezerae rapidly approaching. Father's facial expression, releases waves of laughter, just strong enough for Dezerae to detect.

"Good morning Father, what's so funny?"

His green eyes, and red hair perk up, intrigued by her insight, as he confesses.

"Children make me laugh, that's all Dezerae."

She grabs his right hand, and gently squeezes, a look of desperation strikes her face.

"Will you have a minute to spare after mass?"

He squints his eyes, finding that place within her soul, to communicate.

"I have a breakfast meeting at ten. I suppose I could be a little late unless you care to join us."

She releases his hand.

"No thank you. I have to get home after mass, but it won't take but a minute."

He answers kindly.

"Alright then, meet me in the sacristy after mass."

She smiles with gratitude, "Thank you Father" and walks into church. Fr. O'Donnell shuts the church doors, behind him. The tallest altar boy, in front of the precession line, raises the cross high above his head. The pipe organ compliments the harmony, expelled from the church's choir. Two altar girls, hold white lit candles, standing behind them and the lector. The Lector raises the book, and they proceed down the center aisle. The congregation rises and joins in the opening hymn, and Fr. O'Donnell follows.

At the same time Mass is being said, others take advantage of this beautiful morning, down by the beach. Crystal clear green-blue water, crashes down on the shore, creating foam, engulfing kids body surfing. Three girls in bikinis, play volleyball against three guys in Bermudas; people of all shapes and sizes, sunbathe with their new stylized sunshades. An overweight middle-aged man lays on his stomach, and his wife rubs sun tan lotion into his wobbling skin.

Just to the right of them, the perfectly curved tan creature, in a white G-string bikini, rolls onto her stomach and unties her top. Her wet blond hair, splits around her neck, as beads of water glide down, her rock-hard body. A little kid running with a bucket of water, trips *spilling* the water onto the girl's back. The old man, thanks God under his breath, as she sits up. Two teenage boys walk by. Caught by surprise, one quickly covers his growing erection, with the palm of his hand.

The other spots his growth, laughs, and noticing the girl's bouncing breasts, he materializes an even larger one. As they lock eyes, the girl screams, and covers her breasts, while the guys cover their masculinities, pushing out their backside, as if they got punched in the stomach. The girl degradingly labels them.

"Perverts..."

They hurriedly walk away, embarrassed. The kid with the empty bucket runs away screaming.

"Mommy, mommy."

A billboard of "The Lizard" with Zyra and Dezerae's image, hovers over Pacific Coast Highway, and reads, "'The Lizard', Starring Zyra Jordonello and Dezerae Nelson, coming March 2nd, to a theater near you."

Cars speed through the yellow light, under the sign, as Zyra straddles his Harley, stopped at the red light. Beachgoers scramble along the crosswalk, Zyra's stare pierces through the dark visor, as he sizes up two gorgeous babes, strutting their stuff. He lifts his visor and greets one of them, who walks over, strokes his revving engine, and locks his eyes. The other babe, runs her fingers, up his leg, with a welcoming smile, seducing him, with her voluptuous lips.

"Nice hog."

The other molests him with her words.

"I'd sell my soul, to feel your hog between my legs."

Zyra lifts his left hand, waves his wedding ring, and then drops the visor when the light turns green.

"Not anymore…"

Peels out leaving them coughing in the exhaust. One of them screams out.

"Asshole!"

Impatient drivers honk, and scream.

"Move it."

Zyra laughs to himself, rides away, and receives a flashback of him and Dezerae, about to make love. He tiger-crawls up her body, growling under his breath, and whispers into her ear, "Your hormones smell delicious." Dezerae smiles lying naked under him; she growls back, and bites his nipple, as her legs, wrap around him.

He snaps out of the vision, HONK, swerves around an on-coming car, slows down, puts on the left blinker, and turns into the parking garage, of an office building. He stops in front of the wooden security arm, and grabs a ticket, from the long-haired teller, reading Zyra's book. Zyra looks at his name tag, "Charlie." Zyra lifts his visor and asks.

"Hey Charlie, how do you like the book, so far?"

"Best book I ever read."

Charlie lifts the security arm, and Zyra nods.

"Cool."

He drives past the booth, around the cement pole, and up the incline. Charlie looks at the cover of the book, and shakes his head in disbelief.

"Nah."

At the same time, in a nearby local pub, two drunken bikers, play pool in the back. Its black walls with mirrors, stretch across the length of the bar. The white pony-tailed biker, Eagle, in ripped jeans, wears a Harley Davidson eagle across his back, on an old beat-up jeans jacket. He hits the cue ball, as smoke rises from his cigarette, into his eyes.

"I'm gonna *pop* that bitch, when I get home."

The other biker, Snake, dressed in worn brown leather pants with, a tattoo of a snake wrapped around a naked girl, encircles his upper arm and waits for his shot.

"The only thing you're gonna *pop* is another beer for me when I kick your ass."

Eagle looks up, locks eyes with Snake, and sings his response to the music blaring in the background.

"I'll kick your ass all over the place, singing 'We will...I will...Rock you.'"

He *slams* his fist, down onto the pool table.

Sitting on a back stool, at the corner of the bar is Elizabeth. Her eyes, glued to the television, elevated behind the bar. She ashes her cigarette, blows smoke from her mouth, lifts her Long Island ice tea, to her lips, and takes a sip. Her stone-cold stare, at the television, never changes. She drops the glass, from her lips, leaving a maroon lipstick, imprinted.

Garth staggers out of the bathroom, beer in his hand. It *slips* from his fingers, and pours onto the floor, "Shit." He bends over, picks it up, wipes off the dirt, with his shirt, and finishes the bottle. His eyes are bloodshot, his breath stinks, and his composition is off balance. He takes a seat next to Elizabeth, *slams* the empty bottle down, onto the bar, and looks over at her. The Media, Holly Gossip, attacks Zyra in the parking lot, on television. The camera, and microphone, were shoved in his face.

"Is it true, you see Dr. Von Hildonberg, the noted psychoanalyst, who receives visions from the devil?"

Zyra remains silent, shakes his head, and continues to walk up the stairs, as they follow. Sitting on the other side of Garth, Babel appears out of thin air, dressed in his Victorian white, three-piece tuxedo. Garth turns to Babel and slurs his words.

"I know this idiot. I just worked with him, "The Lizard.""

Babel taps his long fingernail on the wooden bar, slightly turns his head, from his peripheral, and confronts Garth.

"Is it?"

Garth looks over at him.

"Iz't what?"

"Is it true? Does Von Hildonberg receive visions of…*me*?"

Garth shakes his head, not sure if he heard him correctly, and laughs.

"Look man, all I know, working on this movie…I didn't feel right. Like out of nowhere, I feel *cold*, kinda, what I feel *now*. Eerie man. Anyway, Zyra's one messed up Dude."

Babel continues his sly smile, digesting every word. Garth continues his ramble.

"Something's wrong with that boy. *Nah*, I guess I shouldn't say that. Who the hell knows, I could be sitting next to his mother, for all I know."

Is coincidence, that Garth speaks the oddly strange truth, without knowing it, or did Babel, set this up? Elizabeth takes a hit off her smoke and blows it in the direction of Garth's face.

"Excuse me, I couldn't help, but a...to *overhear* your conversation. So, you know Zyra, hu?"

Garth looks up at Elizabeth. She takes a seat, next to him.

"Yeah, why? You *wanna blow'em*, get in line."

He laughs obnoxiously, she puts her cigarette *out,* on his hand, and watches it sizzle into his skin.

"OUCH, WHAT THE. FUuu..."

She cuts him off.

"That's my son, asshole! You were right, should pay attention to your instincts, next time."

She gets up, and walks out, Garth screams at the top of his lungs.

"What the *fuck BITCH*!?"

The bartender, a large bald man with piercings on his face, looks up from wiping the counter.

"Garth, watch your language."

"That bitch just put her cigarette out on my hand..."

The bartender walks over to Garth, and gets in his face.

"I told you, watch your language."

Behind the bartender, on television, Holly Gossip and more journalists persist in Zyra, following him to the doctor's office.

"Aren't you worried about your soul, Zyra?"

Another News Caster interjects.

"'The Lizard,' your most controversial work of art, yet, a lizard human playing the king of kings? Are you the Anti-Christ?"

Zyra turns around, grabs the microphone, from the News Anchor's hand, and sticks his face in the camera.

"What the *hell* is wrong with you people? Worry about your *goddamn* souls!"

Zyra throws the microphone down, walks off the frame, and *slams* the door shut, in the cameraman's face.

"What about the youth, who look up to you, Mr. Rock Star?"

The newscaster turns around and confronts the camera.

"You heard it here, first, folks, 'Worry about your god...(beep)...souls.' I'm Holly Gossip reporting live, from Southern California, where we bring you Hollywood's latest troubled souls."

In a commercial for General Hospital, Felicia's character fills the spotlight, Babel grabs Garth's burnt hand and miraculously heals it. Garth pulls away.

"How'd ya do that!?"

Babel's dark seductive eyes, and deep soothing haunted voice, find their way into Garth's drunken stupor.

"Do you believe in the devil, Garth Blackwood?"

Garth releases a nervous laugh and rests his hands on the bar, to stabilize the spinning room. He looks down, at his healed hand, through Garth's eyes, the bar *rises*, and spins around, showing him an image of last night's massacre.

"What the…who are you, Satan?"

Babel laughs.

"It is you, who says I am. I believe people are their gods. They become who they envision, themselves to be."

Garth relaxes, feeling at ease with Babel's response. The spinning stops, and Garth toasts Babel.

"Amen, brother. Hey, how did you know my last name?"

Babel continues to hypnotize Garth.

"What do you want, from life, Garth?"

The atmosphere fades around him, Garth becomes absorbed in his inner thoughts, guided by Babel's voice. Garth thinks to himself again, *how did he know my name?*

No words come out from Garth's mouth, his eyes, stone-cold, lost in the abyss, he imagines himself sitting at Tartarus' poolside, with the naked playmates running around. The black tiles at the bottom of the pool, bleed out the word.

"MURDERER."

The bartender walks over to Garth and *snaps* his fingers in front of his face, no response. Babel lingers his left hand in front of the bartender and continues to stay focused on Garth.

"Bring my friend a Coke, with a double shot of Captain Morgan's Spiced Rum. I will have the same."

The bartender immediately denies service to Garth.

"He's had enough Sir, but yours is coming right up."

A deep subtle growl rises from Babel.

"Bring my friend, a Coke, with a double shot, of Captain Morgan's Spiced Rum. I will have the same."

The bartender overtly agrees.

"No problem."

The cigarette slowly burns in between Garth's fingers, and the ashes elongate. The bartender grabs the bottle of rum, and makes the drinks, Garth breaks his stare and looks over at Babel.

"A friend of mine, in Boston, shat himself drinking that stuff. His roommate found him passed out on the front lawn, covered in his excrement."

Garth wipes his mouth, and slobber drips down his chin, from laughing at the visual. Through his peripheral vision, he stares at Babel, flares his nostrils, and takes a hit off his cigarette.

The two bikers, finish their game of pool and walk past them in a drunken stupor. Garth overhears.

"Yo Snake, that Zyra character, more messed up, than your Momma."

"Don't talk about my Momma."

Garth ashes his cigarette, turns his stool around, and looks Snake in the eyes.

"It's true Snake, Zyra is more fucked up than your Momma."

His friend punches Snake in the arm. Snake takes him on for a brief moment, and chooses not to respond. His friend chimes in.

"Told you. He's badass, that's why he's making millions."

They walk out of the bar, Babel grins to himself, raises the right side of his upper lip, and pets down Garth's head.

"I'm the hand that rocks the Buzz, my friend."

The bartender drops the two drinks down, onto the counter, in front of them.

"There you go, two Captain Morgan's and coke."

Garth takes another drag off his butt and puts it out in the ashtray. Babel pulls a money clip, full of hundreds, from his pocket, and lays one down on the counter. The bartender looks at it, then back at Babel.

"I can't break that. It's too early in the morning."

Babel generously slides it over to him.

"Keep it."

The bartender grabs it, thanks him, and walks away. Garth shakes his head, not believing what just took place.

"Dude, you just gave him a hundred. You're weird man, but I like your style. Now we'll get service all day."

Babel gently slides his long fingernail thumb, over another crisp hundred-dollar bill, pulls it out, and lays it in front of Garth. Garth questions his gesture.

"What's this for?"

Babel's dark pupils unclasp Garth's attention.

"I'm a soul collector."

Chills rise Garth's spine, forcing him to make the decision, take it or leave the money. Garth reaches out and grabs the money. Babel forces him into a vision. Garth, a young boy, takes money from a stranger, that looks exactly like Babel, as his words reverberate.

"That stranger was me. The deal was already made."

Garth's soul cries out.

"I didn't know any better."

Laughs.

"Whatever you say, Master."

Garth picks up his drink, Babel picks up his own, and they make a toast.

"To Eternity."

Garth smiles and meets Babel's glass mid-air. CLANK! Everything around him stops, his heart races, and the sound of his heartbeat is about to explode from his chest. Everything comes back to normal, Garth continues his drink until the glass is empty.

He burps and shakes the buzz into existence. He gets up from the stool, catches his foot, in the rail, and *slams* his head on the counter, the glass from his hand, *shatters* as it hits the ground. Garth *hits* the ground and slices his head on the jarred pieces of broken glass.

Garth is laid out on the floor. Babel gets off his stool, and black smoke rises from his feet, forming into little fairies, dancing around his boots. He bends down, and picks Garth up, from underneath his arms. Making eye contact with the bartender, he nods his head and pulls him along.

"I got'em."

Babel drags him, out of the bar, scrapping the metal heels, from Garth's boots, across the wooden floor.

* * *

Inside Dr. Von Hildonberg's office, people are seated on the couch, in the waiting room. The bubbly cute Puerto Rican secretary, Rosa, answers the ringing phone with, a very strong accent.

"Dr. Von Hildonberg's office, how may I help you?"

She looks at his schedule on the computer.

"Yes, there is an opening on March Second, 3:30 pm. Alright, we'll see you then."

She hangs up the phone. On the television, in front of her desk, is the other News Anchor confronting America.

"You heard it folks, 'Worry about your goddamn souls,' straight from Mr. Hollywood himself, Zyra Jordonello."

Zyra busts through the office door and flies past Rosa, entering Dr. Von Hildonberg's office. Rosa jumps up.

"You can't go in there."

She follows him in, and with panic struck across her face, she tries to confront the Doctor.

"I tried to stop him, Doc., but he flew past..."

The doctor looks at his female patient, crying hysterically, on the brown leather couch.

"I'm sorry, Trish, but we have to finish tomorrow. I will give you a free session. Same time."

She gets up, wipes her tears, and exits without saying a word. He turns to Rosa and waves her off.

"It's fine, thank you, Rosa."

He looks back at Zyra.

"You will pay for her session tomorrow."

Zyra lays down on the couch.

"Fine."

Rosa leaves shaking her hips, throwing up her hands, in disbelief. Zyra throws his hands, behind his head, puts his feet up on, the arm of the couch, and sings.

"My dope left me in Mexico...

My dreams and screams are all I know...

My heart opposes hell but my mind drinks its soul...

My desert cactus high just won't let me go..."

Doctor Von Hildonberg interrupts.

"Ah...okay Zyra, did you come here to sing?"

Zyra sits up, touches his fingertips together, and enters into a long cold stare. Finally, he speaks.

"I can't stand these idiots, Doc. They have nothing else better to do, with their time, than to make my life, a living hell."

The Doctor sits back in his chair, takes a deep breath, and chooses his words wisely.

"First of all, who are you talking about? And second of all, I was not expecting you, for another hour. Why couldn't this wait?"

Zyra blurts out.

"The media, Doc. I got the money, don't worry. I'll pay for two hours, fine three for crying Jane."

Zyra pulls out his money clip, flips past hundred dollar bills, walks over to his desk, and throws down six hundred dollars.

"Two an hour, right? That should cover it."

Doctor Von Hildonberg leans over, grabs the money, and puts it in his desk drawer.

"That's not the point, Zyra. You can't barge in on me like that. There's patience and confidentiality."

Zyra lays back down.

"I'm sorry. I know it's just, I'm, I'm receiving demonic paroxysmal visions. So can you help me, Doc.?"

The doctor puts his pointer and thumb to the bridge of his nose, and drags his hand down his face, ending at his chin.

"Just relax, Zyra. Paroxysmal, meaning spastic or attacking?"

Zyra gets up, and walks over to the waist-high globe, next to the window, overlooking the beachfront; he spins the globe, and talks to Dr. Von Hildonberg, through his reflection in the glass.

"Exactly, but this time, they manifested, while I was awake, not sleeping."

He stops the globe, landing in California.

Zyra laughs to himself.

"The city of Angels? Where the hell are they? It's more like the City of Demons."

The doctor does not respond as Zyra continues.

"Look at all of these people, Doc. They're no different than anyone else. We're all stuck here, in this crummy world, trying to make heads or tails out of it. All I ever seem to encounter, are beasts that live inside man. Who stabs who in the back, as your belly gets fed, with a smile. They stroke your hair, on your way down, saying *It's alright, everything's just fine*. Then they leave us as prey, for the wolves. Wolves Doc., what the hell is that? You tell me."

Doctor Von Hildonberg, spins his chair around, stands up, and pulls out an antique leather-bound book, from his red oak shelves. Zyra turns around, waiting for a response. He walks back, to the couch, and sits down. The doctor lays the book out, on the coffee table.

"I've done some reading from this book, since our last encounter."

Zyra picks it up.

"What is it?"

The doctor sits next to Zyra and opens the book to Acts 2:17.

"Let me read this to you. *It will come to pass in the last days, that I will pour out a portion of my spirit upon all flesh. Your sons and daughters shall prophesy, your young men shall see visions, your old men shall dream dreams...The sun shall be turned to darkness and the moon to blood, before the coming and great splendid day of the Lord.*"

Anger rises inside Zyra.

"Why do you revert to a book, written thousands of years ago, that has nothing to do, with me?"

The doctor remains calm.

"This explains why you receive visions. You are one of the chosen."

He flips through the pages, and lands on Revelations 18:2. He reads the title.

"*The Fall of Babylon*, you said the man in your dreams was Babel. When the Spirit speaks, one word can represent an empire. Listen to this."

He continues to read.

"*Fallen, fallen is Babylon the Great. She has become a haunt for demons.*"

Zyra interrupts, "My demon, Babel, is a He, not a She."

The doctor lifts his finger.

"He, she is the master of disguise. *She is a cage for every unclean spirit...a cage for every unclean and disgusting beast*, your Dragon-Whale."

Zyra turns away.

"That's right Zyra. *Depart from her, my people, to not take part in her sins and receive a share in her plagues, for her sins are piled to the sky, and God remembers her crimes.*'"

Finished reading, he looks up at Zyra, "This explains your tower of bees."

Zyra shakes off the chills and denies the presence within the room.

"No, this is wrong. This is...too surreal for me."

Dr. Von Hildonberg's confident tone relaxes the opposing tension.

"Let me put you under hypnosis."

"No."

Zyra immediately stands up and walks out. His commanding German tone vibrates the room and shocks Zyra.

"Zyra, there is nowhere for you to hide. Nowhere for you to run. You have to face your demons, so you can move beyond them. Unless you want to continue chasing your tail like a dog."

Zyra thinks to himself, *what am I doing?* Raising his hand to the doorway, he turns around, slowly, walks back to the couch, and sits down. The doctor scoots his chair in next to him.

"Lay down, just relax."

Zyra lays down.

"Are you sure you know what you're doing?"

The doctor gets up, grabs his notepad from his desk, and takes a seat.

"Just relax, close your eyes. I will walk you through every step of your journey."

Zyra relaxes, trusting Dr. Von Hildonberg's treatment.

Chapter 16

OTHER SIDE OF THE SUN

Back at St. Charles Catholic Church, mass just ended, and the congregation slowly walked out. Dezerae walks against the flow of people, up to the altar, genuflects, makes the sign of the cross, faces the tabernacle, and enters the sacristy. A crucifix hangs on the wall above Fr. O'Donnell's head, where he disrobes his vestment. He hangs it up in the closet, as the altar boys say goodbye on their way out. Father thanks them for serving and greets Dezerae as the boys leave.

"Good morning again."

She nods her head and compliments the mass.

"That was an excellent homily you gave today, Father. You were right on target. I don't believe in coincidences either. I want to talk to you about my husband."

He smiles at her.

"How is Zyra? I never get a chance to see him."

"Well, that's sort of what I wanted to talk to you about. Zyra has been receiving...(*unsure of how to put it*)...visions."

"What kind of visions?"

He closes the closet door.

She nervously crosses her legs and plays with her thumbnails.

"Well, demonic images...in his dreams. Yesterday, they materialized, amid a scene. He's scared Father, and, honestly, so am I. I know I must sound crazy, but my marriage is suffering. I don't know where else to turn."

She breaks down.

"I'm so scared. I can't take it, Father."

The usher walks in, places the money in a bag, and gives it to the priest. Father, nods in gratitude, and the usher walks out. Dezerae sits down on the chair, Father O'Donnell sits next to her.

Dezerae wipes her tears.

"I'm sorry for breaking down. You know in the book of Acts, where it says, men will receive visions, and dream dreams, in the end times?"

Enlightenment sprouts from the priest's mouth.

"I don't believe we are living in end times, Dezerae. First of all, God promised not to destroy the earth again..."

Dezerae interjects.

"He promised never to flood the earth again."

He continues.

"...besides He is a loving God, and there is too much work, that needs to be done before His Son can return. Tell Zyra to come and speak to me. It sounds like the two of you carry the weight of the world on your shoulders. You don't have to. Take up the yolk of Christ, He lets you rest."

Dezerae puts her hands to her heart.

"He won't see you Father, it would take a miracle. I can't even get him to come to church with me."

Father looks at his watch.

"Tell Zyra the only end times he needs to worry about is his own life."

He locks eyes with Dezerae.

"We will be held accountable for everything we do on earth. When we meet our maker, our lives should complement, and glorify His existence. If Zyra is being attacked spiritually, I believe, God is watching over him, waiting to show him the right path."

Dezerae interjects.

"From what it sounds like, Zyra is placed in the middle of spiritual warfare, well, we all are, but specifically for Zyra, his manifestations are now controlling his life."

Father drops his head and prays on his next words of wisdom.

"All he has to do is ask. God *calls* each one of us, to *fulfill* His plan for our lives. We must *align* God's Will with our own will, so we can accomplish His eternal plan, which is always the greater good. And as humans, we must surrender, to His existence, to grow spiritually."

Dezerae takes in a deep breath, finding that inner peace. She grabs Father O'Donnell's hand.

"Will you pray for me?"

"Certainly. Dear Heavenly Father, I pray before you today, with your fellow servant, Dezerae Nelson, asking you to send the Holy Spirit into the heart, mind, and soul of Zyra and Dezerae, to fulfill your plan for their lives. We ask this in the name of our Lord Jesus Christ. Amen."

They bless themselves, closing out the prayer.

"Amen. Thank you, Father, I feel a little better."

He lets go of her hand, and they both rise.

"Keep me updated."

Dezerae agrees, "I will, thank you again, Father."

"You're welcome. God bless you, Dezerae…and tell Zyra, don't be a stranger."

Dezerae smiles and walks out of the sacristy, Father O'Donnell follows closing the door behind himself.

* * *

Meanwhile, back in Dr. Von Hildonberg's office, Zyra is lying on the couch, entering hypnosis. The doctor's voice dissipates into Zyra's subconscious.

"Allow your thoughts, to become one, fluid funnel of information."

In Zyra's mind's eye, his body crystallizes, reflecting rays of light. His cavity shatters into thousands of pieces, and his spirit flies out the window, over the ocean. The cool breeze rushes through him, energizing his spirit, during his flight. The clouds darken, blood drips from the darkest parts of the clouds, moves mysteriously, covering the sun, and thunder roars. The sun opens, and lightning strikes Zyra's spirit.

This lightning is Nazareth, who instantly enters Zyra, once again forcing out his wings of flesh. Charged with life, and heavenly power, doves encircle his presence, releasing a protective glow. One voice speaks from the choir of angels, sweeping through the illuminated light. All of the surrounding church bells ring, recognizing this spiritual awareness. Nazareth's voice, speaks through Zyra, as he hovers, above the anxious ocean.

"Do not fear, Zyra. I will stay with you until my hour is called. I am Nazareth, your guardian angel, sent by God."

His hair and wings linger in the wind. Yellow white light, from within his eyes, sprays out as rays, connecting a gravitational pull, towards the sun. His wings, move in a fluid rhythm, and his arms remain open, as his heart, is overwhelmed with love. The light from the sun blinds Zyra. The heat *energizes* and *purifies* his soul, as he approaches the sun. The choir guides him through the infinite tall arches, which flashlights, as they pass through.

While in the sun, white flickers of light, within the brightness become focused. Crystal castles thrust up, underneath him, as streets of gold are paved. The golden ponds separate the vast rolling hills, filled with dragons and dinosaurs. The winged creatures, fly through the air, practically knocking Zyra off course.

"Where are we?"

Nazareth answers.

"Majestic Truth, the land of extinct, earthly creatures, roaming free."

The animals communicate in their angelic language. Nazareth raises Zyra's finger, to his mouth, and speaks through him.

"Shh...listen closely, you will understand."

Zyra's ears widen, instantly knows his presence is being summoned, by a creature looking up at him, from beneath the golden pond. Zyra asks Nazareth.

"What do I do?"

"Drop your wings."

As the words are released from his mouth, he dives down and enters the golden pond. The golden water *splashes*, and twinkles away, as tiny stars. Under the water, Zyra moves methodically, absorbing his surroundings. He turns his head, his knee lifts to his chest, and his wings stop his momentum. He reverses his direction and dives deeper into the illuminated water.

Smaller dragons, fire lizards, swim past him. At the bottom of the pond, huge eggs are being nurtured, by their mother dragons. Zyra sees an egg, shaking in the distance. Its mother, the queen dragon, locks eyes with Zyra. She calls his soul, tenderly over, to witness the birth. A glow radiates from within the egg, through the cracks. Zyra, in awe, floats wide-eyed, mouth open, towards the egg.

The fire lizard breaks its head through and starts eating away its shell. The heart of the mother dragon, overwhelmed with love, for her child, awaits the child, to finish its first meal. Free for the first time, the fire lizard swims, over to his mother, and touches her nose to nose. She speaks to him, in their angelic language, as bubbles *rise*, from her mouth. Zyra interprets her language.

"Zyra."

Lyrics instantly appear in his mind.

"I lay my eggs inside your head

Warning you of the beast in bed

I come to you within your dreams

I'm Zyra, your fire-lizard

Gotholic culture

Live the dream

Ancestral congregation

I'll make you scream"

Tears fill his eyes, acknowledging rebirth within his soul. For the first time, thoughts start to organize, in his mind, to where things start to make sense. His wings of flesh are similar to the wings of the fire lizard. The baby creature turns its head and faces Zyra. A transaction of comfort is exchanged. The fire lizard, licks his face, with its rough, yet soft, reptilian sandpaper tongue. Zyra smiles, Nazareth speaks within his mind.

"It's time to go."

Zyra takes in the fire lizard, one last time, and rises through the water, waving goodbye to his miraculous soul mate. He looks up and sees angels flying above the water. His hands and wings reach the warm atmosphere, as he pulls himself out of the water, and into the air.

The second his feet leave the pond, the golden water instantly dries as tiny stars fly off. Another Angel on the same course as Zyra, arches her back, about to crash into him. He quickly turns, and she changes her direction, before colliding with him. Zyra glides back, finds the composer, flips around, rising into the air. Nazareth releases his fear.

"That was close."

Across the vast heavenly city, as far as the eye can see, Zyra notices the second sun, lingering in the sky.

"Nazareth, why two suns?"

He responds.

"The brighter sun is an exit to this realm, and an entrance to another."

"How many realms are there?"

"As many Kingdoms as Christ needs. I want you to meet someone."

Up ahead, the most brilliant crystal castle of this realm, hovers above the rest. They circle the peak and fly down. The arch doorway stands hundreds of feet high. As they descend, Zyra reads down the golden doors, which are engraved with the history of this realm.

Zyra's wide-eyed wonder continues to expand every second. They land in front of the doors, as Nazareth separates from Zyra, for the first time. Zyra's wings disappear, and Nazareth's wings manifest into full-feathered, pearl-white wings. He folds them into his back and turns to Zyra.

"If you choose to accept your mission, we will work together, to fulfill His plan, for your life."

"Who?"

Nazareth puts his finger, to his mouth.

"Shh, don't say another word unless you are spoken to. Do you understand?"

Zyra nods his head.

"Follow me."

Nazareth touches both doors, and they open. A long white carpet flies out, and flaps down in front of them, leading to a large white throne, up ahead. Zyra, struck by wonder, takes in this magnificent beauty. They enter. The doors *shut* behind them. Zyra looks around and sees the walls, filled with life-sized carvings, of angels.

Zyra's knees tremble, as he continues to follow Nazareth, down the aisle. Moving past stone carvings, of winged gargoyles, flapping their wings, and angels protecting their domain, Zyra feels the overwhelming waves, of love, pouring forth from the moving statues. At this moment, Zyra surrenders, encompassing the love. They finally reach the throne, and see, who is sitting on it. Nazareth drops to his knees, in silent worship. Zyra does the same.

Four living creatures, covered with eyes, each with six wings; a lion, a man, a calf, and an eagle, praise the One sitting on the throne. Nine choirs of Angels, surround Him. A scroll opens behind Him, then another and another. The second scroll is the Book of Life. As it opens, Zyra instantly knows, the dead are judged, according to their deeds, by what is written, in the scrolls. The One Who sits on the throne speaks.

"Behold, I make all things new. Write these words down, for they are trustworthy and true. They are accomplished. I am the Alpha and the Omega, the beginning and the end. To the thirsty, I will give a gift from the spring of life-giving water. The victor will inherit these gifts, and I shall be his God, and he will be my son. But as for cowards, the unfaithful, the depraved, murderers, the unchaste, sorcerers, idol-worshipers, and deceivers of every sort, their lot is in the burning pool of fire and sulfur, which is the second death."

> The Kingdom of Heaven is within you, obey God's
> commandments. Align your will with God's Will.
> Become the person God intended you to be.

Zyra weeps, begging mercy, from Him, forgiveness in his heart, for the sins, he has committed. The Alpha and Omega reach out His hand towards Zyra. Zyra takes it and rises to his feet. In an instant, Zyra is made new, and the weight of the world is lifted. They embrace. Tears of blood drip down Zyra's soul. Nazareth rises to his feet. Zyra feels the tree of life, grow, within him. He smiles, turns back around, and notions to Nazareth.

Nazareth and Zyra approach the Gates. The doors open, then close behind them. Outside, Zyra *falls* to his knees, paralyzed in praise, yet some confusion, as to why he didn't see this before. Nazareth spreads his wings, and lifts his arms, praising, the One Who sits on the Throne. Zyra looks up, and sees the sun, illuminating Nazareth's presence, Zyra speaks.

"Nazareth, what just happened to me?"

Nazareth lowers his hands and rises above the ground. His soft welcoming tone comforts Zyra's heart and *trembling* spirit.

"Your mission, use the gifts He has given you, to spread His words, He has spoken."

Zyra looks down, at the ground, and wipes the tears, with his forearm.

"Where do I start?"

Nazareth glides over and touches his head.

"You already started. The kingdom of heaven is within you."

Zyra shakes his head, takes in a deep breath, and looks up towards the golden miraculous sky.

> "I can't do this alone. It's a cruel world, not like this place, with a lot of temptation. How do I fight it?"

Nazareth smiles.

> "That's why you have Dezerae, and me, as your Guardian Angel. Think of her during times of temptation, then pull from that inspiration. I will always look after you."

Zyra stands up, and looks out, at the vast beauty.

> "What's the purpose of all this, Nazareth?"

Nazareth steps into Zyra, forming his wings of flesh.

> "Look up Zyra. Do you see God's creatures at work?"

He answers Nazareth within his mind.

> "I see the mystical creatures of the earth. I watch them build a bridge that connects one sun to the other. Why?"

Zyra lifts his arms, and gives life to his wings, as they rise as one, into the air.

> "The One Who sits on the Throne will return to earth, on the bridge. The bridge grows, when people find and live in and generate from, that inner love and peace, that they found today. The birth of a new creature is a soul once lost, but now found. When love matures, the fire lizard *grows* into the dragon. The more one loves, the quicker the bridge, will complete. Once this happens, only

God the Father knows when He will send His son. Come on, it's time to go."

Zyra stands there, for a brief moment, lets Nazareth's words sink in, and flies towards the sun, from which they came. A dragon flies underneath them, and Zyra grabs its neck, as the flying beast, escorts them through, the other side of the sun. A flash of light, through the arches, leaves them, gliding over the bridge, into the earth's atmosphere. They reach the end of the bridge and look down upon the vast sea below. They dive off the bridge.

"Here we go again. Tuck your knees into your chest, lower the top part of your wings."

Zyra does what Nazareth tells him to do. He *somersaults* through the air, enjoying his flight down. He closes in on Los Angeles, airplanes fly by. An ongoing, red and white glow, opposes each other, hovering above the city, which Nazareth explains, reading Zyra's quizzical mind.

"The red, Zyra, is the absence of love and truth; the evil that men do. The white light is love and truth. Matters of the heart, create the playing field. Angels oppose demons, every second of every day until He returns."

Zyra sweeps down, skimming the ocean water, with his chest, arms, and wings, out-spread, his legs slightly bent. He glides against the wind, as mist presses against his face. He releases a long breath of air, rises above the beach, overlooking Pacific Coast Highway, and up the coast, towards the top floor window, of Dr. Von Hildonberg's office. He enters, through the glass, hovers over his physical body, as the doctor calls him back.

"On the count of three, you will enter your body. One, two, three."

On three, Zyra, instantly, drops into his body and opens his eyes. A jolt of fear, surges through. He screams.

"Shh, it's ok…you are safe."

Zyra sits up and looks over at the doctor, who greets him.

"Welcome back."

Zyra remains silent. Dr. Von Hildonberg expresses his concern.

"Are you alright?"

Zyra gets off the couch, and walks out of the office, in a trance-like state. Dr. Von Hildonberg shouts out.

"I'll call you tomorrow, Zyra."

He looks down at his notebook, every word spoken from Zyra, Nazareth, and the One Who sits on the Throne, is written down, in blood, from his right pointer finger, and specialized pen.

Chapter 17

BOB & BOB

The deep blue sky, welcomes the fiery, blood-red dusk, as birds warn the earth, of the evil presence on the prowl. Babel guides Garth, by the hand, as the sand stirs up around their feet, they shuffle down the beach, towards the black lagoon. The voodoo spirit encompassing the sixty-nine human sacrifices, grows stronger.

What is left of the sun, disappears behind the horizon, and the full moon illuminates the darkened sky. Babel walks out onto the water, and Garth follows, lost in a hypnotic trance. Babel walks backward, placing one foot in the back of the other as if walking a tightrope. Like a puppet on a string, he *twirls* Garth like a ballerina. His other arm, roams freely, as he orchestras and hums a tune. Garth spins around, faster and faster, like a figure skater, and water shoots up around him, under Babel's spell.

The second Babel releases, Garth snaps from the spell, and his world continues to spin. A piercing scream, and howling of the wind, enter his body, and travel through rapidly. When sanity surfaces, through his dizziness, he *drops* below the cold water.

"Help me! I can't..."

He sinks below the surface and bobs back up.

"...swim."

He coughs up the salty water. Babel remains calm and watches him fight for his life. Babel's smile advances into laughter, as he reaches out, dangles his fingers, inches from Garth's face. Babel's laughter grows stronger, and Garth sinks beneath the surface again, splashing uncontrollably.

Babel raises his arms and *spins down* into the water. As his feet go under, they transform into its dragon tail, and his body lengthens and widens, forming into Dragon Whale. Wings extend from its back, as the neck elongates, and forms the head, of a tiger and alien eyes, bugged out from its white slimy face. Fully submerged underwater, Dragon-Whale continues its descent.

Garth's panic transcends into shock, his tears mix in with the ocean water, eyes protruding from his skull in disbelief. He stops struggling, and welcomes death, peacefully in shock, as he sinks into the dark, cold abyss. Thoughts and images of his life, *flash* before him.

He sees himself, as a little boy, waving goodbye, walking into the darkness. Babel's face, exposing his white and gold teeth, engulfed in laughter, intermixing with Garth's soul, walking away. Air rises from Garth's lungs, through his esophagus, and out his mouth. The air bubbles, filled with anger, rage, and sorrow, rise through the water, and *pop open*, at the surface, releasing his last cry.

"Help..."

Dragon-Whale, swiftly ascends, through the water, and in one gulp, *chomps* down biting Garth in half. His right eyeball explodes from his face, and swims to the surface, like a lost sperm, finding its way home. The tiger head, unlocks its jaw, *ripping* apart his mutilated body, licks its sharp canines, with its green snake-like tongue, finishes Garth's torso.

Garth's blood warms the beast. Fiery hell, reflects in the alien eyes, as Garth's torso, spins back into infinite sadness, nerve spasms fighting every step of the way.

The surrounding sea life, voraciously circles around the beast, waiting for a piece of the sacrifice. Dragon-Whale *GROWLS* scaring them away. The pool of blood rises to the surface and embeds Garth's eyeball, which stares endlessly at the moon.

In the distance, a small fishing boat approaches. On board are two identical twin brothers, Bob and Bob. One, an overweight slovenly American, drinks a beer. The other, anorexic, dressed in military fatigues, and dog chain, steers as the captain of this boat. The moonlight strikes, Garth's eye just right, attracting Bob's attention.

"Hey Bob, stop the boat."

Skinny Bob's pale skeleton face, and mirror shades, are focused on shore.

"No way, Bob. It's dark. We're not supposed to be out, after dark."

Big Bob walks to the side of the boat, and leans over, trying to get a better look.

"I'm serious, Bob. Where's the flashlight?"

Big Bob burps, crushes the beer can against his head, and throws it with the rest of the empties, at the back of the boat. He spots the flashlight, picks it up, and flashes it in his brother's eyes, trying to gain his attention.

"I found it. Thanks to you, not."

Skinny Bob turns around, Big Bob turns on the light, and sees his reflection, in Skinny Bob's sunglasses.

"Look Bob, when I ask you for something, I expect an answer. I see something abnormal in the water."

Skinny Bob speeds up the idol, Big Bob loses his balance, and the flashlight goes overboard.

"The only thing abnormal is your fat ass falling overboard."

He laughs at his joke. Big Bob leans over the side, making the boat practically tip over. Skinny Bob freaks out.

"Whoa, Whoa..."

Big Bob's pants slide down his crack, exposing himself to his brother. Skinny Bob moves his head, back and forth, watching Big Bob, and the front of the boat. He can't restrain his comment.

"Thank God that light's a floater, otherwise, I'd grab your fat ass like a bowling ball, and toss you over."

Big Bob howls.

"Holy Cocka-doodle-doo..."

His voice vibrates off the surface of the water, as Skinny Bob responds.

"Oh that's...that's good Bob."

Big Bob's hand sweeps down into the water and misses the eye.

"Slow down."

Skinny Bob finally does. Big Bob, grabs the flashlight, floating in the water, lighting the eyeball. Big Bob screams out.

"I knew it. A human eye."

Skinny Bob responds.

"Quit smoking your crack Bob, it's probably a fish eye."

Big Bob grabs the eye by its tendons.

"Oh yeah, check this out."

He points the light at the eyeball, that dangles in Skinny Bob's face. The eye reflects, in his mirror glasses. Skinny Bob screams out.

"Jesus Christ, Mary, and Joseph!"

Big Bob soberly states.

"You're right Bro, this one requires the whole Holy family."

Skinny Bob, still in shock, screams out.

"That's a human eye."

Big Bob *slaps* Skinny Bob with the flashlight.

"I told you. But you never listen to me."

Skinny Bob, grabs the flashlight and points it down at the water. The boat idols, making it circle.

"Holy shit, we're in the middle of a bloodbath."

Big Bob leans over for a better view. The water surrounding the boat is deep red. Skinny Bob immediately, throws himself on the lever, giving the engine gas; the boat takes off, and he tries to straighten it out, as it heads towards shore. He hears his brother's feet, slam against the bottom of the boat, THUG, trying to keep his balance.

The eye flies from Big Bob's fingers, and lands in the back of the boat, rolling under the empties. Big Bob pugnaciously shouts.

"I dropped the eye."

Panicked, Skinny Bob screams.

"You dropped the eye!?"

Big Bob says again.

"I dropped the eye."

Skinny Bob shakes his head in disbelief.

"Find it."

Big Bob gets on his hands and knees, searching, as his stretch-marked belly, hangs over his pants, still showing off half his backside. He pushes the cans out of the way and pokes his finger in the eye.

"Ah, man."

He grabs the eye, it squishes out of his fingers.

"Gross."

Skinny Bob screams out.

"What?"

"Nothing, I found it. I found it."

He cuffs the eye with both hands, gets up, and walks over to his brother.

"Do you think it can see me?"

Skinny Bob slaps his younger brother upside the head.

"Shut up. Put it in the cooler."

Big Bob walks it over to the cooler and places it in. Skinny Bob gets a wave of excitement.

"This is big time, bro. We're gonna be on the news."

Big Bob puts the cooler top-down and sits on it.

"Yeah, maybe I'll get discovered."

Skinny Bob shakes his head in frustration.

"You're so stupid. The only thing they would discover about you are all your favorite bakeries."

He laughs at his joke, yet again, pondering the different possibilities of what to do.

Chapter 18

SIXTY-NINE CORPSES

Under the same glowing bright full moon, Zyra drives down Sunset Blvd. contemplating whether he should attend *The Nephilim* party or not. Thoughts circulate in his mind as he hears Garth's voice repeat, *It's exactly like the fallen angel.* He looks down at the gas tank, it reads empty. *I must have not looked at it before*, he thinks to himself as he pulls into the local gas station, and fills up. He runs his red leather glove through his hair, as he takes in the scent of the gasoline, thinks back to the time of his descent from the sun.

Again, he hears Garth's voice, *Fallen Angel.* He thinks back to his dream, of the little boy turning into the demon, *Hey mister, you that fallen angel everyone keeps talking about?* Feeling an uncomfortable presence, Zyra looks up, across the street, he sees a man, dressed in black, staring him down.

"That'll be $16.58. How are you gonna pay?"

Zyra looks at the gas station attendant.

"Huh?"

"The gasoline Buddy, how you gonna pay for the gas?"

Zyra snaps back to reality.

"Sorry. Um...cash."

He hands him a twenty.

"Keep the change."

"Thanks. Hey, aren't you playing tomorrow night?"

Zyra walks away not answering. He looks back at the man, across the street who is now gone. He takes a deep breath, and retrieves *The Nephilim* card, from his back pocket. He flips it over, and reads the back, *North on Coldwater.* He looks at the sign, where the man is standing, *Coldwater* whispers to himself. He gets on his motorcycle, crosses the street, and drives up the road. Just as Zyra passes, a black car flips on its headlights and pulls out behind him.

Zyra looks in his side view mirrors, notices someone following, but decides to continue anyway. He follows the directions on the back of the card, leading him through winding roads, and slowly climbing the hill. The mysterious black car continues to follow. Zyra makes his final turn onto Fontinelle Way, as the iron gates open. Zyra looks in the mirror, the headlights blind his view, and his heart begins to race. Trying to contain his composure, he gets off the bike, and confronts the man in black, getting out of his car.

"Hi, I'm here to meet Garth. I'm Zyra."

The gates close. The man walks past him.

"Follow me."

Zyra follows, passing the dark, unwelcoming walkway, of molten lava rock. The front doors open, and one of the servants greets them.

"Just in time."

Kanniballations plays over the sound system, as Zyra thinks to himself, *I never heard my music sound so good.* They sit Zyra down, on the leather couch, in the pit, by the interior pool. In the corner, illuminated in black light, is a twenty-foot albino python, wrapped around a tree branch, protruding from the wall. Whips thrust out, and linger down, making it look like a black leather willow tree. Zyra stares at his reflection, in the dark glass, over the water. He crosses his legs, as the servant brings him over a dry martini, with a green olive.

"No thank you."

Tartarus blazes forth in a cloud of smoke, with a martini in his hand.

"Have a drink Zyra."

Giving into Tartarus' seductive spell, Zyra accepts the drink and takes a sip. Tartarus sits down next to him, a bit closer than Zyra would like.

"Welcome to my home, I'm Tartarus."

The drink starts to kick in, and a smooth creeping buzz slithers into Zyra's world. Zyra looks at Tartarus's eyes, a dark, very dark soul, seduces him.

"Is there something in this?"

Tartarus smiles.

"Of course."

Zyra takes another sip, almost forgetting where he is, and why he is there.

"Where's Garth?"

Tartarus's black fingernails, gently push Zyra's hair, behind his ear, and caress down his cheek.

"He's here."

Zyra's music sounds even more crisp, alive than ever before, as he relaxes, deciding not to fight the first wave of his spiked drink. Tartarus pulls out a joint, lights up, and passes it to Zyra. As he hits the joint, Zyra stares off into the black glass, reflecting the movement of the water, sending Zyra's mind, into another dimension. Zyra shakes off the paralysis.

"I call this work *Soul Collector*. You see why."

Zyra looks over at him, "Who are you?"

"The abyss of all ages."

Zyra finishes off his drink, as two beautiful women, approach from behind Tartarus, drop their hands, down his chest, and squeeze themselves into him.

"Close your eyes..."

Tartarus demands Zyra. Within his hyper-sensitive senses, more aware of the sensations, pouring through his body and mind, Zyra creates a safe place to mind travel. Soft massaging hands, press against Zyra's back, releasing tension. He falls deeper into relaxation, her hands find their way down his pecks, grabs his chest, squeezing his right nipple ring.

A warm moist sensation, beyond this world, forces Zyra to open his eyes. He looks down, sees the top of the other girl's head, and pushes her off.

"I gotta go..."

She looks up at him and wipes her mouth.

"So soon?"

He zips his pants back up, the drugs climb to their peak. He stands up and falls back down, and the room spins.

"What am I doing here?"

Zyra rolls off the couch and claws his way to the pool. He breaks out in an instant sweat, Tartarus laughs at this pathetic sight. Zyra drops into the water, and Tartarus commands his servants.

"Get him. He can't die."

The woman, Angel, dives in, lifts Zyra's head above the water, and he coughs it up. She lifts his dead-weight body, out of the water, onto the black and red cross-tiled floor.

"Are we ready boss?"

She locks eyes with Tartarus.

"I'll say when we're ready. It is not yet time. Take off his clothes."

Angel rips off Zyra's shirt, exposing his tattooed torso, and arms. She licks his shaven chest and unzips his pants. They untie his laces and pull off his black platform knee-high boots. They peel his wet leathers, off his body, exposing his naked flesh.

"Excite him."

Tartarus commands one of the servants. Simply the touch of the woman's hand brings life back into Zyra. She lifts her white lace dress, grabs his manhood, guiding herself down upon him.

"Stop, just before he climaxes."

Tartarus moves his hand behind her head and kisses her. She starts to ride Zyra, swaying to her rhythm, increasing speed, and getting lost in her ecstasy. Tartarus slowly slices above her breasts, with his pointed finger ring, blood drips down her body and mixes in with her and Zyra's bodily fluids. Another servant snaps photos of this unholy situation. Her moans fill the air, as Tartarus' eyes, manipulate color, radiating rage.

He backhands her across the face, and blood flies from her mouth, knocking her off Zyra.

"You do as I say, tramp."

He stands over her, and she curls into a little ball, like an abused animal. To his other servant, he commands.

"Put this blindfold on him"

He hands her a black leather mask, she places it over Zyra's head. Tartarus interjects once again, handing her a metal ring.

"Slide this on him."

The servant listens and does what she is told. Tartarus hands her a white rope.

"You know what to do."

The servant ties the rope, around Zyra's waist, brings it down, between his buttocks, next to his enraged manhood, up between his legs, around his testicles, and firmly tightens the rope. She brings the rope up, ties it into the belt, wraps the excess around his wrists, and pulls him forward. Pleased with what he sees, Tartarus points to a burning candle, and locks eyes with the other servant, on the ground.

She gets up, walks over to the wall, grabs the burning candle, walks over to Zyra, and pours hot wax down Zyra's chest. Zyra gasps as it burns his flesh, then hardens. She continues to pour down his stomach, over his throbbing manhood, and caps him off with the wax. The sensation, drives Zyra deeper into his state of psychosis, created from whatever Tartarus put into his drink. Tartarus grabs the other woman, kisses her passionately, and throws her down to the ground by the tree of whips.

"Grab one."

She grabs a whip and uses it against Zyra's flesh, *whip*. Welts rise from his flesh, and Zyra screams with pleasure and pain, internalizing the burst of energy. Tartarus murmurs.

"Let's go. It's time."

The servant leads Zyra, down the stone spiral stairwell, leading to the dungeon. She *whips* him again. Zyra takes the pain, not being able to fight the seduction of the drug. The lit torches, lighting the path, brush against Zyra's flesh as he passes, drying the sweat from his moist body. In the distance, echoing throughout the pathway, Zyra hears what seems to be tigers growling. Zyra takes in the smell of burning incense, intermixed with the deceased. They enter the dungeon.

"What's that *smell*?"

They walk Zyra across the center of the dungeon, and throw him down, before the tigers, pacing inside their cages. Zyra's hands drive forward, stopping the tiger from getting too close, which results in tugging on himself, with the rope, tied to his wrists, and sacred dwellings. Zyra gasps with pain.

As if in slow motion, Tartarus throws up a metal blade, it flips midair, drops straight down, and lands between Zyra's wrists, slicing his hands free, and sticking into the cement. He walks over to Zyra, zig-zags his pointed full finger ring, up Zyra's spine, lightly slicing him open. Tartarus pulls the metal blade from the cement and *slices* Zyra's upper arm. Zyra weeps with pain and fear, but is almost in a state of paralysis.

Tartarus brings the blade to the tiger and lets him lick Zyra's blood, which slices open the tiger's tongue. The tiger reacts, stirring up the other beast. Their ferocious growls, uncontrollable behavior, and again, whatever they put in Zyra's drink, goes through him, causing Zyra to defecate. The servants grab Zyra, from underneath his arms, and lift him to his feet. The woman grabs the hose, turns it on, and washes Zyra off. Waste and blood, glide down his legs into the drain.

The servants drag his body, over to the altar, lift him, and throw him face down. They tie his hands and feet to the altar. Tartarus grabs his black book and opens it to the marked page. The rest, circle Zyra and hold hands. Tartarus quotes scripture.

"Men's hearts failing them for fear, and for looking after those things which are coming upon the earth: for the powers of heaven shall be shaken."

Tartarus turns towards Angel.

"Angel, rise above the chosen one."

Angel, the woman who took advantage of Zyra earlier, levitates into the air. Tartarus guides her over Zyra, and sets her down, standing above him. She cuffs her hands with the chains, that dangle above her, she straddles Zyra's twisted, sensationalized, bleeding body. Tartarus continues.

"For the Mystery of Iniquity doth already work: only He who now hindereth will hinder until he is taken out of the way. And then shall that Wicked One be revealed...whose coming is after the working of Satan with all power and signs and lying wonders."

Tartarus glares at Angel's naked body and then commands her.

"Lower yourself upon Zyra."

She squats down only allowing the head of his organ to enter hers.

"And when they shall have finished their testimony, the beast that shall ascend out of the bottomless pit shall make war against them, and shall overcome them, and kill them."

A black energy rises, from the drain, and takes the form of Babel. Tartarus continues as The presence grows stronger.

"The beast that thou hast seen was, and is not: and shall ascend out of the bottomless pit, and go into perdition: and they that dwell on the earth shall wonder, whose names were not written in the book of life from the foundation of the world when they behold the beast that was and is not, and yet is."

Babel's spirit possesses Angel's body. Zyra gives into the deception, slowly losing his soul, through this act of intercourse with the devil. In a moment of enlightenment, Zyra, instinctively, fights the orgasm, images fade into his mind, reflecting the loss of everything, if he gives into this temptation. Tartarus cries out louder as the intensity builds.

"And with all deceivables of unrighteousness in them that perish: because they received not the love of the truth, that they might be saved. And for this cause, God shall send them strong delusion, that they should believe the lie."

Angel's body and Babel's spirit, bring Zyra's soul, closer to the peak of ecstasy. Zyra cries out, knowing he cannot be restrained.

"Nazareth help me!!"

Nazareth instantly speaks to his mind.

"Finally, my brethren, be strong in the Lord, and the power of His might...Put on the whole armor of God, that ye may be able to stand against the wiles of the devil...For we wrestle not against flesh and blood, but against principalities, against powers, against the rulers of the darkness of this world, against spiritual wickedness in high places...Wherefore take unto you the whole armor of God, that ye may be able to withstand in the evil day, and having done all, to stand."

Zyra believes his words, *breaks* free his hands and feet from this bondage, and slides himself out of Angel. Babel releases a hellacious scream.

"NO!"

Zyra jumps off the altar, rips off his mask, and pushes through the encircled people. He grabs the battle axe, hanging on the wall, and starts *swinging*, screaming at the top of his lungs. Chopping and slicing anything in his path. Temporarily insane, Zyra drives the battle axe between the eyes of one of the indulgers. Blood splatters over his naked body. Zyra kills every one of the cult members.

Tartarus is paralyzed in fear, as death grips his throat, he gasps for air. The axe comes down *splitting* his chest in two. Black blood squirts from his heart, over Zyra and Angel.

Tartarus falls to his knees, wide-eyed, Zyra pulls the axe from his chest. In one sweeping motion, he *chops off* Tartarus' head.

He pulls back the swing of death and jumps up on the altar, crazed, ready to chop Angel in half. Babel's spirit leaves, through her eyes.

Angel's soul begging Mercy, locks eyes with Zyra.

He *swings* the axe.

"Ahhhhhhh…"

It breaks through the chains, cutting her free, the axe sticks in Tartarus' book. Zyra takes a moment to collect his thoughts. For the first time, Zyra sees the fresh new bloody corpses, hanging as sacrifices from the gathering before, on the walls.

The number *69* appears in his mind, as he *mumbles* it under his breath. He falls to his knees, and sobs like a baby.

Angel grabs her clothes, and takes off, terrified. Zyra tries to block the images from his mind. He grabs the hose, from the dead person's hand, and washes himself off. In total shock, Zyra sees the picture of himself, and his father, hanging on the wall.

He walks over to his father's old picture and turns it around. Writing on the back marks the present date and time. Zyra shakes his head in disbelief and *smashes* the picture to the ground. Pieces *shatter* everywhere, he fights back more tears. As if in slow motion, silence walks him out of the dungeon.

Zyra looks around the empty living room, picks up his clothes, puts them on, and exits Tartarus' haunted house. He looks up, at the full moon, falls to his knees, in prayer, in front of his motorcycle, and breaks down crying. His wife pops into his mind.

"Dezerae."

He feels a hand touch his shoulder, looks up, and sees no one. He hears a voice and feels quick movements.

"It is I, Nazareth. I have come to escort you home."

Zyra gets on his Harley and rides home.

Chapter 19

BURIED EVIL

Just past the witching hour, that same night, Zyra by the hand of God and Nazareth's guidance, makes it home and pulls into the driveway. He parks next to Dezerae's black luxury SUV, and staggers in, carrying a bag. He walks into the kitchen, puts the bag and keys on the table, drops to the tile, and sprawls out across the floor.

There is no response from Zyra, he is out cold. Dezerae lays in bed, under the covers, furious with puffy, bloodshot eyes, the television barely audible. She grinds her teeth, vibrating her skull, not believing his behavior. Her body trembles, not knowing where he has been, she can't take it anymore, and tries to control her anger, but screams out.

"Where the *HELL* have you been? You didn't call! Don't you think I worry about you? Why do you do this to me? You have the nerve to show up at four in the morning, and not answer me."

She loses it, her voice cracks with volume, anger persists even more.

> "I'm through, Zyra. I can't take it anymore. I'm going to my mother's tomorrow and filing for a divorce. I don't want you sleeping in here tonight."

She pulls the covers over her head and slams the bedroom door shut. Still silence from Zyra. After an hour or so, curiosity finally lifts her from the bed and walks her into the kitchen. She sees Zyra sprawled out on the kitchen floor, his shirt ripped open, and she kicks his boots.

> "Get up. I said get up, Zyra."

She kicks him again. No movement. She falls to her knees and shakes him.

> "Zyra."

Still no response. She slaps his face.

> "Hey, are you on drugs again? I can't believe you. Where have you been? Why is your shirt ripped open? I'm not putting up with this anymore!"

She walks back to her bed, slams the door shut again, and cries herself to sleep. On the wide-screen television in her bedroom, Bob and Bob are being interviewed on the news.

> "This is Holly Gossip, live from Redondo Beach where two twin brothers, Bob and Bob, were returning from their fishing trip, and spotted a floating eyeball. There is no confirmation on whose it is, or if there is even a body connected to it."

Dezerae puts the remote down and thinks to herself *this whole world has gone mad.* She shakes her head in disbelief, grabs the remote, and turns up the volume. Big Bob is on camera, speaking with a Southern accent.

> "I told my brother, Bob, I knew it was a human eye. He thought it was a fish ball, you know an eyeball 'cause fish don't have balls. Anyway, after I dangled it in his face, he knew I was right. It was a human eye. Oh, hi ma, I'm on TV."

He smiles large, showing off his blackened, yellow, spaced teeth. Skinny Bob *pops* him upside the head.

> "Now, why you gotta go n' ruin the mood, ma's been dead for years. I knew it was real. I could smell the stench of death in the air. I'm an ex-marine..."

Holly cuts them off. The cameraman fills the screen with her image.

> "Well, thank you both very much for sharing your story. We will bring you more updates on *Danger in the Deep...*"

A "Danger in the Deep" graphic scrolls across the screen, accompanied by the Jaws theme song.

> "Don't go away, coming up next, Zyra, front man of the goth metal band, Sacred Witch, and also Hollywood's hottest star, tells the American public, *worry about your goddamn souls.*"

A mad image of Zyra fills the screen. Dezerae lowers the sound, the news reporter comments.

> "Thank you, Holly."

Dezerae, still blazing with anger, mumbles under her breath.

"I don't believe this!"

She turns off the television and falls asleep.

A couple of hours pass, shadows creep across the room, then disappear into the morning rays, piercing through. Dezerae enters into REM sleep as an angelic voice lingers in, shedding light into the darkness. In this dream-like state, Dezerae trusts in God, allowing Him to guide her, on His journey for her life.

"Turn away from the sorrow, I am not there."

A friendly male passionate tone replies, Zyra enters her dream, spoons her from behind, and whispers in her ear.

"I need to see Amir."

His long fingernails, slowly scratch up her stomach and tickle around her belly button ring. He grabs her breast and imitates Amir's thick Spanish accent.

"I am Amir, the executive producer of Haunted Shadow Records."

She grabs hold of his masculinity and squeezes firmly. He gasps, she releases, squeezes again. She turns her head and locks her eyes with Zyra. Dezerae enters Zyra's mind, being able to see his thoughts. She sees Amir, dressed as Santa Clause, sitting up in a coffin attached to his reindeer goats. His facial expression is ruthless, about to take flight. She asks Zyra within his mind.

"Why are you meeting with Amir?"

Zyra's tone deepens.

"He wants me to tour *Kanniballations*, I can't; You said it yourself. It's my darkest work."

She releases the pressure, Amir pulls back on the reigns, and the goats run, pulling the coffin.

"I know what I said, but you can't break the contract. He'll sue you for everything you've got."

Zyra takes a deep breath, as the pleasure builds, she increases her hand speed; the goats increase their speed.

"He left a message tonight. I'll call Robin, my lawyer, tomorrow. He'll get me out of it."

She slows down, waits for a moan, to seep from his soul, increases her speed, and the goats lift off in flight. Still, inside Zyra's mind, Dezerae asks.

"Your book lawyer?"

The sensation builds. He can hardly speak.

"Yeah."

She throws her leg over his and nestles in. The goats fly higher and higher, approaching the moon, as her breath quickens.

"Yeah...call 'em...see what he says."

He gasps for air, she rides Zyra as Amir rides the midnight air.

"Uh...oh..kay."

In the darkness, her hips move in rhythm, thrusting forward, and back, she grabs onto his wrists, which firmly squeeze her breasts.

"I love you."

Amir grips the reigns as tight as he can and approaches the center of the moon. Tears fill Dezerae's eyes, as she realizes she is dreaming. The only sense, she atones to, is the aroma of sensuality buried deep, within the darkness of her mind. Amir rides across the moon, as all three, Zyra, herself, and Amir orgasm, at the same time, in Dezerae's mind, feeling each of theirs as her own.

At this same moment, still sprawled out on the kitchen floor, Zyra enters his mind's eye. Sounds of metal chains attack, slithering towards him, cuffs, bite down, onto his wrists, and ankles. In one sweeping motion, they yank his arms and legs, shaping his body into an X. The clunking permanently embeds into his memory. The stretching of his body, forces his mouth open, as his soul cries out for freedom.

In Dezerae's moment of ecstasy, she looks up, and sees in the ceiling mirror above her, a funnel of wind, storming from the angry black sky. Thunder bellows, lightning strikes, cracking and shattering the ceiling mirror, in her dream. Pieces of glass, spray over the bed, slicing her up. Nazareth flies forth, from the center of the tornado, lightning detonates behind him. His hair is wild, and full of life, matching the glare in his eyes. He grabs Dezerae from underneath her arms, presses her naked body against his chest, and pulls her off of Zyra.

He lifts her back up, through the shattered pieces of fallen glass, her fingers shake, and her face distorts, crying, but nothing comes out, only silence. She leans over, Nazareth's locked hands around her waist, her soul dissipates, and she wakes up screaming.

"Zyra...."

She watches the image decrease, reflected in Zyra's hazel eyes. Forbidden music, weighing down the soul, takes over Zyra's world. In a flash, he is back in Tartarus' mansion, amid debauchery. Zyra remains gagged and handcuffed, under the moon, shining through the skylights. He sees Amir and the flying goats in the distance. He summons the strength to rip the chains loose. He lassos the head of the first goat, YANKS, rips its head off. One by one cut off their heads. One goat head after another, falls to its summoned grounds. The chains take a life of their own, strap Zyra back down, hands and legs spread out.

The bleeding goat heads fly through the sky, and land at all five points around Zyra. Their blood moves over Zyra's body, connecting each head, and forming a pentagram. Candelabras instantly light the background, as an undressed woman covered in blood, crawls over to Zyra, and bites down on his nipples.

A dark-haired beauty grabs a candle and pours hot wax over his shaven blood blood-red body. Horns grow from her head, and she settles down, on his throbbing manhood. She *whips* him, making the welts grow, from his ribs. She rocks his world harder and takes more and more of his soul. Zyra stands back from his dream, and sees his body, hovered over the lake of fire, chained to the goats, forming a star. The goat heads elevate above him and come to life.

The dark beauty's legs elongate, down into the lake of fire, her thigh muscles tare, and her bones crack, forming into the legs of a goat. This beast continues to ride Zyra, with animalistic passion. Her hands form into hooves, her breasts grow thick black hairs, her beautiful face, shape-shifts into that of a goat, with powerful horns protruding. His black breath covers Zyra, and his snarl commands attention when it speaks.

"Everything you do glorifies me. I can make you king of this world. All you have to do is ask."

The goat's tongue slithers up Zyra's cheek. Zyra tries to conjure enough strength to confront the demon.

"Leave me, Satan, in the name of Jesus Christ."

A familiar soul weeps, deep within the goat.

"Help me Zyra."

Tears immediately fill Zyra's eyes, "Gabriel?"

The goat's mouth widens, and flames rise from the lake of fire. Gabriel, Zyra's brother, claws his way up, from the goat's esophagus, amid the flames. His fingernails, dig deep, into the goat's tongue, as he lifts himself higher. His blood-beaten eyes, lock with Zyra's, and with every ounce of energy, Gabriel speaks.

"He won't let me go."

A hand reaches up from behind Gabriel's head, clenches his hair, and pulls his head back down, exposing his neck. Gabriel's father appears, from behind him, with his mouth salivating, his teeth sharpened. Sweat pours down his father's face, he gives Zyra a sinister grin, sinks his teeth into his son's neck, and watches the blood saturate his body.

The father moves in rhythm to the synthesized eerie sounds, he continues this sacrilege with his son. Tears stream down Gabriel's face, as an angry look dries out, the father gives one last jolt. The goat closes his mouth, swallows the image, and turns back, into the beautiful dark seductress, who is in the same rhythm as the father. They are back in Tartarus's dark circle, Zyra agonizes screaming in terror!

"NO! Get off me. It's not fair!"

The woman bites down on his nipple again, drawing blood. In the goat's voice, the seductress speaks.

"You never cared. Don't try to care now. You don't know how to love. You knew your father was destroying your younger brother, and you chose to do nothing about it."

Zyra enters into a flashback of his childhood. In the basement of his old wretched house, spider webs cover the corners of the cold concrete walls. The moonlight pierces through, the raised rectangular cracked window. Young Zyra tip-toes down the wooden stairs, absorbing the squeak from each step. Fainted light strikes his black and white spooky clown make-up, Gene Simmons style, and KISS make-up.

He bends down, just below the wooden beam, and watches his father, swing his two fists together like a baseball bat, into Gabriel's stomach, knocking him against the wall. Gabriel cries out for his life. Gabriel leans over and tries to catch his breath, the father drops his head, in an evil grin, grabs Gabriel by the back of his pants, with both hands, and rips them off, exposing his son.

Zyra bites his fists, and shakes in fear, while the father backhands Gabriel across the mouth; blood explodes against the wall. His front tooth hits the concrete and slowly slides down. Gabriel screams as the father growls, possessed by his demons.

"I said shut up."

Gabriel hits the ground and tries to crawl away, one hand in front of the other. His other front tooth hangs on by a strand of gum, and he coughs up blood. The father kicks him in the ribs, making his body jerk. Gabriel finds the strength to continue to crawl, crying like a baby, as Zyra less than ten years old, witnesses this event. Gabriel's pants are wrapped around his ankles, the father unzips and enters Gabriel from behind. The goat demon's voice can be heard.

"You just sat there. Did nothing."

The father looks up with ferocious beastly eyes and stares Zyra down. He then licks the back of Gabriel's head and confronts young Zyra.

"You're next."

Gabriel wipes the blood from his eyes and sees Zyra sitting there afraid. Gabriel moves his lips, asking *why* as the father stays concentrated on Zyra during the act. Gabriel reaches under the army cot, next to him, grabs the loaded gun, cocks it. In one sweep, he turns his body, puts the gun on his father's face, and pulls the trigger.

His brains explode out the back of his skull and scatter across the window. The impact drives his father away, then drops him to the floor. Gabriel drops his head, to the cold concrete, and closes his eyes forever. Zyra, not knowing what to do, wide-eyed and terrorized, curls up in the fetal position, on the current stair, and cries.

"Momma."

Tears wash away Zyra's Gene Simmons, KISS, demon make-up.

Dezerae jerks up out of bed, looks at the alarm clock, and reads "7:15 AM." She packs her bags and walks into the kitchen. The sun pierces through, highlighting Zyra's ghost-like face. He sits up in a roar.

"He's buried evil."

Zyra's nipples bleed off the sides of his pecks, and Dezerae backs away. She notices the cut across his arm but chooses to not give in to the curiosity. He turns his head, and now with a wide-eyed, crazed stare, he penetrates her soul.

"He's buried evil."

She jolts with energy, and the hair on the back of her neck rises. Terror passes through, as she receives a flash image of Zyra's father, then instantly it's gone. The stare strengthens, and their spirits connect. Finally, the adrenaline diffuses, she takes a deep breath and calms down a little. Zyra rolls his eyes and focuses in on the silence.

She bends down next to him, he turns his head to meet her. He grabs her face, with both hands and gently kisses her on the lips. They remain quiet. He looks at her, with compassion and loss of character, just humility. She *slaps* him across the face, pushes his hands off of her leg, and walks out of the house, with the bag in her hand.

Chapter 20

LAND OF THE LIVING

The coffee pot in the kitchen turns on, as the clock strikes 8:15 am. The Hazelnut aroma finds its way into Zyra's brain, waking him up for the second time. Zyra slowly sits up and wipes the sleep from his eyes.

"Dezerae."

He looks around, and thinks to himself, *where the hell am I?* He stands up, loses his balance, and falls against the kitchen table. He picks up the bag on the table, opens it, and pulls out a crystal frame surrounded by angels. He pridefully states.

"My baby's gonna love this."

He walks into the bedroom, the bed is dressed. Dezerae is nowhere to be found.

"Dezerae...Dezerae..."

He hears no response, walks back into the kitchen, reaches into the cabinet, and pulls out a Jim Morrison coffee cup, with a green lizard handle. The caption reads, "I am the lizard king." He pours himself a cup of coffee, as sickness rises to his throat.

"Oh shit."

The cup falls from his hands, shatters onto the floor, runs to the bathroom, throws up in the toilet.,

"Oh my God, I don't feel good."

He drops to the floor and thinks to himself, *I gotta meet Amir today*. He passes out against the sink.

Meanwhile, Dezerae pulls up to her grandmother's quaint, cozy house in Long Beach. She alludes herself to be strong, fighting back the tears, she had cried for the past hour driving down there. Her grandmother, a heavy-set older friendly woman, Grandma, can be heard.

"Coming Dear."

She answers the door and kisses her.

"Welcome Sweetie, I wasn't expecting you today, was I? You know how old age gets. But it's always a delight to see you."

She kisses her grandmother.

"I needed a place to stay for a couple of days, Grandma. May I stay here, otherwise, I can go to a hotel?"

Her grandmother leads her to the kitchen as she asks.

"Of course, Dear, you stay here. What's wrong? Did something happen?"

Dezerae sits down at the table.

"I just need a break, that's all."

Her grandmother pats her on the back and nods in confidence.

"Well, we all need breathing room. Would you like some coffee?"

Dezerae's face cracks a smile for the first time.

"Please, I would love some, thank you."

"Don't worry about it, stay as long as you want. I could use the company around here."

Dezerae smiles brighter, as her grandmother slowly walks over to the coffee pot.

"So how do you like your coffee?"

Dezerae snaps from her thoughts and realizes her grandmother is speaking to her. She instantly picks up the conversation, where she thought they would have left off.

"I didn't get much sleep last night. After coffee, I think I'm gonna crash. I'm just so tired."

She looks up at her grandmother, who has a dumbfounded look on her face.

"That's nice Sweety, how do you like your coffee, though?"

Dezerae laughs to herself, embarrassed for foreshadowing their conversation.

"I like my coffee with cream and sugar, please."

Her grandmother pours the cream and sugar, into her cup, and stirs as Dezerae sits back, watching her grandmother, carry the cup over to her.

"Here you go, darling."

She takes it gracefully. Her grandmother sits down next to her and grabs her hand.

"How's your husband Zara...Zylar?"

"Zyra."

She says with a forced smile, fights back tears, but is not successful.

"I'm sorry Grandma, I didn't mean to bring this on you."

She squeezes her hand tighter, and with true compassion.

"What happened?"

Dezerae lifts her knees to her chin, sitting in the chair, sipping her coffee. She wipes her runny nose on her jeans and brings her slowly into it.

"He left yesterday morning to see his psychiatrist and didn't get home until 4 in the morning. His shirt was torn open and passed out on the kitchen floor. He had some cuts on his arm. I just can't take it anymore, Grandma. I don't know what to do."

She breaks down on her shoulder, and her grandma welcomes her with open arms, holding her tightly.

"Do you think he is cheating on you?"

"I don't know. He just can't beat his drug habit, it's coming between us."

Her grandmother kisses her hand and stands up.

"Well, I'm going to let you sleep. A nice nap will be good for you. Remember Dezerae, you have dragon blood in you, now get some rest."

She leads her through the wooden antique motif, into the guest bedroom. Dezerae enters the brightly lit room, with an oak post bed frame, puffy yellow pillows, and a comforter. She pulls down the cover, kicks off her shoes, and snuggles into bed. She looks up at her grandmother and smiles.

"You did always talk about that Grandma. I love you. When I wake up, I'll go see Fr. O'Donnell. Maybe he can give me some advice as well."

She kisses her on the forehead.

"Okay Sweetie, there is food in the fridge when you get hungry. I love you. It is great to see you again."

"Yeah, thank you, grandma. I love you too."

Dezerae rolls over and goes to sleep, her grandmother walks into the living room and watches television in her Lazy Boy.

Meanwhile, Zyra wakes up, and looks down at himself, sitting on the bathroom floor. His insides are warm against his flesh.

"Oh Jesus Christ, I puked all over myself. What happened to me last night?"

He thinks back trying to remember. He sees a flash image of himself at the gas station, another flash image of the Nephilim card, *I must have gone to the party* he thinks to himself. He stands up, walks into the kitchen, and sees coffee and glass shattered everywhere. He starts to clean up, bends down, and picks up a piece of glass. He sees his reflection, in the oven, as he continues to clean.

"Dezerae, are you home yet, baby?"

No answer.

He finishes cleaning the glistened floor and hops into the shower. After he is done, Zyra gets dressed and sees a phone message on their house phone. He listens. A thick Spanish male accent rises from the speaker.

"Zyra, it's me, Amir. Call me, we need to talk, I tried your cell, no answer. You're on tonight."

A couple more messages go by, but then he finally gets to the last message.

"Dezerae, it's your mother, your father was worried about you and asked me to call. I was worried too. Anyway, Hi Zyra. We love you guys. Bye."

The phone rings, scaring him for a second, Zyra answers.

"Hello, hey, what's up, Doc?... Two's fine. Alright, see you then."

He hangs up the phone and finishes getting dressed. He puts on his favorite shirt, walks out, grabs his helmet, and revs his engine.

Upon the blood of dragons, wings of flesh are born. Generation after generation.

Chapter 21

ROCK STAR

The lights grow dim, over the illuminated skull, overlooking the rowdy crowd, in Hollywood Amphitheatre. Down in the front of the stage, two guys, and a female leach, fight their way into the front row. The long-haired wild-eyed tattooed creature turns to his main squeeze, pressed up against him, as she whispers into his ear.

"Could you imagine if Zyra strips on stage?"

"What?"

The crowd roars, as the guitar strikes a heavy haunting sound. She repeats it louder, as someone else interjects.

"Yeah, he's done crazier things than that."

"Like what?"

The boyfriend asks.

"I went to a show last year in Boston. He pulled some chick up, from the audience, had sex with her, right there in front of everybody."

"He didn't get arrested?"

"The guitarist grabbed a goat, sitting behind the stage, and forced it upon her. "

The girl freaks out.

"WHAT?"

"Yeah, it was at some underground concert. Zyra snapped the goat's neck, as the girl tried getting away."

The boyfriend finally realizes he is in for the show of his life.

"This guy who we're gonna see right now, did all of that last year? At an underground concert? Oh my god, this place is gonna rock tonight."

Zyra comes walking out, dressed in a silverish green lizard costume, with wings of flesh, protruding from his back, as he sings.

"I'm evil...yes, I am...I'm evil now you understand...I'm evil, there's nothing you can do but wait for God's existence, to burn me through and through...I'm evil...I'm evil…el..el..el...I'm evil."

Zyra strikes a pose, staring off into space, living the dream, but now morally conflicted about the lyrics he is forced to perform. Zyra stares into the lights, blinding him. He screams from his core, shattering any nearby glass to pieces. His mind and eyes, were far from the crowd, soaring beyond the horizon. Zyra concentrates energy into balls of fire, within his hands, and throws them at the audience, singing.

"God will baptize you in fire."

His over-drawn face and wicked jaw, penetrate the souls, of those within his sight. Praying over them, as a fire lizard, Zyra breathes tongues of fire, down upon them. He flies over the crowd, by the jimmy-rigged, pulley system, getting them to try and touch him, as he flies over their heads. The crowd is going berserk. People rip off their shirts, forming mosh pits, every five feet. Those lining the walls are being pleasured by their dates.

Another song kicks in, one more driving than the song before. Zyra's sporadic cries and darkened weeps, flood the atmosphere, with emotion to its peak, from everyone in the club. Outside the concert, fans are still trying to get in. Holly Gossip is reporting.

"People are going crazy for Zyra. The controversy is enormous surrounding this man, but the peace he has off stage, says it all, married to the beautiful starlet, Dezerae Nelson, It is just like he says, *I'm just doing my job.*"

Back inside the concert, it is Zyra's grand finale. Everything gets black. There is no sound, only the power charging through the amp. The crowd slowly dies to silence, and Zyra speaks.

"Yesterday, I gave my heart away, to the dying sun. Now, that I have conquered here, my words have already won. If you see me, watch your grave, your moment may come, behave. I offer your soul, to the chosen one, for the kingdom, has more fun. I'm Zyra, the spirit of fire lizard. I crucify your brain, make you feel the pain, drain the blood from your eyes, give your heart a mind."

He growls at the crowd, the bass bounces off his voice. The guitarist feels his rhythm, take him to another place. A guillotine is wheeled out onto the stage. Two leather-bound demon males, carry a girl towards the guillotine. They tie her up, each hand pulled away from her head, and the wood harness around her neck forbids movements. The blade rises, Zyra releases the rope, and waits anxiously for the blade, to scalp her. As it flies past, blood squirts against Zyra's face. He takes in the moment, and roars at the crowd again.

He sticks his hand into her head and pulls out her brain. People in the audience, puke thinking it is real. The fans who got sprayed with blood pressed against the stage, went berserk, screaming at the top of their lungs. Zyra holds the brain, high above his head, showing the audience what he did. The place goes silent, Zyra takes a bite from the brain, ripping off a piece, and chewing it. He spits it on the audience, and throws the brain as far as he can, which crashes down on someone's head. He spreads his wings, finishes his song, and flies out of the room.

The music continues for a minute, as the audience bolts out the door, trying to catch him. Zyra disappears, gone from their sight. The curtains close. The girl on stage gets up from the guillotine and says to herself, *There's another two hundred dollars*. The stage manager hands her two bills. Pocketing the money, she walks off stage. By the time the band is done playing, Zyra is in his limo, and on the road, getting as far away from his show as possible.

Zyra takes off the costume and leans over crying as if he is in a lot of pain. He only repeats three words over and over, as he rocks himself back and forth in fetal position.

"Forgive me, Jesus...Forgive me, Jesus..."

His voice is strained from being overworked, the pain continues to intensify. He thinks to himself, *Who am I, Lord? Who am I?* In his mind's eye, he sees walls, crumbling around him, as he shakes like a leaf, and continues to soak in his sorrows. A friendly voice enters his mind.

"Your pain is self-inflicted. Come with me to a better place."

An image of a pierced hand rises in his mind. Zyra jumps back, thinking it is real, takes a deep breath, and tries to calm down. The driver drops Zyra off at the studio, where he has his motorcycle. He changes inside the limo, leaving the wings and costume behind. He exits the vehicle and walks out in a pair of jeans and a leather coat. He hops on his Harley and takes off.

Chapter 22

GOTHOLIC LIGHT

The grey cool overcast sweeps through the streets of Hollywood, and Zyra walks against the breeze this next afternoon. The wind catches his black trench coat, fanning it out, as he strides up the boulevard. Some fans shopping, notice him, and snap pictures. A tour bus releases a bus full of tourists, on the corner of La Brea and Hollywood Blvd..

Zyra reaches the cross streets, Hollywood and Vine, and hangs a right. Goth punk kids walk past him, coming out of "Witch-Kraft Kettle," a gothic witch store painted black, on the outside. Zyra throws them a look, as they hold up a baggy of red spell potions, spooking each other out with it.

Next to the store, Zyra opens the door and walks up a narrow black stairwell dimly lit. At the top of the stairs, another black door reads, "Haunted Shadow Records." He opens the door and immediately is greeted by Liz, the secretary with long black and red dreadlocks, which complement her facial piercings. She sits behind the free-standing reception desk, chewing gum, and playing with her nails, and as always, her head bounces when she speaks.

"Zyra, it's so nice to see you. Kanniballations is number three, you know. And your show was fucking amazing last night."

Zyra smirks.

"Yeah, the world's screwed up for liking it. Where's Amir?"

She laughs.

"He's almost done with a meeting. I'll let him know you're here."

"Thanks."

Zyra sits down and grabs the latest, "Rolling Stone," issue sitting on the table. His image is on the cover, and the walls behind him are filled with gold records. Next to the reception desk, is a black leather couch, which sits two freaky guys, holding their cd, waiting anxiously. One of them whispers to the other.

"Hey dude, that's Zyra."

"Holy shit, you're right. Watch this."

He stands up and walks over to him.

"Excuse me, Um...Mr. Zyra."

Zyra looks up.

"Yeah."

The guy tries to contain his excitement.

"You've influenced my music, more than any other musician. It's an honor for me to meet you."

He puts out his hand, and Zyra shakes it.

"Thank you..."

The guy does not release his hand. A long odd moment delays his senses. Feeling the oddity from Zyra, he finally releases.

"Kanniballations is the best album in the world."

Zyra looks at the magazine, then back up at him.

"Thanks."

The guy is bug-eyed, lost in awe, drool creeps down his chin. Zyra gestures for him to wipe it, and he does.

"Well, I'm here to see Amir. He wanted to hear our demo. Maybe we could open up for you if we get signed."

Zyra takes a deep breath, having to deal with this guy.

"Yeah, maybe."

Zyra gives him a cold stare, as the guy is relentless.

"Well, it was nice meeting you. I'm just sitting right over there."

Zyra nods his head, and raises his eyebrows, as the guy walks back to his seat, and hits the other guy in the arm.

"I'm such an idiot. I lost it."

"Whatcha say?"

"Maybe we can open up for you if we get signed."

"You're an idiot."

Amir dressed in black pants and, a flowing shiny black shirt, walks out from behind the wall, relaxed and always confident. Zyra stands and greets him. Amir pats him on the shoulder. Zyra comments about his long black fingernails and silver dragon full-finger ring.

"Just get those done?"

Amir smiles.

"Yesterday, you like?"

Zyra smiles as Amir continues.

"In another week, 'Kanniballations' will be numero uno."

They walk towards his office.

"So what brings you here unannounced? I didn't mean for you to come down here."

They enter his all-black office, with a huge silver eight-foot alien, erect in the corner.

"Please take a seat."

Zyra sits down, and crosses his legs, waiting for him to speak.

"So, how was the shoot and your concert?"

Zyra puts his fingertips together and forms a triangle with his hands.

"It went well. Look, Amir, the reason I'm here is because of our contract. Starting the tour off with twenty-two..."

"This record is doing better than we expected...Zyra."

Zyra interrupts.

"There's something I need to tell you."

Amir remains quiet, waiting for his words, the tension in the room, grows thicker.

"There's no easy way to say this so, here it is. I found God. And, 'Kanniballations' corrupts all that is good. I decided I was not doing the tour. I want out."

Amir, waiting for the punch line, looks amusingly confused.

"I want to go back into the studio and record another album. I've been writing new songs lately. Spiritual songs, uplifting songs. I'm getting sick of this darkness. I need out."

Amir busts out laughing. His laughter crescendos hurting his stomach. Tears fall from his eyes, as he repeats Zyra's words.

"I found God. 'Kanniballations' corrupts all that is good. You're fucking hilarious. You make a better comedian."

Zyra immediately reacts.

"Whoa, whoa...Amir, I'm serious."

He laughs even harder.

"I'm serious. I haven't laughed this hard since, since the first time, I jacked off on some dead bitch's face."

Zyra gets up and walks out. Amir tries to control his laughter.

"Where are you going?"

Amir gets up and follows him out. Zyra reaches the bottom of the stairs, Amir opens the door.

"Zyra, seriously, stop!"

Zyra keeps walking and feels a huge weight lift from him. Amir screams.

"I'll ruin you, ZYRA! No one walks out on me!"

He slams the door shut, his face is beaten red, and veins pop from his neck.

"I'll rip his vocal chords, straight from his throat!"

He releases his demons on Liz and shakes frantically.

"Call his agent, producer, director, chicks he slept with, everyone associated with that filth. Tell them what he did. Do it NOW!"

He storms past her and slams his door shut. The other employees in the office, peak their heads out, paralyzed in fear.

The two dudes look at each other, scared, then look at Liz. Liz shrugs her shoulders and doesn't say a word. The two stand up, on their way to leave, when Amir opens his door and shouts out.

"Bring me those two assholes. It's the luckiest day of their lives!"

Zyra walks down Hollywood Blvd. and sees a family of tourists taking a picture by his star. He squats down and gets in the picture. The young teenage girl starts freaking out.

"Oh my God. Oh my God. It's him."

Zyra smiles with excitement, the girl grabs his face and kisses his cheek.

"Thank you. I'm very flattered. God Bless."

He walks away feeling an excitement, he hasn't felt in a long time, as she jumps up and down.

"That was him. That was him. I knew it. I knew we would meet him. I told you, Mom. I told you."

Her mother smiles, recognizing the daughter's excitement.

"Crazy, you did say that."

Zyra glides down the street, with a smile, lighting up the boulevard. He walks down Western and hands the valet his ticket. As he waits, Zyra grabs a joint from his pants, and looks at his watch,

"12:01, good I got some time."

He takes a hit after lighting it. The sound of his Harley approaches, and the valet stops and gets off the bike. Zyra gets on, puts down the kickstand, and continues to smoke his joint. The valet asks.

"I've never seen one like this before."

"Had it custom made."

"Yeah, I'd say. You look familiar. You on TV or something?"

"I've been on TV before."

"Anything I've seen? Or just an extra trying to make it?"

Zyra laughs.

"Yeah, just trying to make it."

"Me too. That's why I'm parking cars."

Zyra looks at him with curiosity.

"You believe in God?"

The valet smiles with caring eyes.

"I can't stand condemning bible preachers, but yeah, I believe there's some higher power. Why?"

Zyra gathers thoughts and releases them as if he were expecting him to ask.

"I believe we're all screwed up, trying to find our way. But if we're truly sorry for our sins, ask forgiveness, God has no choice but to forgive, and unconditionally love us."

The valet appreciates Zyra's willingness to share his philosophy and is somewhat taken aback by what he said.

"Well put, my friend, what's your name?"

Zyra stretches out his hand.

"Zyra, and yours?"

"Johnny Douglas, my friends call me D.J. cause they think I'm a bit backward."

Zyra laughs.

"That's funny. I'll see you around D.J."

Zyra puts his helmet on and stamps out his joint, before pulling into traffic. Zyra looks over, as he is about to get onto the freeway, and sees a local bar, remembering a time before he was famous, hanging out after hours, with his good friend, Dan, one of the owners.

"Zyra, you'll make it. Always remember, acting is believing the lie. If you can do that, you can be anyone you want. I grew up out here, the people who make it are those who persist. Never give up, man. One of the many things I learned from my parents, believe in yourself and others will believe in you."

He shakes the memory, not realizing St. Charles Church, came up a lot faster, than expected. He pulls in. He gets off his bike, looks up to heaven, before entering thinks to himself, *thank you,* walks through the grand dark oak wooden entrance. He takes a seat towards the back, while a few older women are scattered praying the rosary.

Zyra looks around, feeling uneasy, but tries to settle in, as he walks down the center aisle, three-quarters of the way down, and takes a seat in the pew. He drops the kneeler, kneels, and says in a whisper.

"Dear Lord, I don't know what to say. I haven't been faithful to you. I've denied you."

As he stares up, at the larger-than-life crucified Christ, elevated about twenty feet in the air, he fidgets feeling the uncertainty of what he is doing.

"Thank you for Dezerae. She's my angel!"

He starts to break down.

"Forgive me, Lord, for the pain, I've caused. Teach me to forgive. Help me forgive myself and..."

He takes a deep breath.

"family. We were victims of evil, greater than our love for you. I know that now. With all the money, and fame this world offers, it never compared to the love I felt for you when my father died and released me from his family curse. But I blamed you, for taking my brother, and I turned against you. I'd give it all if you would show me the way."

No longer fighting back tears, Zyra lets them go, completely taken over with humiliation, as he thinks back to the night before.

"I don't know what happened to me last night, Lord. I don't even know, where my wife is."

He breaks down even harder.

"I don't expect miracles. I just wanted to talk. Thanks for listening. Amen."

Zyra remembers being a little boy, making the sign of the cross. He cracks a smile and makes the sign of the cross.

"In the name of the Father, and of the Son, and the Holy Spirit. Amen."

He kisses his pointer, after reciting these words, as if he was kissing the cross. Sitting behind him, he hears a woman sobbing. He turns around, and to his surprise, Dezerae welcomes him with her moist forgiving eyes.

"How long have you been here?"

"Long enough to know you love me."

He gets up, walks around the pew, and sits down next to her. He puts his arm around her and hugs her. They both say at the same time.

"I love you."

Zyra whispers into her ear.

"There's something I want to talk to you about."

"Do you want to sit outside?"

"Yeah."

They walk out to the side of the church and sit in the middle of the grotto, where a statue of the Virgin Mary, is surrounded by roses, which fragrance the air.

"I want to tell you more about my childhood. I never told you the worst of it. I miss my brother, Gabriel, so much. I just realized that, this past week, since he's been on my mind. Dezerae, do you know why I fell in love with you?"

Catching him off guard she replies rather quickly.

"I ask myself that question every day."

She gives him compassion, slightly turns her head, and touches his cheek.

"When I met you at that coffee shop, I knew you were the one for me."

"You've said that before."

She smiles and continues.

"You were so nice, and never once, did I feel like you were hitting on me."

He interrupts her.

"Not that I didn't recognize your beauty, oh I did. It was just a crazy day, a lot was on my mind."

She laughs.

"I know, it was that devotion that drove me crazy. I wanted you, but I remember fighting that feeling. It was too strong."

"You were just another pretty face at first, but when I recognized you, I felt like I already knew you."

He sees in his mind, a statue of Christ bleeding from his palms.

"... the One Who Sits On The Throne had this exact plan for us."

She gives him a weird look.

"I'm not sure if that's a compliment, or…?

He puts his head down, composes his thoughts, and looks up at her.

"When I was ten, my younger brother, Gabriel was eight. My father, the bastard that he was, used to beat us. He was rougher on Gabriel since I fought back. Gabriel, just took it, believing his lies. I remember telling him, Gabriel, *Dad lies to you to make you feel the way he wants you to feel.* He'd agree but, nothing ever really changed. The reason he tolerated the pain, was because he was doing *Daddy's penance.*"

Dezerae's heart swells, feeling what Zyra is saying.

"You believe that? Eight years old, and he loved his father so much, he was willing to suffer for his father's sins."

Dezerae grabs his hand.

"I'm sorry your father brainwashed Gabriel."

Zyra jumps in.

"He brainwashed him, I remember if he ewasn't killing him with kindness, he was abusing his body mind, and soul. My father got off on it. Love and hate. A twisted kind of love, a sorrowful fate. Sometimes, I wanted to kill him, become the monster I saw transform, before my very eyes. I know I've made wrong choices in my life, Dezerae, but you are the best thing that ever happened to me."

Tears fall once again from the eyes of Dezerae, as she confronts him.

"You manipulated death, by spitting it out. I was the light, to fill the darkness. But you *dimmed* that light in me, Zyra, and, I can't go on, if this is the way it's going to be. I can't die to my spirituality, lose everything I've gained because you won't straighten out."

There is silence as Zyra finally responds.

"That's why I told Amir, I'm done with the tour."

"What? When did you do that?"

Zyra drops his head.

"Today, before I came here."

She lifts his chin, with her hand, locks eyes.

"What did he say?"

Zyra laughs.

"Say?! He was pissed. Anyway, on Halloween night, in 1983, my brother and I, were getting ready for trick or treating. I was dressed as Gene Simmons from KISS, and he was going to be Paul Stanley. My mother was working late, so my father said, he would take us trick-or-treating around the block. I was upstairs putting on my make-up when I heard Gabriel scream… for my father to stop. I remember feeling this, sick to my stomach feeling, so I ran downstairs to the basement, where I heard my brother."

His lip starts to quiver, she holds him tighter, never seeing him this vulnerable before.

"...by a...by the time, I got down to the basement, my imagination couldn't have added to the horror, I heard coming from my brother's being. Clenching the rail, I remember that vividly, I was shaking like a leaf. The light was dim, so I squatted down, just behind where the stairs, separate from the floor. I saw my…my Dad *mole   sting* my little brother, and I did *nothing* to stop it. I was *struck*, paralyzed in fear. Time stood still, sound faded, then, POW, gunshot. My father's face and brain exploded against the window, and my brother looked at me with, a confused smile and, at that same moment, asked me for forgiveness. He dropped his head, which fell motionless, in a pool of blood. The last I remember, my mother arrived, shoved my head into her bosom, and rocked me back and forth, repeating over and over, *I'm sorry, I'm sorry*...her tears soaked my head."

Zyra's chin rests on his knees, his arms, wrapped around his shins, drool drips down his lip. He slowly stops rocking and glares up at Dezerae, whose eyes are now bloodshot, with tears, streaming down her face. Zyra continues.

"I woke up ten days later, in a hospital. It all seemed like a bad dream. My mother was nowhere to be found. Some people were there, who I didn't know, I was told...I'd be living with them. My family never mentioned it again. Not a single picture, or trace, could be found. I haven't seen my mother since…*then*. It's not that I blame her, I guess I understand, I mean, who would want me, as a son, after letting that happen? There were so many times, I forced that memory, *deep* **deep** down, not allowing it to surface. That part of my life… just, a figment of my imagination."

He repositions himself, parishioners walk by, nod acknowledging them.

> "In High School I started writing poems, singing them, at local poetry song competitions. I'll never forget it, my very first poem."

"What is it?"

Zyra leans in, pressing his fingers, to his temples.

> "In the land of the living
> I am dead
> Days before darkness
> I am Red
> Night becomes laughter
> In my forsaken dreams
> And tears become stranger
> Even in my wildest dreams
> Numbness restricts my sight"

Dezerae leans in, and rests her hand, on his knee.

"If I ever knew pain...it was when I woke up, that morning, and my family was *taken* from me, at ten years old."

Dezerae puts her arm around him, squeezing him tightly.

> "I'm sorry, Zyra. My words can't heal your past, but God can. That much I know. He did it for me, and I know He will do it for you."

He looks at her, and shakes his head, recalling an experience, fulfilling her point.

"You know, I remember having dreams, about my mother, during my teenage years. It was strange, because sometimes I felt, like, I don't know, I know it sounds crazy, but that she was just around the corner, watching over me."

Dezerae rubs her nose, and sniffles as Fr. O'Donnell walks by.

"Good afternoon you two."

Dezerae looks up.

"Hi, Father."

"It is very nice to see you both here. How's everything going?"

Dezerae smiles at his compassion.

"Good, we're just talking...straightening things out."

Father presses his hands together, in prayer form.

"Great. Just allow the Good Lord Shepherd, to guide you, and everything will be alright. Take care, and Zyra, don't be a stranger, God Bless."

They both say goodbye. He walks on. Zyra continues his thoughts.

"That was nice...anyways, yesterday when I was at Hildonberg's office, he put me under hypnosis. My guardian Angel, Nazareth, that's his name, brought me, to a...awe man, I haven't verbalized this yet, he brought me to the other side of the sun."

Not expecting that, she quickly responds.

"The other side of the sun?"

Zyra's hands start to get sweaty, he rubs them together.

"You may not believe me, Dezerae, or you may want to
believe, I *believe* it truly *happened*, either way, I just
wanted to let you know. It was the first time in my life, I
felt love so powerful, so real and so caring."

"From the Doctor?"

She says smirkingly. He laughs.

"No, from The One Who Sits On The Throne. A spiritual
bridge is being built. It connects our world, to their world,
and this kingdom is found, within each one of us, at the
same time, existing on the other side of the sun."

She looks at him with contentment, awe, and disbelief.

"What are you talking about, Zyra?"

Zyra takes a deep breath, trying to figure out another way, to
rephrase his point.

"It's like the sun, was His heart, pouring out his love,
created in the first realm, of heaven. His heart, awaits each
person, each living organism. He was life, pure life, energy
waiting to be welcomed in."

Dezerae interjects.

"Through acts of love."

"Exactly."

She takes a deep breath and changes the subject.

"So finish telling me about, Amir."

"After the concert last night, I just broke down and cried like a baby. The tour is *too* dark. I need light in my life. That's why I did it."

Zyra gets lost in his thoughts, as he says out loud.

"I forgive my mother, my brother...but it seems next to impossible to forgive my father. It would take a miracle."

Dezerae remains silent.

"Oh, I forgot I need to call Robin, about Amir."

He takes out his cell phone and dials. She looks at him, not knowing what to think, as he travels from thought to thought, not grounded or focused, on one thing.

"Stacy, hey, it's Zyra. May I speak to Robin, please? Alright, just tell him I called. He's got the number. Bye."

He hangs up the phone and looks at Dezerae.

"He won't be in for another hour."

He looks at the time on his cell.

"1:40, I got to go Baby. I have a two o'clock appointment with Hildonberg. I'll be home after that. What are you gonna do?"

She looks down with tears in her eyes.

"Zyra, do you know why I left and went down to my grandmother's?"

She looks up at him. He shakes his head.

"No, I heard a message from your mom, on the machine, but that was it."

She leans into him, and talks with her hands.

"You got in at 4:30 in the morning and passed out on the kitchen floor. I called your name a million times. I even tried to *shake you*, out of it, but nothing. I couldn't take it. I left you. You seemed drugged. I told you, I wanted a divorce. Do you remember any of this?"

Zyra drops his head in shame.

"No, I didn't know where you were. Last night's a blur. The last thing I remember was I was going to a party, Garth wanted me to go to. It was called, *the Nephilim*. That word appeared in my dream, Dezerae, so I went. I was served a drink, and the last thing I remember, waking up, on the kitchen floor, puke everywhere."

He touches her shoulder.

"I'm sorry Dezerae, please forgive me. I should have never gone."

She remains silent, lets the moment pass, then speaks.

"Robin's going to freak out, about you cancelling the tour. You'll lose *everything* you've worked so hard for. You know that, right?"

He stands up.

"I've already made my decision. Better my material possessions, than my soul."

Dezerae hugs him.

"I forgive you Zyra. You need help. Alcoholics Anonymous. I have to go to my grandmother's, pick up my stuff. I'll meet you at home, this evening. We'll talk more about it then."

"I love you."

He kisses her goodbye.

"I love you too."

They hug for a long minute, kiss again, and part their ways.

Chapter 23

DANGER IN THE DEEP

After flying through the side streets of Los Angeles, Zyra turns onto Pacific Coast Highway. An overcast settles in up ahead, and a crowd of people is gathered on the beach. The road is blocked off, cars are backed up for miles. Sirens create Doppler's effect, passing Zyra as he thinks to himself, *What the hell is going on up there?* He lifts his visor and pans the coast. Seagulls flock around the crowd, as he reads on his cell, *1:55.*

"I'm gonna be late. Traffic isn't moving."

He dials the Doctor's office. Putting a finger in his left ear, so he can hear.

"Hello, Stacy, it's Zyra. I'm stuck on PCH. There's a huge accident up ahead. It's backed up miles. Alright, I'll hold..."

Classical music plays over the phone. She gets back on.

"Zyra, are you still there?"

"Yeah."

"He has another appointment at 3, so if you just want to reschedule, that would be better for him."

"That's fine. Let me call you when I get home. Bye."

People are getting out of their cars, and walking to the scene. Zyra thinks to himself, *"This reminds me of that REM video."* He turns off his bike, puts the kickstand down, and dials Dezerae.

"Hey, baby."

She screams out over the phone.

"Where are you? There is so much noise."

Cars are honking, people are screaming out profanities, revving their engines.

"I'm stuck on PCH. I had to reschedule with Hildonberg. It looks like there's a huge accident up ahead, I want to check it out."

Cops block off the scene, and people are gathered, trying to see what happened. Zyra asks some surfer dude, while he is still on the phone with Dezerae.

"What's going on?"

The surfer turns around.

"Holy crap, you're Zyra. Some dude got washed up on shore. His body was bitten in half. I guess jaws are real, man."

Zyra looks beyond him, not believing a word he says. Dezerae's voice can be heard over the cell.

"What happened?"

Zyra talks to her.

"I don't know. Some dude said Jaws bit somebody in half. I'm gonna get closer. It's probably some beached whale or something. I'll call you when I know more."

As he is about to hang up, looking over people's shoulders, she quickly responds.

"No, keep me on the phone. I want to know."

Zyra pushes past the crowd to the front. The medic's back, faces Zyra, as he squats down. The other medic is on the opposite side. The medic closer to Zyra says.

"On three, one two three."

They lift with their legs and stand up with the body. A third medic holds open a body bag, as the two medics place, Garth's bloodless wrinkled torso, missing one eye into the bag. Flesh is torn away looking like fish dabbled for dinner.

Zyra screams out.

"Holy shit!!!"

Dezerae screams over the phone.

"What is it?"

"You're never going to believe this! Well, they just put..."

Zyra pukes up all over the place. Everyone around him pushes away as Dezerae shouts out.

"Baby, what's wrong?"

Zyra's complexion turns ghostly, he gets back on the phone and walks away from the scene.

"I don't feel good. I'll call you back."

He hangs up the phone and connects it to his belt. The medics lift the bottom half, of the body, shredded at the waist, flesh torn from his legs. They dump it into the bag, professional, yet disturbed, and place the body bag in the back of the ambulance.

Holly Gossip runs to the scene. One of the policemen, blocking off the scene, screams out.

"Alright folks, the show's over, please disburse. Nothing to see here."

People start to break away, as Holly and her camera crew, rush the cop. Through the viewfinder, Holly questions him.

"Do have an explanation for why half a person has been washed up on shore?"

The cop answers.

"At this time, we have no information. Thank you."

He walks out of the frame. The grey clouds release a drizzle, Holly turns around and runs smack dab into Zyra. She is pleasantly surprised, she speaks to him on air.

"We meet again, Zyra. What a pleasant surprise! Do you know what took place here today?"

Worry strikes his face, Zyra takes a deep breath and confronts the issue.

* * *

Dezerae arrives at her grandmother's house, storms in, turns on the television, flipping the channels, until she lands on the news. K.N.O.W. as news anchor, Dick Bishop, interrupts the program.

"We interrupt this program, to bring you a live update on, *Danger in the Deep*."

The jaws theme song fades in, under his voice.

"Holly, you there?"

The screen splits, showing Holly Gossip on location, and Dick from the studio. It rains harder in Holly's background.

"It looks like you're getting wet out there. What's going on?"

Holly responds.

"Yes, Dick it just started raining here, a few moments ago, when the paramedics arrived on scene. I am here, believe it or not, with Zyra Jordonello, front man of Sacred Witch."

The screen fills, with the shoulder shot, of Zyra.

"Zyra, do you have any information on *Danger in the Deep*?"

The graphics ripple onto the screen, and Zyra's pale face, and dizzy eyes, stare off into the camera.

"You people disgust me. Somebody died here today, you make it out to be, some kind of miniseries or something."

He walks off the frame. Holly interjects.

"Thank you, Zyra, for your input."

Zyra walks back and grabs the microphone from her hand.

"May God give strength, to this person's family, and friends. May he rest in peace."

He hands the microphone back to Holly and walks off. Dezerae's eyes are glued to the television, as a wave of excitement and grief, hit all at the same time.

"That's my baby, maybe he is changing."

Dick gets back on the air.

"That was Holly Gossip, reporting live, from the west coast of Southern California."

Dezerae mutes the volume, and the program comes back on. She picks up the phone and dials Zyra.

* * *

Back on the beach, people are walking to their cars. They shuffle passed Zyra, he answers his phone.

"Hey, baby."

Dezerae sits Indian-style on the couch.

"Are you okay? I just saw you on the news."

"I don't feel well. I don't feel well. What time will you be home?"

Zyra arrives at his bike, throws his leg over the seat, and lays his head down on his gas tank. He envisions Garth's torso, and gets sick again, thinking to himself, *Was Garth at the party last night?* Zyra shakes off the vision, and tunes back into Dezerae's voice.

"I called Robin for you. He wants to talk to you. Amir had already talked to him."

Zyra realizes he missed part of the conversation.

"Whoa...I didn't hear you...what happened?"

She speaks louder.

"I said, I talked to Robin today. He wants to talk to you."

He puts his finger deeper into his ear.

"I heard you say that. What did you say before?"

She gets off the couch and walks around the house.

"I was upset, Zyra. I don't want to lose everything, we've worked so hard for. He agreed with me. He doesn't think it's a good idea, to not uphold the contract. He suggests you work it out with Amir, you know get rid of some of the extreme acts."

Zyra shakes his head in disbelief.

"I can't believe you said you support me, and this is what you go and do. So...what? You called him on the drive down?"

Her voice can be heard.

"Yes, I first checked voicemail, and Amir had left a million messages threatening you."

He revs his engine.

"I'm coming home now."

He hangs up the phone and attaches it to his belt. He throws on his helmet, inches along, following, the slow-moving traffic. The ambulance pulls away, sirens fade, and doves *dive* down over Zyra. The police wave on the cars to pass by, Zyra looks up, sees the doves, and feels a tinge of comfort.

Immediately, his thoughts come together. *There is so much I don't understand. How am I to see the light, when I've lived in darkness for so long?* He drives passed the scene and turns onto Topanga Canyon, through the winding road, filled with trees and cliffs. His mind journeys, as he travels through, this James Coleman atmosphere.

The doves continue to follow Zyra, as he thinks back to his dream, Dragon-Whale ruling underwater. Its ferocious tiger head, jets forward, ending face to face with Zyra.

In his mind, talking to this spiritual beast right now, *visual communication transfers.* Dragon-Whale's eyes reflect Garth in the local bar, handing over his soul to Babel, for a hundred dollars. *Why?* Zyra questions Garth's gesture, as a dark gentle voice, breaks through the silence. As he continues his ride home, he hears.

"To get closer to you my dear."

Dragon-Whale's presence no longer threatens Zyra, he slowly continues to grow, in faith, feeling strength from within, allowing him to confront the beast.

"How did you manifest?"

The voice tickles his ear, as it gets louder, more piercing.

"I am an angel who fell from grace. Those who disbelieve, choose to ignore, or are too caught up in this world, strengthen my existence. Greed, lust, envy, gluttony. Shall I continue? These principles are my children, a doorway to your reality."

Dragon-Whale continues to speak to Zyra's curiosity.

"I am who you say I am, who you think I am, who you feel I am. I am your thoughts. I am your, Dragon-Whale. I am your, Tower of Babel."

Zyra refuses the sweet bitter temptation, of entertaining Dragon-Whale's thoughts. It swings its tail around about, trying to slam Zyra off his Harley, as he goes around a turn. Zyra stops the tail in his mind.

"You have no control over me. I am now, love, not fear. You cannot touch me."

Dragon-Whale releases a deep condescending laugh.

"You fool. You think you know it all."

His words penetrate Zyra's mind, grabbing hold of his soul, for a split second. Zyra calms himself, finding that inner peace, then confronts him, once again.

"It's a game to you. A battle, not worth fighting. For years, I gave in to you and received nothing, but heartache and pain in return. You gave me fame but at the price of my soul. You strung me along like a puppet."

The voice becomes more welcoming.

"Wisdom grows within side you Zyra, but I've existent before man was created. You, my friend, are nothing, less than a speck of dust."

Dragon-Whale's image fades, blowing fire from his mouth, and flying back into infinite darkness. Zyra snaps from the vision, and finds himself on top of Mulholland Drive, looking down at the valley. He pulls off to the side of the road, turns off the bike, and just sits down, overlooking this magnificent view. He grabs a joint, from his vest, and lights up. Tears rise, then fall from his eyes. In slow motion, he feels every bit of moisture, streaming down his face.

Cars drive by. The doves still hover, then land on a branch, sticking out over the cliff. The sun graves down, upon his flesh, he puts his hands around his knees and presses them against his chest. He starts to sing, and imagines himself, free as a bird, his wings of flesh appear, and he takes off in flight, flying over the valley, with the freedom to be, the one he dares to be.

> "Life becomes our choices
> Living love buried in the voices
> I've come to see my wicked ways"
> He stops singing for a moment, then starts again.
> "If only you could see my faith
> I'd rise from my grave
> To prove my love for you..."

He reflects upon Dezerae's beautiful smile and thinks of all the torture, he has put her through.

> "I cry to you within my dreams
> Only you can hear my screams
> Only you can heal my friends"

His cell phone rings, scaring him half to death. He answers it.

"Hello, baby. I'm on Mulholland and Topanga...Meditating. What? Already."

Zyra takes a deep breath.

"This is crazy. Calm down. I'm coming home. Don't worry about it. Where's your faith? I need you to be strong. Trust me, everything will work out. I love you. Bye."

Zyra finishes his joint, puts on his helmet, starts his bike, and takes off. As he drives home, he thinks back to their conversation. Dezerae is hysterical crying. Her words repeat over and over in his mind, *They could easily get forty-five million dollars for not doing this tour.* He thinks about how she looks. Her eyes were swollen red from crying, sipping a glass of red wine. He prays within his soul, *Give her the strength and faith she needs, Lord.*

Zyra finally arrives home and parks his bike in the garage. Dezerae opens the door, and stands there in tears, holding a glass of red wine, and a piece of paper. Behind him, a car pulls up in the driveway, a man in a grey suit, gets out of the car, with an envelope in his hand. He walks up to Zyra.

"Zyra Jordonello?"

Zyra turns around.

"Who's asking?"

The guy walks into the garage and hands him the envelope.

"You've been subpoenaed."

He walks away. Zyra looks at Dezerae, and opens the letter, skimming through it.

"You are commanded to appear in the United States District Court at the place, date, and time specified below to testify in the above case."

Zyra looks up at her.

"Keep reading."

He drops his head and continues.

"Los Angeles Court House, March 2nd, 8:00 am."

"I did the numbers, Zyra."

She hands him the piece of paper, with handwritten numbers on it.

"This is how I came up with forty-five million."

He pushes past her.

"Let me clear my head, and deal with this inside."

He walks into the kitchen, grabs himself a glass of wine, from the bottle she left out, and sits down on the couch, looking over the paperwork.

"Fine, let's say this is true. Do you love me?"

She quickly answers.

"Yes Zyra, I love you, but that's not what it's about. We worked so hard to get where we are. If you just do this one tour, and leave the label after, you never have to go back there and deal with this asshole."

Zyra shakes his head.

"Are you now telling me to compromise my soul, for money?"

She takes it in, thinks about her response, and speaks calmly but firmly.

"No, what I'm saying is, you don't have to do the show, the way he wants. You can alter the show, to fit your beliefs."

He rubs the bottom of his chin.

"How Dezerae, when the show opens up with *Eat the Dead*? I start the show at an altar, eating the brains of Christ. I can't do it. I want *nothing* to do with it anymore."

She doesn't respond, except to reposition herself. But then the thought comes.

"What if, the scripture about, you must eat my flesh and drink my blood, to gain eternal life, plays in the background? You know stuff like that."

Zyra takes in the idea for a moment.

"When Amir and I sat down, for the first time, discussing the special effects needed, to pull off this hour and a half of blasphemy, I was excited. We thought of the darkest images, then it got progressively worse from there. The show ends with me chopping off the scalp of a little girl, as a human sacrifice. How am I supposed to do this, and have a relationship with God? This is a test. If you want to leave, I understand. I'm not asking you to go through this with me. I need to cleanse my soul, this is part of it. My sins are piled to the sky."

He shakes his head, laughs to himself, and takes her hand.

"It's going to be okay. I love you. I will let you go if that's what you want."

Tears rise to her eyes.

"I love you, Zyra. I'm just scared. I don't know what to do."

She grabs his face and kisses him.

"I will never leave you. I will die with you. I love you so much."

He hugs her.

"We need faith, Dezerae. That's what we need, right now. I am going to be going through withdrawal. I need your help."

She gains her composure and sits back on the couch.

"Yeah, you're right. This is a test, we will pull through."

He sits up lifting his knee to the cushion.

"Dezerae, just think about how much you started with, compared to now."

She looks at him with an evil eye.

"What are you saying, easy come easy go?"

Zyra replies and sips his wine.

"Maybe, we'll see what happens."

The grandfather clock in the corner, STRIKES six times as Dezerae reacts.

"Oh shoot, we have to get ready. The screening's tonight."

Zyra responds.

"It starts at eight. Do you want to go?"

She gets up and pulls him along.

"We have to be there at 7:30. Let's shower."

Zyra follows her into the shower.

"Alright."

They get ready for their big night at Mann's Chinese Theater.

Wings of flesh across my back, lizard skin across my face,
Sacred Heart of Christ, Heal my every wound. Jesus the Healer
manifest your love. Forgive my sins, let my voice be heard
above. Protect my thoughts, control my actions, do with me as
you please! I am your servant.

Chapter 24

THE PREMIERE WITH GHOSTS

The sunlight dims, and night settles in on, Highland and La Brea, the heart of Hollywood. Guards stand by, blocking off Hollywood Boulevard, only allowing those guests, to the premiere. Mann's Chinese Theater, stands tall, lighting a larger-than-life poster of Dezerae and Zyra, "The Lizard."

A red carpet is rolled out from the entrance, and Paparazzi line the carpet, snapping away at everyone who enters. Many controversial celebrities are on the guest list. Howard Stern who just flew in from New York, escorts some new hot girlfriend, dressed in a red satin dress, and high heels, "Snap!" Behind them, Brian Warner (Marilyn Manson), dressed in red leather pants, and a white cowboy hat, attends with his loved one, dressed in black lace and red high heels. Flashes go off. People shout out, as they walk by.

"The Beautiful People...The Beautiful People..."

Zalman King's family walks in, behind Sting, the director, dressed to kill in his latest fashion suit, draping his arm, a new starlet. Hollywood's latest stars, one dressed hotter than the next, enter. Paparazzi are having a field day.

The next limo pulls up. The limo driver walks around and opens the door. Dezerae, hair up in tendrils, steps out of the limo, with her long firm legs, slinking out of her silky black dress, barely covering her. She elegantly waits for Zyra, who steps out of the limo, wearing black snakeskin boots, velvet black pants, white ruffled lace shirt, under his black velvet-tailed coat. His top hat presses firmly against his long dark hair and lizard eyes. He throws out his elbow, and Dezerae grabs his arm.

They march forward, as everyone goes crazy, calling out their names. A paparazzi jumps in front of them; they stop, he shoots their picture, and they continue. The guards holding the doors open, smile and nod, as they walk by. Ozzy and Sharon Osbourne, and the Rhoads family, follow behind them.

The dimly lit theater, full, houses the little conversations that slowly diminish. Zyra and Dezerae, take the best seat in the house, as the producer walks to the front, stands at the podium, and waits for everyone's attention.

"Thank you all for coming out tonight, and supporting us. We worked very hard on this film, over the past year. When Zyra came to me, with this idea, I looked at him, with a very disturbed smile, and said, *You are the Anti-Christ.*"

The crowd chuckles.

"He gave me a look I'll never forget, it sent shivers down my spine, and paralyzed me in fear for a second."

Zyra screams out.

"I'm the repenting Anti-Christ now."

Awkward moment.

"Anyway, he said *Jim's dead, and I'm the Lizard King.* You'll understand this statement, after viewing the movie. Well, I've talked enough. *The Lizard* Everybody, starring Zyra Jordonello and Dezerae Nelson, directed by Christopher Sting."

He walks off with the podium, and everybody applauds. The back doors close, as last-minute crew members shuffle in. The house lights go down, and the large red curtains open, as the countdown on the screen begins…*5, 4, 3…*

As the movie fades in, we hear jungle tribal metal, as we see an aerial shot of Southern Florida, sweeping down into the Everglades, following an airboat. Gators, the size of monsters, chomp down, on their prey, as water moccasins, and other creepy tropical animals, flash on the screen.

We close in on a mosquito, flying through the air. It races the airboat, and lands on the extremely short man's nose, driving the airboat, dressed in camouflage; his name is Little Person. He slaps the mosquitos, and blood splatters across the screen. His voice can be heard over the blood.

"Got ya sucker."

He lifts it off by the tiny leg and flicks it into the wind. We follow the dead mosquito through the air, it lands on a rock, protruding from the water. Above the dead mosquito, on a tree branch, a male lizard bites down onto a female lizard's chest. It sticks its hemipenis into her.

Title: "The Lizard." Roll Opening Credits.

The movie continues as people in the dark theater squirm in their seats when they see a priest, played by Ozzy Osbourne, deliver a human lizard, from a woman, in a cathedral church. The disturbed, confused life of the human lizard, played by Zyra, goes through many obstacles. Dezerae grabs onto Zyra's arm and digs her nails into him.

"Owe"

Zyra whispers in her ear.

"What are you doing?"

She turns to him.

"You're insane. Look at you up there..."

Zyra floats off into thought. *I can't believe this is going to be released worldwide next week.* The house screams and jumps as Marilyn Manson's music intensifies, and Zyra's eyes are in agony. Dezerae squeezes his arm again.

"Look at you. You're crazy."

Zyra feels overwhelmed. The last scene keeps everyone on the edge of their seat, as the Lizard hangs on the cross, giving birth to his new species. Dezerae walks out of the church, credits roll. The first credit reads, "This film is dedicated to Garth Blackwood." A new song, "Beware of the Lizard King," sung by Ozzy and Zyra plays over the credits.

The house goes crazy, clapping, cheering, hooting, and hollering, as they give the film a standing ovation. The house lights go up, curtains close. The producer gets back up in front of the crowd.

"Thank you. Thank you all very much. There were so many people involved in this film, that I don't know where to begin. Zyra and Dezerae come up here please."

Everyone cheers, as Zyra turns to Dezerae.

"I don't know what I'm going to say."

She kisses him on the cheek.

"Well, better think of something."

They walk up to the front, as people pat them on their back, and grab their hands. Zyra grabs the microphone, there is dead silence, after hearing the peak of the roar, from the crowd.

"Thank you. I don't know what to say. This movie is...pretty disturbing."

People laugh.

"Right before I came up here, I thought to myself, what are all of you going to think, when I tell you the truth, about how I *truly* feel about this film? Then I thought screw it, don't say anything, but here it is. I hated it."

The crowd laughs even harder.

"I'm serious. Here's my wife."

He hands the microphone to Dezerae. People laugh out of confusion.

"Um…"

Giving Zyra a weird look.

"..you could have explained yourself a little better. I think what he's trying to say..."

Zyra grabs the microphone.

"Ever get tired of all the bullshit? What I've learned, love, is the only thing, that's real. Something, you can't even touch or explain. That quote from Natural Born Killers, *Love kills the demon.*"

Someone screams out.

"Yeah, you are a demon, that's real!"

Everybody laughs, and the same guy screams out again.

"So where's the party?"

Zyra hands the microphone back to Dezerae.

"Um, thank you Zyra, yes, love does kill the demon, but I also think there is a deeper message here. After watching the film on the big screen, I couldn't help, but see the metaphoric correlation, how the sub-plots, intertwined themselves with current events, and yet, paralleled scripture, the dark reflected image of scripture, but scripture."

She hands the microphone back to the Producer.

"Thank you, Dezerae and Zyra. The party will be at the Billboard Live on Sunset. If you don't know where it is, ask the person next to you. See you all there."

They walk off together. Time passes as they all gather outside the after-party. Limos are lined up on Sunset, waiting to drop off their clients. A tall muscle-bound guard, dressed in a yellow suit, greets the guests in line, takes their invitation, and allows them to enter.

The large dance floor is overlooked by two levels. A huge movie screen, plays The Lizard film, as techno rock, blares from the speakers, lining the back wall. The party increases every minute. Everybody grabs their free drinks from the bar, and cocktail waitresses, as others hang out talking, and dancing. A few loosen up, after a couple of drinks, join their friends on the dance floor. Zyra and Dezerae walk in, go upstairs, to the second level, and grab the corner table.

They scoot in and take in the scenery for a moment. With a tap on Zyra's shoulder, Zyra looks over and locks eyes with Nazareth.

"What are you doing here?"

Dezerae looks over at Zyra.

"Who are you talking to?"

Zyra looks back at Dezerae and mumbles under his breath.

"Nazareth."

Dezerae shakes her head in disbelief.

"What does he want?"

"I don't know Dezerae, let me talk to him."

Zyra turns back to Nazareth.

"Why can I see you now?

"Zyra, what film comes to mind, when I say, *Christmas Classic*?"

"Um, I don't know, the Scrooge?"

Nazareth taps his fingers on the table. The sound starts to echo, enveloping Zyra's surroundings.

"Like in the movie Scrooge, you will be visited by three ghosts, spirits of souls, familiar to you. Listen to them, anyone else who can see them is anointed."

Nazareth disappears. Dezerae became annoyed.

"Is he gone?"

"Yes."

"What did he want?"

Zyra grabs her hand.

"He said we will be visited by three ghosts tonight."

Dezerae looks at him.

"What are you talking about?"

He pulls his hand away.

"I don't know, he asked me my favorite Christmas movie, and I said The Scrooge, he said just like him, you'll get visited by three ghosts."

Dezerae getting fed up.

"You know what? I, *I'm done*, you said you weren't doing any more drugs."

"Dezerae, look."

The ghosts of Zalman and Patricia King, appear at the table.

"May we sit?"

Zyra and Dezerae, lock eyes with each other, smile, then greet them, with a warm embrace. They sit down as Zalman King speaks.

"I've done some freaky films in my life, but this one, Zyra, takes the cake."

Zyra laughs, shaking his head in agreement.

"I've spent years studying your film techniques. Your work influenced this film. It makes sense why *you* would appear to us. But how is this made possible?"

Zalman King points behind him, Zyra looks over and sees Nazareth in the corner.

"Nazareth."

Dezerae gets the chills. The waitress comes over.

"What can I get for everyone tonight?"

Patricia asks for an ocean spray vodka and cranberry. Dezerae orders a glass of Beaujolais. Zalman orders an Angel Beer, and Zyra orders a glass of water. The waitress responds.

"I'll be right back."

She walks away as Kelle and Veronica Rhoads approach.

"Great movie Zyra."

"Thank you Kelle, and thank you for the vocal lessons. You improved the hell out of my vocal range. Greatly appreciated. Can't wait for you to hear my new material. Please, guys, have a seat."

They take a seat at their table. Zyra and Dezerae, give them a warm welcome. Zyra is not sure if Kelle and his wife see Zalman and Patricia. Kelle interjects.

"Ozzy and Sharon had to go, but they said to tell you, they loved the movie and Ozzy's role."

Zyra smiles.

"So who are your friends? You guys look familiar."

Zyra introduces everybody.

"Kelle, Veronica, this is Zalman and Patricia King."

Kelle shakes their hands.

"Zalman King. Oh, Red Shoe Diaries, 9 ½ Weeks. Some of my favorites."

Zyra can't believe, Kelle and Veronica can see them, as well, remembering what Nazareth said, *whoever can see them is anointed.* The realization hits Kelle.

"Wait a second, aren't you guys, *deceased*?"

Zalman and Patricia smile. Kelle and Veronica, get the chills, sort of spooked. The waitress comes back, with everyone's drinks, pleasantly surprised to see Kelle and Veronica Rhoads.

"What can I get you guys?"

Kelle orders.

"Coke."

"Diet Coke, please."

The waitress gives them an above average, smile, and walks away. Pointing to Zalman and Patricia, Kelle stops the waitress.

"Wait a second, Ma'am, can you see them?"

The waitress turns around.

"Mr. and Mrs. King? Of course."

She walks away. Kelle shakes it off and asks Zyra.

"This is happening?"

Zalman King confronts Kelle Rhoads.

"Kelle, for whatever reason, God has allowed this encounter. There's one more guest."

Randy Rhoads appears. Kelle and Veronica's mouths drop, and their hearts race. Randy walks over and gives his brother the biggest hug in the world. Tears rise in Kelle's eyes.

"I've missed you so much, little brother."

Randy responds.

"I know, scoot over, let me sit."

They make room for Randy. Now this is a table to be sitting at: Zalman King, Patricia King, Kelle Roads, Veronica Rhoads, Randy Rhoads, Zyra Jordonello, and Dezerae Nelson.

Zyra looks over at Dezerae, back at Randy.

"Randy, it's, it's an honor brother, truly."

Randy smiles.

"So Zyra, you got the best filmmakers in this world and beyond, the best musicians in this world and beyond, sitting at your table. What is it, you think, God wants from this encounter."

Zyra goes deep into thought. Tears rise.

"Um, as you all know, I recently gave my life to Christ. I'm receiving visions, that no one should receive. God has a plan for my life. This new life is fulfilling His Destiny, so I can be a catalyst in His return."

Zalman locks eyes with Zyra.

"Why you, are you the soul saver?"

Zyra thinks about his words.

"Yes, Zalman King, I am a soul saver. I save souls for Jesus Christ."

The waitress brings back their drinks. Zyra nods and continues.

"I found God. I told my producer, I won't promote *Kanniballations*. It's becoming clear to me now. I must work with all of you, to accomplish, what Christ has in store, for this world. I needed to learn music and filmmaking, from your families, not only because you are the best, but because you are a family, who truly inspires out of love, and together we all focus on one path, laid out before us. Forces unite, binding Heaven and earth."

A disturbed look, crosses, Zalman's face, Kelle chuckles.

"I'm a walking dichotomy myself, Zyra, but how can we, help you, from Heaven."

Dezerae interjects.

"Zyra's had life, changing experiences, occur recently."

Zalman expresses concern.

"Another demonic attack?"

Zyra puts his head to his hands.

"It's nothing, forget it, please. Let's talk about something else."

He gulps down a huge amount of water. Randy's curiosity is peaked.

"You got me interested, Zyra."

Zyra places the glass back on the table.

"I've had disturbing dreams lately. Honestly, you are not the first among the dead to visit me. My brother Gabriel visits me as well. I've never been afraid, of *anything* in my life, but this...this is different. Visions manifest right in front of me."

Dezerae jumps in.

"We don't know what to do. The other day, when we were shooting, do you remember the scene toward the end, when the camera closes in on Zyra's eyes?"

Kelle answers.

"Yeah, it even gave me chills."

Zalman looks at him. Dezerae continues.

"Well, during the scene, while we were filming, the devil, or what's his other name, Babel? appeared to him. So that presence you felt, *the chills*, is real."

Zalman shakes his head in disbelief.

"Let me get this straight. You and Zyra believe the devil, Satan, the prince of darkness, the fallen angel himself, is present, captured in your film, and that's why Kelle Rhoads got the chills?"

Everyone cracks up. After the laughter settles, Zyra answers.

"Yes. It's true."

Zalman locks eyes with Kelle.

"Well, you did get the chills, when you realized we were real, so maybe it is true. How about when your brother appeared?"

Kelle nods. The mood changes. An eerie presence is felt as Veronica shouts.

"BOO..."

Everyone jumps and starts laughing. In the distance, Amir is spotted, dressed in black, walking over to their table.

"Am I disturbing anyone?"

Amir looks at each person and ends on Zyra. Kelle notices, he glances over at Zalman, Patricia, and his brother, as if he doesn't see them.

"Congratulations on your film, Zyra. When you get a minute, I would like to speak with you, alone."

Zyra nods.

"I'll find you."

Amir tilts his head, to the side, locks eyes with Zyra, silence. He rubs his hands together, and slowly lifts his head. He walks away without saying a word. Zalman looks over at Zyra.

"Who's the creepy guy?"

Zyra laughs.

"I wish he was my only problem. Lately Z, I've been writing some eccentric music, Randy, I wish I could record you playing some guitar. I need to get into the studio."

Kelle quickly responds.

"That's what I'm talking about."

Veronica interjects.

"What about *Kanniballations*? It's your best work. That's the album, he helped you on."

Zyra firmly states.

"Thank you, I know, we'll just keep making better and better music."

He downs the last sip of his water and gets up.

"I'll be right back."

Zyra walks away. Zalman looks over at Dezerae with a concerned look.

"Isn't his album number three, on the charts?"

"Yeah."

"I've never heard of such a thing, *I can't promote my number three album, because I found God.* Wouldn't you think, God is the one who gave him, a number three album?"

Patricia hits him on the shoulder.

"Don't judge him."

Zalman shakes his head.

"I'm not, I just don't understand."

Kelle interjects.

"I may have to agree with you, but I don't know."

Zyra walks downstairs, and spots Amir talking to a supermodel. Sting passes behind them, down another flight of stairs, leading to the restrooms. Zyra walks over to Amir and taps him on the shoulder. Amir turns around.

"Do you want to speak now?"

The music blares, Amir reads his lips and answers.

"Let's go downstairs, where we don't have to scream, at each other."

They find a psychedelic purple couch downstairs, in the waiting area, and take a seat. Amir starts.

"I'm apologizing for not taking you seriously. But it struck me *very funny* that you out of all people, would tell me those words."

Zyra just listens. Amir leans forward and rubs his hands together, again.

"I will take back the subpoena if you agree to do the tour."

Zyra shakes his head, no.

"What do you want, Zyra?"

Zyra finally speaks.

"I want to record a new album, pretend like this one, never existed."

Amir clenches his fists, anger, and frustration.

"You don't make sense to me. The whole world loves your album."

Zyra answers.

"Parents hate it. Christians hate it. Anyone with any kind of morality hates it. It tears down the walls of decency. It decays the mind of the youth."

Amir tries another approach.

"We are all damned, Zyra."

Zyra gives him a blank stare, Amir raises his hands, to say forget about it.

> "Fine, you don't have to start the show, eating the heart or brains of Christ. Eat whatever the hell you want, just do the goddamn tour."

Zyra tunes into Amir, trying to penetrate the walls, blocking him from seeing the truth.

> "You don't get it, man. My message needs to be positive. No more death and destruction. I need to enlighten souls not bring them down."

Amir strains for words.

> "You...you're off your rocker, man. You don't know what you're talking about. Enlighten souls? Decayed youth, sells."

Zyra stands up.

> "That's my point. I don't care what sells. I care about doing the right thing, and the money will follow. God provides."

Amir stands up and throws down his bottle, it *shatters* on the floor. Security runs over, and Amir, full of rage, leaps for Zyra, like a vampire attacking its prey, screaming a hellacious roar. Zyra raises his arms to defend himself. On the big screen behind them, the lizard attacks his victim, rips off his face, and eats it.

Amir *slices* Zyra's face with his full finger ring, and blood gushes from the wound. The lizard's yellow, green eyes and orange pupils, fill the screen. Riding the adrenaline, Zyra instantly grabs Amir's wrists, rage stares him down to the ground.

"You still want me to do your tour!?"

Security jumps on Zyra's back and wrestles him to the ground. Other security guards do the same to Amir. Everyone gathers around, to see the commotion. Dezerae's voice can be faintly heard.

"Zyra."

Zyra backs off holding his face. The faceless victim, on the screen, grabs his face. Amir ravenously breaks from his cage, the guard's grip, and screams out to Zyra.

"I'll see you in court. I made you. I'll break you."

Security walks Amir, out of the building. The club manager approaches Zyra with a damp towel and presses it against the wound.

"I apologize. I didn't know you had bad blood, otherwise, I would not have let him in."

Zyra shakes his head.

"I know. It's alright. Where's my wife?"

Dezerae squeezes her way in.

"Are you okay? Baby, let me see."

Zyra, pulls the blood-soaked cloth, from his face. The sliced flesh, two inches or so in length, started at his cheekbone, and ending diagonally down by his lips. Dezerae screams.

"Oh my God, we need to go to emergency, now. You need stitches. Keep pressure on it."

She guides him out of the club, into the limo, waiting outside the front door. They hop into the back seat, and Dezerae tells the driver.

"Bring us to Cedars Sinai."

The limo driver closes their door, jumps into the driver's seat, and pulls away. Kelle, Veronica, Randy Rhoads, Zalman King, and Patricia watch the limo pull away. Randy turns to Zalman.

"Another day in paradise."

Randy hugs Veronica, and then his brother goodbye. Zalman King, Patricia King, and Randy Rhoads twinkle away as heavenly stardust. Nazareth stands behind Kelle Rhoads. Nazareth's wings open, he flaps them, rises from the ground, and follows Zyra to the hospital.

A toast from Heaven, may your will align with God's Will, blessings upon you.

Chapter 25

SHROUDED DENSITY

"Controversial Rock'n'roll, Zyra Jordonello claims, *I found God.*"

Broadcasts over the news, radio airwaves, and printed on the front page of the Los Angeles Times, with a close-up of Zyra's bloody face. Zyra is sitting on the toilet, the next morning reading the newspaper. He reads the article.

"Last night, after the premiere of Christopher Sting's, *The Lizard*, held at Mann's Chinese Theater in Hollywood, California, at the after party, Amir, CEO of *Haunted Shadow Records,* drew blood from his client's face. Amir claims Zyra Jordonello will not tour, his number three album, *Kanniballations*, costing Haunted Shadow Records, millions. Zyra has claimed, he *found God,* and will not, have anything to do, with the violent nature, of this project. Zyra was taken to Cedar Sinai, late last night, after Amir sliced open his face. He has seventeen stitches, down his cheek. Amir comments, 'I will sue him for everything he's got.' No comment, yet, has been made from Zyra, whether or not, he will counter sue, Amir, for the assault."

Zyra folds up the newspaper and throws it down on the bathroom tile. He pulls toilet paper from the roll, and wipes. After flushing the toilet, he washes his hands, and lifts the gauze, covering the stitches.

"I can't believe he *scarred* my face."

Zyra realizes he needs to call Robin.

"Hey, Honey."

The morning sun, pours through the glass window, onto Dezerae, still lying in bed.

"Yeah."

Zyra still examines the stitches in the mirror.

"What did I need to talk to Robin about?"

She thinks to herself. *Just look in the mirror.*

"Amir jacked you up, remember?"

"I'm talking about from the other day when he called back and talked to you. Oh yeah, forget it. I remember."

She sincerely asks.

"Zyra are you alright?"

Her eyes remain closed, she screams out.

"Don't touch your stitches. I don't care if they itch. I have to see your beautiful face every day, so you better do, what the doctor tells you. Don't take off the gauze, yet, you can't get it wet, remember?"

He turns his head and nods as she comments.

"And don't give me that look."

He puts the gauze back on.

"Yes, mother."

He opens the shower door, turns on the water, adjusts it to the perfect heat, and steps into the running water. It slams against his chest, racing down his stomach, and legs making his flesh red. The steam rises, from his body, he grabs the soap, shower sponge, and soaps up. Dezerae surprisingly opens the shower door, steps in, and presses her naked body, against his.

She grabs what she wants, squeezing gently, as it ripens in her hand. The soap rinses off his body, she kisses his lips, and the water moistens their flesh. She kisses down his chin, her nails scratching down his back, exciting him even more. She brings him into her and bites down on his nipple.

Goose bumps rise on his chest, she slowly kisses down his stomach, and rubs her cheek, against his lower abdomen. Reaching around, she caresses his backside, her soft voluptuous lips, pressing against his shaven skin, just below his bellybutton. Her fingers tickle, between his thighs, teasing him even further, and his skin tightens.

Zyra's head falls back, into the water, soaking his long black hair. The steam rises, clouding the glass door, as her passionate lips, drive eagerly around him, burning with desire.

Ecstasy engulfs his being, his fist tightens, against the tiled wall. He strokes her hair, words rise from his soul.

"Oh my God."

His stiff body relaxes, and his thoughts drift, into another universe. The water rushes down her face, he begins to breathe normally. She looks up at him.

"I missed you."

He smiles.

"I missed you too."

She stands up, presses herself into him, and they kiss again.

The phone rings, and as they both let the answering machine pick it up, Zyra's voice can be heard.

"If you have reached this voice-activated device, we are not here, or we don't want to answer your call, either way, leave a message."

It beeps, Amir's thick Spanish voice, speaks.

"Zyra, Amir. Let's talk. Let's work this out, without the officials. Call me."

Dezerae asks.

"Are you going to call him back?"

Zyra thinks about it.

"Yeah, I told you, he doesn't want the police involved. There's too much at stake. I know everything about his company. I'll call him back, if he drops the charges I won't contact the police."

They step out of the shower, dry off, and get dressed for the day. Zyra picks up the phone and calls Robin.

"May I speak to Robin, please? Zyra. Thank you."

Inside Robin's office, hangs his Law degree from Harvard University. Robin is a mid-western-looking guy, from Indiana. His brown hair parted, to the side, his thick coke bottle glasses, high school nerd stereo-type. On his desk, sits the Los Angeles Times. Headshots of many famous clients, cover his walls, and he sits at his desk, using his computer. Over the loudspeaker, Stacy's voice arises.

"Mr. Urltimer, Zyra is on the phone for you."

Robin tells her to connect him, and greets him with a warm welcome, as he lays the newspaper, with Zyra's image, onto his desk.

"Hello Zyra, had an interesting night I see. So, how can I help you?"

Zyra sits at his office desk, staring out the window, overlooking the ocean.

"Amir just left me a message. I have a feeling he'll drop the charges if I don't contact the authorities. What's your advice?"

Robin grabs his pen, and jots down some numbers, on a scrap piece of paper.

> "Well the way I see it, Zyra, you cost him about twenty-five to thirty million dollars. For him to eat this, will set him back a few weeks. He could plug the rest of the money, from your tour, into a new band, and make his money back, eventually. So give him a call, hear what he has to say, and if he's smart, he'll drop the charges. Pretty ironic, anyway, call me back, and let me know how it goes."

Zyra hangs up the phone, and looks at Dezerae, handing him a cup of coffee, and sipping her own.

> "Thank you."

She sits down on the lazy boy, next to his desk.

> "Well? What did Robin have to say?"

He takes a sip of his coffee.

> "He thinks I should call him back. He thinks if Amir, puts the rest of the money, that was not used for 'Kanniballations,' into another band, he could break even. It will save him, the hassle of going to court, paying the fees, keeping me quiet, about all the dirt I know."

Dezerae sees in her mind, a shroud flowing down, covering a pile of dirt. She responds.

> "It's almost like, we are shrouding his density."

Zyra looks at her with an impressed smile.

> "Wow, that was very profound. Shrouded density. I like it."

She hands him the phone.

"Call him."

He dials the number.

"Amir, please. Zyra returned his call. Thank you. Amir, it's Zyra."

In Amir's office, in front of his desk, sits those two guys from before. Amir and Zyra work out the details, then Amir sums it up.

"...So we have a deal, I drop the charges, and you don't contact the police. I'll take the blow for your tour. I lost control, it cost me."

Zyra agrees.

"Yeah, that's fine."

Amir drops his feet, from on top of his desk.

"Good. Legal forms will be mailed to you tomorrow. I don't want to hear your voice on my phone again."

Amir hangs up the phone, grabs the remote, and blasts these two guys' albums, dark eerie death sounds, fill the air. Amir turned into Zyra's mind and picked up on the phrase, *Shrouded Density*. Amir sits up and raises his pointer.

"...that's it. I'll you *Shrouded Density*. It's brilliant."

The lead singer looks over at the guitarist, shaking his head.

"Shrouded Density? That sounds cool, man."

The guitarist responds.

"It's like, we're covering up our fate, or something?"

Amir demeans him.

"No, you idiot, not destiny, density. It means ignorance. To cover up your ignorance. Now get out."

They exit his office. He turns off their music and stares out his window.

Chapter 26

INTANGIBLE REALITY

A few days pass while Zyra and Dezerae lay low, as *Kanniballations* takes flight, and reaches number one. The newspapers, Television, and Magazines plaster Zyra all over the media, hyping him up as another modern-day, anti-Christ, even though, Zyra made his position clear to the media. His agent is overwhelmed with calls. The more fame Zyra receives, the more controversy spreads, as he and Dezerae spend time in morning mass, continuing to live a low profile. His agent calls at least twice a day, with new information.

Dr. Von Hildonberg receives calls about Zyra and leaves them messages as well. While the world is Zyra crazy, Zyra and Dezerae drive east to Big Bear, a cozy mountain resort to get away. About two and a half hour drive from Los Angeles. Inside a wooden cabin overlooking the lake, they lay by candlelight watching the news. A stand-in for Holly Gossip reports.

"I'm Turner Dee, reporting live from outside the Cine dome on Sunset Strip. 'The Lizard' grossed over 20.9 million dollars opening weekend, still Zyra Jordonello and

Dezerae Nelson, have not yet commented, on the film's release creating pandemonium across the Nation."

Zyra turns to Dezerae.

"They didn't look here."

"...He is keeping a low profile"

As his agent Todd Deader, comments.

"With a number one album, number one movie, and best-selling book, according to the New York Times, Zyra has been on top of the world, driving chaos and spreading evil. A tragedy has hit our news station. Reporter Holly Gossip is in Miami, where her thirteen-year-old nephew, Jose Gonzalez, stabbed his parents to death, while they were sleeping. He said, 'Kanniballations,' Sacred Witch's latest album, 'is my inspiration.' Jose believes Satan spoke to him through the lyrics of the song, 'Eat the Dead.' He was found eating their flesh. Here are the lyrics that created this little monster."

Zyra looks over at Dezerae in disbelief.

"Rise destroy the spine

Claim your throne

I'll make you mine

Chop off your guardian's head

Drink their blood and

Eat the dead"

An image of Holly Gossip is shown at the funeral. Tears fill Zyra and Dezerae's eyes, sickness rises from his gut, he rushes to the bathroom, getting sick in the toilet. Dezerae sits on the bed paralyzed, by what she just saw. The silence in the room is eventually filled with a sizzle, coming from the television. A cold dark presence sweeps through the room, Dezerae glances down and sees a thick black cloud, creep across the room.

It serpentines through the air, into the bathroom, where Zyra is leaning over the sink, washing out his mouth. This presence rises his spine and manipulates his aura. He gazes into his eyes, and through the mirror, a demon of great power disfigures his face. Zyra's eyes rush with blood, anger encompasses his spirit. He throws his hands down to the sink and tries to stop the spinning. The demon confronts him, with a very high-pitched piercing tone.

"If you answer questions, I explain ways of the world."

Zyra fears for his soul, "ways of world," float around his brain.

"How do you weigh out a pound of fire?"

Zyra looks confused and does not respond.

"How do you measure a bushel of wind?"

Again, no answer.

"How do you bring back a day that has passed?"

Zyra answers.

"No man can answer these questions?"

The demon speaks in Arabic. Zyra discerns his words.

"How can you ask, 'Why does this happen to me?"

The demon leaps out of his eyes, into the mirror, being brought back down into hell. Zyra gets weak in the knees, and falls to the ground, crying. Dezerae runs in, and puts her arm around him, squeezing him tightly.

"It'll be ok."

Zyra looks up at her.

"No, it won't. A kid killed his parents because of me. How many more have to die because of ME?"

He breaks down even more.

"It could be years, before the evil I spread, diminishes."

Dezerae comforts him.

"It has to play out. That's how God works. We just pray, that people will not act upon evil impulses when they are being entertained by you. You need to start producing positive messages, for His glory not your own."

Zyra wipes the tears from his eyes.

"I'm sorry, baby. I should have listened. The truth is slowly revealed to me. I feel like a paranoid schizophrenic. Where's that inner peace, you talk about?"

Dezerae sits down, Indian-style, on the floor, in front of him.

"Your soul has to cleanse itself. Tonight we'll pray to St. Michael, the Arch Angel. I believe he will help you get through these times."

Zyra drops his face to his hands and grabs his chin.

"Ok, I'm hungry, let's go into town, and grab some food."

"I love you, Sweetheart."

The sun settles, dropping over the lake, as beautiful vibrant colors stream across the dark blue sky. Zyra and Dezerae eat at a nearby Country Inn, and their waitress, a young sweet local, recognizes them.

"Oh my God, you're Zyra and Dezerae. Oh my God, Oh my God. I never thought in a million years I would be serving you. My friends are going to freak out. I need to gain composure. Ok, I can do this. So, what would you guys like to eat?"

Zyra looks over at Dezerae, waiting for her to order. Just as she's about to order, the waitress speaks again.

"Do you like chicken, 'cause we have the best chicken pot pie, in all of Southern California? It is so good, trust me."

Dezerae responds.

"Alright, you sold me, I'll take the chicken pot pie."

Zyra interjects.

"Well, if you're that excited over the chicken pot pie, I'd be a fool not to order it."

Her hands shake, as she writes down the order.

"I'm sorry, I'm just a bit nervous. What would you like to drink?"

Dezerae orders.

"A coke please."

The waitress looks over at Zyra.

"And for you, Zyra?"

"What kind of beer do you have on tap?"

She thinks for a moment.

"Bud, Bud light, Coors, Coors light, and our import is California Angel."

Zyra raises his eyebrow.

"I'll try the California Angel."

She adds.

"It's a lager."

Zyra smiles.

"Ok."

She excitedly repeats back the order.

"So we have two chicken pot pies, a coke, and a California Angel. I'll be right back with your drinks."

She walks away talking to herself.

"I can't believe I'm serving Zyra and Dezerae. Thank you, God."

They overhear her excitement as Zyra laughs.

"Our friend is pretty star-struck."

"She's cute leave her alone."

The waitress brings out the drinks. A few minutes pass, and Zyra orders another beer, for his meal. A group huddles in the doorway of the kitchen, watching her serve them. The waitress puts down the beer, and hands him a magazine picture, with an image of himself as the lizard.

"Could you, please, sign this, please?"

The old guy, who must be the owner, screams out in now a silent restaurant.

"Don't bother the customers."

"I know I'm being extremely rude right now, but if I don't do this now, I will cream my shorts."

Zyra looks at Dezerae and laughs.

"Well, we don't want that to happen, so why not spare the girl the orgasm, and sign the piece of paper, Zyra."

Zyra signs the magazine. After their meal, Zyra and Dezerae, walk through the quaint little town. The high-contrast moon, lights the shadows, haunting the night. As they pull up to their cabin, in Dezerae's Range Rover, Zyra gets out of the car, laughing, obviously having a good time. He throws his arm around her and kisses her passionately.

"I love you."

He whispers wholeheartedly. She looks at him with mysterious welcoming eyes, as the moonlight pours down upon her face.

"I've never heard you say those words to me, with as much love, as you did right now."

His smile brightens, happy she picked up on the sincerity.

"Did you want me to stop?"

She grabs him and brings him closer.

"Are you crazy? Those words are candy for my soul."

He throws her up against a tree, which overlooks a pond in the front yard. The owls raise their voices, to the sky as the squirrels, fly from one tree to the next. The dim lights on either end of the cabin door, silhouette them, as he lifts her hands, above her head, and unbuttons her shirt with his mouth. He bites down on her neck, breathing heavily as she takes it in. He rips open her bra and grabs her breast. She lifts her left leg around him, then the other. He grabs her hips underneath her skirt, rips off her underwear, unzips his pants, and enters home.

He makes love to her aggressively, as she claws her nails down his back. He turns her around, makes her grab the tree, bends her over, and continues his rhythmic movement. At the moment of reaching ecstasy, Zyra receives a flash image of himself, making love to the woman, from the "Nephilim Party." He pulls out and pushes her away.

"What's wrong?"

Zyra does not know what to say.

"Nothing."

She turns around and pulls up her underpants.

"Why'd you pull out? I almost came."

"Sorry."

She pulls herself together, and walks passed him into the cabin. Zyra collects his thoughts, pushes the memory away, throws her on top of the bed, and gets on top of her, making it impossible for her to move. She stops him, puts her finger over her lips, rolls him over, and straddles him.

"We're gonna pray."

Zyra sighs.

"Right now. Can't it wait?"

She nods, gets off of him, and grabs the incense, candles, and her rosary beads from the bag. She turns to him.

"Do you have a lighter?"

He reaches into his pants and pulls out a lighter.

"Thank you."

She lights the candles and incense.

"So, what are we doing instead of making love?"

She walks over and plays spiritual hymn music on the little boom box, they brought from home.

"We have to get into the spirit before we can pray. This atmosphere helps us get to that level."

Zyra looks at her quizzically.

"I was getting into the spirit just fine. Sounds like some Wiccan ceremony, though."

She looks at him and decides to mess with his head.

"I know, and the three wise men brought Jesus frankincense. So what's your point?"

He laughs at her quick-witted remark and repeats what she said with sarcasm. She sits down Indian style and asks him to do the same. She grabs his right hand with her left hand, as they sit facing each other. After grabbing the other hand, she walks him through some breathing exorcizes to get them in tune. Dezerae's soft rustic voice, opens spiritual pathways, within their meditation.

"Now that you have entered this new world, in the distance, picture yourself standing behind the brightness. Your complexion, becomes apparent, as you step forward, and see St. Michael, the Arch Angel. Tell me, what he says to you."

Zyra jerks, as energy rushes through his body, and his spirit elevates to a different place within his mind.

"I see myself flapping my wings, as he comes closer."

Zyra jerks back again, then continues.

"He lands in front of me, like an eagle on top of a mountain."

Dezerae quickly responds in a low tone.

"Ask him to give you the strength to conquer your demons."

Zyra pulls away from Dezerae, she fights him, squeezing his hands tighter. Zyra takes in the information, from the Arch Angel, and delivers it to Dezerae.

"There's going be a meteor shower tonight, between moonset and dawn, three or four in the morning."

Dezerae, not expecting him to say that, is taken aback, and left with nothing to say. Zyra settles into his body, from his highly erect seated position, when the spirit within the flame of the candle, St. Michael, rises, manipulating its movements.

She takes in a deep breath and tells Zyra she will be counting back from three, when she reaches one, he will be awakened with a new direction.

"Three, two, one, wake up."

Zyra slowly opens his eyes and takes a deep breath.

"So are you ready to start?"

Dezerae refrains from laughing.

"We already did it."

"Did what?"

She releases his hands, and stretches out her legs and back, lifting her arms above her head. He gets up and sits on the bed, Dezerae follows.

"You just said to me, that there will be a meteor shower, at three or four in the morning."

"When did I say that?"

"Just now."

She replies, with a frightened strange look across her face. Zyra curls up, pain shoots up his stomach, and he screams out. In agony, Dezerae leans into him.

"Are you alright? What's wrong?"

He relaxes.

"Oh my God, that just felt like somebody stabbed me in the stomach."

He throws his arms back, onto the bed, and lays down. She opens the closet door, takes out her white lace lingerie, and puts it on. Through Zyra's eyes, her face elongates, distorts, then goes back to normal.

She dances around the room, waving her arms delicately, through the air, to the soothing music. Her elegance and beauty radiate, driving him to want her again, but with more animalistic tendencies. He takes off his shirt, calms himself down, and lights a joint.

"I think I'm going through withdrawal."

"Withdrawal of what? you smoke, you drink."

He sits on the bed with the ashtray, watching his wife perform. She hums her song, to the music, and stretches out her arm, asking him to join her. Zyra keeps the joint in his mouth, and joins her, a very per evocative dance. They move in unison, never missing a beat. He spins her around, pulls her back into him, they embrace with a kiss, he gazes into her eyes, and seduces her soul.

He grabs her face, his fingers stretch out, caressing her cheeks. Her smile lights up the room, illuminating the night. She closes her eyes, drops her head back and around, then opens them up again.

A red rose is pressed against her face, when she opens her eyes, causing tears to arise. She takes in the scent of the rose, with grace and elegance, enjoying it, as if it were the last rose she would ever smell.

"It's beautiful."

She grabs it gently, brings it to her heart, and passionately kisses him. He allows the feeling to overwhelm his senses, taking in every touch, every ounce of pleasure, known to flesh and spirit. She brings her finger to his lips, he kisses it, sucks on it, and quietly whispers.

"I love you."

He releases her finger, places the rose in a cup of water, opens a bottle of red wine, and pours three glasses. They sit in a circle, as she puts the extra glass of wine, into a space. Zyra unzips his pants and takes off his jeans. He throws them to the side, and she reaches over, grabs the rosary beads and candle, and places them in the middle. She turns off the lights, the candles and moonlight's elegant glow illuminate the atmosphere. Zyra's curiosity is peaked.

"What are we doing now?"

"My right palm will face down, on your left palm, and vice versa. The right hand, gives energy, while the left hand, receives it."

Zyra laughs.

"Ok, where did you learn this?"

She answers.

"I read books. It will bring back, that inner peace, you were talking about."

He squeezes her hand.

"What else do you do, that I don't know about?"

She smiles, Zyra sees her smile, transform into an evil grin. Zyra shakes off the manipulation and finds her sweet face again.

"Why do we have three glasses of wine?"

Zyra takes a sip. She answers with sincere faith.

"Jesus."

Zyra, wide-eyed.

"Whose our spirit guide?"

The flame flickers, glowing, accenting her facial features, and eyes. Her sweet serene voice lingers above the flame.

"The Holy Spirit."

Chills, rise Zyra's spine.

"I just got the chills. I don't want to conjure up another demon."

She reassures him.

"Zyra it'll be fine. Before we start, I want to switch the music."

She gets up, flips through the music, and finds Pope John Paul II, music album. The soothing spiritual sounds, elevate the presence in the room, as she sits back down. She blesses herself.

"In the name of the Father, and of the Son, and the Holy Spirit. Amen."

She grabs his hands and takes a deep breath.

"Just relax, breathe deep with me."

Zyra does.

"We will take ten deep breaths. Close your eyes, and with each breath, imagine falling deeper into love."

Zyra closes his eyes, takes in a deep breath, then another, then another. The smell of Nag Champa incense, calms his heart rate, as he listens to Dezerae, visualizing everything she says. Her words are like crisp, cold water, flowing over a stream of rocks, refreshing to his soul.

"Allow yourself to feel the energy, circulate through my body and into yours. Welcome it, give it strength, let it pass through. As it passes through us, we enter into the spirit. Find that place, within your soul, that gives you your inner freedom."

Zyra imagines the sky and ocean, moving rapidly, as the sun spins, and is pulled back from the center, opening the sky, as it bundles around. The wind picks up pace, in a circular motion, faster and faster. Dizziness surrounds chaos, as the impurities funnel through, creating a little tornado. This tornado grows by the second, twice its size, every second.

Now even faster, the monstrosity of this tornado, cannot be described in words. It connects the sky, to the water. Zyra sees flashes of different familiar faces, going through this same cleansing experience. Moments of confusion unravel, revealing his inner thoughts. Confusion becomes clarity. Revelation after revelation, untangled in his mind. He thinks *this experience is different than the others. I see what happens around me. I should be scared but I'm not. I even understand my visions.* The fear dissipates.

Inside Dezerae's mind, she enters sleep, and sees Zyra in her mind's eye, with his arms out-spread like Jesus Christ, lingering above the ocean. The wind blows through his long flowing hair, as peace surrounds him.

Excitement starts to build, as love overwhelms her body, mind, and soul. She wants to touch him, to be with him, but her thoughts run wild, in the wind, escaping her mind, like a lost child. She sees unicorns galloping towards her from the sky, as the ocean waves break into song waiting for their arrival. The moisture drips down from Zyra's pores, Birds take flight and form into eagles, messengers of God. Mountain tops, in the distance, explode with inner life, as the lava flows down the mountain, forming into dancing skeletons, their bones are free of constriction.

Boa constrictors wrap around Dezerae's ankles, slithering up her legs, waiting for their moment to enter, sending her into complete horrific ecstasy. Her arms elongate and form into wings, and she stares off into the horizon. She feels her crippled mind, healing, and her dying eyes, reflect the sun, in his eyes.

Zyra's eyes liquefy, into the silver mesh, as they capture her soul, transforming her thoughts, and allowing her to believe, the impossible. Dezerae glides through the air, hypnotized by Zyra. She enters into the invisible bubble, encircling him, protecting them. Their hearts beat as one, her arms wrapped around his body, and the water below them rages into a fiery ocean. Faces of demons, press against the bottom of the bubble, faintly hearing their piercing screams. Zyra and Dezerae raise their arms and intertwine.

They kiss magically, becoming one, as a baby fetus with wings, grows in Dezerae's womb. The flame below continues to dance as Zyra and Dezerae snap out of the vision and find themselves in each other's arms, hovering above the lit candle. The second reality hits, they fall to the ground, putting out the flame, and knocking over their glasses. Zyra snaps back from the shock.

"We just levitated."

Dezerae looks at him in fear. She tries to speak, but her tongue is mute. Her eyes water, tears drip down her cheeks, and she cradles her legs into her chest, curling into a small tight ball. Not knowing what to expect, a cold chill passes through. Zyra doesn't move anything but his eyes, as they pan from the left, to the right, and back again. He stands up and turns on the light. The illuminated darkness disappears, he grabs another joint, lights up, and doesn't say a word. Dezerae prays.

"St. Michael the Arch Angel, defend us in battle, be our protection against the wickedness and snares of the devil. May God rebuke him I humbly pray to thou prince of the heavenly host. By the power of God Thrust into hell Satan and all the other evil spirits who prowl around the world seeking the ruin of souls. Amen."

Zyra looks at Dezerae.

"Think that'll work?"

She stares back at him, lost in a glare, speaking very slowly.

"That has never happened to me before. It was incredible. Beyond words."

Zyra breaks out with laughter.

"This is the weirdest thing that ever took place."

He takes another drag off his joint, walks over to the phone, and picks it up.

"Who are you calling?"

He dials their home phone number.

"I'm checking our messages."

He punches in a code, and listens to the messages, Todd Deader, Zyra's agent, left three panicked messages.

"Zyra where the hell are you? Why haven't you returned my calls? Have you seen the news? You're all over the television, man. Everywhere I turn, it's you, and no one seems to know, where the hell you are. They all blame me cause, I'm your agent, now call me. We booked you for Letterman, in two days. Your flight leaves tomorrow. Call me."

Zyra hangs up the phone, nonchalantly.

"Who was that?"

Zyra drops his head.

"We have to leave tomorrow morning. Todd booked us on a flight to New York, to do the Letterman Show, in two days."

Her confused smile questions him.

"I thought you didn't want to do interviews?"

He shrugs his shoulders and looks up at her.

"It's inevitable, time to face my demons."

She grabs his hand.

"I'll be next to you the whole time."

"Thank you Dezerae, I need your support. It's my mess, and now I have to clean it up. I can't bring back Holly's sister, but I can apologize to her publicly."

Dezerae hugs him.

"I'm here for you, Luv bug. I love you."

He squeezes her tighter.

"Thank you, Babe, I love you."

They get their last night of peace before the storm hits.

Upon the witch's glow, heavenly snow dresses the soul, vampire bite, oh this sacred night.

Chapter 27

NEW YORK

Meanwhile, the earth is in between two worlds, the place where spirits run free, fighting principality, almost reaching its peak in the battle, and those completely oblivious, to the spiritual warfare happening around them. Zyra, on many occasions, has been called to join Nazareth, in fighting and destroying, demons in their path. Nazareth finally explains to him, his life spiritually up until this point.

"Zyra, many angels and spirits have been sent, to help you complete God's Will, for your life. Souls once on this earth, were allowed to visit you, to give you the faith, and courage you need, to do what God has asked of you. Your willingness, to align God's will, with your own, is why Heaven can progress. Each of us is called to align our will with God's Will. When we do this, miracles take place, as you have witnessed in your life. The battle of principalities is fought for you. This is God's Holy War, not yours!"

The physical manifestations, resulting from this warfare, have finally given Zyra the strength he needs to stay off drugs and alcohol. With this extra amount of energy, gushing through his pores, the sun releases its wings, and drives out the spirit bridge, being pulled by thousands of Angels.

Directly below them, Dragon-Whale continues his plot, in destroying the bridge. The tower of bees continues to rise, on par to intersect the bridge. Within Zyra's soul, he notices as he cleanses his soul, fasting from demons, Angels conquer them, but when Zyra gives in to temptations, many demons conquer Angels. This same principle exists for each, and every living soul.

An airplane carrying Zyra and Dezerae, fly through this spiritual battlefield, on their way to the east coast. Zyra stares out his window. The Statue of Liberty below them, their plane finally arrives at J.F.K. airport. They grab their suitcases from baggage claim, as their driver, Curtis, a tall slim, African American male, greets them.

"Mr. and Mrs. Jordonello, Hello, I'm Curtis, your limo driver, for the Tonight Show, with David Letterman. May I take those from you?"

Curtis grabs their luggage, and opens the door, the cold brisk air, reddens their cheeks. They walk to the limo parked in front.

Curtis places the luggage in the trunk and opens the door for them. Dezerae grabs Zyra's arm, and squeezes it, trying to keep warm. They enter the limo.

"I didn't know it would be this cold here. I guess we get spoiled in California."

Curtis responds.

"From what I see in the movies, California seems like paradise all year long."

Zyra adds.

"Trust me it's just the movies."

Curtis laughs and shuts the door. He enters the driver's seat and lowers the window separating them.

"Excuse me, Mr. Jordonello?"

Zyra responds.

"Zyra."

"Zyra, there's a brand new Harley Davidson waiting for you at the hotel. Mr. Letterman knows how much you love your motorcycle. I will also be on call for you, this entire trip."

Zyra smiles and squeezes Dezerae's hand.

"Thank you, Curtis."

The limo drives through the streets of New York City, they take in the lights, standing up through the open moon roof. Curtis pulls up to Waldorf Astoria, on 301 Park Avenue and 50th. Curtis opens the door, and hands their bags to the bellboy, Curtis hands them his card.

"You can reach me on my cell. There will be an itinerary for you at the front desk. I have you scheduled for a pickup, tomorrow at two pm. Have a nice night and welcome to New York."

Zyra hands him a tip and says goodbye.

"No Sir, I can't take that."

Curtis gives the money back to Zyra. Zyra and Dezerae approach the front desk and check in. This elegant, four and a half star, Hotel creates a fruitful ambiance. The flamboyant Russian connoisseur greets them.

"Hello, welcome to the Waldorf Astoria. I am Serge. How can I help you?"

Zyra places his hands up on the counter, and answers.

"My name is Zyra Jordonello and this is my wife..."

Serge cuts him off and raises his hands like he wants to caress Dezerae's face.

"...Ah yes, your beautiful wife Dezerae. You are even more beautiful in person."

Dezerae blushes.

"Thank you."

Serge drops his hands and continues.

"I have your agenda for the Tonight Show. They made sure we put you up in our best suit."

Zyra smiles.

"Thank you."

He hands him a blue shiny folder with, the "The Tonight Show With David Letterman" logo on it, and two room keys. Serge winks at Zyra.

"Your room is on the top floor overlooking Park Avenue. Our bellboy will show you the way. Anything you need, to make your stay more comfortable, please call me at the front desk. Thank you and have a nice evening."

Dezerae holds in her laughter, at his charming feminine gestures. She looks over at Zyra and whispers.

"I think Serge likes you. Did you catch that subtle wink?"

Zyra squeezes her hand, returning the subtle disposition. They follow the bellboy to the room. Upon entering the room, Zyra tips the bellboy, he nods acknowledging his gratitude. Zyra shuts the door and jumps onto the bed.

"I'm exhausted."

Dezerae opens the curtains, exposing Park Avenue below.

"Look at this view. It looks like it may even snow."

The grey overcast and icy ground chills the air. Zyra gets up and looks at the view.

"It's beautiful. You don't see this in LA. Maybe we should move here."

Dezerae surprisingly looks at him.

"Are you crazy? I can't take the cold."

"Ah, my poor baby, can't take the cold brisk air."

"Shut up."

Zyra looks around the room, enters the bathroom, and calls for her to come in.

"Hey, check this out."

She enters the bathroom.

"Yes! A hot tub. Turn it on. We'll go in before we grab dinner."

Zyra turns on the jet spays, and rips off his clothes. Dezerae laughs and undresses, she drops one toe in, and feels the warmth, allowing the chills to rise on her body. She steps into the hot tub and sits down. She spreads her arms out and takes in every second. Zyra does the same.

"So where do you want to eat?"

She stares into his eyes and runs her finger up his leg.

"I want the best sushi from the Atlantic, money can buy, in New York City."

Zyra leans back, grabs the phone by the tub, and calls the front desk.

"Serge, hey, it's Zyra. It's perfect. Listen, where is the best Sushi restaurant in all of New York City? Azuma Sushi Restaurant in Hartsdale. Can you make an eight o'clock dinner reservation for us? Thank you, oh Curtis, our limo driver said to...you have his number, great thanks again. One more thing, Curtis also said that there is a Harley Davidson here for me. I'll see how I feel. Thank you. Bye."

He hangs up the phone, Dezerae gets on top of him, and they make love in the Jacuzzi. He locks eyes with her, and whispers.

"Azuma Sushi sounds good."

She growls at him.

"You sound good."

She dives down and kisses his neck, water splashes out of the tub, soaking the white tile floor.

* * *

Meanwhile, at the very desolate, Miami International Airport, Holly Gossip stands alone, on her cell with her assistant, holding a carry-on.

"The Tonight Show. Perfect. Thank you very much. Book me on the next flight."

A sweet evil grin crosses her face, she hangs up the phone and walks inside the Airport. Zyra and Dezerae are back in their hotel, down at the bar, having a few cocktails. Holly's plane arrives, she finds a cab and tells him to take her to the closest hotel to David Letterman's building. He drives through the city, and drops her off across the street from the "Tonight Show." She checks in under Bertha McClain and goes up to her room, to plot out her plan.

At the bar Dezerae is tipsy, leaning on Zyra's arm as she whispers into his ear.

"While you're rehearsing tomorrow, I'm going shopping."

Zyra looks at her and laughs.

"Oh yeah."

Slurring.

"Yup."

"So what's your limit?"

She thinks about it.

"Well, I figure with all the publicity you'll get from Letterman, I'm good for at least, thirty grand."

"Thirty grand!? Are you nuts?"

Her wobbling head and bloodshot eyes, lay into him, as she slurs her words.

"Looking is good, ain't cheap."

She laughs, and Zyra looks at her very seriously.

"Promise me, no more than ten."

She looks at him like he's crazy.

"Ten grand in New York City? I'll be lucky if I can buy one shoe for that. How about Twenty-five?"

He gives in.

"Twenty, no more."

She smiles.

"All those auctions I went to, paid off."

"You better be good."

"Yeah, yeah, I will."

Zyra pulls out his dragon pocket watch and looks at the time.

"3:33 Where did the time go? I'm going upstairs."

She gives him compassionate eyes.

"I'm going too."

He tells the bartender to charge everything to the room, she grabs his arm, and stumbles trying to keep her composure. They enter the elevator, with an older couple, Dezerae throws Zyra up against the wall. She kisses him aggressively. The older couple, embarrassed, look at each other, but you can see the hidden excitement in their faces. The older man covers his growing manhood, his wife slaps him on the shoulder.

"Harry."

The elevator reaches the top floor, and the door opens. Dezerae jumps up on him, wrapping her legs around him, as he walks her to the room. He fumbles with the card key to open the door but finally manages. He places her down on the bed, as the city lights highlight their room, to the perfect setting.

Back in room 333 across the street from the "Tonight Show," Holly sits at the end table, with a layout of David Letterman's building. She marks it up with a red pen, plotting out her plan. Her thoughts drive forward like a mad truck, *if he enters from the back, I can dress up homeless, slit his throat, and continue on my way. But there's security. I could dress as security, wrap a phone cord around his neck, and strangle him. No, that won't work, where will I get a security uniform? I could walk up to him, and blow his head off, although this would be my favorite, I don't have a gun. Better yet, I think a slow torturous death is more deserving. Maybe I'll become the beast in his music, eat his flesh. If I file my teeth...*

She sees an image of her sister, lying in her coffin. She regresses, to a time when she and her sister, were playing as children by a lake. A little boy, is down by the water, with a stick in his hand. He raises it above his head, his friend cheers him on.

"Do it. Do it."

The little boy screams, and as hard as he can, *slams* the stick down, onto a baby duck's back, snapping it in two. Holly's sister screams.

"NOOOOOOO!"

Running over to it, the duck's quack, lingers in the air, as she cries like a baby, and freaks out on the little boy. The other ducks swim away, leaving it to drown. It sinks into the water, the boys laugh, and the boy murderer throws the stick into the water, and they run away. Holly relives the moment, as tears stream down her face. She grabs the pillow and cradles it between her legs. She thinks out loud, *"What am I doing here? I'm not a killer."*

Her doubt is overwhelmed with rage.

"I love you, sis. He will pay."

The cover of Zyra's book appears in her mind.

"That's it."

Chapter 28

LIGHTS OUT

The following morning, the phone rings in Zyra's room, he leans over Dezerae and picks it up.

"Hello, already? Thanks."

He hangs it up. Dezerae wakes up.

"Who was that?"

"The front desk. It's nine o'clock."

She turns back over.

"Already? I don't remember calling for a wake-up call."

He responds.

"I did before we went to bed."

She cuddles the pillow.

"Hmm, I don't remember."

Zyra gets up, makes coffee, looks at her, sprawled out across the bed.

"You got pretty wasted last night."

Her words are barely audible.

"Shut up."

Zyra pours two cups of coffee.

"It was fun like old times. Do remember sneaking a quicky in the woman's stall?"

She immediately responds.

"We did not."

Zyra places the cups on the end table.

"How can you not remember?"

She starts laughing. In her memory, she sees her face pressed against metal, her hands firmly grabbing the top of the stall. Zyra loves her from behind, sweat moistens the wall, and she muffles under her breath.

"I remember. That was fun. We've been making love like crazy lately."

He quickly responds.

"Don't complain about it."

He sits at the end of the bed, rubs his hand, along the inside of her leg, and tickles her, while she lies on her stomach.

"We've done crazier."

She sits up.

"Can you bring me a glass of water, please?"

Zyra gets up, walks over to the refrigerator, and pours her a glass of cold water.

She grabs it, gulps it down, then kisses him on the lips.

"Thank you. What time do you have to be there?"

Zyra answers.

"Two o'clock is a rehearsal, then a two-hour break, before we shoot."

She responds.

"That's right. I forgot they shoot these shows at five."

Zyra takes another sip of his coffee.

"I have to call and cancel Curtis. I want to take the bike out this morning, for a couple of hours. Do you want to come, or are you going shopping?"

She sips her coffee.

"I'll pass on the bike ride, cowboy."

He walks over to the window, opens the curtains, light floods them out, for a split second.

"It's snowing."

She jumps up.

"Really."

She runs over, looks out the window, and sees a white layer, covering the streets. Zyra takes it in.

"It's beautiful."

She folds her arms, and puts her hands, under her armpits.

"I'm freezing."

He writes on the foggy window, 'I love you' with his finger as he speaks.

"It's not that cold."

He stares out into the distance.

"I should have just enough time, to ride out to the countryside, and back by rehearsal. I'm gonna take a shower."

She looks at him like he's crazy.

"You'll never make it."

He shakes his head in disagreement.

"Yes, I will. An hour each way. I can ride an hour into the mountains, and be back around one. It's perfect."

She doesn't feel right about it.

"I don't know Zyra. It's snowing out. You're not used to it. I'm gonna worry about you the whole time."

He cuts her off.

"...then come with me."

She quickly responds.

"I can't."

He walks towards the bathroom.

"You won't be worried, you'll be thinking about what dress to buy next."

She laughs, at the truth hidden, underneath the sarcasm.

"It looks like a perfect day to be walking around. I'll meet up with you after rehearsal. We'll grab a bite, then go to some club after. Hey, we should see Phantom of the Opera."

Dezerae gets all excited.

"I want to see 'Cats'

Zyra agrees.

"Alright, call and order the tickets, with the credit card, while I'm in the shower. Oh, can you have Serge' cancel Curtis for me?"

She nods. Zyra hops in the shower, and Dezerae calls for tickets. He screams out to her from the shower.

"Dez, call your parents, and let them know I will be on Letterman tonight."

He hears her scream back.

"Alright."

* * *

Back at Holly Gossip's hotel, she sits at the edge of her bed, with dark circles under her eyes, as if she was up all night. Her hair is greasy, her jaw tightened, and anxiety oozes from her, superseding any thoughts of rationale. Her fingers shake, and her mind drifts, into untouched territory. She imagines herself hungry for blood. Vampire/wolf-like, she prowls the earth, seeking revenge.

The beast within, raw with human emotion, creeps away from her, like a man shot down, crawling away from his killer. She rises from the bed, grabs an old ragweed coat, and walks downstairs, to the lobby. The cold brisk air reddens her cheeks, and her boots crunch into the snow, and she exits the building. The busy morning atmosphere paints the picture of black slush, filling the sides of the streets.

Holly enters "Calvin's Coffee" at the corner. Business types, as well as, homeless sip their coffee, as Holly orders a large Hazelnut, and a bagel, sits down next to a guy, reading the "New York Times." On the front cover, an image of Holly's sister and brother-in-law, are being escorted in body bags to the ambulance. The caption reads, "Music Spawn From Hell, Makes Child Slaughter Parents In Miami." Holly's blood boils, she drops her head, and weeps. The guy lowers the paper and confronts her.

"Are you okay, ma'am?

She locks her blood-shot crazed eyes, into his, gives him the stare of death, stands up, and walks out of the restaurant. The guy mumbles under his breath.

"Jesus Christ, excuse me for caring."

He puts his head back in the paper, she takes off walking, down the street. Not paying attention, she slips on the icy sidewalk and falls to the ground. Her coffee darkens the ice around her, her bagel rolls into the street.

"FUCK!"

A car runs over it, and she screams at the top of her lungs.

"Can't I get a break?!"

She tries to get up. A small child holding his mother's hand turns around, and eyes Holly. The mother pulls him along.

"Mommy, I know that lady. She's on TV."

The mother continues walking.

"Let's go, she looks like someone you've seen on TV, but she's not. She homeless."

The little boy continues to look back at her, as they walk forward. At this same moment, Zyra drives by on his bike, but

Holly does not notice him. She reaches the outside of the Tonight Show and sits out front. Gazing at her watch, she reads.

"9:36."

Impatient, she gets up, walks to the corner of the street, and grabs the paper from the newsstand. She walks back, behind the building, sneaks into the parking lot, and finds a seat outside the door, which reads "Stage." A large security guard stands outside checking the IDs of those who enter.

Under the same grey overcast, Zyra enjoys his ride, as he travels the countryside. A white dove, flies above him, escorted by Nazareth. His thoughts become visions in heaven, as he converses with his maker.

"I am putting all of my faith in you. Forgive me for my sins."

He imagines himself, floating on his back, in the ocean, under the sun. His wings of flesh, stretch out in the cold crisp sea, as the saltwater stings, and cleanses the battle wounds. He closes his eyes and absorbs the heat. The water turns to warm blood. Zyra lies submerged, in a pool of blood, the sun opens, and white doves fly out against the dark grey sky, encircling him. A voice radiates from the hole in the sky, commanding his attention.

"I am telling you the truth: if you do not eat the flesh of the Son of Man and drink his blood, you will not have life in yourself. Whoever eats my flesh and drinks my blood has eternal life, and I will raise him to life on the last day."

The doves act as a magnetic force, keeping the voice in an invisible cylinder, from the sky to the ocean. The sky immediately closes, the doves disappear, and Zyra shakes off the vision. He pulls the bike over and looks out at the valley below. Taking off his helmet, he runs his glove through his hair and takes a deep breath.

The air thickens around him, and he sees little white flickers of light, dancing in front of the grey snow sky. He reaches out and tries to grab them, they move, as his black leather gloves, pass through. Zyra pulls out his watch, at *12:02,* he thinks to himself, *I have to go.* He puts his helmet on and acknowledges God's presence.

"Thank you."

He drives away, heading back to the studio.

Dezerae walks out of Versace's, with a bag in her hand, a smile across her face. She thinks, *where now*? She mixes in with the shuffle of the crowd, walking along the sidewalks. Zyra pulls up to the Letterman Building, and parks in the back lot. Holly spots him from a distance, and hides herself, watching every move he makes.

A man in a white three-piece tuxedo, whom we recognize as Babel, walks through the parking lot of "The Tonight Show," and up to the security guard. Zyra pays no attention, walks passed the two men. The security guard, who wears a gold crucifix around his neck, welcomes Zyra. He informs the second Assistant Director, over the walkie, that Zyra just arrived. Babel distracts the guard, Holly makes her move. The two men converse.

"Excuse me, sir."

The guard stands erect, hands folded in front.

"Yes."

Babel continues.

"I seem to be lost. I'm looking for Central Park."

The guard responds.

"May I suggest you catch a cab? It's a pretty decent walk, especially in the cold. Don't want to mess up those brand new shiny white shoes of yours."

Babel glares into his eyes, making him feel sick to his stomach. The guard grabs his stomach and quickly gets on the walkie.

"This is Mark. I need someone to release me now, 10-20 break."

Holly walks over to Zyra's Harley, grabs a knife from her pocket, and cuts the brake line. Babel nods his head, acknowledging Holly's actions, and smirks at the guard.

"You're right. I don't know what I was thinking. Thank you. You better go take care of your problem."

The other guard opens the door, Mark blows passed him.

"I'll be right back."

Mark turns around, Babel is gone. He runs to the bathroom, the pressure builds in his intestines. He slams the bathroom door open, right as David Letterman is walking out.

"Whoa. Take it easy, will ya?"

The guard throws open the stall door, and drops his pants, releasing an explosion. Letterman turns back around and sees puke fly out from underneath the stall. Letterman runs. The other guard outside the studio, spots Holly walking away from Zyra's bike.

"Hey, what are you doing?"

She turns, sees he is talking to her, and takes off running through the snow. She mixes in with the crowd on the sidewalk. Back in the studio, the Assistant Director escorts Zyra to the waiting room.

"We'll call you on set when it's your turn. It should only be about 20 minutes or so."

Zyra says.

"That's fine."

The Production Assistant stands outside his room, watching every move he makes. A television plays their network, in the corner, as a table of craft service, fills the back wall. Zyra walks over, grabs a handful of nuts, and pours himself a cup of coffee. He puts in cream and sugar and walks out of the room.

Zyra confronts the Production Assistant.

"What's your name?"

The Production Assistant surprisingly answers, forcing down a mouth full of M&M's.

"Phillip, I'm sorry. You caught me off guard. I'm not used to the guests talking to me. They usually don't acknowledge my existence."

Zyra answers.

"People can be strange. So who are the other guests tonight?"

Phillip smiles.

> "Donna Delory. She used to be Madonna's backup singer, but now she's a solo artist. They're playing tonight, they're pretty good."

Zyra thanks him and heads over to the next guest room.

> "I want to meet her."

Phillip follows him in, people walk passed them in the hallway, Zyra peaks his head into her room, and knocks on the door.

> "Hello."

Donna has long dark hair, and is beautiful, dressed in leather pants, a red flowing lace shirt, and platform boots.

"Yeah."

Cameron, the other band member, walks over to Zyra. Zyra introduces himself, Donna walks over.

> "Hi, I'm Zyra. I just wanted to introduce myself. I saw you in Zalman King's film
>
> *Radio Silence*, which changed to, *Women of the Night.* You were amazing. I just wanted to meet you, since we both had a mutual friend."

Donna shakes his hand.

> "I'm Donna and this is Cameron."

Zyra shakes his hand.

> "Nice to meet you."

Donna continues.

> "What a small world. I miss him a lot. May he rest in peace. I've seen your music video, Zyra, it's out there. Zalman would have loved that for sure."

Zyra laughs.

> "Eat the Dead."

Donna smiles.

> "Yeah that was it, *Eat the Dead.*"

Zyra sips his coffee.

> "Well, I just wanted to peek my head in and say hi. I can't wait to hear from you guys tonight."

She drops her hand, from against the door panel.

> "Hold on a second."

She walks away, grabs a CD of hers, and hands it to him.

> "Check us out. I know it's on all digital platforms, but there's still nothing like holding music in your hand. It's nothing like your music, but I think you'll like it."

Zyra takes it from her and looks at it.

> "Bliss. Thank you."

She smiles.

> "God Bless."

Zyra walks away. She looks at Cameron with an intrigued smile.

"He seems nice."

Cameron answers.

"Yeah, not what I expected, after seeing his work."

Phillip calls for Zyra.

"Hey Zyra, it's time to go."

Zyra follows him to set, as David Letterman greets him.

"Hello, Zyra, thank you for coming on the show, on such short notice. They said you were out of town, so I appreciate your sacrifice."

Zyra answers.

"No problem, David, I have to face my demons somewhere, might as well be on your show."

A surprised unsure laughter rises from David's gut.

"Oh, is that what we're doing? Well, take a seat my friend, and a...we'll start confronting demons."

Zyra takes a seat, the crew gets into position, and the first Assistant Director gives him the go. David asks his first question.

"So welcome, we are here with goth rocker, Zyra Jordonello of Sacred Witch. What is this I hear, Zyra? You found God, and now you won't promote your tour, *Kanniballations?*"

Zyra crosses his legs, sits back, and rubs his hands together, formulating an answer.

"Have you ever felt anger so palpable, that you don't even think about suicide, cause you don't want to give the devil, the satisfaction? Your blood *boils*. Your temperature rises so high, you feel like, bursting out of your skin."

David ponders the thought.

"Well, when I don't get my way."

Zyra interrupts.

"Dave, You don't understand."

David laughingly defends himself.

"I was kidding, go on."

"While making Kanniballations, anger led me to the wolves, paralyzing me beyond fear. In retaliation to society, for allowing a person like my father to exist, I ate the god of flesh, the one who led me there. I destroy the maker of evil, in my life, by dying to his inflictions, not glorifying the hatred. *Kanniballations* was hatred, breathing hatred, for the one person, I needed to get to know and love, that's Jesus Christ. So you tell me, David, how am I to go on contradicting the faith, it took 20-something years to find? If you were me, what would you do?"

David remains silent, does his infamous smirk, and Zyra continues.

"I no longer believe this is the right path to be traveling."

David, trying to follow his train of thought.

"How did this radical change come about, Zyra? I mean it is almost like overnight this transformation occurred, and you expect everyone to drop what they are doing, and follow along. Not everyone is ready to give up everything, they worked so hard to get. And trust me, when I tell you, I see how hard you worked, to achieve the level of success you have. Any idiot can see it, in your acting, and by watching your concerts, but my question to you is, how can a man one day wake up, and say, it's over, life as I know it, is over?"

Zyra leans forward in his chair and locks eyes with him.

"The Immaculate Heart of Mary and the Sacred Heart of Jesus Christ."

David turns towards camera number two.

"You heard it here first. When we return, Zyra will continue confronting his demons."

The director screams.

"Cut."

David sips his water and confronts Zyra.

"I can tell already this is going to be a heavy night. I don't know if my audience is ready for you yet, oh well."

Zyra screams out.

"May I have a glass of water please?"

Phillip flies in a glass of water for Zyra. Zyra takes a sip, and sits back in his chair, as the first Assistant Director confronts the crew.

"Alright, quiet on set, we're back in five, four, three..."

Two and one are silent as he points to David, giving him the hand signal for you're on. The director, back in the control room, tells the switcher to record the rehearsal.

"If David feels this strongly about him, we'll get things that cannot be repeated, trust me."

The band kicks in, and David confronts his audience.

"Welcome back to tonight's show. Our guest tonight is Zyra Jordonello, today's hottest, most controversial Hollywood rockstar/actor. Zyra, before the break, you mentioned you were in a pit of darkness, filled with anger and rage, and Jesus Christ is the one who saved you from self-destruction. Now, you refuse to tour your number one album, *Kanniballations,* and I read a quote from you in Time Magazine, saying how you did not even want to promote the movie, that Siskel and Ebert said caused more ruckus than any other film to date."

Zyra grabs his chin, gazes off into the vast emptiness, within his mind, and starts to speak.

"My father literally sacrificed my brother, Gabriel, tortured him first, when I was ten. I never publicly announced that before. I witnessed it on Halloween night in 1983. I was petrified, paralyzed by fear, and could do nothing to stop him. I live with this memory, haunting me every day. I have been receiving visions lately. I believe them to be the devil, manifesting from my dreams. I thought I was crazy, until the darkness was eaten away, and my soul cracked open, light poured in. I've been given a gift. I can fly within my dreams, led by my guardian angel, Nazareth. I know others have the gift too. I see them. My wife, Dezerae, has been by my side, as I've walked on coals, metaphorically speaking of course."

The cameraman chuckles.

"Many times, I wanted to give up, but she wouldn't let me. She left me because I couldn't get my life under control. Not that I have all the answers either. I just know this is what I need to do right now. By the grace of God, Dezerae not only came back and stayed my best friend, but she also stayed my wife, whom I love eternally."

David looks dumbfounded.

"I'm speechless Zyra. Unbelievable. This is the first time in television history, that I don't know what to say."

Zyra doesn't bat an eye, he just continues.

"I'm sorry for contributing to the decay of society. I publicly ask for forgiveness from the family, whose child killed his parents, and for all other parents, going through hard times, with their teens, because of the influence my music had on them. I know people make their own decisions, however, influence is a major factor in behavior. There are two types of people in this world. Those who contribute to the demise of society, and those who build it up. Those who choose to do nothing, add to the chaos. I, now for the first time in my professional career, choose to help restore the brokenness this world creates."

David sits back in his chair, lost in Zyra's words. He finally speaks.

"Zyra Jordonello everybody."

David stands up and claps.

"You're a man on a mission. You have our support. I hope you find what you're looking for."

David turns to his audience and reaches out to Zyra.

"Zyra Jordonello."

Zyra humbly thanks them, and sits back down, as the audience continues to cheer. David finally comments.

"My audience has never been this supportive of a guest before. This is truly one powerful show folks."

He turns to the floor manager.

"Are you guys getting this?"

He answers.

"The red light's on."

David turns back to Zyra.

"Thank you for a wonderful show."

Zyra puts his head down, not expecting this kind of response.

"When we return, Donna Delory of Bliss will take the stage."

The director screams.

"Cut."

Twenty minutes pass before Zyra finally has an opportunity to leave. He calls Dezerae on the cell, tells her how the rehearsal went, and to meet him back at the hotel. He leaves the building and walks out to the valet. He looks up and sees a white dove hovering above him. He reflects on the show and thinks to himself. *Truly a blessing. Now I have somewhat of an idea of what Ozzy went through, leaving Sabbath, and going solo.* Zyra confronts the security guard.

> "Things are different from what I expected. People got excited about the truth. I thought exposing the scum of the earth, is what people wanted, but they hunger for light."

The security Guard nods.

> "I left David Lettermen speechless."

He looks up towards the sky and gives credit where it is due.

> "They were your words, not mine. Please, continue to show me the way, I will follow."

Zyra hops on his Harley, puts his helmet on, sees an eighteen-wheeler up ahead, but has enough time, and drives out of the parking lot.

Zyra enters onto the main street and applies his brakes, the bike does not stop, and the truck is barreling down the road. Zyra watches the grill of the truck, get larger, the truck *slams* on its brakes, and the back half, filled with fumes, hits an ice patch, swerves, its back half, swings around, and SLAMS into a parked car.

EXPLOSION! A young couple, at the wrong place, at the wrong time, burn to a crisp.

The truck slams into Zyra's motorcycle, Zyra is thrown through the air, bounces off the ground, and rolls to a stop, in the oncoming lane. His bike lifts off the ground, flies through the air, skids on its side, and sparks follow its trail. A car, slams on its brakes, swerving through the ice, and stops inches from crushing Zyra's skull.

A pick-up truck slams into the back of that car, and pushes it passed Zyra's head. A mid-50s Asian woman jumps out of the car, numb from shock, and runs over to Zyra.

"Oh my God. You okay!?"

Zyra looks at her, in a daze, and sees the Asian woman from his dream, a while back, the one who lost her boy. A homeless man, walks over, from the other side of the street, sees Zyra laid out, motionless on the ground, and turns to the Asian woman.

"It's a good thing to wheel's turned, otherwise, you would have crushed his skull."

People from the surrounding area, gather around, fire blazes in the background. Finally, someone screams.

"Someone call the police. It ain't the fourth of July!"

An elderly man jumps, on his cell, and dials 911. After another moment passes, someone else screams out.

"Call' em yourself."

Within minutes, the police and ambulance, arrive. People still gathered in shock, the police backed everyone away, and the fire trucks siren in. The firemen, jump out of the truck, wheel out the hose, and start to put out the fire. The police mark off the area, keeping people behind the lines, and cars honk in the distance.

The grey skies darken, covering the sun, thunder roars at the city, scattering everyone, and lightning strikes, lighting up the sky. The guy in brown leather screams out.

"RUN!"

People run for cover. Those who stayed, witnessed the sun, from behind the clouds, open. The bridge is being released. The wings at the end of the bridge, FLAP pulling the bridge from the first realm of Heaven, beyond its furthest point. Another lightning bolt, which is Nazareth, *strikes* Zyra's body. The paramedics, fly back. Zyra's body, convulses, on the stretcher. A cold storm melts the ice and puts out the remaining fire.

Holly Gossip stands in the furthest distance, watching her creation. Tears fill her eyes, and she falls to her knees and weeps.

"I'm sorry God. I didn't mean for this to happen."

Like a shadow passing in the night, Babel glides by, through the cold brisk air, and disappears making Holly, turn around, feeling his dark presence, chills shoot up her spine. Zyra's body spiritually comes alive, leaving his flesh body. His wings of flesh, grow, expanding far beyond, what he imagined. Zyra and Nazareth, reconnect, interlocking spirits.

"You're back. I feel more alive than ever. Where to this time?"

Zyra's body finally finishes convulsing, and one of the paramedics screams out.

"Don't touch him yet."

The other paramedic, pulls away, as the rain falls harder. The media van pulls up, and the anchor and reporter burst through, the police line. The police stop them, dead in their tracks.

"We don't have any information for you at this time."

The anchor persists.

"Can't you just tell *us*, what happened, here?"

The cop, stressed from the situation screams.

"No!"

The news anchor, sees the Asian woman, shaking, walking back to her car.

"Excuse me, ma'am? Can you tell us what happened, here today?"

She looks at the camera, with a blank stare, and keeps walking. She reaches her car, and climbs in the front seat, asking her son, who is strapped in his seat belt, if he is alright. Tears stream down his face.

"Yes Mommy, just scared."

She hugs him.

"Me too. Thank God you're alive."

Zyra flaps his wings, gazing down upon the scene, as a heavy fog, surrounds the area. He smiles, realizing, his dream was a premonition for this moment, and he was able to help save his life, by Nazareth putting the thought into her head, to double-check her son's seatbelt, before they left. They ascend through the fog, leaving the accident behind. The paramedic checks his pulse, feeling nothing.

"Nothing. He's dead."

He takes off Zyra's helmet and gives him CPR. Zyra and Nazareth fly towards the sun, guided by the dove. They reach the end of the bridge, in the sky, and land down upon it. Zyra falls to his knees in worship, asking God's mercy, to enter his heart. Nazareth separates from Zyra, standing behind him.

The cops block off the accident, telling everybody to go home because it is not safe.

The news anchor captures the moment of the little boy, and his mother, who almost crushed Zyra's skull with her car, and lost her son.

* * *

Meanwhile, inside the Waldorf Astoria, Dezerae is in the bathroom, fixing her hair, in the background, she hears the news report, on television. Shopping bags are scattered on the bed.

"Outside, the Tonight Show, there has been a terrible accident. An eighteen-wheeler has just exploded, burning two people alive, who have not been identified, and crashed into a Harley Davidson motorcycle. The person riding the motorcycle has not been identified. Medics are trying to resuscitate the body."

Dezerae turns off the hair dryer, runs into the room, and watches the TV. She sees an aerial shot of the accident, and they go into a close-up of Zyra's dead body, lying motionless, in the street. She loses it and runs out of the room.

"NOOOOOOOOOOO!"

The news jumps back to the main anchor and shoots over to Los Angeles, where they report a huge rain storm, causing many landslides along the cliffs. Dezerae flies down the stairs, out of the hotel, as Serge witnesses her hysteria.

"Is everything ok, ma'am?"

She blows passed the guard, and down the street, where she can see, the accident from afar. She runs as fast as she can, reaches the accident, and a cop stops her from crossing the border. She punches him in the face.

"That's my husband asshole!"

She forces her way through. The paramedics lift his body, onto the stretcher, and wheel him over to the ambulance. She pushes one of the paramedics out of the way, hugs his body, and sobs.

"Zyra, you can't die on me now baby...Pull through baby, please, I can't live without you... please Zyra."

The cop approaches her.

"Ma'am, you need to come with me now, for assaulting an Officer."

No movement, she hysterically cries.

"Nooo...Jesus, I beg you, please don't take him...Not yet...I can't live without him. Take me instead. ZYRA!"

The paramedic grabs her hand, pulling her into the ambulance.

"Come with us. We're taking him to the hospital."

"Excuse me, she will be coming with me to the police station."

The Paramedic confronts him.

"Listen Officer, please, she didn't mean it, this is her husband, let this one go, please."

The cop looks over at Dezerae.

"Fine."

He walks away. Dezerae climbs into the ambulance, and sees the oxygen mask, and intravenous drip, pumping into him. Dezerae grabs his hand, shaking, praying. The ambulance pulls away from the scene.

"Now faith is the substance of things to be hoped for, the evidence of things that appear not. For by this the ancients obtained a testimony. By faith we understand that the world was framed by the word of God; that from invisible things visible things might be made." Hebrews 11: 1-3

Chapter 29

TOWER OF BEEZ

Across the country on the west coast, Los Angeles at the same moment, has rain storms flooding the streets. Cars are pulled off to the side of the highway, and a chilling breeze sweeps through the city streets, passing by each accident. Chaos and fear, align the streets, palm trees sway in the wind, fighting for their lives. Pandemonium, runs rapidly once again, growing at every turn.

On top of Malibu Canyon, Zyra and Dezerae's house, stands weak in the knees, confronting its demise. Landslides occur across the cliffs, pulling down, one house after the other. Some families make it out, just in enough time. Others find their eternal sleep.

Eventually, underneath Zyra's house, the earth, landslides down the cliff, as their house hangs over. An eerie cracking of the wood vibrates throughout, and in an instant, the living room glass wall, *shatters,* into a thousand pieces. The rain invades the empty nest, as the roof bends and cracks. Finally, the back half of the house breaks off, and hangs on for a single moment, before descending, *crumbling down* the cliff, *smashing* into a thousand pieces, onto Pacific Coast Highway.

Angry waves, pound the shores, people run for their lives, trying to escape the storm, and falling debris. An overweight woman runs for cover. She looks up for the last time, and a metal door flies down, from the cliff, *slicing* her in half. It digs its way into the earth and stops holding half her body on one side. Her torso from shock screams for bloody murder and falls to the ground, her brain shuts down, her eyes bug out of her face, and into the sand, and she faces plants.

A teenage boy who witnessed the freak accident, pukes, pisses his pants, runs off. The news reporter stands in the middle of Pacific Coast Highway filming as much as he can. A loud wind howls across the coast, and the power in the camera dies, during their Electronic News Gathering (ENG). The camera guy screams out to the anchor.

"We lost power."

He screams back.

"WHAT?!"

The camera guy takes off, with the camera, towards the van, and the news anchor follows. His life flashes before his eyes, as they drive through this natural disaster.

About two hundred yards offshore, Dragon Whale creates a whirlpool, by swimming rapidly in a circle. The center of the hole deepens, until the earth below the water, is exposed. The angry ocean, crashes down onto the shore, destroying all in its path. Instantly, Dragon-Whale slams its tail, down onto the earth, and cracks open the surface.

The vibrations descend towards the earth's core, the lake of fire, releasing millions of bees, from its possession. They travel up through the earth, out the opening, created by Dragon Whale.

"BUZZZZZZZZZ..."

Millions of bees protrude up from the surface, forming a tower, rising in the air. Directly above, coming towards the earth is the spirit bridge, being pulled by wings, from the sun. Meanwhile, inside Dr. Von Hildonberg's office, he stares out at the rain, overlooking the ocean. In the distance, he sees houses and, a landslide off the cliff.

Within his mind's eye, he sees and enters, into the spirit, allowing him to enter this realm and see the tower of bees, rising, through the air, in the middle of the ocean. He thinks to himself, *this is the end.* Reminiscing on his life, about how straight-laced he was, creeps into his memory. Something alcoholics call a moment of clarity, reveals within his mind, balance. In the distance, he witnesses the spirit bridge, heading straight toward the tower of bees.

A palm tree lifts from the beach is carried through the air and is headed straight for him. The doctor stays pressed against the window, in his trance. Just as it is about to hit, his secretary runs in, and at this very moment, things seem to slow down, as the palm tree, *slams* against the window, BANG, cracking the glass. Breaking the trance, the doctor is thrown back into his secretary, reality hits that they may die, and she screams as they both hit the ground.

"Didn't you see it coming? What are you trying to do, kill yourself?"

He looks at her, crazed in his eyes, and drops his head, in her bosom. The rain pounds against the window, and moisture and humidity, fog the glass. He makes his decision, slides his hand up her leg, grabs what he wants, and then kisses her passionately. Electricity, transpires between their lips, charging their hormones. Morality vs. Sensation.

The crucifix above his desk falls to the ground, Christ breaks off, and lands face down, next to him. He rips off her G-string, unbuttons his pants, pulls himself out, and enters her aggressively. Before she realizes what is happening, his right-hand covers her mouth, she bites down, taking it in, feeling the shock and excitement, all at once.

She gives in to the overwhelming pleasure, wraps her arms and legs around him, squeezing tightly around him, he thrusts into her. He lets go of her, sucks her breasts, forcing her into pure ecstasy. The other hand reaches down, slaps her buttocks, squeezes, her hips, ramming deep into him.

"Uhhh...Uhhh..."

He tickles her half-dollar pink erect nipple, with the tip of his tongue, their rhythm in perfect unison, juices flow, they climb holding their breath, reaching orgasm at the same time.

"Oh God...oh God."

* * *

Back in New York, the ambulance pulls up to the emergency room. The paramedics jump out of the ambulance and open the back door. The doctor is already at the door to meet them. The medic instantly confronts the Doctor as they wheel him in.

"Zyra Jordonello, critical condition. Fractures in his right wrist, and collarbone. I'm not sure if there are other breaks and fractures at this time. We moved him, as minimally as possible, and got him breathing on the way over here. It's a miracle he's still alive."

The doctor takes over and wheels him into surgery, and Dezerae hysterically follows.

"Is he gonna live doc? Please tell me...he's gonna live."

They wheel him passed the double doors, the nurse keeps Dezerae out of surgery.

"You can't come in here, ma'am. We'll keep you updated on his progress."

She throws her hand up and blocks the door.

"No, I have a right to be in there. He's my husband."

She barges passed the nurse, into surgery screaming.

"Zyra."

The doctor calmly asks Kim, a large male nurse, to handle the situation. He walks over, grabs Dezerae around the waist, lifts her, and walks her out of the room. She kicks and screams.

"Get off me!"

He sits her down, in the waiting room.

"It's your choice, ma'am. I can stand here, and watch you, or you can calm down, and let me get back, to my job, so your husband doesn't die."

She stares at him, with her bloodshot eyes, and shivering hands, but takes a deep breath, and calms down. She drops her head to her knees and cries. The nurse calls in security to watch her and gets back into surgery, as Dezerae prays, asking the Lord to get her through this.

* * *

Back in Doctor Von Hildonberg's office, his secretary rolls off of him. Her shirt is torn, and she looks up at the ceiling, in between breaths.

"How do I explain this to my husband?"

They both start laughing, she sits up, and the wind *breaks* through SHARDS of GLASS and slices them to pieces. The Doctor instantly covers his eyes, and she screams, he dives back on top of her. Blood drips down her face, she falls back to the ground, and light twinkles off the pieces of glass protruding out from her face and body, like a human sacrificial masterpiece.

The wind forces the rain in, flooding out the office. He looks around and tries screaming, but nothing comes out, only a faint whisper, which crescendos into a deep horrifying yell, as he gains strength. The yell mixes with the howling of the wind, which travels in circles, making its way out towards the ocean. The sorrow within the yell gets caught in the whirlpool and spirals down the tower of bees.

"BUZZZZZZZZZZZZZZ...."

Demons from within the tower, torture the lost souls, trying to escape their prison. Their cries are heard among the powerful ambiance of Dragon Whale's voice.

"RISE. Destroy, the bridge connecting that world to mine."

His words summon the energy from the ocean, and force it up through the tower, as it increases in height and power. Tortured souls, ride the coattails of his voice, to the top of the tower. They reach out for hope, demons hold them back with chains, starved for blood.

The wings at the end of the bridge, continue to work, pumping through the air, pulling the bridge closer to earth, and in direct path of the tower of bees. An aerial shot of Los Angeles, warm glows of light, pour throughout the city, meaning people are *acting* out of pure *love* for God and humanity.

The battle cries, from the trapped souls within the tower of bees, get sucked into the sun, and enter *through* to the other side. At this same moment, thousands, maybe millions, of Angels with mature wings, are lined up mid-air, one right after the other, militant-like. The light within their hearts brightens enough to connect each Angel's heart, to the next. The last Angel, connects the train of light, through the first realm of heaven, to the larger sun, behind its presence.

The One Who Sits On The Throne stands on mountain tops, with His arms fully extended, from one end of heaven to the other. The sun shines through, the piercings in his hands, as Angels *hover* above his arm-span. His head hangs low, staring down at His beautiful creation, as the perfect harmony travels through. The crystal castles illuminate.

Zyra flies over peaks, and valleys, gathering up the dinosaurs, and dragons, and leading them into the train of light. Less mature Angels, ride the dragons as warriors, Nazareth, at the other end of heaven, does the same. These earthly extinct animals, now heavenly creatures, enter the light, charge forth through, the smaller sun, into the earth's atmosphere, galloping on the bridge. The fluttering wings at the end of the bridge, pull its extension even further, as the animals approach. The heavenly choir accompanies the illuminated bridge.

Nazareth and Zyra lock eyes, after gathering the last of the animals. They face the sun, leading to the earth's atmosphere, and extend their arms. The light summons them together, and they reunite as one spirit, in the Sacred Heart of Jesus Christ. All three beings as one, Zyra, Nazareth, and Jesus, their eyes focus on the light, Zyra thinks, *what now,* the voice can be heard over the heavenly music, and the galloping of dinosaurs and dragons. The three hearts beat, as one, when Nazareth communicates to Zyra.

"Sing from your heart, with the strength of the Holy Spirit."

Zyra opens his mouth, and instantly the angelic language drives through, forcing them to the light, and the name, "GOTHOLIC" is born. They pick up speed, pass through the piercing, in Christ's right hand, and enter the earth's atmosphere. They travel passed the animals, towards the end of the bridge. As images fly by, Nazareth says.

"We will lock into the wings, at the end of the bridge. Then we will pull the bridge, and connect it to the earth."

Zyra, obviously filled with excitement, and wonder, asks the question he did not want to know. "Where's our destination?"

"The City of Angels."

They reach the end of the bridge and pass through the wings. The wings of flesh enter the spirit wings and lock in.

"Whoa..."

Zyra looks down, and sees their body, dangling in front of, and above, the tower of bees, rising below them.

"What is GOTHOLIC?"

Nazareth, excitement pouring through his words.

"Welcome to Gotholic Warfare."

* * *

Meanwhile, back at Forest Lawn Mortuary, in Los Angeles, Garth's body is being prepared for viewing. The mortician just finished sowing his body together and is now cleaning off his tools. He turns around, and to his surprise, Garth is gone. The mortician blinks, reassuring what he sees, but the body is still gone.

"HOLY SHIT!"

He looks around, but the body is nowhere to be found. He panics and runs out of the room.

"I've been doing this *shit* way too long."

Babel, stands in the corner, smiling, then disappears midair.

* * *

Subsequently, we sweep over the angry ocean, and rise, the tower of bees. As we approach the top, Zyra is seen, flapping his wings, pulling the bridge. On top of the tower of bees, the sounds of screaming souls, cry for mercy. A toilet bowl manifests above them. The base of the tower widens, and a force travels up through it. It rises to the top and forms into the face of Babel. Strapped over Babel's mouth, with chains, is the toilet bowl.

Garth sitting on his toilet throne, attached with hooks, pierced through his skin. His body was possessed by thousands of souls and demons, making their presence known, through Garth's eyes. They take control of his body, like the puppet, as moans and evil screams, permeate, above the sound of the bees. Round weights with protruding spikes, attached to the end of the chains, wrapped around Garth's arms; they dangle below the toilet bowl, in the center of the tower, weighing him down.

Babel's face, encompasses the surface below the toilet bowl, making the tower of bees his neck; he coughs, summoning up, from the depths of hell, through his long esophagus, the soul of Zyra's father, the original TARTARUS. The soul flies up, through the center of the bees, curves around bends, in the neck, and eventually reaches the end. He is released out of Babel's mouth, up through the toilet bowl, into Garth's carcass, and transforms Garth's face into Zyra's father's face. Zyra approaches the figure, wide-eyed, in disbelief.

"Dad?"

Zyra's father is tortured and demented as his spirit speaks.

"It's been a long time my, son."

Zyra, exhausted, and lost in the illusion, continues to pull the bridge. He reaches out for his father, he *shakes* with rage. Babel speaks, with powerful words, manipulating his father's face, but delivered, as his other son's voice, Gabriel's voice.

"Help me, Zyra."

Zyra lets his guard down, for a split second, as it registers. Out of love, compassion, and faith, Zyra decides to speak.

"Gabriel?"

His next words confront Nazareth.

"What do I do?"

Nazareth answers.

"There is nothing you can do, Zyra. Babel is the master of disguise."

Zyra thinks back, to the time of his brother's death. Shaking his head, he thinks to himself, *I will not let him go a second time.* He conjures up the strength, and fights back, as Nazareth quickly opposes his decision.

"You can lose your soul forever, Zyra. You can't change the past."

"My brother needs me. I will not let him die again. I'll take his place if I have to."

Zyra screams with vengeance, every muscle, and vein stretch to its maximum.

"I command you, Satan, in the name of Jesus Christ, to release my brother, Gabriel Jordonello, to me."

Babel speaks through the father's face, with a force equally as powerful, straight from hell.

"He's mine."

Zyra's determination and self-sacrifice, filled with faith and love, will not accept Babel's lie.

"NOOO! Take me instead."

Gabriel's spirit is instantly released, from his father's eyes, pulled in through Zyra's eyes. As Gabriel passes through Zyra's soul, he feels Gabriel's gratitude.

"Thank you, brother."

Furious, Babel ROARS, possesses Garth's body, stands up on top of the toilet, swings the weights, and SLAMS, and Zyra in the head. The tower of bees rises even higher, just a few feet from stopping the bridge. Nazareth screams.

"Duck!"

Zyra shakes off the blow.

"You're a little too late."

Babel swings the weights around, gaining momentum, making it look like a well-oiled machine. Nazareth screams.

"It's now or die, Zyra."

Zyra summons the power of God.

"May the power of our Lord of Heaven and Earth REIGN FOREVER."

During "Forever," a rush of lightning surges from the sun, through the bridge, and charges through Zyra's fingertips, knocking Babel out of Garth's body. Zyra's body convulses with energy, his wings stretch beyond their previous state. Babel's long green tongue slithers out, and swallows Garth, on the toilet bowl, down its long, thick neck. Babel *strikes* at Zyra like a poisonous serpent. The light flowing through Zyra's fingers, catch Babel, at just the right moment, stopping him dead in his tracks, inches from biting off, Zyra's head. The struggle is *nothing* he has ever felt before.

Zyra's concentration, forces Babel down, with the strength of God. In a slow hard push, Babel starts his demise. Zyra's wings work even harder, pulling the bridge over Babel. Looking into the eyes of death, Zyra sees in the distance, Garth's dead body, being spit into the bottom, of the illuminated bridge, by Babel.

His skin boils, the weights melt, souls and demons, cry out for mercy, forced into the light, sizzling, burning, yet constantly rising, into the illuminated light. Babel's face drops down its long neck, and the tower of bees elevates, turning into black smoke, as they submerge, into the bottom of the bridge. The smoke clouds their surroundings. Zyra and Nazareth, continue their mission, towards Earth, as people witness, a black smoke spreading throughout the sky.

* * *

On the other side of the sun, Gabriel passes through, and the piercing in Jesus' hand, travels through the light, connecting the Angel's hearts. The harmony of heaven, escorts his soul, through the first realm of Heaven, and the other piercing of Christ's hand, entering into the Second Realm of Heaven.

* * *

Sinking the tower of bees, Babel hits the ocean bottom, and transforms into a Dragon Whale; it stops swimming. The whirlpool fills in, with rushing water, separating the tower of bees, from the center of the earth. The bees continue to rise, burning into the bridge, expanding the black cloud, hovering over Los Angeles. People continue to witness this spiritual event. The stench alone, forces vomit from their stomachs.

Meanwhile, like the hand of death, creeping into Dr. Von Hildonberg's office, black smoke enters their noses, and down into their lungs. Coughing, choking on the smoke, the doctor and secretary, release their warm insides upon each other, as he pulls the glass, from her face.

* * *

Back in New York City, in a hospital room, Dezerae sits by Zyra's bedside. She watches the news, as the reporter from the helicopter reports.

"There is a black cloud, which appeared out of nowhere, that continues to grow, hovering over the City of Angels. The rain has caused many landslides, along the west coast of Southern California, the worse hitting the cliffs of Malibu Canyon."

The helicopter sweeps down, over the falling homes. Dezerae cries knowing their house was destroyed.

* * *

The rest of the tower of bees, diffuse into the bridge, finalizing their demise. The smoke lingers above the dark ocean, people run for cover. Just as the waters start to calm, the tiger head of Dragon-Whale, rises, from out of the water. Its mouth is wide open, its canines are exposed. It lashes out its tongue, rising from the ocean, with a horrific ROAR.

Gravity, pulls the excess water back down, as this white, slimy beast, continues its ascension, squirming its long anaconda-like neck through the air, pulling its massive body of a blue whale, straight up. Its wings flutter, lifting itself higher and higher into the sky. The tail pushes a final time against the water before it is completely out of its terrain.

Zyra looks down and sees the beast flying up, through the air, straight for him, still connected to the bridge. His eyes and mouth widen, paralyzed in awe, Nazareth breaks him from his hypnotic state.

"Keep going, it can't touch us."

The beast reaches Zyra, face to face, each part of its body, rises in slow motion, beyond its evil black oval alien eyes. This is the first time Zyra, sees the belly of the beast. The only words to describe this awesome sight, are extracted from Zyra's soul.

"My god."

Nazareth quickly responds.

"Not your God."

Its gills flare, at the same time, as a huge gust of wind, collides with its body, from the after swing, of Zyra's wings. Dragon-Whale barely makes it over the bridge, like a dolphin diving over a rod. It lingers in the air, over the spirit bridge, connecting Heaven to Earth. Dragon-Whale speaks these words.

"But woe to you, earth and sea,

for the Devil has come to you in

great fury..."

On its descent, its wings catch the air and glide down. It takes a nose dive, then straightens out again. It dives a final time, entering the water, with an awesome, SPLASH!

Zyra and Nazareth reach the west coast of the United States. The bridge disconnects from their back, and SLAMS into the ground, causing the templates to split all along the coast. The big 10.0 earthquake finally hits California.

Zyra and Nazareth separate, they both have their wings. Zyra's wings, fresh as newborn pedals, remain as those wings, received from the end of the bridge. A Tsunami builds in the distance, and gains power as it heads for shore. EXPLOSIONS, one right after another, light up the sky. The earth *breaks off*, water rushes in.

People scatter trying to flee the city by car, foot, bike anything to get them out of there. Across the media, helicopters report the tsunami, about to destroy the city of Los Angeles.

> "The horrific sounds of the roaring and rumbling, created from this natural disaster, one could only speculate, has not been heard since the time of the flood."

Zyra and Nazareth fly above the tsunami and overlook the whole city. The wave crashes down, over the cliffs, flooding out the neighborhood streets. Cars and houses, crumble instantly on impact, buildings *crumble* to the ground. All over the world, people are tuned into this live natural disaster. Over the airwaves, messages can be heard.

> "Between the earthquake, and the rushing water, anyone along the coast, if not instantly dead will be short."

The news broadcasts images of loved ones dying.

> "It is a sad day in the history of the United States. Humanity suffers as nature reconstructs itself. The state once known as California is almost completely submerged."

Tears build in the reporter's eyes, getting choked up, reporting the news.

"Scientists have been telling us...for years this would happen, but we didn't believe them. For the millions lost, our hearts pour out to the families and friends. May your souls rest in peace."

On televisions across the world, the San Francisco bridge, breaks in half, and the bay slowly sinks. News reporters line the new coast, as people crowd around them, crying, praying, some in shock, some just silent. They watch this huge land mass, once their home, sink into the water. The rain continues to pour down, as strong winds blow off the surface of the Pacific.

Zyra and Nazareth, fly over the submerged land. Zyra's face, seriously disturbed, cries like a baby. He lands on the bridge, hovering over the water, of God's new canvas. Zyra breaks down.

"I wouldn't have done His will sooner if I knew everything was going to be destroyed."

With a caring smile and gentle spirit, Nazareth wipes the tears from his cheeks and locks eyes with him.

"Zyra, the sins of man create natural disasters. Man and nature are connected. There are two sides to tragedy. You can stay in darkness or live in the light. Where there is darkness, life cannot exist."

Zyra looks up at the sun's rays, breaking through the clouds. Doves fly, as a peaceful ambiance finally settles, within Zyra. The bridge stands strong, connecting the first realm of Heaven to Earth. Zyra sees the thousands of souls, lost to this tragedy, being called home into heaven. A sadness comes over him.

"What about those who never had a chance?"

Nazareth looks up, at the sun which is held open by the hands of Christ.

"The fall of man is a choice made by each individual. To say a person, never had a chance, is to deny God's existence. You cannot deny what is."

Zyra's revelation causes time to reverse, as the west coast starts to resurface. Everything goes back to the way it was, just before the bridge hit. Like Atlantis rising from its grave, the coast of California is once again filled with life. Dumpster trucks ride the streets, cleaning up the landslide residue. Zyra shakes off his vision, thinking *it's all a dream*, but everything is the way it was, when the rain storm hit, before the Tsunami and earthquake, hit the coast.

"What's real Nazareth?"

Nazareth looks up at the sun, Zyra's eyes follow, as they see protruding out, the hands of Christ, with rays of light, shining through His piercings. Hypnotized by the illusion, Zyra's soul hungers, as his mouth salivates, tasting the sacrifice of God. Blood pours down from the hand, in the sun, and finds its way into Zyra's mouth.

Zyra drinks His everlasting blood, which pumps life through his veins. Nazareth, snaps him, from the vision, and points down, Zyra sees another drop of blood, land in the ocean.

It enters the water without a splash, from that same place, Babel rises, dressed in his three-piece white tuxedo. Water, instantly dries, as the air touches his skin. From Babel's back, black wings grow, Zyra looks at Nazareth, knowing what he is going to ask. So Nazareth answers.

"Only God the Father knows when He is going to send his Son, to claim his reign from Lucifer, the fallen angel."

He nods at Zyra, and they fly down, from the bridge, and land on the water, a hundred yards or so, from Babel. In the blink of an eye, Babel is upon them.

"I'm impressed, but I still have the one soul, who gave you life, my friend."

Stone cold, Zyra's look, freezes Babel's words, in the middle of the air.

"I'm not your friend. We all have the freedom, to make our own choices."

Babel smiles, and the frost line cracks, evaporating into nothing.

"Yes, you see now, it is my world. As long as you are in my world, you play by my rules."

"Lucifer, get behind me. I am with Christ now."

Babel raises his long pointed fingernail at Zyra, then pauses, and drops his hand, changing Zyra's train of thought.

"Well, I better go. I have a lot of souls to tend to."

Babel's black wings flutter, and he walks on water. Zyra and Nazareth part, letting him pass, as he heads towards shore. Babel disappears into the fog rolling over the sea.

"MY WIFE! I have to get back to her. It's not...too late Nazareth, is it?"

Nazareth smiles.

"I'm going to miss you, Zyra."

Nazareth takes in the moment, hugs him, and kisses Zyra on the cheek.

"When will I see you again, Nazareth?"

"When your spirit passes through the sun for its final time."

Tears muffle in Zyra's eyes.

"Thank you for showing me the way. I love you Nazareth, my Guardian Angel. God be with you."

With that, Zyra takes off in flight, allowing the doves to guide him back, to the hospital. Nazareth watches Zyra fly away, he thinks to himself, *I will always be with you.*

Chapter 30

VALLEY OF HALOS

The golden sunrise, bounces off the snow in New York City, finding its way, up through the cracks, in the window, of the third floor, at New York City's Hospital. A crowd of people, fans, and news reporters are gathered outside. Three days have passed, since there was movement in Zyra's body, which lays paralyzed in bed, a few stories high. People have sleeping bags, tents, burning candles, and singing "Amazing Grace," outside of his window.

Zyra's oxygen mask continues to fog and clear. The machines keep him alive, as intravenous cords, stick out from his arms, feeding his appetite. Zyra slowly opens his eyes, to the faint singing of "Amazing Grace." Surrounding him, beings of light, protect his soul. An Angel illuminates, at the foot of his bed. Under the oxygen mask, Zyra mumbles.

"Where am I?"

As he comes to consciousness, the Angel materializes into Dezerae. She runs around the side of the bed, grabs his hand, and squeezes tightly. Tears fill her eyes, her voice flutters.

"Oh my God, you're alive. Thank you, God, thank you."

She caresses his face and kisses him tenderly.

"I love you, baby. I thought you...I love you."

A surprised look on his face, eases into relaxation, as he realizes his situation. A slight smile breaks his sleepy stare, and she brings his hand, to her bosom.

"I thought I lost you forever."

"What happened?"

"You were in a terrible accident."

Zyra thinks back to the last thing he can remember, and sees a huge semi-truck, heading straight for him. He jerks.

"How did I survive? I didn't see it coming."

"It's a miracle, baby."

"What about the earthquake?"

Zyra asks. She looks at him bewildered.

"What earthquake?"

"The 10.0 that hit California."

She shakes her head, not understanding.

"10.0? That would knock California off the map."

Zyra closes his eyes, and with a sigh of relief, she comforts him.

"Did anyone die in the accident?"

Dezerae lays down next to him, snuggles her chin, into his chest, and squeezes him tightly.

"It was a very bad accident. It has consumed the news for the past three days."

It hurts him, and he gets upset.

"Did anyone die?"

She breaks down.

"Yeah...a young couple."

Zyra fights back his tears.

"It was my fault."

"No baby."

"I'm killing everybody. What's happening to me?"

She squeezes him, he starts to cry.

"There's something I have to tell you."

The doctor, a Danny DeVito type, with thick black glasses, walks into the room.

"Well, good morning. Welcome back, Zyra. How do you feel?"

Zyra turns his head and looks at the doctor.

"You're my doctor?"

"Yes, Dr. Clark. It's a miracle Zyra, that you are here with us today. And I don't use that word lightly. You must have someone upstairs looking after you."

He turns his head back, and stares up at the ceiling, the doctor continues.

"We tried to get rid of your fans, and the Christians, who've been praying for you, non-stop, for the past three days. I've never seen anything like it, honestly. To the point, where it got me thinking about my death, and who would show up outside of my window, praying. So I let them stay."

Zyra looks at him, with a puzzled grin. The doctor walks over to the window and opens his curtains, the sun pours in, and Zyra squints holding up his hand, to block the light. He sits up slowly and gets out of bed.

Dezerae helps him, grabs the I.V. pole, and walks over to the window. Out in the distance, and below his window, people are gathered, in the yard and parking lots. People are singing "Amazing Grace."

Overwhelmed with emotion, Zyra instantly breaks down, and Dezerae hugs him. Zyra turns to the doctor.

"What do I do?"

The doctor smiles.

> "Talk to them. Show them you're alive."

Zyra opens the window, and on the television in his room, a news break shows this exact moment with a News Reporter.

> "People have been gathered outside the hospital room of Rock Star and Actor, Zyra Jordonello, for the past three days, praying for him. Here's a young man, why are you here?"

The young teenage boy proudly speaks.

> "After I saw Zyra on Letterman, he gave me inspiration and hope. My cousin used to sexually abuse me. After I saw what Zyra said, I started praying. My cousin the very next day turned himself in, because of a guilty conscience. That's power. I'm not leaving until..."

Zyra is in the background, his arms outstretched, welcoming everybody. The sound begins to diminish, until silence. The boy runs towards the window, and Zyra confronts the crowd.

> "Thank you all, for your prayers. They worked. Even the doctor admitted it, my waking up was a miracle. Well, this is very overwhelming."

Everyone cheers. He stops himself from breaking down again.

> "I don't know what to say. I'm at a loss for words. May God Bless you all. I love you. Thank you again, keep the faith, God is real!"

Dezerae hugs him and kisses him in front of everyone. The doctor leaves the room, the crowd picks up where they left off singing.

"Amazing Grace, how sweet the sound to save a wretch like me..."

Zyra closes the window and gets back into bed, there is a knock at the door. A woman's voice can be heard.

"Hello, Zyra?"

Dezerae walks over to the door and opens it a crack, to see who is there. The Italian woman, Elizabeth, Zyra's mother, enters the room. Dezerae hugs her.

"Hi, you must be Dezerae."

Zyra asks.

"Who's at the door baby?"

Dezerae smiles, releasing Elizabeth, she walks her into the room. Zyra stares at her, and waves of truth hit him at once. Vulnerability in his voice.

"Mom?"

She smiles.

"What are you doing, here? I thought you were dead, or something."

Dezerae jumps in.

"I told her to come."

Zyra looks at her.

"What are you talking about?"

Elizabeth walks closer to the bed.

> "When I saw you were in critical condition, on the news, I didn't know what to do. I went for a walk to clear my mind and found myself entering a Catholic Church. A kind man approached me. He said, 'You don't know me, but I know your son and Zyra needs you.' Nobody knew I was your mother, Zyra. To keep me out of jail, for not turning in your father, I was forbidden by the court, to have any contact with you. Something happened to me, when this stranger, Nazareth, approached me. I believed him."

Zyra interrupts her.

> "Did you say, Nazareth?"

She continues.

> "I called the hospital, spoke with Dezerae, got here as soon as I could."

Elizabeth gets choked up, feeling humiliated. She tries to continue, but it is as if there is someone there, speaking for her.

> "I couldn't bear to lose another son. I've begged God for forgiveness, for not protecting you, and Gabriel. I had to learn, to forgive myself, and now I, I am here, asking you for forgiveness."

Zyra puts his head down.

> "You know, I just woke up from a coma, and this, this is not, what I expected to wake up to. I haven't seen you, since I was ten."

She sucks in her humility, puts her hand over her face.

"I'm sorry for bothering you. I don't know what I was thinking."

She runs out of the room hysterical.

"MOM! MOM, COME BACK!"

Zyra gets out of bed, and Elizabeth meets him in the doorway. They lock eyes and share tears. When they finally hug, it is like two worlds colliding. Zyra whispers into her ear.

"I love you, Mom. I forgive you. I know Gabriel loves and forgives you too."

They squeeze each other tightly, and their tears intermix. She kisses his cheek and wipes her tears away. Dezerae hugs the both of them, figuring now is a good time to mention, what she's been waiting to tell, at the right moment.

"By the way, I'm pregnant."

They both scream out.

"WHAT!?"

Zyra breaks away, she looks at him, with a serene smile, painted across her face, with a pregnant motherly glow.

"You're going to be a Daddy."

Zyra stands there paralyzed, by the news, then after a while, after it registers, he hugs her, picks her up, and twirls her around, as the I.V. cord entangles them. Elizabeth interjects. "Watch out for the baby."

Zyra kisses her passionately.

"I love you. I love you, so deeply, it hurts."

Elizabeth's bottom lip flutters, holding back these confused emotions, of whether or not, Zyra will want her, in his new life.

"Congratulations Zyra and Dezerae."

Zyra slowly coming out of the shock, asks.

"When did you find out?"

"Yesterday."

"I can't believe this."

Dezerae drops her head, and Zyra confronts his concern.

"What's wrong Sweetie?"

She looks up at him.

"Well, besides this good news, I have something, I have not been looking forward to telling you, but..."

"What is it? What baby?"

She finally answers.

"Before Elizabeth, Mom flew out here, she told me she lived in Los Angeles, and that they were in the middle of a horrible storm, which I had seen on the news. She said she wouldn't be able to get out here, for a couple of days..."

Zyra looks at his mother, then back at Dezerae.

"...I asked her to drive by our house, to check up on it, because on the news, I saw houses all along P.C.H. crumble down the cliff."

She breaks down, and Zyra jumps in.

"I don't care. I don't want to raise a family in Los Angeles anyway, Dezerae. This is our free ticket. We can go anywhere in the world. It's a new beginning."

She looks at him, surprised at his understanding.

"But we lost everything, Zyra. Our house, our belongings."

"No baby, I lost nothing. I gained everything. My life, you, my mother, and now our child. We can finally be the family, you always talked about. A real family, like you see in the movies."

Dezerae smiles at his joke. Dezerae faces Elizabeth.

"You should come with us. Where do you want to live, Elizabeth?"

She looks at Zyra, waiting for his approval.

"Yeah Mom, where do *you* want to live?"

Elizabeth stands proud.

"Well, I don't know, how you feel about, *Florida*, I visit there, and I think you guys would like it. Good place to raise kids."

Zyra looks at Dezerae in interest.

"Well, they always had the hottest chicks."

Dezerae hits him in the arm.

"What, I mean fans."

"I can't believe you."

"I'm just kidding."

"No, you're not. I'm gonna get fat and ugly."

Zyra puts his arms around her.

"No, you will never be ugly to me, no matter how big you get."

He kisses her on the forehead.

"So do you think we're having a boy or a girl?"

Dezerae and Elizabeth both say.

"Girl."

Zyra at the same moment says.

"Boy. Unless we have twins. So Dezerae, where would you like to raise our child?"

She quickly answers.

"As long as I'm with you, I don't care where we live."

"It's settled then. When I'm able to get out of here, we'll find a place in Florida...maybe some college town."

Outside the window, the crowd starts to sing.

"Our Father Who art in heaven..."

Dezerae raises her finger to her lips.

"Shh...do you hear that? They're singing *The Lord's Prayer?*"

Zyra walks over to the window, and opens it, turning back to Dezerae and Elizabeth.

"From here, it looks like, Valley of Halos."

"Valley of Halos, that's a great song title, or maybe even album title."

White doves hover above the crowd and a rainbow jets across the sky. Their voices contribute to the song, as Zyra, Dezerae, and Elizabeth, wrap their arms around each other, standing in front of the window, singing along.

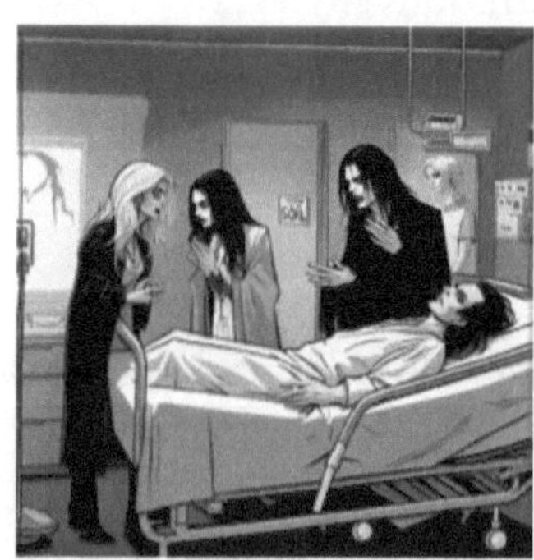

May the soul weep when the devil sleeps, protected by God's Sacred light. Within the mind, within the spirit, within the soul, I see more clearly, my heart lays worship at your feet, Lord Jesus Christ. My blood has returned.

Chapter 31

EPILOGUE

A year later, Zyra and Dezerae, find themselves, nestled into a comfortable home in Northern Florida. Except for a plane ride back to Los Angeles, where Zyra had to straighten out all the legalities with his lawyers, they have had a peaceful year. Their large Colonial House sits off the dirt road, amid a forest, in a small little town located outside of Tallahassee.

Deer and rabbit run through their yard, on this bright early morning. In the backyard, a wooden playground, stands erect, next to a two-story, wooden deck, which wraps around and leads to the kitchen, on the second floor. Antique furniture compliments the Gothic atmosphere, even in this rural setting. Red oak walls, line the foyer, down the creaking old wooden stairwell, leading passed the grandfather clock, down another flight of stairs, to the sunken family room, which is overlooked by a stone fireplace. Black velvet and red lace drapes, flow over the windows, overlooking the backyard.

On the black carpet, Dezerae kneels, changing her son's diaper, Zyven Jordonello. Zyven laughs.

> "Come on, spread those legs...Hold still. Ah dang it, I can't believe you just peed on me. Zyven quit being crazy like your daddy. Hold still."

Zyven cries, kicking his legs, she lifts his legs and wipes underneath.

> "Pew, this is a stinky one."

He releases a jet stream, onto her face, just as she grabs for the diaper. The phone rings, and she lets the answering machine, pick up.

> "You have reached Dezerae, Zyra, and Zyven, leave a message. One of us will call you back. God Bless."

Zyra's voice comes over the machine, after the beep.

> "Hey baby, it's me..."

She quickly finishes putting his diaper on and answers the phone.

> "Hello, hello...hey just changing the baby. He peed all over me twice. Yeah real funny. Oh...cool, alright, see you soon. I love you too. Bye."

She hangs up the phone and crawls over to Zyven.

> "Daddy will be home soon. Aren't you excited? Tonight, you're gonna see Daddy's first theatrical production."

Meanwhile, on the campus of Florida State University, old historic tall brick buildings, stand tall as Zyra walks out of the Burt

Reynold's Theater. One of his students, the star of his production, Johnny Wildfire, stops Zyra before he gets into his car.

"Mr. Jordonello."

Zyra turns around.

"Yeah...oh hey Johnny. So are you ready for opening night?"

"Yeah, I just wanted to thank you for everything you've taught me this year. You have been an inspiration to me, for many years, and to be taught by you, is beyond a dream come true. I have found my faith again, because of you. Anyway, I don't want to get all mushy on you. I just wanted, to thank you, for giving me this opportunity."

Zyra is very taken aback by his kind words.

"You're welcome, Johnny. Thank you for working so hard. You deserve it. Good luck tonight. Break a leg. That's what they say in theater, right?"

Johnny smiles.

"Yeah, that's what they say."

Zyra takes out his keys, before entering his brand new, metallic blue pick-up, he turns back around.

"God Bless."

Johnny smiles and walks into the theater. Zyra gets in the car and drives off. Dezerae is in the kitchen making Zyra a sandwich for when he arrives. He opens the door and shouts out.

"Where are my two babies?"

Dezerae calls down from the kitchen.

"Up here, Mr. Writer, Director."

Zyra walks up the stairs, hugs her for a long minute, then kisses her on the lips. He walks over to baby Z, sitting in the high chair, at the table, lifts him, kissing his dirty face. Zyven spits up baby food, all over him, and Dezerae cracks up.

"Ah, man."

Dezerae walks the sandwich over to the table.

"You're lucky it didn't come from the other end."

She starts laughing, at the food, *clumping* down Zyra's face.

"This is nasty."

Dezerae laughs even harder, he approaches the sink and cleans up.

"Johnny paid me a very nice compliment today."

"Really? What did the man playing my husband have to say?"

She wipes Zyven's face clean.

"Well, he said I was an inspiration to him."

"Uh ha, and..."

She nibbles on the baby's ear lobe, trying to contain her reaction, to the baby's cuteness.

"And ah...well, I have inspired him for many years, and it was more than a dream come true for me, to be teaching him."

She lifts the baby from the high chair and lets him run loose, within the gated area. She walks over to Zyra tickles her fingers down his chest, jokingly.

"A wet dream?"

She pushes Zyra onto the kitchen table, unbuttons his shirt, she bites down on his pierced nipple.

"Hey, there's a baby over there."

She laughs and sticks her hindside into the air.

"Your loss."

A couple of hours pass, the sun settles, and Zyra gets out of the shower. He throws on a shiny black suit, and silky white shirt, and looks over at Dezerae. She is fixing her hair, and wearing a form-fitting red dress.

"If beauty burns, you're scorching me."

She laughs at his cheesy line and dresses Zyven in black leather pants, and a white silk shirt to match his Daddy. Zyra interjects.

"I have to call my Mom, tell her what time to be there."

Dezerae quickly responds and lifts the baby.

"I already called her. Oh, and my parents called earlier to wish you luck."

Zyra smiles. They shut the lights off, and exit their home. They put Zyven in the back seat of Dezerae's new silver Lexus, get in the car, and take off. Dezerae pulls out Zyra's new C.D. from the glove compartment. On the cover, the heavens are open, shining light down on Zyra, with his wings of flesh.

The name of his new album, GOTHOLIC "WINGS OF FLESH." She puts it in the CD player, as an angelic choir of bells, creating the atmosphere, for to Zyra read scripture. An electric guitar and synthesized drums ease their way in.

After the intro, Zyra screams, and as the music kicks in heavy, they drive out into the dark desolate road, leading them to the campus. They park in the back, of the theater, and enter the building. Zyra walks Dezerae and Zyven to their seats.

"I'll be right back, Sweetie."

He kisses her on the cheek, looks up, and sees a full house. Zyra enters backstage, wanting to make sure everyone is in their proper places. The curtains are closed, and the actors settle into their roles, during the last-minute commotion. Zyra gathers everyone in a group, on stage, behind the curtain. He speaks very energetically but controls his tone.

> "Alright, everybody. I would like for each of you, to grab the person's hand next to you. I pray that God will guide this production tonight. And that no one will forget their lines."

The actors laugh.

> "And finally, we give our audience, a show they will never forget. Let's pray. Our Father who art in heaven Hallowed is Thy name..."

They finish the Lord's Prayer, Zyra waits behind the curtain, for the house lights to go down. The audience quiets, and the house lights dim to darkness. A spotlight shines center stage, in front of the curtain, Zyra clears his throat and steps out to begin his introduction.

> "Hello and welcome to the opening night of 'Wings of Flesh,' written and directed by yours truly, Zyra Jordonello."

The crowd applauds.

> "Thank you. I hope this evening, will be as exciting for you, as it is for me. This is a very personal story, that inspired my life, and I hope it inspires you. Well, enough said, WINGS OF FLESH."

The spotlight turns off, the curtains rise, and smoke shoots out, fogging the stage. Eerie music chills the audience, and Gothic attire, decorates the bedroom in reds, blacks, and greys, on a white silky bed. Johnny, playing Zyra, sleeps next to his wife. Instantly, he wakes up, screaming, bloody murder.

> "DIE, DIE, DIE!"

His muscles are flexed, to their maximum, his legs and hands, distorted, as he fights off some kind of invisible entity. Sweat pours from his flesh, and his wife sits up, scared. Afraid to wake him, from his night scare, and afraid to fall back asleep.

The show continues, telling his story. It is a smashing hit! After the standing ovation, critiques and reporters, give it a rave review.

> Dezerae is overwhelmed, not being able to stop talking about it, in the car, on the way home. She puts the baby to bed,

Zyra pours two glasses of wine, and burns some incense, down by the fireplace.

He lights the logs, gets undressed, and lays on the bear skin, waiting for his lovely wife. Dezerae walks down the stairs, holding the monitor, for the baby's room. She smiles at Zyra's little plan, walks over to the stereo, places the monitor on top, and plays classical music. She steps out of her dress, walks over to Zyra, and cuddles up, next to him.

"You were amazing tonight."

"I...didn't do anything. It was the students."

She smiles at his humility.

"You know what I love about you, Zyra Jordonello?"

"What Dezerae Jordonello?"

She rubs her fingers, along the side of his naked body.

"I love your modesty. I love your brilliance. I love you."

He kisses her passionately.

"You know what, I love about you?"

"What?"

"I love your modesty. I love your Brilliance. And I love you."

They hold each other close and make love as she whispers into his ear.

"Are you going to bring me with you tonight?"

He smiles.

"I'll see what I can do."

They fall asleep in each other's arms, on the white bear skin, as the fireplace crackles in the background.

The End...hmmm, or is it just the beginning? Or maybe it's the beginning of the end?

AFTERWORD

"WINGS OF FLESH: Gotholic Warfare" could not have been written without scripture from, "The Holy Bible" and Chuck Missler's, "Return of the Nephilim." The first draft of this novel was completed on January 4th, 2001, then rewritten, completing the rewrite on April 25th, 2002, then a final revision on August 12th, 2002. Now 22 years later, in the same amount of time, my daughter, ZYLA FAUSTINA NYAHAY, was on this earth, I revisited this story, and completed it today, February 24, 2024. All characters are fictional except for Zalman King and Patricia King, Ozzy Osbourne and Sharon Osbourne, Randy Rhoads, Kelle Rhoads, Rhoads Family, Marilyn Manson and other celebrities mentioned. Marit contains real people in made-up events. All those mentioned, and more, I greatly admire, but these beautiful souls, helped cultivate me as an artist. Thank you, I am eternally grateful. God bless you all, and your loved ones.

Most importantly, I want to thank Jesus Christ and all of Heaven, for using me as a vessel, to reveal this story, to the world. I also want to thank my family, Jacqueline, Zyla, and my Mother, Rosemary Nyahay, and father Dr. Edward Nyahay, for putting up with me, as I wrote the first draft in their home, twenty-two years ago. Now after going back into this story, first, I'm about twenty years or so, ahead of my time, Second, I realized, that a lot of my metaphors came true, this piece seems timeless, even though, it reflects the modern day. Zyla never read my book, while she was on this planet, but I felt her every step of the way, guiding me through this rewrite. Zyla is in everything I do. I originally saw this as a trilogy, but now, I believe this is a pilot, to many ongoing stories, that will branch off, and become part of human literature, known during this period.

One of the best guitarists in the world, Jonathan Natal, was another inspiration for my musical journey, and after all these years, we still make GOTHOLIC music. I love you all, and thank you, for supporting my efforts, including you Christopher Zell, my best man; you are a true inspiration, and one of the best writers around, God bless your soul, and have a drink with Zyla for me. Thank you Mom for editing my first draft, Published through Xlibris. I inherited my writing from you. Thank you to my grandparents, Anita and Emanuel Barattino, who also is a daily inspiration to me. All of you make up the Ancestral Congregation, living and deceased, all who put God first in their lives.

Align your will with God's Will, for your life, let Him bless the fruits of your labor. I want to thank my old college roommates, who inspired the Hanover College Chapter, Andy Jankowski and Michael Hemmelgarn (4 WHEEL DRIVE CHRISTMAS). One person, who truly lives the way of the cross, is my older sister, Carrie Magalski, whom I am honored and blessed to be your brother. You have always been there for me, in dark times and joyful. You never abandoned me. You are a true testimony of how we should live life on this planet. God bless you and your family always.

If your life seems empty, you know where to find fulfillment. Seek God. Manifest your creative spirit, always. There is a reason for everything. I know this was a dark crazy journey I led you on, but maybe, it's through our pain and suffering, that we truly begin to live, grow, and become who we are meant to be, while we have the time to make a difference, in this world. Love conquers all. In the midst, of GOTHOLIC WARFARE, which side are you on? God is calling, we choose to hear His voice or shut it out. Time is at hand. Illumination of the soul.

May God Bless You All,

Edward Francis Nyahay Jr.

Author

WINGS OF FLESH
"Gotholic Warfare"
Edward Nyahay